Praise for Elmer Kelton

•

"One of the greatest and most gifted
of Western writers."
—*Historical Novel Society*

"Elmer Kelton is a Texas treasure."
—*El Paso Herald-Post*

"Voted 'the greatest Western writer of all time' by
the Western Writers of America, Kelton creates
characters more complex than L'Amour's."
—*Kirkus Reviews*

"Kelton writes of early Texas with
unerring authority."
—*Fort Worth Star-Telegram*

"One of the best."
—*The New York Times*

"A splendid writer."
—*The Dallas Morning News*

"A genuine craftsman with an ear for dialogue
and, more important, an understanding
of the human heart."
—*~~ok~~list*

Forge Books by Elmer Kelton

SHADOW
OF A
STAR

— AND —

PECOS
CROSSING

ELMER KELTON

FORGE®

A TOM DOHERTY ASSOCIATES BOOK | NEW YORK

This is a work of fiction. All of the characters, organizations, and events portrayed in these novels are either products of the author's imagination or are used fictitiously.

SHADOW OF A STAR AND PECOS CROSSING

Shadow of a Star copyright © 1959, 1984 by Elmer Stephen Kelton Estate

Pecos Crossing copyright © 1963 by Elmer Stephen Kelton Estate

All rights reserved.

A Forge Book
Published by Tom Doherty Associates
175 Fifth Avenue
New York, NY 10010

www.tor-forge.com

Forge® is a registered trademark of Macmillan Publishing Group, LLC.

ISBN 978-1-250-17785-8

Our books may be purchased in bulk for promotional, educational, or business use. Please contact your local bookseller or the Macmillan Corporate and Premium Sales Department at 1-800-221-7945, extension 5442, or by email at MacmillanSpecialMarkets@macmillan.com.

First Edition: March 2019

Printed in the United States of America

0 9 8 7 6 5 4 3 2 1

CONTENTS

SHADOW
OF A
STAR

1

They had shaken the last sign of pursuit two days ago. Now they had to stop riding, for Curly Jack was dying on their hands.

They eased him to the warm ground beneath the thin shade of a mesquite. Because the sun still came through, Dencil Fox unsaddled Curly Jack's horse and draped the wet saddle blanket across the branches to deepen the shade. Dencil poured water from a canteen into a handkerchief and gently touched it to Jack's fevered face.

"You just need to rest a spell, pardner," he said. "You'll be all right directly."

But he knew he was lying. There was the smell of gangrene about Curly Jack—the smell of death.

He wondered how Jack had managed to stay in the saddle as long as he had. It wasn't such a bad wound, they had thought. A bullet high in the shoulder, nothing fatal. But they hadn't dared hunt for a doctor. And the posse hadn't given them much chance to probe for the bullet the first couple of days. When at last they'd had time for Dencil to try, he hadn't been able to extract the slug. If anything, his efforts had made things worse.

Jack weakly motioned toward the canteen, and Dencil touched it to his lips, lifting Jack's head.

The other three men stood around uncomfortably, a deep weariness in their eyes, the droop of their shoulders. They were dusty and bearded. The oldest two were silent, but the youngest began to complain.

"We could have left him off someplace the first day. They'd have found him and took care of him."

Dencil Fox frowned quickly at his younger brother, then looked back at Curly Jack. "They'd have taken care of him, all right. Jack had rather go this way than at the end of a rope."

"If he was goin' to die anyhow, at least we wouldn't have been saddled down with him."

Sharply Dencil said, "Shut up, Buster!" He knew Curly Jack could still hear all that was said.

Buster kept talking. "If he'd shot that bank teller, he wouldn't have caught a slug himself."

Dencil said, "We didn't go in there to kill anybody."

"You *didn't* kill anybody. And you didn't get any money, either."

"We didn't figure on that gutty teller. And we never did know where he got that gun so fast."

Buster Fox said bitterly, "Leavin' me outside to hold the horses . . . If I'd been in there, things would've been a right smart different."

"That's why we left you outside."

"Well, you won't leave me outside next time!"

Curly Jack died without ever speaking a word. Because there was no shovel, they had to carry him to an arroyo, roll him in his saddle blanket, and cave a steep bank in on top of him. This way, at least, no one was likely to find him for a while. Later, if a rise came down the arroyo and washed the body out into the open, the four riders would be so far gone that the discovery would not put them in danger.

Dencil Fox stood with hat in hand, gravely looking down on the pile of fresh-caved earth at the bottom of the arroyo.

"Mighty poor way to leave you, Jack." His voice was sorrowful. "No marker, no preacher to read over you."

Buster spoke dryly, "Jack wasn't exactly the church-goin' kind."

Dencil said, "He was a good man, and don't you forget it."

"Too bad he wasn't a good shot."

They rode on then, leading Jack's horse for an extra, putting miles between them and the place where the fifth outlaw had died.

In time Dencil Fox said, "We got to find us a good spot to lay over. These horses will die under us if we don't rest them a few days."

A tall rider named Hackberry said, "We crossed the railroad tracks late yesterday. I figure we're about half-way between Grafton and Swallowfork. There's a big draw runs through a ways this side of Swallowfork. With the wet spring they had here, there ought to be good grass in it, and plenty of water. We could camp there as long as we wanted. Ain't anybody apt to see us except maybe a stray cowpuncher or two."

Dencil said, "You don't reckon they've heard about that bank job?"

"That was a long ways off. Last time I was in Swallowfork, it didn't have no telegraph or nothin'. Who'd be lookin' for us down here?"

"Nobody, I reckon. And I could sure use me a good rest."

The younger Fox pushed his horse up close to Hackberry's. "What kind of a town is this Swallowfork? Chance a man could find himself a little entertainment?"

Hackberry said, "The kind you're lookin' for?" He shook his head. "Last time I was there it was just a dull lookin' little cowtown. You could get yourself somethin' to drink and maybe a quiet game of cards, low limit. Nothin' fancy. And no wheeligo girls."

Buster was plainly disappointed. "Ain't that a shame!" Then, his face brightened again. "I wonder if they got a bank . . ."

A loud clatter was going on at the shack's old cast-iron cookstove.

"If you don't quit polishin' that tin star and go chop some firewood, there won't be any breakfast!"

Sitting on the edge of his cot, Jim-Bob McClain turned about with a youthfully sheepish grin and waved a hand at the young man who had spoken. "Hold your horses, Dan. I'll get to it directly." He pinned the deputy badge on his left shirt pocket, catching the Bull Durham sack with the pin the first time he tried. He reached down and pulled on his long-eared, high-heeled boots. He already had his hat on. It was the first thing he looked for when he got up of a morning: an old cowboy habit he had developed sleeping on the ground in wintertime, dressing from the head downward as he worked up out of the warm blankets.

Dan Singleton stood at the black stove, poking remnant woodchips in on top of the reluctant flame he coaxed out of dry kindling. Ashes filtered out around the sprung door and fell at his feet. "Thought this was your week to chop the wood," Dan prodded Jim-Bob good-naturedly. "Or do I have to call out the law?"

"I meant to do it last night, but with the dance down at Sothern's barn and all, I flat forgot."

"Then you better get at it, or it's goin' to be a long, hungry day."

Jim-Bob walked out of the little frame shack and paused to enjoy the clean freshness of the early morning. This was the summertime's best hour in the West Texas range country, just at sunup. The cool air of a brand new day braced a man and gave him vigor, made him imagine he could ride horseback a hundred miles without his shoulders ever sagging. It gave him all manner of grand ambition, notions the noonday heat would later bake out of him.

Along the wagon road just hollering distance away lay the beginnings of the town of Swallowfork. A scattering of frame and adobe houses first, thickening up and bunching closer together the nearer they lay to the rock courthouse and jail and the dozen or so business buildings that made up the core, it sprawled out haphazardly like a big *remuda* of horses loose-herded across half of a valley.

Jim-Bob listened. About all he could hear was a couple of roosters crowing the sun up, and a shut-in milkpen calf bawling for its mammy.

Quiet town, most of the time. Sleepy livestock town, drawing its livelihood from the good rolling rangeland that lay about it; from the tall bunch grasses that made the hillsides wave green in the gentle south breeze; from the valley's short, tough curly-mesquite buffalo grass; from the leggy, longhorned cattle that roamed and grazed there; and from the scattering bands of free-ranging sheep that were edging in on the cowman's domain, winning him over by pressure of economics if not from liking for the animal.

Quiet town it was, but one with ambitions, and one with a future. Jim-Bob's town. Like the town, he had ambitions. He could only hope *he* had a future, too.

He stood with hands shoved deep in his pockets, jingling the coins he carried there. Pay from his first month as a deputy sheriff of Coldridge County. He had hoped and worked and planned for a long time to pin that badge on his shirt. Now he had it.

"Jim-Bob," Dan Singleton's impatient voice insisted through the open door, "how about that wood?"

"Comin'."

A big red dog, ugly as a mud fence, sidled around the shack and came up wagging his tail. "Mornin', Ranger," Jim-Bob greeted him, patting his broad head. "Where'd you spend the night? Liable to be a scandal around here if you don't take to stayin' home."

Jim-Bob unwedged the ax from the big mesquite limb that served as a chopping block and pulled a smaller limb down from the woodpile. He and Dan Singleton had taken a couple of Sunday afternoons and a borrowed wagon to haul in this supply of dry wood from a brushy draw a ways out of town. His strong back and hard-muscled arms made short work of the wood. In a few minutes he walked into the shack with a good armload.

"Hope you didn't cut it too long this time," Dan said. He had once accused Jim-Bob of trying to do such a poor job of it that Dan would take over in disgust. He wasn't far wrong. Jim-Bob never did go much for wood-chopping and the like. He preferred something he could do a-horseback. But a man who made up his mind to live in town and be a deputy sheriff also had to make up his mind to do some menial chores he didn't care for.

Outside for another armload of wood, Jim-Bob paused to squint down the south wagon road that led in from Dry Creek and from ranches like the C Bar. There, in the reddish glow of the sun just up, he saw two riders trotting their horses purposefully toward town. Recognizing them, he waved.

"You-all come on over and have breakfast with us," he called.

They only acknowledged his offer with a quick wave of their hands and rode on. By the rigid way they sat their saddles, Jim-Bob could tell they meant business. He frowned and looked down at rusty-hided old Ranger, who had moved out a little way to size up the pair. "Somethin' the matter, Ranger? They've had to ride half the night to get in from the C Bar. And they're both packin' guns."

The way the country had settled up and closed in, folks weren't wearing their guns much anymore. When they did, it was usually because they felt a genuine need for them.

"Now what would Walter Chapman and Tom Singleton be needin' with guns?" he mused.

Walter Chapman owned the C Bar. Tom Singleton was his foreman and Dan Singleton's older brother.

Jim-Bob had worked on Chapman's ranch for several years after his father had died and left the growing boy to shift for himself. Excepting maybe Sheriff Mont Naylor, there wasn't a better man to work for, anywhere, than Walter Chapman. He was a solid old ranchman of the longhorn school. When he said work, now, he meant *work,* but he'd be right there beside you, or maybe out in front of you. He paid well and never abused man or horse. Always an easy mark for a hard-luck story, he was forever picking up dogies like the orphaned Singleton boys or Jim-Bob McClain, giving them a chance to work out their own way. But if he ever caught you lying to him or cheating him, there would be hell among the yearlings.

Dan Singleton stood in the door, watching the riders move on toward town. "That looked like Tom," he said, puzzled.

Jim-Bob went on picking up wood. "It was him. Never even stopped to say howdy."

"Awfully early for him to be in town. Must be something wrong out there."

"I reckon we'll hear about it soon enough." Heavily loaded, Jim-Bob strained to pick up the one remaining piece of wood and spilled half of his armload. He muttered something under his breath and made two trips of it.

He had the woodbox half full by the time Dan called him. He brushed the dust and chips away from his clothes and poured fresh water into a basin on the soap-slick washstand. Lathering his hands as best he could in the strong soap, he took a long whiff of the bacon and black coffee smell. Dan was a heap sight better cook than Jim-Bob ever even wanted to be.

Jim-Bob liked Dan, and he liked this place they shared here on the edge of town: an ancient shack, a small barn, a couple of corrals and a creaky windmill that needed new leathers and a greasing. The shack wasn't much, as houses go. They had painted it inside and out, but the job had been done several years too late to keep the place from weathering beyond redemption. One corner sagged gently where the cedarpost foundation had sunk. The windows didn't fit well anymore, and the west wind whistled in around them. The roof leaked in a couple of places, but this was a dry country where a leaky roof was only an occasional inconvenience. For two happy young bachelors in the springtime of life and the first glow of real independence, the place was more than adequate.

Dan Singleton was getting a good start as a teller in the bank. He'd always been a good-enough kid cowboy, but it had been easy to tell that he held promise of better things. He liked to read, and he had an unusual aptitude with figures. There wasn't an old-time cowman around who could do a better job of tallying cattle. Dan never dropped a count. Walter Chapman had finally fired him off the C Bar for his own good, forcing him to accept the job which old man True Farrell had been offering him at the bank. Dan Singleton was going to amount to something someday, people said. And everybody knew that one of the things West Texas needed most was more bankers who knew something about the cow business.

They weren't all sure about Jim-Bob McClain. He was a pretty fair cowboy, a little on the wild side. He would ride any horse they led out to him, or at least would try to. He would rope anything that would run from him, and he would stand tied to it. But he would never make a banker, or a storekeeper. Most people figured he would just end up another stove-up cowpuncher.

But old John McClain before him had been sheriff of Coldridge County for many years, and a good one.

Sheriff Mont Naylor had the idea that young Jim-Bob McClain might have the makings in him, too, if he had a little of the rashness stomped out of him. Jim-Bob had pestered him long enough about it, anyway.

Jim-Bob's chance came when Mont had to fire Chum Lawton for pistol-whipping a harmless old Mexican sheep-herder whose only crime had been taking on a little too much tequila. Mont rode out to the C Bar and swore Jim-Bob in.

If he lived a hundred years, Jim-Bob would never again know the great swell of pride that came when Mont pinned the deputy's badge on him.

Yesterday was a month he'd worn that badge. "Here's for your first month," Mont had spoken simply as he paid him. And that was all he had said. Not a thank you or a howdydo, just that and nothing more. The young deputy had tried to see something more in the sheriff's eyes, for nothing in the world mattered like pleasing Mont Naylor. He listened to those five words a hundred times in his mind, and still he didn't know. He had done his best. Maybe that hadn't been enough.

Good thing about living close to town this way, they could always buy fresh food like vegetables and eggs, something they had often missed on the ranch. Jim-Bob liked his eggs. He was so busy eating that he didn't pay much attention to Dan Singleton. He finally noticed Dan watching him with humor in his eyes.

"You were sure havin' a good time at the dance," Dan said.

"Had to stay around and be sure things stayed peaceful. It's what I'm hired for."

"I think you were goin' far beyond the call of duty. I noticed you takin' mighty good care of Tina Kendrick. You never gave anybody else much chance to dance with her."

Jim-Bob felt his face coloring. It had never occurred to him that anybody would notice. Looking away from Dan, he dropped a strip of bacon into Ranger's eager jaws.

Dan said, "Chum Lawton was plenty burned up. After all, he brought her, and you danced with her all night."

His dancing with Tina Kendrick wasn't all that had Chum Lawton riled, Jim-Bob thought. There never had been much love lost between them, and especially not since Jim-Bob got Chum's old job. Chum was out breaking tough broncs for a living now. It wasn't something a man enjoyed after soft living around town.

Dan commented, "That little girl, Sue-Ellen Thorn, from up the creek, had her eyes on you a lot. You could have her, I think, if you wanted her."

Jim-Bob grunted. "I was scared to death she was goin' to come right out and ask me to dance. You know, they tell me there's girls that will do things like that."

Dan shook his head, smiling. "Must be awful tough to have so many girls on the string."

Sheriff Mont Naylor rode up as Jim-Bob carried his dirty dishes to the washpan on the kitchen cabinet. Walter Chapman and Tom Singleton sat beside him on their horses, their faces grim.

The sheriff said, "If you've finished breakfast, Jim-Bob, you better go saddle your horse. We got a job to do."

Jim-Bob didn't like the undertone of worry in the sheriff's voice. He looked at Walter and Tom, expecting one of them to offer an explanation. They didn't. Well, they would tell him in their own due time, he figured.

"You fellers get down and come on in," he said. "There's still coffee on the stove."

Dan Singleton stepped to the door, his face brightening as he looked out at his older brother. They quietly shook hands. No words passed between them, for sometimes brothers know little to say to each other. Just being together was enough.

Tom Singleton was tall and stiff-backed, a severe man who looked older than his thirty years. He wore a black vest and a black moustache and a solemn mien that he never relaxed. He wasn't an easy man to get to know, but there was this about him: he was honest and worked hard, and he had little patience with anyone who did not. To him, black was black and white was white. People knew that, and they respected him for it whether they agreed with him or not.

Only one thing ever softened Tom Singleton's eyes. Talk about his younger brother Dan and you could see a glow of pride start there. Tom Singleton had been in his teens when the responsibility for Dan had been thrust upon him. Tom had worked harder than two men, had missed the happy, youthful years to which he himself was entitled. But Dan had borne out all his hope, had justified all his sacrifice. Tom might never speak of his pride, but it showed in his dark eyes.

Jim-Bob walked to the little barn out back, Ranger following along with his stumpy tail twitching. Most of the time they let the horses run free on the town-section grass when they weren't using them. Everybody did. They made it a point to feed a little grain first thing after breakfast every morning, rain or shine.

That guaranteed that the mounts would always be up in case they needed them.

The sheriff and Walter Chapman came around in a minute. Looping his bridle reins over a post, the sheriff felt of the rough bark on a big mesquite tree to be sure there wasn't any sticky sap on it. Then he squatted stiffly and leaned his back against it, grunting with the effort. At his age, and with his growing weight, his knees popped when he bent very far.

People in Coldridge County always said they'd been blessed with good sheriffs. John McClain had set a strong pattern. He had usually found a peaceful way to handle the problems that came up. But when something demanded rough treatment, McClain had been able to administer it.

Mont Naylor was an old-time cowman, like John McClain before him. He had brought his own herd up with him from the brush of southern Texas in the early days and had settled in the upper end of the county. Eventually, drought and low prices got a stranglehold on him and left him flat broke. But people didn't want to see him go. Because Mont Naylor had always been a good horse trader, banker True Farrell lent him money to buy out the Swallowfork livery barn and wagonyard. Later, when John McClain died, folks prevailed on Mont to take over as sheriff on a temporary basis. It was the longest temporary job he'd ever had.

Mont was a broad-shouldered, deep-chested man with a square face hard-bitten by a lifetime in the hot, dry wind and the sullen punishment of the Texas sun. The creases in his face, always deep enough, bit even deeper this morning as he frowned over the trouble that had brought him here.

Jim-Bob itched to ask what they were going to do,

but he had learned better years ago as a kid around a cow camp. The button who asked a lot of fool questions would find himself jingling horses, holding the cut or trotting the mountain oysters back to camp for the wagon cook.

Jim-Bob noted that the sheriff had his saddlegun along. It was the first time he had carried it since Jim-Bob had been working for him. Mont sat with his back to the mesquite, his lips puffed out while he worried. He absently sketched cattle brands in the sand and then changed them over the way a rustler would. Mont had seen it all done in his time.

Presently Mont said, "We're goin' out to Jace Dunnigan's. We all know he's been butcherin' C bar beef. This time Walter and Tom think they can prove it on him."

That was no great surprise to Jim-Bob. Jace Dunnigan had a ratty little place some distance from town. He kept a few cattle, bought a few occasionally, and—it was generally believed—stole a lot more than he bought. Jace supplied beef to a good many townspeople. Though it was basic knowledge that there were but four quarters to a beef, it was a common joke around Swallowfork that Dunnigan cattle grew seven or eight apiece.

Mont said, "Tom Singleton spotted him yesterday out on the C Bars, nosin' around just a little before dark. He followed him and saw him pick up a fat heifer yearlin'. He trailed Jace right on to his place. Jace killed the heifer, skinned it and buried the hide a little ways from the house. Tom says he's sure he can find that hide this mornin'."

Jim-Bob pointed his chin at the sheriff's saddlegun.

"You don't think you'll need that thing with a man like Jace . . ."

"You never can tell."

Jim-Bob walked back into the shack and strapped on his gun. It was a single-action Colt Frontier .44 with black rubber grips. John McClain had left his son little but a gold pocketwatch, a fond memory, and this heavy old six-shooter.

Nobody did much talking as they rode out. To Jim-Bob it was as if they were going to a funeral. He tried to make conversation, but he soon realized he was the only one doing any talking. As the youngest, he knew it behooved him to shut up, and he did.

They rode back south down the wagon trail, toward the C Bar. Jim-Bob watched Tom Singleton as they rode. It struck him that Tom would always be the standout in whatever crowd he might ride, his back so rigid that it made anyone else look slovenly beside him. He was a handsome man, even in his severity, with steady brown eyes almost black, a straight nose, and that strong black moustache. He wore a flat-brimmed gray hat, its tall crown barely pinched toward the top. Even in dusty ranch clothes he always seemed better dressed than the others around him.

Tom Singleton had been known to go for days without saying anything other than the bare necessities for getting the work done. On roundup, he usually took the lead and rode a length or two ahead of the other men as he led them around the outer part of the circle to drop them off for the drive. Even now, he rode a little ahead of Mont Naylor and Walter Chapman.

The men's silence was not broken until they happened across a calf that showed a wound infested by screwworms. The calf carried someone else's brand, but it was unthinkable that it should be left to die untreated simply because it belonged to another man.

Tom Singleton shook down his rope, built a small loop and gently edged toward the calf. He took it slow and easy, easing the calf a little way from its mother. At the crucial moment when the calf suddenly turned to bolt, Tom touched rowels to the horse. The loop swung around his head only once, then dropped like a rock and fitted perfectly over the calf's neck. No sweat, no strain, the way Tom Singleton did things. Jim-Bob watched with admiration. Dan Singleton had always been his pal, but Tom had been his ideal. Tom was a cowboy for you, now. Anything he set out to do, he would do it better than anyone else.

The calf's mammy was bawling and working around with her head low, trying to get up the courage to charge in. Jim-Bob moved to keep her away while Tom was down pouring chloroform into the wound. Freed at last, the calf ran to her. With all the concern a mother can show, the cow sniffed around on it to be sure it was all right. Then she shook her head threateningly at the riders, turned and trotted away with the calf.

Somehow the incident loosened up Tom Singleton a little. He said nothing, but he winked at Jim-Bob as he swung back onto his horse. It loosened Walter Chapman a little, too. He seemed to feel a need to explain the reason for this ride out to Dunnigan's. "It's not as if he was some hungry nester, Mont, butcherin' a beef once in a while for his young'uns. They've done it many a time, and I've never said a word. But Jace Dunnigan's been killin' our cattle for sale, stickin' the money in his pocket and gettin' drunk on it. He could find him an honest job if he was a mind to. He's just too sorry to do anything but drink and steal."

The sheriff nodded. "The state'll find him a nice permanent job over at Huntsville, I expect. There he'll sweat or go hungry."

There wasn't an adobe hovel in the west end of town that looked half as bad as Jace Dunnigan's place. He lived like a boar hog in a swaying frame shack that had cardboard in place of half the glass windows. A scattering of tin cans and old bottles made a horseshoe-shaped pile out behind the house. The rustiest ones lay the farthest away, indicating that the junkpile was edging closer to the house as the man got lazier.

Tom Singleton reined up. He hadn't spoken since they had left town. Now he said, "Right there, I think it was, Mont. See the dried mud on some of those cans? He buried the hide under there and kicked the cans over to hide the fresh dirt."

Jim-Bob caught a movement at one of the dirty windows. "Somebody in the shack," he said. The head bobbed and was gone. "Looked like a woman."

"Mrs. Dunnigan," Mont replied.

Walter Chapman nodded. "I saw her. Always puzzled me, why a woman would live like this, in the midst of all the filth, with the likes of Jace Dunnigan."

Jim-Bob shook his head. "No woman could love a man like that."

Mont glanced his way. "You're too young to know much about women, son." He paused, then added, "I wonder if any man ever gets old enough."

"Do you really think a woman could love a man who makes her live like this?"

Mont shrugged. "I've seen fine women fall in love with men that weren't fit to breathe the same air. I've seen good men go plumb out of their heads and fall into the mud over some common dancehall floozy. You just take a good look, Jim-Bob, and let it be a lesson to you."

A brown mongrel dog crept out from under the shack and set up a racket. His ribs showed like bed slats through his coarse hide. Sheriff Mont Naylor stepped down out of the saddle, careful to keep his horse between himself and the house as he did so.

"Jace," he called. "Jace Dunnigan."

Jim-Bob stayed in the saddle, hand close to the old gun on his hip. Excitement kindled in him. This was the first time in his month as a deputy that he faced even the remote possibility of using a gun. He watched the front door. Jace Dunnigan might be inside, or he might not. But Mrs. Dunnigan was there. He wondered why she didn't answer.

The dog kept on barking. Presently Jace Dunnigan walked around the corner of the house. He reached down and picked up a rock. "Git!" he shouted at the mongrel. He hurled the stone, striking the dog so hard that Jim-Bob flinched at the flat *whu-u-mp* of the rock against bare ribs. Yelping, the dog tucked its tail between its legs and slunk back under the house.

Jace Dunnigan turned then to his visitors. His yellowed teeth—what there were left of them—protruded a little. His lips were perpetually pulled back, his mouth open. He stood slackly, lank shoulders drooping. His clothes were filthy with grease and dried animal blood. Jim-Bob could smell him from six feet away.

Jim-Bob wondered suddenly how many times he had eaten beef butchered by this dirty man. The thought made him a little sick.

"Howdy, Mont," Jace said lazily. His red-veined

eyes flicked to the other three men without any particular friendliness, for he knew full well what Walter Chapman and Tom Singleton thought of him, and Jim-Bob was just a big kid who didn't matter. Puzzlement came into Jace's eyes, and a trace of worry. But he tried to cover it up.

"I got a little shot of whisky out at the barn," he said by way of invitation.

Mont replied evenly, "I don't think I'd care for any right now. But I *would* like to take a look around that barn. I reckon you got some beef hangin' up?"

Suspicion narrowed Jace's eyes. "Matter of fact, I butchered one of my calves last night. Got the beef in the barn, coolin' out. Figured I'd haul it into town this evenin' when the heat of the day was past."

"Mind if we look at it?"

Dunnigan hesitated. Then, voice lower, he said, "I don't see as it would hurt nothin'." He looked uneasily at Walter Chapman. His glance barely touched Tom Singleton, then flicked away. Tom's dark eyes were boring a hole through him, loathing him for the sneak thief that he was.

Dunnigan led the way out to the barn. A couple of thin calves stood waiting pathetically beside an empty feed trough. It would be a long time before these were ever fat enough to butcher.

The beef, sawed down the spine, hung in two halves on rope suspended from a sagging rafter. There was no tarp cover. Flies buzzed around.

Jim-Bob felt his stomach turn over.

Mont Naylor nodded in satisfaction. This carcass was a lot fatter than any cattle Jim-Bob had ever seen wearing Jace's brand. Mont said, "Where's the hide off of this animal, Jace?"

A tremor was beginning in Jace's voice. "Why, I hung it out over a corral fence." He showed them a hide, laid flesh side up. Dry and stiff as a board, it hadn't come from any fresh-killed animal. Jace said, "The brand's right there if you want to turn the hide over and read it. My brand, Mont, you can see for yourself."

Mont paid little attention to him. He poked around a little and found a shovel. He held it out to Tom Singleton. "Go see if you can find that hide you were talkin' about."

Jace Dunnigan seemed to wilt as he watched Tom Singleton walk toward the pile of rusty cans, the shovel in his hand. Sweat popped out on his forehead. His tongue worked constantly back and forth over his lips. His hands shook as he took a tooth-marked cut of plug tobacco out of his pocket and tried to chew it. He spat it out in a moment, still as dry as when he had stuck it in his mouth.

His wife moved out onto the back step of the house, watching. She was a thin, pale woman with hair almost completely gray. Yet she couldn't have been forty years old, Jim-Bob reasoned. He thought he could see a dark bruise marring her face. Life with Jace Dunnigan was far from easy.

Tom Singleton dropped to one knee and began to scoop out dirt with one of the rusty cans. He stood up again and came back, dragging a dirty hide by the tail. It was still soft and pliable.

"Looks fresh, Jace," Mont commented quietly. "Last night fresh."

Glaring at Dunnigan, Tom dropped the tail and toed the bloody hide over, revealing the brand. "There you are, Mont. C Bar."

Jace Dunnigan trembled. He cleared his throat. "Now looky here, Mont, maybe I made a little mistake."

"I reckon you did."

"It was gettin' dark," Dunnigan argued desperately. "I thought it was mine till I had it shot. It was too late then, and you wouldn't want me to let that meat go to spoil. It's the first time it ever happened."

Seeing Mont didn't accept that, Dunnigan turned to Walter Chapman. "Look, Mr. Chapman, tell you what I'll do. I'll give you one of them calves yonder for it. Fair swap, even up. What you say?"

"I say you're a dirty liar. I say you've killed more C Bar cattle than my whole crew could brand in a day. And now you're fixin' to pay for every one of them."

Sick fear was in Jace Dunnigan's red eyes. Not many years ago, he would probably have been hauled out to the nearest tree, had a rope put around his neck, and a wagon rolled out from under him.

Jim-Bob figured that thought was running through Dunnigan's mind.

Jace's voice quavered. "Mont, what you goin' to do?"

"Goin' to take you in, Jace. Try you, ship you off to Huntsville penitentiary for six or eight years."

"Penitentiary." The word came off Dunnigan's lips in a dreading whisper. "Ohmigod, Mont, no." He was shaking like a thin dog in a cold rain.

Mont Naylor looked levelly at him. "I wish I could say I'm sorry, Jace, but I can't. Fact of the matter, I don't know as I ever enjoyed an arrest more. Jim-Bob, come over here and put your handcuffs on him."

Jim-Bob moved up with the cuffs. He had never seen a man in a spot like this before. For a moment he felt a tug of sympathy, looking into the hopeless eyes of this miserable thief. "Let's see the hands, Jace."

Dunnigan lifted his shaking hands. Jim-Bob got one cuff on him, but he found he was almost as nervous as Dunnigan. He had accidentally locked the other cuff. He looked around, fishing in his pocket for the key. The instant he felt the gun jerked from his holster, he knew he had made a mistake.

Dunnigan pushed him hard. Caught off balance, Jim-Bob landed on his hands and knees and rolled in the dirt.

Dunnigan stepped back, the .44 gripped tightly in both hands, the one loose cuff dangling. "Just you hold still now, Mont," he said excitedly. His eyes were wild. "You ain't sendin' me off to no pen to rot. I never stole enough cattle to break anybody."

Mont Naylor was caught by surprise, but his voice was still even and strong with authority. "You're makin' it harder on yourself, Jace. Be sensible and put that gun down. You let it go off and it won't be just cow stealin' anymore. They'll hang you for murder."

Mont took a step forward. Jace steadied his hands, and for a second it looked as if he was going to fire. Jim-Bob lay frozen in fear for Mont.

Mont said, "I'm givin' you just one more chance, Jace. You can't get away, so don't hurt yourself any more than you already are. Drop the gun."

Dunnigan held it, retreating another step. Mont started to move forward, pressing him. Dunnigan's eyes widened in wild resolution, and his finger went tight on the trigger.

Mont threw himself to the ground, drawing his own gun as he fell. The .44 roared in Dunnigan's hands, but

Mont already had dropped beneath the path of the bullet. Mont squeezed his trigger just once.

Dunnigan doubled over as if hit by a sledge. He went to his knees, groaned once, then pitched forward in a loose heap.

Jim-Bob still lay where he had fallen. For a moment all the strength seemed to be drained out of him. He couldn't even get up. In that last instant of life, Jace Dunnigan had looked straight at Jim-Bob. Jim-Bob clenched his fists and squinched his own eyes shut as if the pain had been his. Never, as long as he lived, would he forget the mortal fear and agony he had seen in Jace Dunnigan. And it had been Jim-Bob's fault. Shame flooded him.

Deadly silence followed for a long moment that stretched like eternity. Then a woman's voice lifted in a wail. Mrs. Dunnigan came, screaming as she ran. She threw herself down across the slack body and squalled.

As a precaution, Tom Singleton leaned over and picked up Jim-Bob's gun that Dunnigan had dropped. Then he helped the young deputy to his feet, his dark eyes asking if Jim-Bob was all right. Jim-Bob only nodded. His throat was drawn up in such a tight knot that he couldn't speak. The men stood helplessly watching the woman. They looked at each other, and no man had any suggestion. Mont Naylor tried to put his hand comfortingly on her thin shoulder, but she jerked away from him, eyes ablaze in hatred.

"Murderers!" she screamed. "Murderers!"

Jim-Bob could tell now that he had been right about the bruises on her face. One eye was swollen half shut. How, he asked himself, could a woman carry on so about the death of a husband like that? The wonder was that she hadn't killed him herself.

To Tom Singleton he said tightly, "Looks to me like she's better off with him dead."

Tom told him what he knew he should have seen for himself. "She's simple, Jim-Bob. She's got the mind of a child. He could beat her and starve her, and still she stayed with him because she was afraid to be alone. Now she *is* alone."

Mont Naylor stood white-faced and shaken. Only then did Jim-Bob fully realize how this had affected him. Mont was the kind of man who would lose many a night's sleep, seeing Jace Dunnigan die again and again.

"I'm sorry, Mont," he said. "It was my fault you had to do it."

Mont looked through him as if he didn't see him. Then he said quietly, "There's a wagon out back of the barn. Go see if you can find his team and catch them up. We'll take him to town."

2

Jace Dunnigan's funeral was an awful ordeal to Jim-Bob McClain. The one good thing about it, it didn't last very long. Almost no one was there. Just the widow, the minister, Mont Naylor, Jim-Bob and a couple of the elder town leaders who went only out of sympathy for the widow.

Walking back alone from the graveyard on the hill, Jim-Bob could feel people watching him. He thought he knew what was running through their minds. It wouldn't have happened if this wet-eared deputy hadn't been careless.

Some of the townsmen quietly made up a collection for Mrs. Dunnigan. Jim-Bob stood off at a distance, miserable, and watched her board the mail hack for Grafton. She wore a plain black dress that some thoughtful woman had given her, for she had owned nothing fit to travel in. At Grafton she would catch a train and return to her own people in East Texas.

Jim-Bob leaned against a porch post in front of the bank, savagely whittling down a piece of white pine with the sharp blade of his pocketknife. Feeling a hand touch his shoulder, he looked around at Dan Singleton.

"Stop blamin' yourself, Jim-Bob. You didn't sleep last night, and you haven't eaten. You know she's better off with him dead. Maybe he's better off too. He'd probably have died in that pen."

Jim-Bob nodded bleakly. "I reckon so. But still, he'd be alive now if I hadn't pulled that stupid stunt and let him get ahold of my gun. Mont Naylor wouldn't have him on his conscience, either."

"Has Mont said he blames you?"

Jim-Bob looked down. "He hasn't said anything at all. He doesn't have to."

Dan's voice was quiet but sincere. "I make a mistake at the bank once in a while, but True Farrell doesn't blame me for it. He says the best lessons you learn are through the mistakes you make. I don't ever make the same one twice. Neither will you."

"None of your mistakes ever cause a man to die."

"Mine's not that kind of a job. Yours is."

Jim-Bob sat down on the edge of the high porch and flipped the pine stick away. He absently thumbed the point of the knifeblade. "It may not be my job very long. Old man Trumpett and a couple of the merchants were in to see Mont this mornin'. I reckon they wanted me to hear every word they said. They told him I was too much of a kid for a job like this. Told him he ought to fire me and get somebody with enough experience to wear a badge right and proper. Maybe hire back Chum Lawton."

"What did Mont say?"

"I skipped out while Trumpett was still talkin'. But I expect they were right, and Mont knows it. He'll get around to tellin' me in his own good time."

Dan listened sympathetically. At length he said, "Maybe not, Jim-Bob. But if he does—" he hesitated a moment "—this isn't the only town in West Texas.

We could go off, you and me, and we'd find something."

"Dan, you've got a fine job here."

Dan shrugged. "What're partners for? We've been partners a long time."

Jim-Bob swallowed. He remembered what his father had told him years ago about friends being worth more than any amount of money. He hadn't been able to figure that one then. But he could see it now. He shook his head. "You're not goin' to leave here, Dan. I'm not goin' to stand for that."

He walked on down to the jail and found Mont there. Only one prisoner had spent the night in the jail. He was a cowboy who had been breaking up furniture and bottles at a little adobe *cantina* on the west end last night, trying to pick a fight with the Mexicans. Jim-Bob had tried to stop him, but the cowboy made a lot of noise about the kid deputy who had bungled a job and caused a man to get shot. Jim-Bob had backed off a little. It had looked as if the only solution was to pistol-whip the man, and he didn't want to do that. Little as one might think about it, a heavy gunbarrel could brain a man. But Mont Naylor had shown up in time. With that quiet, deadly way he had when he meant business, he just looked the cowboy straight in the eye, disarmed him and marched him off to jail. He hadn't said a word to Jim-Bob about it.

Now, with Jim-Bob standing by, Mont unlocked the cell door. "You can come on out now, if you're ready to pay for the damage down at Francisco's."

The cowboy didn't look nearly so salty today. Sheepishly he counted out the fifteen dollars Mont asked him for. "It's that tequila," he apologized. "I go out of my fool head on that stuff, and I ought to know better than drink it. I'm sorry it happened, Mont."

Mont nodded patiently, but his voice was firm. "Just be glad it was a deputy like Jim-Bob. One like Chum Lawton would've beaten half your brains out with a gunbarrel."

The cowboy turned to Jim-Bob. "I said some things last night that I didn't mean. Forget them, will you, kid?"

Jim-Bob said, "Sure." But he didn't fail to catch that last word. *Kid!*

After the cowboy was gone, Jim-Bob hung his head. "I reckon they all feel about me the way he did last night—that I'm just a dumb kid who oughtn't to be wearin' this badge at-all."

For the first time since the shooting at Jace Dunnigan's, Mont Naylor looked directly at Jim-Bob. "Son, I won't lie to you; there's some talk goin' around. But I'll tell you what I told John Trumpett after the funeral this mornin'. You're only young, not dumb. What you did was from lack of experience mostly. Give you time, and you'll be all right."

Jim-Bob stared hopefully. "You're givin' me another chance?"

Mont nodded. "Never was any question about it. Only, you better watch yourself a while. Step like you was walkin' on eggs. Someday you'll get a chance to prove yourself. Just don't let folks squeeze you out of this job before that chance comes."

Jim-Bob's throat was tight. "You don't know how much this means to me, Mont. I always remember Dad, and the way he wore that star. The only thing I've ever wanted was to be able to wear it half as good as he did."

Mont smiled. "You will, son, you will. Now I think it might be smart to get you out of sight a day or two. Out of sight, out of mind, they say. How about runnin' a little errand for me, a personal errand?"

"Sure."

"I got a little bunch of broncs over at the corral—swapped for them the other day. I'd be much obliged if you'd take them out to George Thorn's ranch in the mornin'. He's goin' to break them for me."

Jim-Bob nodded happily. "I'd be tickled, Mont." A sudden thought dampened his enthusiasm a little. "Say, Mont, Chum Lawton's workin' out there, ridin' broncs for Thorn. He doesn't like me much."

Mont frowned. "I know that, but I still need you to go. You just keep an eye out for Chum, you hear me? Don't let him sucker you into a fight. He'll jump at the chance to make you look bad, because he knows the ice is a little thin under your feet right now. You watch him, Jim-Bob, and whatever you do, don't fight with him."

It was good to get away from town and the feeling that people were watching him. Jim-Bob left Mont's corrals at daylight, angling the horses northward up the wagon road toward Grafton. The Thorn outfit lay roughly halfway between the two towns, a little to the east of the road along the dry fork of Paint Horse Creek.

The red dog Ranger followed a while, chasing rabbits and barking at the broncs whenever they strayed off the road. Finally, when he figured Ranger had gone as far as he safely could without getting sore-footed, Jim-Bob ordered him to return home. It took twice to get the job done. Jim-Bob turned in the saddle and watched the dog trot disconsolately back along the wagon road toward Swallowfork, tail tucked under a little. Presently a jackrabbit bobbed up, and Ranger was off after him, his hurt feelings forgotten in the joy of the wild chase.

Jim-Bob grinned and gave his attention once more to the horses. They were young broncs and acted like a bunch of kids would act, running at first, kicking and biting and playing in the cool air of the early morning. And like kids, they tired of it after a while. They settled down to a long, steady trot. Each horse found his own place and more or less stayed in it.

Jim-Bob trailed along behind them and let them have their heads so long as none of them tried to pull away. For a while he felt like a cowboy again, jog-trotting across the wide mesquite flat in the dusty wake of the broncs. He had long since decided there was no future in cowboying if a man wanted to build something that would really be his own. But as a way of life, if he was willing to work for someone else, it carried a lot of satisfaction.

About four miles out of town, along the Grafton road, lay the Kendrick ranch. In size it was second only to Walter Chapman's C Bar. Where everything on the Chapman outfit was built for stout rather than for looks, and everything had a purpose or wasn't tolerated, the Kendrick outfit was something of a showpiece. A big white two-storey house stood out on the open flat, rising up beyond the straight lines of planted trees like a toothpick out of a pie. The paling fences gleamed with white paint, and even the barn was white.

As a common working cowhand, Jim-Bob had never

been invited up to the big house. But cow country rumor had it that the family ate its meals on a large white linen tablecloth, with a young Mexican maid standing there to keep the coffee cups full and carry off the dishes as quickly as they were used. They said Mrs. Kendrick never had to cook or wash her own dishes. The story was told that once her own cook fell suddenly ill, and Mrs. Kendrick had gone without food for a whole day rather than eat anything that came from the cowboys' cookshack. There was supposed to be a white porcelain bathtub in the house, too. Old Ox Quisenhunt, the freighter, once told Jim-Bob he had seen it himself, had hauled it down from the railroad at Grafton behind a "grass freight" team of oxen.

But naturally the prettiest thing about the place was Tina Kendrick, the rancher's daughter. When Ox had told Jim-Bob about the bathtub, Jim-Bob had immediately pictured Tina sitting in it. The idea brought a blush and a quick surge of shame. Somehow now, every time he saw Tina Kendrick he thought about that bathtub, and about her sitting in it. It was a naughty thought but a pleasant one, and that faint tugging of guilt was never enough to banish it from mind.

Tina Kendrick fitted with a big white ranchhouse, white tablecloths—and yes, even with a white porcelain bathtub. She was as pretty as a china doll. Just looking at her around the dances was enough to take most men's breath away. To a working cowhand like Jim-Bob, she had always seemed like a beautiful prize, far away and unobtainable. Small wonder it shook him when she had paid so much attention to him at Sothern's barn dance the other night. It was like a broke and hungry cowboy suddenly discovering a hundred dollars in his pocket.

Coming upon the white buildings of the Kendrick ranch with his string of broncs, Jim-Bob didn't really mean to stop. But he found himself angling the horses up the dusty road to the house before he realized what he was doing. He felt suddenly foolish. He had no real business here. Now it was too late to turn the horses back, for chances were he had already been seen. And what was it Mont Naylor had told him one day? "Once you've started down the hill, it's safer to go ahead than try to turn around and go back."

He saw an open corral gate near the barn and eased the horses through it. Jim-Bob stepped down inside the corral and shut the gate behind them, wondering what in thunder to do next. In an adjacent pen, nearest the barn, he saw an old pensioner shoeing a horse in the cool of the morning. The aging cowpuncher finished up. He dropped the horse's forefoot and slipped the rope off its neck, turning the animal loose. He was too busy to notice Jim-Bob.

"Button," he called to someone in the barn, "Button, you git yourself out here where you belong."

In a moment a cowhand a couple of years younger than Jim-Bob stepped out of the barn. He looked like a cat caught with its paw in the birdcage. The old man was bawling him out. "The boss left you here to help me with these horses, not to be lollygaggin' in the barn with his daughter. Now you pick up that rope and go catch me another horse."

Tina Kendrick appeared in the doorway of the barn. As the young ranch hand hurried off, building a loop in his rope, the old man testily turned to her. "Your daddy won't like it, you down here at the barn makin' fools of these kid cowboys. Now why don't you git yourself back up to the big house where you belong?"

Tina Kendrick smiled and tickled the old man under the chin. She let her slender fingers run through his short gray beard. "Now Papa John, you don't mean to lift your voice to little old Tina that way."

The old man said sharply, "You can wrap the rest of the men around your little finger, but I'm too old to bend thataway. I've known your tricks ever since you were a little girl." His voice softened, though. She had him, just like she did the rest.

Tina's eyes lifted and found Jim-Bob, coming through the gate afoot. "Papa John, we've got company."

The old-timer turned and glared. "Another one. It ain't enough you got all the cowboys on *this* place tongue-tied. Now you got to go and bring them in from someplace else."

Jim-Bob hastened to explain. "I just stopped in to water my horses. I figured they were gettin' a little dry . . ."

The old man snorted. "Only four miles from town, and this early in the mornin'? They wouldn't drink if you kicked them off in the river."

The young cowboy led up another horse. He was eyeing Jim-Bob suspiciously. Papa John caught the look and sniffed. "Nothin' makes me tireder than to hear some old fool wishin' he was a kid again. Believe me, I'm glad I got all that foolishness far behind me." He turned away from Jim-Bob and began petting the horse, easing his hand down the hind leg so he could pick up the foot.

Smiling, Tina walked up to Jim-Bob, her skirts

swinging just a little. She had that kind of walk. She stopped a full pace away, putting her hands behind her and rocking back on her heels a little. She looked him full in the eyes a moment, her own eyes dancing. "What brings you all the way out here?"

Jim-Bob remembered his hat and took it off. "Well, I was just drivin' these broncs out to the Thorn ranch, and I saw your place, and—well, it's like I said, I wanted to water the horses."

The pen where Jim-Bob had turned the broncs had no water in it.

"I know better than that," she smiled. "You came by to see me."

He reddened. "I hope you don't mind."

"Of course I don't mind. Why, I was just thinking about you when you rode up. Isn't that a coincidence?"

Papa John snorted again.

Jim-Bob just nodded, glancing at her, then looking shyly away as an electric thrill worked all the way down to his toes. "It sure is."

Tina caught his arm and said, "Let's go up to the house and see if there's some coffee and cake left. You do like coffee and cake, don't you?"

He would have eaten coffee grounds and raw dough if Tina Kendrick had been serving them.

Tina looked back at the young cowboy who stood beside Papa John. "Willy, would you mind taking Mr. McClain's horses down and watering them in the big trough?"

The young man nodded. "Sure, Miss Tina. I'll be glad to do it." But the look that stabbed at Jim-Bob showed he had rather take the deputy down to the trough and throw him in it.

The big house was even more sumptuous than Jim-

Bob had imagined. Lace curtains, fine mahogany furniture, linen tablecloth. He was afraid to walk on the carpets with his high-heeled boots and spurs, and he started to skirt all the way around them. Tina caught his arm and led him across.

"Silly," she teased, "this is all very plain. You can't hurt it."

He met Tina's mother, and he got an uneasy impression she disliked him right off. He decided this was a foolish notion. How could she dislike somebody she hadn't had time to get to know? Just the same, Jim-Bob sat thoroughly awed, afraid to touch anything because it all looked so fragile. He ate cake and sipped weak coffee in delightful misery with Tina, and felt as out of place as a bronc in a boarding school.

A most disrespectful thought crept unbidden into his mind. He wondered where they kept the bathtub. He tried to shut the thought out, but it clung stubbornly while his face reddened. He caught Mrs. Kendrick staring severely at him. A panicky notion struck him that she might be reading his mind, Tina and soap bubbles and all. She *was* a cold-eyed old sister.

He was glad when Tina at last led him out the front door. They stood on the porch together. She frowned, but her eyes were soft and blue.

"Jim-Bob," she said, "I had to promise Chum Lawton I'd let him take me to the next dance. But I hope you'll be there to rescue me. There's not anyone in town I'd rather dance with than you."

Jim-Bob swallowed. "You just give me the high-sign, and I'll rescue you any time you want me to." He drew a circle with the toe of his boot. "I was hopin' maybe sometime I could take you to the dance myself. Then I wouldn't have to be rescuin' you from anybody."

Her voice was soft. "You just ask me sometime, Jim-Bob."

He walked down off the porch and looked back at her. She threw him a kiss and tore him to pieces inside.

Tina's mother stood watching, well back from the door. When Jim-Bob was gone, she said brittley, "Tina, come here."

The girl came inside, laughter dancing in her eyes.

"Tina, have you no pride? Must you forever be carrying on with men like that? I didn't bring you up to marry some common cowboy."

"Who said anything about marrying one of them, Mother?" Standing in the doorway, she watched Jim-Bob open the corral gate and string out his broncs. Her smile widened as she saw the cowboy Willy follow Jim-Bob out and stare after him.

Her mother said, "I heard about this McClain and Chum Lawton. I heard they almost fought over you at the dance. Disgraceful!"

Tina nodded. "They almost did. Perhaps another time."

"Tina!" Mrs. Kendrick gasped. "You mean you *want* them to fight over you?"

"Why not? Someday you'll marry me off to someone with a rich and dull future, someone like Dan Singleton. But I'll always be able to remember that I once had men fighting over me like two bulls over a heifer."

"Tina!" Mrs. Kendrick gasped again.

"Don't be so shocked, Mother. I'll bet you've got plenty of memories you wouldn't tell Dad about. Well, I'm going to have some memories, too, to keep me warm when I get old!"

* * *

It took a while for Jim-Bob to get settled. He rode with his head down, day-dreaming about Tina Kendrick. First thing he knew, the broncs were completely out of sight ahead of him. He touched spurs to his horse and eased into a lope to catch up.

With time, the mesquite flat stretched out behind him. The land roughened up, going hilly, with mesquite-timbered draws slashing down among the hills. The draw grass stood belly deep to a horse where cattle hadn't stocked it too heavily. Along its edges, he came across Mexican sheepherders drifting their wooly Merino bands on the shorter grass. Sheep would fatten where cows drew thin, yet sheep would starve in tall grass.

The broncs had left the main wagon road and veered east. That was all right with Jim-Bob. He had to leave it sometime anyway. The Thorn ranch lay to the east of the road. The broncs were feeling good. Reining up a moment, Jim-Bob could hear them ahead, breaking into a lope. He spurred the brown again. He almost lost his seat when a startled jackrabbit jumped up right under the horse's hoofs and caused the mount to shy violently to one side. Jim-Bob grabbed at the horn and pulled himself back into the saddle. The left stirrup flopped where his foot had slipped out of it. He was glad no one had been around to see him. It always rankled a cowboy to have someone see him fall off of a horse, or grab leather.

He followed the broncs' tracks up over the brow of a hill and dropped down on the other side, then reined up again. Ahead of him he could see the broncs heading pell mell for a wide draw, where five hobbled horses

stood with heads high, watching. He saw smoke curling lazily upward from a campfire, and men running
out to catch their horses. For a moment it looked as if
Jim-Bob's broncs were going to carry away those in
the hobbles. But instead, they stopped running and
began to mill around, nosing the other horses, getting
acquainted.

By the time Jim-Bob reached the camp, there had
been a brief kicking and biting fight between one of
his broncs and another horse. The older horse put the
young bronc in his proper place, and things settled
down. The broncs began to graze on the thick green
grass and to bite off the long strings of drying beans
that hung down from the scattering of mesquite trees.

Satisfied that his broncs were under control, Jim-
Bob reined toward the four men of the camp. One of
them stood with a rifle in his hands. Another had a
thumb hooked in his gunbelt, fingers touching the butt
of the six-shooter on his hip.

All of a sudden Jim-Bob got a weird feeling about
this camp. He wanted to keep right on going, but he
knew he had to cut the broncs out from among the
hobbled horses. Mont Naylor had told him: "You ever
find yourself in a ticklish spot, you just go right on as
if you hadn't expected anything else. Don't ever look
behind you or start backin' up. Just keep your eyes
open and your hardware handy."

Jim-Bob pulled his horse up thirty feet from the
campfire. He had let his hand ease down to where he
could almost touch his gun, but he hoped the men
hadn't noticed it. He tried to keep his face and his
voice calm.

"Howdy."

They looked him over good, no friendliness in their

eyes at first. Jim-Bob wished he'd watched the broncs a little closer, wished they hadn't picked this spot to drop down into the draw.

Finally one of the men smiled. "Howdy, kid. Git down, and we'll have dinner directly."

Jim-Bob said, "I didn't figure on runnin' into anybody. I was just takin' a bunch of broncs out to the Thorn outfit. I didn't go to let them run through your camp like they did."

The man shrugged. "No damage. Just surprised us a little, was all. The way they came lopin' in here, we thought it might be a—well, it might have been most anything. Horse thieves or somethin'." He looked about him. A somewhat younger man with much the same facial features still stood with rifle in his hand. "Buster," the man said, "put that thing up. You want this boy to think we're unfriendly?"

The one called Buster was frowning darkly. "Ain't we?"

"Put it up, Buster!"

Jim-Bob hesitated, then carefully swung down from the saddle. He followed the example Mont had set at Dunnigan's—got off with the horse between him and the men. Jim-Bob knew just about everybody in this country, but these men were strangers to him, and not very friendly strangers at that.

"Don't mind Buster," the man said. "He's just a little ringy. He thought them broncs of yours was fixin' to run off our horses. He sure does hate to walk." He extended his hand. "I'm Dencil Jones. Buster's my brother."

Warily Jim-Bob shook his hand. The one who called himself Dencil Jones pointed a thumb toward the other pair of men. "That's Pony Sims, there with the bald head, and the other one we just call Hackberry."

Sims and Hackberry shook Jim-Bob's hand, but he could feel their eyes working him over questioningly. Buster Jones stayed back. He had dropped the rifle from its ready position, but he still held it slackly in his hand.

"Ridin' hell-bent into a man's camp like that," Buster Jones said darkly, "how were we to know you weren't tryin' to run our horses off?"

Jim-Bob shook his head. "You don't have to worry about me stealin' your horses. I'm Jim-Bob McClain, deputy for Sheriff Mont Naylor." He reached up and touched a finger to his badge. But he realized they must already have seen it. Something lay cold in the pit of his stomach, and for a moment he wished he'd had that badge in his pocket instead of out in the open that way.

Dencil Jones was pleasant now, but Jim-Bob thought he sensed an undertone of worry in the man's voice. "What's a deputy sheriff doin' way out here?"

Jim-Bob explained his errand. Dencil Jones seemed to believe him. But Buster Jones still scowled. He had gone back beyond the fire and hunkered down well away from the flames' heat. He had laid the rifle down within close reach.

Jim-Bob licked his lips, for they were still dry. He found it hard to take his eyes off Buster Jones, and Buster's rifle. "You fellers are a long ways from any-place yourselves," he remarked, not wanting to ask them straight out.

Dencil nodded, noting how Jim-Bob watched his younger brother. "Don't worry about Buster," he said. "Like I told you, he's just a mite ringy. He don't trust nobody lately that wears a badge."

He poured black coffee into a tin cup and handed it to Jim-Bob, following it up with another cup that had a spoon and some sugar in it. "We just finished drivin' a bunch of cows up to the TP railroad for the Circle Dots down south. While we were in Grafton, Buster took on a little too much of that happy juice and like to've wrecked the place. We decided we'd best hole up out here in the brush a few days till things kind of blew over, then head on south. Buster saw your badge and naturally thought you'd come to get him, was all."

It sounded all right, but Jim-Bob couldn't swallow it, somehow. He tried to keep from showing his doubt. "I hadn't heard anything of it. If it happened in some other county, it's none of our lookout anyway."

Dencil glanced at his brother. "See there, Buster? Settle down now." To Jim-Bob he said, "I could tell you were a right kind of a law when I first saw you. Buster didn't mean no harm in Grafton. He's just a little too playful sometimes."

Jim-Bob nodded. "Sure, I savvy." But he didn't. All he knew for sure was that something was wrong here. But he found his nervousness easing.

Pleasantly Dencil Jones said, "Why don't you stay and eat dinner with us? We'll be fixin' it directly."

Jim-Bob believed Dencil sincerely meant it, although Buster still scowled. Normally it was about half a day's ride to the Thorn place from Swallowfork. But Jim-Bob had lost time around the Kendrick ranch. It was still a couple of hours to Thorn's, and his stomach was growling at him. Moreover, he was curious. "I don't reckon it'd hurt to stay," he said.

Squatting on his spurs in the tromped-down grass, he studied the Joneses. Remarkable how much the brothers resembled each other. Much more than did Tom and Dan Singleton. Dencil was the oldest, and the years had set deeper in the lines of his face than they had in Buster's. But a stranger might easily be confused by the two.

"Easy enough to tell that you two are brothers," he remarked.

Dencil smiled. There was an easy-going quality about him that Buster didn't show. "I don't reckon we can help that."

Jim-Bob looked out toward the broncs to be sure they weren't straying. They were remaining well put, enjoying the good grass. He studied the Jones outfit's horses. Mont Naylor would give his eye teeth for horses like those. It was seldom you saw a group of cowboys so uniformly well mounted.

He said, "You couldn't have a better bunch of horses if every one of them was stolen."

Buster darkened a little. Jim-Bob spoke quickly, "I didn't mean anything by that. Just a manner of speakin'."

Dencil laughed, but somehow it was a strained sort of laugh. "A cowboy workin' for the other man never has a chance to accumulate much of the world's goods, Jim-Bob. I always figure he's at least entitled to own a good horse."

The one they called Hackberry did the cooking. He sliced venison from a quarter hanging up in a mesquite limb and started mixing dough in a flour sack. He punched a hole in the center of the flour with his fingers, then carefully worked it with his hands, adding salt and baking powder as he squeezed water and flour into dough. He had no Dutch ovens, for the men carried only what they could pack behind their saddles. He fried the bread in an open skillet.

Meanwhile, to pass the time, Jim-Bob sat in a card

game with Dencil and Pony Sims. Buster Jones didn't play. He walked off down the draw, looking at the horses. Every time Jim-Bob glanced that way, he found Buster staring at him.

An idea had been nagging at Jim-Bob. Maybe these men *were* horse thieves. There was no getting around the fact that these were mighty good horses for four drifting cow-punchers. Jim-Bob had noted that no two of the horses carried the same brand. He tried to figure out some of the brands, but none of them were familiar to him. He would remember them, though. They might bear a little checking.

When he got back to town, he thought, he'd tell Mont Naylor about these men. Maybe they'd prove out harmless. Then again. . . . Well, it would keep. Right now he had to get these horses out to Thorn's. Time enough in a couple of days to talk to Mont. It didn't look as if these men were fixing to go anywhere anyway.

He saddled up after dinner and prepared to gather his scattered broncs. Dencil Jones stepped out to shake hands with him. "Come back by," he invited. "We'll be around a while."

Even suspicious, Jim-Bob found himself liking this man. "I may do that."

He separated his broncs from the Jones horses and stretched them out again in a long trot. The hobbled horses wanted to follow. Jim-Bob had to push them back twice. The last time he looked, he could see that Buster Jones was still watching him.

Buster scowled as Jim-Bob left. He walked back to the campfire and picked up the rifle. Dencil said sharply, "Put it down, Buster."

Buster replied, "We're makin' a mistake, lettin' him

ride off like this. We could still get him, and nobody would know."

"He'd be missed."

"Not before we finished the job we been figurin' on. Afterwards, it wouldn't matter."

Dencil Fox sternly shook his head. "I swear, Buster, I don't know what ails you sometimes. I do believe you just like to see the blood run. He's only a green kid. He can't hurt nothin'."

"Maybe he's green and maybe he ain't. I wasn't any older than him the time we took that bank in the Panhandle, and there wasn't anything green about me, remember? I still say we oughtn't to take the chance." He took a step forward, toward his horse.

Dencil reached down and yanked the rifle out of Buster's hands. "*I'm* runnin' this outfit, and I say there's not goin' to be any unnecessary killin'. You want us all to hang?"

"Let the wrong people go ridin' around free and we'll hang anyway."

Anger crackled in Dencil Fox's voice. "Any time you decide you don't like the way I run things, you can leave. But as long as you stay with us, I'm the big brother. You savvy?"

Buster tried angrily, but he couldn't meet Dencil's blazing eyes. "Maybe someday I *will* leave," he said and abruptly turned away. He walked to where his saddle lay on the ground. He took a bottle out of a saddlebag and worked the cork out with his teeth.

"You better go easy on that stuff, too," Dencil prodded him.

Buster spat the cork out in the grass, showing that he didn't intend to put it back into the bottle. "You go to hell!" he said.

3

George Thorn's ranch wasn't exactly a poverty outfit, but it wasn't enjoying any excess of prosperity, either. George was a long-time cowboy who had saved his money for years and invested it in mares. In time he had himself a sizable bunch of horses. His TX horses were used all over West Texas. George would sell them either broken or as broncs. Besides that, he would break other men's horses for them if they couldn't or didn't want to do it themselves. He would charge by the head, depending upon the degree of roughness the owner wanted ironed out.

But these days George had to pay someone else to do the really rough stuff. Oh, he could still handle them pretty smartly himself, once the sharp edges had been rubbed down a little. He could still ride a bucking horse better than Jim-Bob ever could, even with his gray hair and the way his shoulders were becoming stooped a little more each year. An old bronc stomper like George Thorn might be forced to slow down, but he was unlikely ever to quit so long as he could still get on one by himself or get somebody to leg him up.

"A new horse is just like a new woman," George

often said. "You can't stand the curiosity. You've just got to see for yourself how they turn out."

The first thing a casual visitor might notice would be George's corrals. They were better than his house. Fact was, they had to be, or the broncs would tear them down. The posts were of good heart cedar, six to eight inches thick across the top, and sunk as deeply into the ground as a man would care to dig with a crowbar and a coffee-can scoop. The planks were of good strong pine, hauled down by wagon from the railroad at Grafton.

The planks in the house appeared to have been leftovers from the corrals. George Thorn had spent half his days out in the open, following a chuckwagon. It didn't take much of a house to look good to him now.

The hot afternoon sun was well along its descent when Jim-Bob put the broncs through the gate of an empty corral and stepped down in the dust to shut it behind them. Narrowing his eyes in the summer glare, he could see two men out a-horseback in the distance. Their horses were crow-hopping around, evidently broncs out of the corral for their first time under saddle. The men rode in circles, yanking the horses around, getting them used to the rough pull of the inch-thick hackamore reins. Every once in a while one of the horses would bog his head and take three or four jumps.

"Howdy, Jim-Bob," a girl's voice called pleasantly. "Come on over and I'll put you to work."

Jim-Bob saw Sue-Ellen Thorn working in the adjacent corral. She had three hackamored broncs tied along the fence. She was sacking out a fourth. Holding the single rein, she gently threw a saddle blanket upon the pony's fear-humped back, then pulled it off again and again, getting him used to the feel of it against his touchy hide. The bronc's left hind foot was tied up so he couldn't jump around or kick much.

"Easy now, be gentle," she was saying softly, constantly talking to the bronc as she moved around in the gray dust stirred up by restless hoofs.

Jim-Bob leaned against the fence and watched her between the planks. At eighteen, Sue-Ellen was a real cowgirl for you. Sue wore a broad-brimmed hat that had been made for a man. Her long brown hair was done up in braids and tied down to keep it from being windblown. A thick coat of dust lay on the brown blouse and the dark split riding skirt she wore. From a distance, one might mistake her for a man. Close up, he wouldn't. Even with this rig on, she was quite obviously a girl. Jim-Bob had seen her in a dress a few times, her hair combed out and prettied up with a curling iron. A man would hardly recognize her as being the same. But even when Jim-Bob saw her that way, he remembered her this way.

Sue-Ellen could be a nice-looking girl when she dressed up. Not really pretty like Tina Kendrick though. Her face was sun-browned, and her hands were a little on the rough side. Tina's blue eyes always held a little of laughter, a little of mystery. They gave a man a vague feeling that she knew something he didn't. Sue-Ellen's large brown eyes looked at you frankly and honestly, and there wasn't any mystery about her. She had been brought up among men. She had the man's way of saying what came to mind, be it pleasant or not. If she didn't like you, you knew it right away and no foolishness about it. If she did like you, you knew that, too.

Maybe that was what made Jim-Bob shy away from

her so much. She liked him, and she wasn't coy about it. It gave him an uneasy feeling, because the way he had always been taught, a girl was supposed to sit back and wait for the boy to make the first move. Or at least make him think it was his idea.

"Well," said Sue-Ellen, "did you come here to loaf? There's some more broncs over here need sackin' out."

Jim-Bob jerked loose his hornstring and took his rope down from his saddle. Walking into the corral where Sue-Ellen was, he said, "I'll help you. It's a man's job anyway."

That was like stepping on a sore toe. Sharply she said, "Oh, it is, is it?"

She let the bronc's hind foot down and retrieved her rope. She led him to the fence and tied him, then walked toward one of the other broncs. Stalked might be a better word. She was angry.

Jim-Bob realized she had declared herself into a contest with him. He pulled the slip knot of another hackamore rein and freed a second bronc from the fence. He saw Sue-Ellen build a small loop in her rope and drop it right in front of the bronc's hind foot, at the same time leading him up so he stepped in it. With a quick jerk of her wrist she took in the slack and pulled the horse's foot up. Doubling and redoubling the rope, she tied it around the bronc's neck. Quickly Jim-Bob moved to do likewise. But Sue-Ellen had her horse's foot tied up before he did. He flushed in vague resentment, letting a girl beat him this way. Corral was no place for a girl anyway.

He thought back to all the times he had ever seen Sue-Ellen, and it seemed she was always conspiring to make him uncomfortable. He remembered one day she had been visiting the C Bar chuckwagon with her father. Jim-Bob had missed two loops at a wormy calf. Sue-Ellen borrowed somebody's rope, rode out and dropped a loop over that calf's neck just as neatly as any other girl might make a hemstitch. The boys around the wagon had razzed Jim-Bob until he'd finally had to bloody one of their noses.

Then the other night at Sothern's barn. He had been trying to dance with Tina Kendrick, but every time he glanced around it seemed that Sue-Ellen's eyes were on him. She wanted him to dance with her, and she didn't make any secret about it. He knew Tina could tell it, and it made him uneasy. But he had never given Sue-Ellen the satisfaction of dancing with him. She ought to learn it was a woman's place to wait and be asked.

"What did you come out here for, anyhow?" she asked belligerently as she began to work the bronc with a saddle blanket.

"I brought out some of Mont's broncs for George to break."

"What's the matter, can't *you* do it?"

"That's not my job."

She said flatly, "From what I hear, you're not doin' too well as a deputy, either!"

Then, seeing the hurt in Jim-Bob's face, she was instantly apologetic. "I'm sorry. I had no business sayin' a thing like that. I didn't mean it."

"I reckon you did," he said tightly. "You were mad enough to say what you thought. And you're right, I did make a mess of things."

She dropped the saddle blanket to arm's length and faced Jim-Bob. "Anybody's goin' to make a mistake once in a while. Even as long as Dad has worked with these old broncs, he occasionally lets one of them get to him. You oughtn't to let it ride you that way."

Jim-Bob said nothing. Sue-Ellen walked over and touched his hand. "Please, Jim-Bob, forget I said anything. You just made me so mad there for a minute, that business about this bein' a job for a man. It really shouldn't bother me, I've heard it so much. It's just that Dad needed a boy to help him, and he never had one. So I've had to learn to be a cowboy for him."

Jim-Bob managed a smile. "Next thing you know, you women will be wantin' to vote!"

Eventually old George Thorn and Chum Lawton came in with their horses. It wasn't an easy ride. One would have to lead or drive the other a little way. Then, when his own bronc began acting up, the other did the leading and driving. By the time they finally got back to the corral, the pitch was pretty well gone from the broncs, at least for the day. But the animals still had a lot to learn before they would ever be cow ponies.

Old George waved his hand at Jim-Bob. The sudden movement almost caused him to lose his seat, for the bronc didn't especially approve it. Thorn had a certain easy grace when he was on horseback. The way he sat there, straight and proud, he looked like somebody sure enough. But when he stepped stiffly to the ground, he was something else again. George Thorn, with more broken bones than he could keep account of, hobbled around so awkwardly that it was almost painful to watch him. He had been thrown, stomped, rolled over on, walloped against fenceposts and tree trunks until it was a wonder he could get around at all. His right leg was bowed out of proportion to the left, result of a compound fracture's crooked healing.

His left arm was drawn up stiffly. The knuckles of his big hands were knotted, and his right thumb had long ago been cut off between a slipping rope and an unyielding saddlehorn.

But he was one of that tough old bronc-stomper breed who loved horses in spite of all they'd ever done to him. He talked them and breathed them, and he mumbled about them in his sleep at night.

"Jim-Bob, *come le va?*" he spoke jovially, his friendly eyes squinted up with turkey-track wrinkles reaching back halfway to his ears.

"Fair enough, I reckon."

"Them the ponies old Mont was a-goin' to send out here?" Thorn asked. He peered at them through the fence a moment or two. When he turned away, he probably could have described every horse in there.

Chum Lawton's bronc was still humped up a little and giving him some trouble in getting out of the saddle. Jim-Bob wasn't much inclined to help him. Chum finally saw an opening and swung down quickly. The bronc pawed at him with one forefoot as Chum stepped clear. In anger Chum started to swing the knotted end of the hackamore rein at him.

George Thorn said quietly but firmly, "Easy now, Chum, it's just pony nature to want to git you. You got to see it his way." Then, uneasily, he added, "Chum, I think you and Jim-Bob know each other." He knew very well that they did, and he was watching them pretty close.

Chum was square-jawed and ruddy-faced. And his eyes always seemed to be angry at somebody. Chum didn't offer to shake hands, so Jim-Bob saw no need to force the issue. He just shoved his own hands in his pockets and returned Chum's glare.

Chum *was* an ornery-looking cuss, Jim-Bob thought. Just an uneducated cowboy who couldn't even talk English right and proper, and who wouldn't never be nothin' but a cowboy or a bronc stomper all his life. He wondered what Tina Kendrick could see in such a man.

George said, "I'd figured on takin' out a couple more broncs before we quit for supper. You're goin' to spend the night with us, aren't you, Jim-Bob?"

Jim-Bob nodded. "Figured on it. I'll take a bronc out with you."

Chum scowled. "You sure you can hang on one? I don't aim to spend all night chasin' after your saddle."

Jim-Bob's face heated. "You couldn't catch it noway, because you'd be afoot before I was."

George Thorn saw it was time to change the subject. He led his horse right in between the two young men and nonchalantly began unsaddling him. Chum and Jim-Bob both scrambled to get out of the way. "If you boys are goin' with me, you better pick you a couple and throw a kack on them."

It was turning dark by the time they got the three broncs back into the corral, unsaddled them and led them out to stake them for the night. Sue-Ellen had taken the others out one by one and tied them around to big old freight-wagon wheels, loose stumps, and anything else heavy enough to be hard dragging but not quite solid enough to break a bronc's neck if he made a hard run against the rope. By the time the broncs had been staked out a few nights, they learned plenty of respect for the hackamore that rubbed all the hide off their noses.

Jim-Bob's right leg was sore. Chum had bucked his bronc into him a couple of times. Jim-Bob was certain he'd done it on purpose. He had tried to return the favor but had been able to get his own bronc to buck only once all the time they'd been out of the corral.

The three men walked into the house with their spurs a-jingle just as Sue-Ellen lighted a pair of kerosene lamps in the small kitchen. "Supper's on the table," she said. "You-all wash up."

Jim-Bob noted that she had changed to a cotton dress. It looked better on her than those outdoor clothes. This was more the way a girl was supposed to look, he thought. She had hot biscuits and real milk gravy and steak. And the coffee—it was the real thing. No disrespect, but that coffee Tina had served him this morning had been as weak as water. Maybe someday he would get a chance to teach Tina how to fix coffee.

"Sue-Ellen," Jim-Bob finally said when he was able to stop eating for a minute. "I didn't have any idea you could cook like this."

She talked angry, but he couldn't tell whether she really was or not. "Any reason why you thought I couldn't?"

Watching his step, he replied cautiously, "No, I didn't say . . ."

"You didn't have to say it, it stood out all over your face. You didn't think I could do anything but handle broncs and rope cattle. Well, I can do that and cook too. I'll bet *you* can't."

"No, ma'am," he admitted quietly, "I sure can't."

This girl was making him about as nervous as Tina Kendrick did, but in a different way. He didn't mean to be setting her off like that all the time. What did she want to be so touchy for?"

George came to Jim-Bob's aid. "Well, to be honest about it, she doesn't cook like this every day, Jim-Bob.

Only when she's got company she likes. If you'd come here a little oftener, I might get a little tallow on my ribs."

Chum stared malevolently at Jim-Bob. "You say you can't cook, and you can't ride. I just been wonderin' what you *can* do, Jim-Bob. They tell me you couldn't even keep out of the way of a stinkin' old cow thief."

Jim-Bob stiffened.

George Thorn said quickly, "Cut it out, Chum. Jim-Bob does the best he can."

Chum said, "That ain't much."

Jim-Bob stood up, his chair scraping back across the floor. "Now you listen here . . ." Then he remembered what Mont Naylor had told him. No matter what he did, he wasn't to let Chum Lawton sucker him into a fight. He sat back down.

But Chum was standing up. "Listen to what?" he challenged. "Seems to me like you got quiet in an awful hurry."

Jim-Bob looked down at his plate, his face flaring. He poked a tender piece of steak into his mouth. But now it was tasteless.

"I can't fight you, Chum."

"Or *won't*."

George Thorn quietly but firmly slapped the palm of his huge hand down on the table. "You two young roosters just settle down there. I can whip the both of you if I have to. There'll be no fightin' in my house."

Jim-Bob glanced up at Sue-Ellen and saw the question in her brown eyes. She was probably thinking he was scared of Chum Lawton. That brought him a flush of shame. He had rather be accused of stealing sheep.

"I made a promise to Mont Naylor," Jim-Bob said.

"I told him I wouldn't fight with Chum, no matter what happened."

He realized suddenly that admitting this was the dumbest stunt he'd pulled all day. Now, knowing Jim-Bob wouldn't fight, Chum would needle him without mercy. Jim-Bob could see that idea working around in Chum's eyes. The way the story would get told, it would make Jim-Bob out a coward.

After supper they sat on the front porch, in the darkness, enjoying the cool of the evening after such a hot day. George Thorn made some effort to start conversation, but it raveled out to nothing, and he finally fell quiet. Jim-Bob sat on one end of the little porch, Chum on the other. Eventually Chum got up and walked out to the shack where he slept.

George cleared his throat and knocked burned tobacco out of his strong pipe. "I'd figured on Chum sharin' the shack with you, but I don't reckon we'd any of us get any sleep tonight. Barn suit you all right?"

"I was going to suggest it myself," Jim-Bob said.

George lent him a pair of blankets, and Jim-Bob walked out to the barn. Presently he decided it was too hot in there, so he carried them outside and spread them in a corral on the off side away from the house. He lay awake a long time, dreaming how good it would be to arrest Chum Lawton for stealing horses or smashing up a saloon. He didn't know when he finally went to sleep, but it was awfully late.

Awakening slowly, he opened one eye and saw that daylight was coming on. He became aware of noise. Sleepy-headed, he raised up on one elbow to see where it was coming from. Suddenly he was wide awake and on his feet. A dozen horses were spilling through the corral gate on the run, headed straight for Jim-Bob. He grabbed at the blankets and sprinted barefooted for the barn, the blankets wadded under his arm. Jim-Bob's shoulder slammed hard against the barn wall, and he turned to see the horses trample across the clothes he'd dropped on the ground. One of his boots went sailing and came down in a shower of sand.

Chum Lawton rode his horse through the gate and drew up, his eyes laughing. "Oh, howdy, Jim-Bob," he spoke with sarcasm. "You up already?"

Anger hit Jim-Bob like a fist, and he started across the corral toward Chum before he thought better of it and stopped. He picked up his boots, his pants and his shirt. It took a minute to find his hat, trampled out of shape and half buried in the sandy corral. He slapped the clothes against the barn to beat the dirt out of them before he put them on over his long underwear. There was a ten inch rip right down the back of the shirt.

Chum said, "It could have been worse. You could have had it on."

"One of these days, Chum," Jim-Bob breathed. "One of these days . . ."

Chum laughed, unsaddled his horse and walked to the house for breakfast.

When Jim-Bob got there, George Thorn stared in surprise at his rumpled, dirty clothes. "You look like you'd been run over by wild horses!"

Jim-Bob glanced sharply at Chum Lawton. "You might say I didn't miss it far."

Chum was keeping his mouth straight, but his eyes were laughing. "Town life's spoilt him. He's got to where he sleeps half the mornin'."

The significance of all this somehow escaped George, but he could tell there had been something between the two young men. He didn't pry.

Chum ate silently a while. Then, "How much they payin' you, Jim-Bob?"

Jim-Bob tried to ignore him, but he couldn't. "None of your business."

Chum shrugged. "Just askin'. Seems to me like with a kid in the office, the county ought to just be payin' a kid price. Save some tax money."

"Tax money never seemed to worry you when you had the job, Chum. They tell me you ruined all the horses the county furnished for you, and Mont finally had to make you furnish your own."

Chum grunted. "Yeah, I been wonderin' about that. I been wonderin' if Mont didn't go ahead and charge the county for horses I didn't use. After all, he's in the horse business."

Jim-Bob dropped his fork. He could swallow an insult to himself. But Chum was treading on holy ground when he began to libel Mont Naylor.

"Mont's never taken anything that didn't belong to him," Jim-Bob hotly declared. Chum studied him keenly, evidently sensing he had found the nerve that was the touchiest.

Chum asked, "Is that a fact? Can you swear he's never stole anything from the taxpayers?"

"You're lyin', Chum. You're eggin' me on because you know I promised Mont I wouldn't fight you."

Chum glanced at George and Sue-Ellen to be sure they were getting all this. Sue-Ellen was watching Jim-Bob, dismay in her eyes. George said quietly, "Let him alone, Chum. He doesn't want to fight you."

Confidently Chum said, "Sure he don't. Maybe he's

gettin' into that county money himself. I been wonderin' why he was so anxious to steal my job."

"I didn't steal your job. You'd already lost it before Mont ever came to me."

"But you'd been finaglin' around to get it. And it seems to me Mont was all-fired glad to give it to you. Maybe you got a deal of some kind worked out between you."

Jim-Bob clenched his fists futilely beneath the table. "You're gettin' way out on a limb, Chum."

Jim-Bob saw how Sue-Ellen was staring at him, and he looked quickly away. She was probably thinking he had no spine at all to sit here and endure this, promise or no promise.

Chum kept shoving the knife a little deeper. "Sheriffin' don't pay any big money, and it's been a puzzle to me why a man like Mont would hang onto it if he wasn't gettin' something extra on the side." A glitter of malice worked into his eyes. "Maybe Mont wasn't the first one. Maybe your old daddy set the pattern, because he had it a long time himself."

Jim-Bob jumped to his feet and went around the table in three long, determined strides. Chum was caught off guard a second or two, for he hadn't really expected Jim-Bob to fight. He was standing up and pushing his chair back when Jim-Bob hit him. He tumbled backward over the chair and hit the board floor with a thump.

George Thorn grabbed Jim-Bob's arm. "You don't need to do this for us, Jim-Bob. We know why you sat there and let him talk."

"I'm goin' to do this for *me*," Jim-Bob flamed. "Get up from there, Chum."

George said, "You made a promise to Mont, Jim-

Bob. He had good reason to ask it of you. But if you're goin' to break it, then do it outside. I didn't build this house to stand up for a fist fight."

Chum pushed to his feet, gingerly fingering his nose that hadn't quite straightened out yet. It was beginning to bleed a little. "Suits me fine," he said. "Outside."

Jim-Bob walked out first. He paused on the bottom step to see if Chum was coming. Right behind him, Chum gave Jim-Bob a shove that caught him off balance and sent him sprawling into the broom-swept yard. As he got up, Chum was waiting for him. Chum caught him a hard blow that sent him staggering back.

Sue-Ellen stepped out onto the porch, but George gave her a quick nod of his chin. "Back into the house, Sue-Ellen. A thing like this isn't for girls to watch."

They fought around the front yard like two young bulls, slamming their bodies up against one another, rolling on the ground, grunting and groaning, hard fists driving. First one had the upper hand, then the other. Both men were bloody and bruised, their clothes torn and dirty. But eventually it began to work Jim-Bob's way. Ranch work had made him lean and tough. Chum had never worked particularly hard at anything. Jim-Bob was moving slowly now, but he still had some strength left. His breathing was labored but steady, while Chum was gasping for breath. Finally Jim-Bob was sitting up on Chum's chest, his knees pinning Chum's arms to the ground. Jim-Bob had Chum by the hair, lifting his head up and drumming it against the earth.

Breathing hard, Jim-Bob demanded, "Say it! Say you lied!"

Chum's bloody face twisted in pain, but he still

cursed and squirmed under Jim-Bob's weight. Jim-Bob hammered his head some more.

"Admit it! It was all a lie!"

Chum alternately cursed and groaned, but finally he gave in. "All right, all right. It was a mistake."

"Mistake, nothin'," Jim-Bob said stubbornly. "You just flat lied! Tell George you lied!"

Desperately Chum admitted, "It was a lie."

Jim-Bob pushed to his feet and stepped back, watching while Chum turned over and got to his hands and knees. "You heard that, didn't you, George?"

Thorn nodded passively. "I heard it. None of it was ever goin' to be repeated in the first place." Shaking his head, he motioned Jim-Bob back toward the house. "You better wash up, then get goin'. We got broncs to ride here, and Chum's the only bronc rider I have. I can't afford to get him all crippled up fightin'."

Jim-Bob frowned. "How can you keep a man like that workin' here?"

"Bronc riders are hard to find. You got to take what you can get, because work's goin' out of style. Ten more years, there won't any of these young folks know what hard work is."

Jim-Bob heard Chum's boots on the ground behind him. Chum shouted, "Jim-Bob!" Jim-Bob turned just in time to catch a hard blow on the head. He dropped to his knees and it hit him again. Head drumming, he could hear a brief struggle and George Thorn's angry voice. A big piece of stovewood dropped to the ground beside him. He heard George say, "Chum, you get away from here and cool off before I take a notion to fire you!"

Next thing he knew, Sue-Ellen was bent over him with a washpan, carefully washing his face with a wet rag. Her lips were drawn tight. He thought she was angry with him.

"It wasn't my idea," he told her. "I didn't want to fight."

Tightly she said, "What'll people say when you show up in town like this? It won't matter what the real reason was, they'll say it all traced back to jealousy over that Tina Kendrick. For all I know, maybe that's what it really was."

"You believe that?"

"It doesn't matter what I believe. They'll say you're too irresponsible to wear that badge. They'll most likely take it away from you."

Jim-Bob gritted his teeth at the raw pain when she touched his left eye.

"Turnin' black," she told him. "You're a pretty sight."

Jim-Bob declared, "I'll be back to see Chum another day, when he can't get his hands on a chunk of stovewood. Then we'll see how pretty *he* is, with two front teeth gone!"

4

Jim-Bob saddled up and reined his pony south again, toward town. He figured to get there by noon. Mont was likely to be disappointed. Jim-Bob knew Mont had hoped he'd stay at Thorn's a day or two and let things blow over a little in town. Jim-Bob had always gotten along fine with George, and he liked to fool around with horses. But Chum Lawton had been too much to take.

Jim-Bob rode along with fists clenched. He thought up two dozen ways he could cheerfully kill Chum Lawton, from rope-dragging him back and forth across a prickly-pear patch to drawing and quartering him between a bunch of wild broncs. They were all highly satisfactory but also illegal, so far as he could see. Bye and bye he managed to shove Chum Lawton from mind, and he thought of the Jones brothers, camped in the draw some distance above the Kendrick place. It occurred to Jim-Bob that it wouldn't hurt to have a look-see, just to be sure they were still around. Mont Naylor would more than likely be interested.

He smelled the mesquite smoke before he got in sight of the camp. Coming into the draw, he sensed that something was wrong. There was one less horse hobbled on the green grass today. Riding in, he could see three men in camp. He wondered where the fourth was.

The sound of his horse brought the men quickly to their feet. Dencil Jones turned, hand on his gun. He recognized Jim-Bob, and the sharp lines of his frowning face softened again. He raised his gun hand in greeting.

"Git down, git down and rest a spell." Somehow his face was not as cheerful as he had made his voice, though. Swinging down from the saddle, Jim-Bob led his horse closer to the camp's center and got a better look. Dencil's right eye was darkening. A bruise discolored one side of his face. The jaw was swelling a little. Knowing better, Jim-Bob asked innocently, "Horse throw you?"

Dencil shook his head. "A young bronc, you might say. Buster got the rings. He started drinkin' and took it in his head to go to town and raise a little cain. I tried to stop him, and I found out how old I was." Ruefully, Dencil rubbed his jaw. "I used to could whip him. But I reckon a few years' difference is bound to show up eventually. Go yonder and pour you some coffee."

It must have been quite a fight. Flour and coffee and sugar were spilled out in the grass where the struggling men had fought and rolled over the camp goods. The coffee pot, now sitting on coals at the edge of the slumbering campfire, was bent so that the lid just balanced on it rather than fit the way it should. One of the coffee cups looked as if a horse had stepped on it.

Dencil was watching Jim-Bob. A smile broke on his friendly face. "Looks like you must've run up against some kind of a bronc yourself." Jim-Bob grinned self-consciously and felt Pony Sims and Hackberry laughing with him. Dencil asked, "You whip him?"

Jim-Bob poured a little coffee into the cup, sloshed it around to wash the dirt out, then filled the cup to the top. "I did for a while. Then he got his hand on a chunk of stovewood. I lost."

Dencil's smile grew. He walked out to where a quarter of venison hung from a limb. He pulled out a butcher knife that was stuck in it and trimmed off two good slices of red meat. He brought one to Jim-Bob, then placed the other over his own darkening eye.

"Try that," he said. "They tell me it'll help take the black out."

Jim-Bob tried it. His eye ached. He couldn't tell that this made it better.

Dencil kept watching him, and finally he broke into a laugh. "We're a funny-lookin' pair, I do declare. A couple of black-eyed losers."

Jim-Bob didn't know that it was so funny, but he found himself laughing too, and he felt better for it. At the foot of a heavy-trunked mesquite lay a broken bottle. Dencil saw that Jim-Bob was looking at it. "That's what started it," he said, serious again. "I tried to tell him he'd had enough. I finally had to take it away from him and smash the bottle on that tree. He swarmed over me like a hive of bees."

"Where did he go?"

"Swallowfork. To get a little drunker and maybe get in another fight. He'll come draggin' in tomorrow, maybe, like a whipped dog." Dencil frowned. "You look like a good boy to me, Jim-Bob. Don't you ever let that bottle make a fool out of you."

Dencil was still nursing a remnant of anger against

Buster. Yet Jim-Bob could see worry deep in the tall man's eyes, too.

"Do me a favor, will you, Jim-Bob?" Dencil pressed. "When you get to town, look around for Buster. Sort of watch out for him. We'll give him a little time to work off his mad, then break up camp this afternoon and drift into town. Chances are we'll get him out of there before he does anything drastic. But just in case . . ." He shook his head. "I don't know what's come over him lately, he's just got plumb out of hand. I'm his brother, but I can't talk to him anymore."

Jim-Bob asked, "How long have you had the responsibility for him?"

A sadness lay in Dencil's eyes. "Since we was little kids, him about eight, me maybe twelve. Our ma and pa, they . . ." He broke off. "It don't matter about them." Looking at Jim-Bob, he asked, "You got a ma and pa, Jim-Bob?"

Jim-Bob shook his head. "Lost them a long time ago."

Dencil frowned. "It's a tough country thataway, throws a lot of boys out on their own long before their time. Some make out fine, and some . . ." He was silent a moment, his mind running back to times long past. "Somebody's done a good job of raisin' you, Jim-Bob. I wish I could have done better for Buster."

Jim-Bob felt a tug of sympathy. There was no doubt in his mind that these men had heard the owl hoot, that somewhere somebody would probably give plenty to get his hands on them. But these men were human, too, and Jim-Bob couldn't help liking them. Especially Dencil. Dencil talked and acted like a half-hundred cowboys Jim-Bob had known, common, friendly, easygoing.

"Sure, Dencil," Jim-Bob promised. "I'll keep an eye on Buster."

Riding on toward Swallowfork, Jim-Bob thought of going by and visiting Tina Kendrick again. But he had run out of excuses. And he didn't want her to see him all bruised up like this, his clothes torn. So he passed up the Kendrick ranch, although he kept glancing toward the white buildings as he rode by on the wagon trail.

The relentless gnawing of his stomach told him it was about noon as he rode into the main street of Swallowfork and turned toward Mont Naylor's livery stable. Mont was sitting comfortably in the little bit of noon shade at the front end of the frame building, his cane chair leaned back against the wall. He had whittled a slab of pine boxwood down to a sliver.

"Didn't expect you back for a day or two," he said, surprise and disappointment in his voice. His disappointment grew plainer as he saw the darkened eye and the bruises on Jim-Bob's face. His lips pursed to form a whistle, but Jim-Bob never heard it. He was already too busy explaining.

"I couldn't help it, Mont. I know I promised you, but Chum was bound and determined. So I finally took him on."

Mont remained silent a moment, studiously whittling on what was left of his wood. "Whip him?"

"Nope. Got whipped."

Mont pondered a little, then shrugged. "One thing about it, you're honest. Most of them would've made some excuse about the other fellow gettin' hold of a club or somethin'."

Jim-Bob had been about to, but he swallowed it quickly. "I'm sorry."

The sheriff looked back to his whittling, his thoughts unreadable. "Can't be helped now. Better unsaddle your horse and give him some oats."

Jim-Bob led the animal through the big front door into the dim hay-dry interior. He silently unbuckled the latigo and slid the saddle off, swinging it up onto a nearby wooden rack. Tonight he would take it back out to his shack.

He heard Mont come up behind to stand and watch him. Mont said, "I know how you feel, son. I put you up to a test, and you feel like you failed it. But maybe next time you won't. There's some hard lessons in this business." He put his hand on Jim-Bob's shoulder. "If you're goin' to be a lawman—and it appears you've made up your mind to do it—you've got to learn self-control. There'll be times you'd give your right arm just to get one poke at a man. But it's mighty often the wrong thing to do. You've got to forget yourself and remember what you stand for, wearin' the star. Let the other man be the one to lose his temper and come swingin'. You keep your wits and never let your temper get the best of your good judgment." Mont smiled. "I'll bet Chum looks as bad as you do. Go get your dinner, son."

Much relieved, Jim-Bob walked up to the bank and stood in the front door, looking around for Dan Singleton. He saw Dan hunched over a ledger in a teller's cage, running a pencil down a string of figures, his lips moving silently. Jim-Bob waited until Dan had finished totting up the sum, then asked, "How about dinner? It's time."

A big wooden clock with a long pendulum began to

strike twelve. The old banker True Farrell squinted up at it from his desk, then pulled a silver watch from his pocket as if he didn't believe it. He nodded then, satisfied, and smiled at Jim-Bob. "You'll never need a watch. You always know when it's time to eat." To Dan he said, "You buttons go ahead. I'll lock up."

Dan laid aside his ledger books and stood up, stretching. "Got so wrapped up in those figures, I didn't even notice how hungry I was."

"Well, come on," said Jim-Bob. "*I* noticed." To Jim-Bob, figures in a book meant nothing. He could never understand how Dan so cheerfully accepted them as a challenge. A wild cow, now, which needed roping— that was something Jim-Bob could understand.

They stepped out onto the porch. In the daylight, Dan caught for the first time the dark marks on Jim-Bob's face. Seeing Dan's eyebrows lift, Jim-Bob headed off the question.

"Chum Lawton. I lost."

Laughter in his eyes, Dan said, "I wasn't goin' to ask."

"You'd have popped if I hadn't told you. Let's go down to Grammon's for a bowl of chili."

The weather-warped boardwalk rattled under the boots of men going home to eat. Jim-Bob stepped down to the ground and walked on the sand by preference, heading toward the little hole-in-the-wall where an old wagon cook named Grammon had set up a chili joint. Grammon's place specialized in Mexican-strong brown chili, and hot Java to cut the grease. It would never crowd the hotel dining room out of business, but it was a favorite with cowboys trying to save their money for essentials and spend as little as possible on such things as food. Five-cent chili stretched the summer wages and perhaps allowed a little extra tobacco or a spare pint. It wasn't the food that a man remembered when he got back to the ranch anyway.

Grammon was a middle-aged, heavy-set man with a deep voice which sounded as if he were talking down a barrel. He looked like he could wrestle a bull. He had cooked for years in the great open-range round-ups that Jim-Bob could remember as a boy. Absolute master around the chuckwagon, Grammon ran his bluff on cowboys and ranch owners alike. Now that barbed wire fences had whittled the roundups down to size, Grammon maintained that the day of real men was past, and he had moved to town. He still ruled his chili joint as he had ruled his wagon. When it came to cleanliness and propriety, he could be as contrary as an old maid. Somebody was catching thunder as Jim-Bob and Dan walked in.

"You watch out there and don't slop that chili all over my clean floor," Grammon was telling a short, stocky cowboy. "Where do you think you're at, a chuckwagon?" When the cowboy started to lick the chili off his fingers, Grammon snorted and pitched him a washrag. "Some outfits, they'd make you eat out back."

The cowboy grinned at a tall man who sat beside him. "Slim, I always knew he was the ringiest wagon cook in the country, but I thought he'd be polite when he got to be a businessman and we was payin' customers."

The one called Slim smiled and said, "We haven't paid him yet," and went on eating his chili.

Grammon frowned at Jim-Bob and Dan, who were hunting a pair of counter stools that suited them. They were all alike. "When the bank and the law git to runnin' together, somebody better watch himself," he grunted. "Did you come to close me out, lock me up, or eat?"

"Just hungry," Jim-Bob replied quickly. He had long ago learned the only defense against Grammon was a tongue as sharp as his own. "Got anything fit to eat?"

Grammon sniffed. "We just serve man-food in here, and I doubt that you buttons can take it." He dished them out some chili.

The stocky cowboy glanced at Jim-Bob's face. "Fall off of a horse?"

Jim-Bob looked him straight in the eye. "If I said yes, would you believe me?"

"Nope."

"Then there's no use me lyin' about it." And he dropped the subject.

The short one elbowed the tall one in the ribs, and both of them laughed. The pair were Harvey Mills and Slim Underhill, partners in a little ranch east of town. They had been young cowboys when Jim-Bob was a small boy. He still thought of them that way even though both were beginning to show some gray, and their eyes were getting the deep turkey tracks that came from squinting against the glaring Texas sun. Jim-Bob faintly remembered that Harvey had once been a deputy for his father, years ago.

People didn't pay much attention to Harvey and Slim. The two had worked quietly for years, saving their money until they had enough to buy a little place of their own. They never spent much time or money around town. Theirs was just a greasy-sack outfit, maybe, but they were proud of it.

Jim-Bob always remembered John McClain saying Harvey Mills was one of the best deputies he'd ever had, although Harvey had decided he liked cow work better than being an officer.

"People like Harvey or Slim Underhill don't make as much noise as some," McClain had told his son. "But always remember that still waters are often the deepest. You ever need help, they're the kind that'll give you all they've got and never ask you any questions." Jim-Bob always thought of himself and Dan Singleton as being like Harvey and Slim. Working together, they'd amount to something someday.

Harvey Mills turned back to pestering old Grammon, who growled and enjoyed it. Jim-Bob and Dan ate silently a while. Finally Jim-Bob said, "Dan, what do you think of Tina Kendrick?"

Dan was reluctant to answer. "Really got you, has she?"

Jim-Bob nodded. "I went by there on my way out to Thorn's. Dan, she's the prettiest thing I've ever seen. You don't know what it is to see somethin' so pretty you've just got to have it."

Dan stared thoughtfully at a horse picture on Grammon's wall. "Maybe I do. I remember one time I wanted a paint pony. Neighbor outfit had it in its horse pasture. I used to ride over there and just sit and look at it over the fence. Tom told me it wasn't near the pony it looked to be, but I still had to have it. So one day Tom bought it. Spent two months' pay, the only real extravagance I ever remember in him. I was so happy I didn't touch the ground for a couple of days. I was just a little kid, and that was the prettiest pony . . ."

He sadly shook his head. "But you know somethin',

Jim-Bob? It was just like Tom said. That pony wasn't much 'count for me. It never did make a cow horse, never was good for anything but show. I finally got so I didn't even want to look at it. I'd think how hard Tom had worked to earn that money, and I'd get sick inside. One day I told him to sell it, and he did. He didn't get all his money back, but he said the education was worth the difference. Maybe it was. I never have worried about paint ponies since."

Jim-Bob said, "You tryin' to tell me Tina is a paint pony?"

Dan shrugged. "Not necessarily. But she's cut out of a different pattern from us, Jim-Bob. Either she'd be tryin' to change you, or you'd be tryin' to change her. Do you think you could ever change?"

Troubled, Jim-Bob rattled the spoon in the empty chili bowl. Unbidden, a picture came to him of Tina eating chili in Grammon's joint, and he could see that it didn't fit. "I could *try* to change."

"And if you didn't make it?"

Jim-Bob hunted around for an answer but didn't find it. He wished he hadn't even brought up the question, and he felt a momentary stirring of anger against Dan. Dan Singleton sometimes had his older brother's way of bringing a fellow down to earth and jarring him hard. Maybe that was why he would make a good banker.

Hearing boots strike the floor, Jim-Bob looked up. In the front door stood Buster Jones. Jim-Bob was startled by the man's sudden appearance. He felt a twinge of conscience, for he had promised Dencil he would look around for Buster soon as he got to town. Other things had come up, and he had forgotten. He noted that Buster's face was flushed with drink, and his left eye was swollen. Dencil hadn't let him off scot free.

"Plenty of room inside, cowboy," Grammon said. "What'll you have?"

Buster started to answer. Then he saw Jim-Bob.

"Howdy, Buster," Jim-Bob said.

Buster stared in surprise, suddenly belligerent. He turned on his heel and stomped back out the door.

"Now what do you suppose made him act that-away?" Grammon asked, puzzled.

Jim-Bob said, "I think he was just born like that."

Dan frowned, trying to remember something. Then his eyes brightened. "I *thought* there was somethin' familiar about him. He came into the bank the other day. Had another man with him. They looked just alike. The other one did all the talkin', said they were brothers. This one watched me like he thought I was goin' to rob him."

In the bank? Alarm began to tingle in Jim-Bob. "What did they want?"

"Had a big bill. Wanted to change it and said they didn't want to try it at a store or saloon which might not be able to handle it."

Jim-Bob rubbed his jaw, his face creased. "They told me they'd never been in Swallowfork. They look the bank over pretty good?"

"I don't know—I guess so. What do you know about them?"

"Ran into them on my way up to Thorn's. They were restin' up after a cattle drive, they said. Names are Dencil and Buster Jones."

Dan said, "I'd have sworn they told me their name was Smith."

Jim-Bob stood up abruptly. "Somethin' queer about

this whole deal, Dan. I think I'll go talk to Mont about it."

"Go ahead. I'll see you later."

"Sure," replied Jim-Bob. "See you later."

He tried the livery stable first. Mont wasn't there. It took some time before he finally caught up with the sheriff at the jail. Mont listened with interest while Jim-Bob told him about the Jones brothers. Or Smith, or whatever it was.

Eyes closed, Mont concentrated. "Dencil, Buster. Something about those names . . ."

He reached in a drawer of his big roll-top desk and took out a huge sheaf of dodgers. Putting on a pair of horn-rimmed specacles, he thumbed through them slowly. At length he pulled one out and peered closely at it. "This is the one. I knew I'd seen it." He passed it over to Jim-Bob.

The name wasn't Jones, it was Fox. Dencil and Buster Fox. There was no picture on the dodger, but the description left no doubt. Wanted up in the Panhandle for rustling cattle and running them across the New Mexico border. Wanted at Wichita Falls for attempted mail robbery. Wanted in Brown County for holding up a bank.

"Think they've got their eyes on this bank?" Jim-Bob asked anxiously, wishing now he had talked to Mont earlier.

"Could be. We better go talk to True Farrell."

Mont stuck the rest of the dodgers back in the desk and folded the one about the Foxes. Jim-Bob felt a sharp pang of regret.

"It doesn't really surprise me none. I had just hoped . . . I liked Dencil right off. He treated me good, the kind of a feller you enjoy makin' a friend of."

Mont smiled, a thin smile of irony. "Time you're as old as I am, Jim-Bob, you won't take everybody at face value. Some of the nicest people I ever knew were crooks." Jim-Bob gave him a questioning look at that, and Mont said, "I know it sounds funny, but it's so. Many an old boy who's good at heart slips off the track someway. Maybe he doesn't intend to at first, but each time it gets a little easier to do it again. Finally he's so far gone that there's no way to ever pull back." He shook his gray head. "I can't help but feel sorry for a man like that. Maybe there was a lot that was good about him, but he's wasted it. It's the waste that's so pitiful."

Mont took his six-shooter and gunbelt down from a hook on the wall where they hung most of the time. Around town, he seldom ever put them on. "Let's go, Jim-Bob."

Jim-Bob was at the door when he heard the shot. For a second he froze, his face draining cold. He sensed immediately where the shot had come from. He struggled for voice. "The bank!" he exclaimed.

He leaped completely over the steps, falling to one knee as he hit the ground. He faltered, got his balance, and headed for the bank in a hard run. Mont followed, but he was too far along in years to keep up with Jim-Bob.

Heads poked out of doors. Alarm whipped up the street as people saw the sheriff and deputy running. Other men dropped what they were doing and followed along.

Old True Farrell groped his way out of the bank's open door and grabbed onto a porch post.

"Doctor!" he shouted. "Get the doctor!"

Jim-Bob was fifty feet ahead of Mont Naylor when

he reached True Farrell. He glanced at the old banker and saw he wasn't wounded. The excitement was probably too much for the man's heart. Jim-Bob rushed into the bank and halted abruptly. In a corner, a ranchwoman customer stood crying softly in the afterwash of terror. On the floor, in a spreading pool of his own blood, lay Dan Singleton!

5

Dan!" Jim-Bob choked. He dropped to one knee beside his friend. Dan gasped for breath. Jim-Bob touched the sticky crimson stain that inched outward from a hole in Dan's shirt pocket. Then he gripped the shock-cold hand.

"Easy, Dan. We'll take care of you." He dropped his chin and began to whisper a prayer. Dan coughed and tried again for breath.

"Hold on, old partner," Jim-Bob whispered, almost crying. "Doctor's on his way."

Dan Singleton tried, but there was no holding on. Jim-Bob felt the weak hand try to tighten on his own. Then Dan lay still. Jim-Bob began to sob.

Behind him, True Farrell was telling Mont Naylor about it. "We didn't notice the man till he was already in here. Came in the back door, I think. Had a gun in his hand. He forced Dan to give him all the loose cash there was around, then go into the vault. He pretty well cleaned us out. Dan said something to him, something angry. And this outlaw stood there cold as ice and put a bullet through Dan's heart. He went out the back door. He had a horse there, I'm sure."

Mont Naylor shook Jim-Bob's shoulder. "Run saddle us a couple of horses, son."

Numb from grief and shock, Jim-Bob stayed down on one knee. Mont shook him again, harder. Jim-Bob looked up angrily. "Leave me alone! Can't you see he's dead?"

Mont's voice went harsh. "He's dead, and there's nothing more you can do for him. Now you've got to remember you're a lawman. Go saddle us some horses, quick."

True Farrell said gently, "Go on, Jim-Bob. We'll take care of him."

Somehow Jim-Bob made himself get up. The gathering crowd made room for him as he moved blindly out the front door.

Old Leather Dryden, Mont's hostler, helped him saddle the horses. In a minute Mont came on to the livery barn, bringing with him four men he had lined up as a posse. There were the two partners, Slim Underhill and Harvey Mills. The chili man, big Grammon. And a broad-shouldered blacksmith. Other men clamored to go, but Mont had chosen his help. He wanted a few men of his choice, men he could depend on, rather than a big mob of men he might not be able to control. He was supposed to have them raise their right hands and swear an oath, but that was book stuff, and there wasn't time. These men knew what it was all about.

They picked up the tracks in the weedy alley behind the bank. The robber had had his horse tied back there, all right. He had headed north, up the wagon trail toward Grafton. There was no question as to who it was. True Farrell's description fit him to a T. Buster Fox!

Afoot, Mont Naylor might show his age. But on horseback, with a driving urgency upon him, he was as young as Jim-Bob. He spurred out in the lead, pushing hard. He had a big, heavy-boned sorrel, built to carry Mont's extra weight. The other men had to struggle to keep up.

Jim-Bob rode woodenly, the shock still heavy upon him. He was like a man asleep in the saddle, his reflexes keeping him on the horse because his mind was far away. He was thinking of Dan, of all the things they'd done together, all the plans they'd had—wild plans, some of them, but happy ones.

Dan Singleton, a fair-to-middling cowboy who was going to become the best cowtown banker in West Texas. Dan Singleton, the nearest to a brother that Jim-Bob had ever had. Jim-Bob was barely conscious of the hot wind rushing by his face, of the laboring of the running horse. But in a little while he began to sense that Mont had slowed down.

He heard Mont say loudly, "We've got no chance to catch up with him in a hurry now, and we can't afford to kill our horses."

It was when his horse heaved violently to one side to avoid collision with Mont's that Jim-Bob jerked himself up to reality. He found himself grabbing desperately at the saddlehorn to keep from going down under the hoofs of the horses behind him. It was like a splash of cold water in his face. Dan was dead, he told himself harshly. There was no way ever to change that. Jim-Bob could only hurt himself, grieving now when there was so much to do. There would be time later to think about Dan, a time when Jim-Bob could more readily accept the grim fact of sudden death. The thing now was to catch up with Buster Fox.

After a while the white buildings of the Kendrick ranch began to bob up above the mesquite whenever the riders topped a rise. Mont hauled up short, so short that some of the others almost ran him down.

"There it goes," he said, pointing to fresh tracks on the ground. "He took off of the trail and out into the brush."

Harvey Mills swung down from the saddle for a close look. Jim-Bob remembered how his father had said Harvey was a first-rate tracker, that he must have some Indian in him. Harvey said, "Same horse, all right."

Mont pulled off the road and spurred out, following the tracks. Harvey Mills and Slim Underhill stayed close beside him now, for this might turn into a task for a tracker. But it wasn't. It soon became obvious where Buster Fox was headed.

"The Kendrick place," Mont said. "He's been runnin' his horse hard, and he'll be lookin' for a fresh one."

Jim-Bob's heart tightened up. Tina! What if Tina was there? What if she somehow got in Buster's way? He felt his mouth go dry. Then he roweled his horse harder, moving out in front of Mont and Harvey and the others.

He was still a quarter mile from the place when he heard what he thought was a shot. A long moment later there came a couple or three more. Heart pounding wildly, Jim-Bob kept spurring, his lips flat against his teeth. He was well out in lead of the posse when he loped through the front gate of the corral and up toward the barn. He could see a couple of cowboys riding in excitedly from the other direction.

Then he heard a girl screaming inside the barn. Jim-Bob was on the ground and running before his horse ever came to a full stop. Gun in hand, he stumbled, got to his feet and ran to the barn. At the door he stopped, eyes wide in fear for Tina. What he saw in the barn was almost a duplicate of what he had seen in the bank. The old pensioner called Papa John was kneeling over a young cowboy who lay on his back on the dirt floor. This was the one called Willy. And he was dead.

Tina stood with her back to the wall, fists clenched against her terror-drained cheeks. She screamed wildly, out of her mind with fear. Running to her, Jim-Bob grabbed her arms. "Tina, Tina, are you hurt?" She seemed not to see or hear him. She just kept on screaming.

The other men rushed into the barn. Mont Naylor had the whole picture in one quick glance. To Papa John he said, "What happened?"

The old man shook his head. "I don't know exactly. I was up at the big house. . . ."

Jim-Bob couldn't hear for Tina's screaming. He shook her gently. "You're all right, Tina."

Papa John tried to go on, but Tina's screaming had unnerved him. Sternly Mont Naylor said, "Jim-Bob, try to quiet her down."

Suddenly Jim-Bob ran out of patience. He stepped back, hands still gripping her shoulders. Sure, she had a right to be scared, seeing something like this. But to go off the deep end that way . . .

"Tina, snap out of it." He shook her, hard. "Stop it, I say."

Then, when she didn't, he slapped her. His hand left an angry red blotch on her face. Tina stopped screaming. But she stood as stiffly as before, her eyes fixed in terror, seeing nothing. Jim-Bob stepped back and looked away from her, ashamed. But not of himself.

He was ashamed of Tina. He had slapped her, and when she came to her senses and realized it, she probably would never forgive him. But somehow, after all that had happened today, it just didn't seem to matter.

Papa John continued shakily. "I was at the big house rakin' the yard. I seen this feller come a-ridin' up to the barn in a big hurry. Willy here was supposed to be trimmin' the tails of some horses that had got tangled up in cockleburrs. I didn't know Tina was here. I've told her time and again not to go out to the barn where the cowboys was workin'."

Jim-Bob felt a cold chill. "She was out here with him?" He pointed his chin toward the dead cowboy. Papa John shook his head affirmatively.

"What for?" Jim-Bob demanded, then realized how silly it sounded.

The old man glanced at Tina, something of disgust in his eyes. He never answered Jim-Bob's question. "Feller must've wanted to change horses, and maybe Willy got in his way, I don't know. But I heard a shot and came a-runnin'. This feller threw his saddle on one of the horses and spurred out like the devil was chasin' him."

Mont turned to his posse men. "We better catch us some fresh horses, too. We been pushin' ours mighty hard."

One of the two cowboys who had come riding in from the other direction told Mont excitedly, "We didn't know what was goin' on. We met this feller ridin' out, and I reckon we got in his way a little. He took a shot at us. I happened to have my saddlegun along, so I gave one back. I was flustered and jammed the gun before I could get a second shot. But I'm pretty sure I hit the horse. I saw it stumble."

Mont said hopefully, "Then he won't get far. Forget about those fresh horses. We better ride."

Jim-Bob hesitated a moment, looking at Tina. He remembered what Dan had said about paint ponies, and he realized Dan knew what he was talking about. She was great for show.

Now there were eight of them after Buster Fox. The two Kendrick cowboys joined up. Mont no longer pushed so hard. He stayed in an easy lope, confident they would soon run the wounded horse down. They followed the tracks out across a broad mesquite flat, then down into the rockier breaks of a big draw that drained all the way to the Centralia. Here gullies spread like long crooked fingers from the rough hills above, where infrequent rains brought runoff water crashing down to eat away at the soil. Beyond, as the draw spread out, thorny mesquite brush grew like a jungle in the deep fine silt washed from the hills and the gullies. A few of the old cowmen like Mont Naylor were saying this was a result of overgrazing by cattle and sheep, that the grass was being grubbed off short and letting the soil work loose. But others said it wasn't so, that it just didn't rain as much as it used to, that the grass would come back as good as ever when season-able times came again.

Occasionally they lost the tracks. Harvey Mills and Slim Underhill would get down and look around. It never took long for them to get straight.

"Horse is beginnin' to falter," Harvey said. "Here he went down. Fox got off and kicked him up again. But he won't get much more out of him, I'm a-thinkin'."

Mont Naylor frowned toward the thickening brush ahead. "Then he's down yonder someplace. He'll be lookin' for cover, and there's plenty of it in that brush."

They came to the Kendrick outfit's outside fence. It was four strands of barbed wire, still so new there was no rust on it. Harvey said, "He went across with his horse, right here."

Buster had knocked the staples out of a couple of fence posts on each side to loosen the wire. Then he had pushed the wires down and held them with his foot while he forced the horse to cross over. Jim-Bob stepped down and helped Harvey hold the wires to the ground so the other men could ride across. The wires sprang partway back up the posts as they turned them loose.

Worriedly Mont asked the Kendrick cowboy, "Did you notice what guns he was carryin'? Anything besides a six-shooter?"

"That's all I saw. But he might've had a saddlegun."

Jim-Bob knew what was going on behind Mont's troubled eyes. It was bad enough to ride into the thick brush after a man who might be anywhere, holding a six-shooter. It was much worse to go after one who might be carrying a rifle.

Mont reined his horse around to face the other men. "You-all know what we're up against. With a rifle and a little luck, he could pick off half of us before we could find just where he's at. If there's any of you want to stay back, I won't think bad of you."

Jim-Bob edged his horse up to the sheriff's. "I'm with you, Mont."

So did Harvey and Slim. The Kendrick cowboys followed suit. There was a grimness in their eyes now. They'd had time to think about Willy lying there on the barn floor. At first, they had been too busy to let it dwell on their minds. The old cook Grammon and the blacksmith were the last. The blacksmith had a family.

Seeing that the others were going, Grammon said gruffly, "We just as well go with them. We'd feel awful lonesome ridin' back to town all by ourselves."

The blacksmith's voice was nervous, but he forced a smile. "I reckon. Anyway, he'll shoot at you first because you're the biggest target." The two pulled their horses up to Mont's.

Appreciation was in Mont's eyes. "We better spread out then, and not give him too easy a target. If we find him, don't take unnecessary chances. He's killed two men today. We don't want any of us added to the list."

Grimly they spread out in the mesquite, a hundred feet or so between each man. Mont remained in the center as guide, following the tracks. His was by far the most dangerous position, and he accepted it without question. This was his job. He slipped his saddle-gun out and touched heels to his horse's ribs, the gun across his lap.

Jim-Bob had no rifle. He drew the heavy old .44 and gripped it in a cold-sweaty hand. Moving into the thick brush, he could hardly make himself breathe. He held his breath until his chest began to ache. He rode slowly, weaving in and out among the thorny branches. His gaze flicked from bush to bush, from Mont Naylor on one side of him to Harvey Mills on the other. This gave Jim-Bob the same cold, sick feeling deep in his stomach that he got when beating the weeds with a stick for a rattlesnake he knew was there.

Looking off to one side, he let his horse carry him under a low limb. The thin green leaves raked his ear. He jerked around, gasping in surprise, swinging the six-shooter up. He came within a hair of pulling the trigger and firing into space. His heart was hammering. The blood roared in his ears. Another time, he would have gotten a big laugh out of it afterwards. But he doubted that this would ever be funny to him, not even when he looked back on it years from now.

It was silent here in the thicket. Not a trace of wind to rustle the leaves, not a bird singing, nothing but the quiet movement of horses through the brush, the swish of a green limb pushed aside, then springing back into place. The summer heat rose up thickly around Jim-Bob. It seemed to stifle him. He found his shirt half wet with sweat. His head itched beneath the leather sweatband in his hat. Sweat worked down into his eyes, burning them.

He came upon the horse then, Buster Fox's horse, standing with head drooped, blood trickling down the left foreleg. The horse was dying on its feet. Jim-Bob looked across at Mont Naylor. Mont saw it and nodded.

"Shoot it, Jim-Bob," he said quietly, then passed the word down the line so the others would know what the shot was for.

Jim-Bob peeled off Fox's saddle and dropped it to the ground. He noted that there was a saddle scabbard, and it was empty. No question about it now. Buster Fox was in here afoot, hiding. And he had a rifle!

The horse stood unmoving as Jim-Bob slipped the bridle off its head. Jim-Bob took a firm grip on his bridle reins, not wanting his own horse to jerk away at the sound of the shot. He hesitated a moment, hating this. He had never shot a horse before. To him, it was almost like shooting another man. Then he pulled the trigger. The horse fell.

The spread-out posse moved again, slower now, knowing Fox could not be far away. Tension drawing tighter within him, Jim-Bob found himself wondering once why he had ever wanted to be a lawman in the first place. There was something infinitely unfair about this, good men having to ride along in the open this way, waiting for a killer to get first shot so that they might, if they lived, have a chance at the killer. Offering themselves up for sacrifice, as it were. Jim-Bob wondered if there were any job in the world that paid enough to justify that. But he knew what old John McClain would have said. With some men it is a sense of duty rather than any thought of pay. Men strong enough to stand up to the risk felt an obligation to their friends to use that strength in making the community safe. This sense of doing a worthwhile service was the job's own reward, a more satisfying one in its way than money could ever be.

A rattlesnake almost always gives a warning before he strikes. Buster Fox gave none. The high-pitched slap of his rifle racketed through the thicket. Jerking around, Jim-Bob saw Mont slump in the saddle.

Without thinking, Jim-Bob instantly spurred through the brush toward the sheriff. He was oblivious of the thorny branches that clawed him, ripping his shirt to ribbons, scratching his face and leaving tiny ribbons of blood on his cheek. He glimpsed Buster Fox crouched behind a mound of silt that had piled up in a many-pronged mesquite. Buster was levering another cartridge into the rifle. Jim-Bob fired at him once, a wild shot to make Buster dive for cover long enough for Jim-Bob to reach Mont and get him away.

He grabbed at Mont, got an arm around his waist at the same time he gripped Mont's bridle reins in his other hand. Spurring, he heard the rifle speak again. He felt the vicious snarl of the slug pass his face.

Right ahead of him was a depression where bulls had been pawing sand. "Drop, Mont," Jim-Bob said urgently. He pulled away from the sheriff, turning his horse between Buster and Mont and letting Mont half fall to the ground. The rifle cracked again. Buster Fox was not taking careful aim now. He was firing rapidly. It might be that he was as near panic as Jim-Bob.

Gun still in his hand, Jim-Bob swung to the ground and let the horses go. They ran away into the brush, frightened by the gunfire. Time enough to catch them later. Jim-Bob dropped to his belly in the sand and noted with satisfaction that he and Mont were lying on the off side of a small rise which would protect them from Buster's fire so long as they didn't raise up.

Mont's teeth were clenched in pain. Jim-Bob ripped away the bloody shirt and saw where the bullet had smashed into the shoulder. Jim-Bob used his handkerchief in a vain effort to stanch the bleeding. "Easy, Mont," he said quietly, "everything's goin' to be all right."

But he found his lips trembling and his voice trying to break. Mont was in agony, that was plain to see. The sheriff's kindly face was going pale. Jim-Bob touched Mont's forehead and felt it cold and clammy. It came to him then that Mont might die.

Strange how different things were when the time really came. Jim-Bob had often pictured a situation like this. He knew that a lawman lived always in jeopardy, that he might be called upon at any time to lay down his life. He had always assumed that when the time came he would simply brace himself bravely and take it.

But now it was here, and it was different. Here lay old Mont Naylor, one of the kindest men he'd ever known, bleeding and maybe dying in a bullhole deep in a mesquite thicket. Jim-Bob could hear the sheriff's labored breathing; felt the lawman's warm blood sticky on his hands. First Dan. Then Willy. Now Mont for a third victim of the ruthless killer who lay forted up only thirty or forty feet away, waiting his chance to make it four.

A black rage heaved up in Jim-Bob. Suddenly then, only one thing was important: to get Buster Fox. There was no time to consider fear. He glanced at the .44 again to be sure he hadn't gotten it clogged with sand. Then he was on his feet, rushing toward Buster Fox, firing as he ran.

Fox raised up and squeezed off a quick shot that tugged at Jim-Bob's sleeve, nothing more. Jim-Bob kept firing. He could see the bullets kicking up sand around Buster. Fox saw it too. One shot, two, three. Buster fought at his rifle. Then he stiffened in terror. Four.

Buster Fox screamed. "Don't shoot me! Don't shoot me!"

Five shots. That one kicked sand into Buster's eyes. Buster still held the rifle, could use it. But he stood helpless in panic, waiting for the sixth shot that wouldn't miss.

Jim-Bob stopped and aimed. At this range it was a certainty. Fox's chest was a broad target. Jim-Bob held the front sight on the third button of the dirty shirt. His finger tightened on the trigger.

Buster Fox sobbed, "No, kid, please!"

For a moment the rage was more than Jim-Bob could contain. It was so much that the gun wavered. He could not hold it true. Finally he lowered the gun. He tried to speak, but his throat was so tight he couldn't bring out a word. He motioned with the gun-barrel, and Buster Fox stepped out haltingly, his rifle falling to the ground, his hands lifting.

The posse men came running. They had been circling around behind Buster when Jim-Bob made his charge. They had had to scatter again to keep out of the way. Now they gathered around, covering Fox. Harvey Mills quickly checked Buster for a hideaway gun in his shirt, waistband or boottops. There was none.

Harvey said appreciatively, "Good goin', boy. If it had been me, I don't think I could have kept from killin' him."

Buster Fox went white. He dropped down in the sand and rubbed his sleeve over his eyes. Jim-Bob thought the outlaw was going to be sick. He gazed at him in hatred. Yet somehow he began to be glad he hadn't killed Buster. He was glad they were going to be able to take Buster to town, to make him pay properly for what he had done.

Jim-Bob got his voice back. "Mont's hard hit."

They walked back to where Mont lay. Jim-Bob knew the responsibility was his now, but he found no strength. He stood wavering, uncertain what to do. Harvey Mills understood, and he took over. There was a solid confidence about this rancher that commanded respect.

"Bullet's high, long way from the heart. Biggest danger is shock. Shock can kill a man even when the wound itself doesn't amount to much. We better get Mont to the Kendrick place as quick as we can. We can haul him on to town in a wagon."

The blacksmith brought up the question. "Where's the bank loot?"

In the excitement they had all forgotten about it. Jim-Bob tried to say something, but reaction had set in from the violent excitement. He found himself shaking, unable to talk.

Harvey demanded, "Where is it, Fox?"

Buster had regained some of his composure. He shook his head. "Go hunt it yourselves."

The men quickly scouted around where Fox had made his stand. They found no sign of the money.

"You didn't have time to hide it," Harvey said to Fox.

Buster just glared at him, not answering either way.

Harvey looked worriedly at Mont Naylor. "A couple of you fellers can stick around and look. We got to get started with Mont. You can catch up with us later."

They tied Buster Fox's hands. With his own horse dead, they put him on one of the Kendrick cowboys' horses. Then two cowboys stayed to search. Later, they would ride double.

Jim-Bob had to do something with his hands, had to get them busy. He started to reload the old .44. He looked at it, then sagged.

"What's the matter, Jim-Bob?" Harvey asked. "You look sick."

Jim-Bob handed Harvey the gun, almost dropping it. "I forgot I'd shot that horse. There wasn't no sixth shot left in that gun!"

6

The hot summer sun had lost its fury and was rapidly dipping into blood-red clouds on the skyline. The horsemen rode with their prisoner past the shack Jim-Bob had shared with Dan Singleton. Jim-Bob glanced once at the shack, thought of Dan, and looked quickly away. He wondered how he would be able to make himself return there. Usually the red dog Ranger would come out to greet him any time he happened to ride by the shack. He didn't see him now, and he wondered where the dog was.

Old Grammon and the blacksmith brought up the rear in a Kendrick wagon, hauling the wounded Mont Naylor to town. The word spread out before them like concentric rings that followed the dropping of a stone into still water. People stood silently on front porches and steps of their homes to watch the passing of the riders and wagon. Moving on down into town, the posse found a crowd gathered around the stores and saloons, the blacksmith shop and hotel. All eyes dwelt on this bank robber who had killed two men as thoughtlessly as other men might kill a rabbit. No one in the crowd had much to say. The quiet anger in their eyes spoke for them.

A disturbing thought began to creep into Jim-Bob's

mind. Harvey Mills voiced it. "I got a prickly feelin' at the back of my neck. That jailhouse may not be any place for honest men tonight."

Jim-Bob asked anxiously, "You think they'd lynch him?"

"Wouldn't surprise me any. I never saw a man deserved it any more than Buster Fox does."

"But he's a prisoner, Harvey. It's up to the law to hang him in its own due time."

Harvey shrugged. "What *is* the law, Jim-Bob? It's nothin' but a set of rules people have made up to help them live with each other. It's not sacred in itself: The people can change it. And these are people. If they decide to rush things up, is that much different from goin' by the law and takin' the long way around? The law does it for them if they don't do it for themselves. It winds up the same."

Jim-Bob had never thought of it in just that light. Fact of the matter, he had never thought about it much one way or the other. As he saw it, a law enforcement officer was not supposed to worry about the merits of the law. He was supposed to accept it as it was and see that it was carried out. He was a man who moved about his job with a quiet pride and an unshakable confidence, standing aloof from those who argued and wrangled. He simply saw his duty and did it. At least that was the way it was with John McClain and Mont Naylor. It was the way Jim-Bob wanted to have it for himself.

"If we were goin' to kill him," he said firmly, "we ought to've done it out yonder when he still had a gun in his hand. Now he's our prisoner. We're duty-bound to protect him till they take him out and read papers over him and hang him legally."

Harvey had a grim smile. "Papers! Did I ever tell you why I quit bein' a deputy? It was those everlastin' papers. It seemed to me that lawyers and law officers in general worshipped those papers the way other folks worship God. A hungry man can go to the pen for stealin' a fat calf, but a land-grabber can steal half a county if he can find himself a crooked judge who'll give him a set of papers. And the sheriff will have to help him throw the widow off the land, like it or not."

Jim-Bob didn't know why, but Harvey's outlook needled him a little. He was a shade too young and inexperienced to understand all there was about it, and maybe when he got older he would turn cynical the way Harvey was. Right now, though, all he had to go on was what he had learned from Mont, and what he remembered of his father. The law had meant a great deal to them. Jim-Bob would not question it. By those standards, Harvey Mills was wrong.

Jim-Bob said, "I'll grant you that the law may be goin' to a great length to protect people like Buster Fox. But maybe at the same time it's protectin' the rest of us, too. Maybe there's no safe way to take a short cut on the lawbreaker without takin' the rights away from the good people at the same time."

Harvey looked at him queerly. Finally he nodded. "I'll bet you learned that from your old daddy."

"I did."

Harvey said evenly, "You just go on believin' in the things John taught you. You'll never go wrong, boy."

Someone in the crowd called Jim-Bob's name. He pulled up, his gaze searching among the faces. Tom Singleton, dressed in black, stepped out into the sandy street. Dan Singleton's brother stopped and stood there, gaunt and straight. Hatred was a cold fire in his dark eyes. The sight of him sent a chill up Jim-Bob's neck. Jim-Bob moved his horse over beside Tom.

"This him, Jim-Bob?"

"It's him, Tom."

He sensed Tom's intention. The man's hand dropped and came up with a gun from the holster at his hip. Jim-Bob had no time to consider. Instinctively he threw himself out of the saddle and landed on top of the tall cowboy. They fell to the ground in a heap. Tom Singleton grunted in anger and tried to heave Jim-Bob's weight away. Struggling with him in the sand, Jim-Bob managed to get his hands on the gun. He hurled it away and saw Slim Underhill pick it up.

"Stop it, Tom," he said. "Stop it!"

Normally he wouldn't have lasted long with Tom Singleton in a fair fight. But much of Tom's breath had been slammed out of him when he hit the ground. He gasped for air, the sweat breaking on his face as he tried to pitch Jim-Bob off.

"Let me go! He killed my brother!"

"Tom, stop it. You're not helpin' anything this way."

The struggle ended. Jim-Bob pulled away, panting, and stood up. Tom pushed onto his knees and rested there, trying to get his breath back. Jim-Bob said, "Tom, he's in my charge. I'm not goin' to let you have him."

Tom Singleton got to his feet. Angrily he dusted his black vest, his black trousers. Jim-Bob reached out, and Slim handed him Tom's gun. Jim-Bob unloaded it and started to give it to Tom, changed his mind and shoved it in his own waistband. He realized it was a futile gesture. If Tom wanted a gun, he wouldn't have any trouble getting one. From the looks of the men who watched, any one of them would have lent him a gun without hesitation.

Jim-Bob said evenly, "Tom, we been friends a long time, you and me. Dan and you were both like brothers to me. I'm as interested as you are in seein' that Buster Fox gets what's comin' to him. I don't want to see you in jail for murdering him. So stand off, Tom. Let things alone."

Tom Singleton's voice was like ice. "I'll get him, Jim-Bob! *You* stand off, because I'm goin' to get him!"

Jim-Bob heard a murmur of approval run through the crowd. He sensed that many were angry with him for stopping Tom. He spoke loudly, "You fellers better go on home and let things alone!"

To himself his voice sounded hollow. He knew it must sound that way to the others. It was just a kid talking. Who was going to listen to a kid? He got back on his horse and headed on toward the jail with Buster, Harvey and Slim.

Buster said, "Pretty fast work you did back there, keepin' that hombre from shootin' me."

Jim-Bob turned on him, eyes ablaze. "I want you to understand this right now, Buster, I don't care what happens to you. Personally I'd be tickled to death to see lightnin' strike you dead right here on the street. I didn't want to see Tom in jail for killin' you."

Hearing the rattle of chains, Jim-Bob looked back over his shoulder. Grammon and the blacksmith hauled the wagon team off to the right and pulled up in front of the doctor's small frame house. Some of the crowd followed along afoot, anxious about Mont Naylor. Jim-Bob waited a moment until sure the pair had plenty of help in lifting Mont out of the wagon. Then he moved on toward the jail.

He clanged the cell door shut on Buster Fox and turned away, not wanting even to look at him. In a second cell sat a man who had been arrested yesterday for fighting. Jim-Bob unlocked the door and swung it open. "You better clear out of here, Punch."

Punch looked surprised. "Mont say so?"

"Mont's not in shape to say anything. I think it's best that you go."

Punch stood up but cocked his head over doubtfully. "You guarantee you got the authority, boy? I'd like out, sure enough, but I don't want to get in no trouble over it. I got enough trouble now."

Jim-Bob's face warmed. "I'll take the responsibility. Now git!"

He slammed the door shut again and pitched the big key ring onto Mont's heavy desk. Harvey Mills and Slim Underhill had followed him into the jail. Harvey watched Punch leave and said, "Still havin' trouble provin' you've come of age, aren't you, Jim-Bob?"

Jim-Bob nodded and walked over to the front door. He leaned against the jamb and looked unhappily out into the street. "It was a mistake bringin' Buster in here. I can see that now. We ought to've taken him straight to Grafton or someplace as quick as we caught him."

Harvey said, "Hindsight's easy. It's foresight we all need more of."

Jim-Bob watched the street. He watched the people on it, the way they walked, the way they stopped to look toward the jail. Twilight, he thought. Won't be long until night. What then?

Jim-Bob asked, "Harvey, how old were you when you were a deputy?"

"A couple or three years older than you are, I reckon."

"Did you ever come up against a situation like this?"

"Never did."

"What would you have done if you had?"

Harvey shrugged. "*Quien sabe?* Who ever knows what he'd do in any situation till he really comes up against it? You study about it, and you think you know yourself. But when the time comes, everything's different. You play it by ear." He paused. "Or maybe you don't play it at all. You just skin out."

His eyes were on Jim-Bob in a level, honest gaze. "You've been up against it twice today. Once when you jumped up and took Buster Fox, and again when you piled off on top of Tom Singleton. You did fine."

Jim-Bob shook his head. "That wasn't thinkin', either time. I didn't have time to think. I just went ahead. They were bone-headed stunts, both of them. If Buster had held his ground, he could have blown a hole in me you could shove a hat through. And if Tom had had a little pressure on the trigger, he might have killed me without intending to. There was an angel on my shoulder both times, that's all. That's too much luck to keep hopin' for."

Harvey said, "Maybe you're not givin' yourself enough credit. You've got a way of doin' things all of a sudden, and doin' them right."

Jim-Bob moved back into the office and sat down weakly in a cowhide chair. His shoulders slumped. "Harvey, for the first time in my life, I think I need a drink."

Harvey frowned. Jim-Bob could see sympathy in his eyes. "That won't help you. Either you've got it in you, or you haven't. Whisky won't put somethin' there that wasn't in you to start with." Harvey started to move out the door.

"Feel like eatin', Jim-Bob?"

"No."

"You better anyhow. I'll go over and see if Grammon will fry up a steak or somethin' for you." He glanced back into the cell. "I better get somethin' for Fox, too. If things don't work out, there's no use him dyin' on an empty stomach."

Slim Underhill shifted nervously from one foot to the other, and Jim-Bob motioned for him to follow Harvey. For a while Jim-Bob was alone with the prisoner. He moved the straight cowhide chair up close to the front door, where he could keep an eye on the long street. He pulled down the window shades and locked and barred the rear door. Pausing at the rear window, peeking around the shade, he saw a man standing back in the gloom, watching. They've put up their guards early, he thought. He walked back to the chair and sat down. He had taken off the heavy .44 for comfort, but he had a shotgun standing up against the wall within easy reach.

In the short period of peace, then, Jim-Bob had his first chance to relax. Or at least to try. It had been a long and harrowing day, and fatigue washed over him. But his nerves were wound up tight. He could not relax. He knew it would be a long time before he did. He had time now to think, to let his mind dwell on Dan Singleton. Now more than at any time today he felt the full impact of the loss. He tried to blink back the burning tears as he thought of the laughing-eyed boy he had known so long. There was an emptiness, a loneliness in him that he hadn't known since his father had died. He remembered how it had been then, like turning his back on a chapter of his life and starting out alone on a strange new road. He had that feeling again now. He sensed that this was another turning point. From this day forward, nothing would ever be quite the same. This morning he and Dan Singleton had been a pair of big young boys together. Now Dan was gone, and Jim-Bob would never be a boy again. He had finished another chapter.

He saw banker True Farrell striding slowly up the street toward the jail, alone. The old man's gray head was bowed. Trouble rode heavy on his stooped shoulders. He walked up onto the small porch and paused.

"Good evening, Jim-Bob." His voice was weary and thin. This was probably the hardest day of the old man's life.

Jim-Bob stood up in respect. "Come in, Mr. Farrell."

"Thank you." Farrell walked in and stared a moment at Buster Fox in the cell. His veined hands knotted into fists. True Farrell could hate as deeply as anyone else. But he would never be a violent man.

At length he looked back at Jim-Bob. "You didn't find the money." It wasn't really a question. He already knew.

"No, sir. He either hid it or threw it away."

"What's the chance of finding it?"

No use lying to a man like True Farrell. He was level-headed enough to accept fact. "Mighty little, sir. We backtracked him the best we could, comin' in, and we never saw anything. A couple of the Kendrick hands scouted all over the area where we found him, and so far as I know they never stirred up nothin'. We'll try again, but it'd take the rankest kind of luck. And we been mighty short on luck today."

Farrell nodded. He had probably known before he

ever got here. He sank into the sheriff's big chair. When he looked up, his eyes were bleak.

"Jim-Bob, I counted up the loss. We've got to get that money back."

"What if we can't?"

"Then it looks like the bank is finished. And it might take half the town with it. People in a place like Swallowfork don't know how completely their fortunes are tied in with those of the bank. We can't pay our depositors back. We'll have to call in a lot of loans and break people who've been here longer than you or I."

True Farrell seemed to have aged a lot in these few hours. "I'm not worried so much for myself. I can always find a position in Fort Worth or Dallas or San Antonio. I won't be my own boss anymore, but I won't be hungry. It's the people here that I'm worried about. This is my town. These are my friends. I don't want them hurt, and I don't want to leave."

Jim-Bob said, "Some of your friends are thinkin' about takin' Buster Fox out and hangin' him tonight."

"They mustn't, Jim-Bob. If he dies without showing us where that money is, the town may well die with him."

"Why don't you go tell them that? Why don't you talk to Tom Singleton?"

True Farrell shrugged. "I've already tried. It's as if he were stone deaf. He just sits there, and you can't tell whether he hears you or not. The rest of them are angry too. Whatever Tom does, they'll follow him. He's that kind of man. I've tried, but I can't get them to understand what they're about to do to themselves."

Farrell looked back at Buster Fox. "Think he would tell us if we explained to him how it is?"

"Would you, in his place?"

Farrell sighed. "It was silly of me even to ask. He has a powerful weapon to bargain with, knowing where that money is."

Jim-Bob said, "Only Tom Singleton won't give him a chance to bargain."

It was getting dark in here, and Jim-Bob didn't want to light the lamp. He could still see Buster well enough, though, hunched over in the cell, dirty, bearded, a misery in his pale eyes. With Farrell gone, Jim-Bob got up and walked over to Buster.

"You heard what Mr. Farrell said?"

Buster nodded weakly, not looking up.

Jim-Bob said, "You've got nothin' to gain anymore. Why don't you tell where that money's at? It'd square you that much, and it might make things go a little easier with you."

Buster grunted. "How easy can you go with a hang rope?"

A plea in his voice, Jim-Bob pressed, "Buster, why don't you think of other folks for once? There's a lot of good people in this town goin' to be bad hurt if we don't get that money back."

The outlaw's voice colored with a flare of anger. "What do I care about other people? Nobody ever cared anything about me."

Shaking his head, Jim-Bob turned away from Buster. He knew he could talk until he was hoarse, and he'd never get anything out of that man. He stiffened as he heard a quiet knocking at the back door. Harvey Mills, he thought at first, and he wondered why Harvey would have come back that way instead of through the front. Then he knew it wouldn't be Harvey.

Drawing the .44 out of its holster on the wall, Jim-Bob lifted the bar out of place. He stepped to one side of the door and cautiously opened it an inch. "Who is it?"

"Jim-Bob, it's me." He didn't see the face, for it was dark outside. But he knew the voice. Dencil Fox!

"What do you want, Dencil?"

"I want to see my brother. You know I can't come to the front door."

Jim-Bob held back, not sure he ought to do it. Keeping his back to the wall and the gun up, he opened the door a little wider. "First," he said, "throw your gunbelt in here, and the gun with it."

Dencil's hand showed as he pitched the weapon in. It and the belt slid across the rough board floor.

"Just you now, Dencil," Jim-Bob warned. "Not Pony or Hackberry. And no false moves."

Dencil walked in, his hands up to shoulder height. Jim-Bob quickly shut the door behind him and dropped the bar back in place. He took a quick look at Dencil, decided he was no longer armed, and said, "You can put your hands down now."

"Thanks." Dencil looked quickly toward Buster's cell. Trouble and worry were in his eyes. "How you doin', son?"

Buster's voice was sullen. "How do you think I'm doin'? You come to git me out of here?"

A little of anger tugged at Dencil's mouth. "You got no business bein' in this kind of a jackpot."

"I don't need any lectures. Just git me out."

"I don't know as I can."

"You always did before."

"This is a worse mess than you ever got in before."

Jim-Bob watched Dencil curiously. Even now, knowing him to be a bank robber and a cow thief, it didn't seem to make much difference. He still looked like an ordinary every-day cowboy. He probably had been, once. Jim-Bob could not help but wonder where he had gotten off the road.

He said to Dencil, "You were goin' to rob the bank, the whole bunch of you, isn't that right? Only, Buster tipped over the milk bucket."

Dencil nodded as if it made no difference anyway. He glanced back at his brother. "It was his drinkin' that ruined it. He didn't like the way we had it planned. He got drunk, and we fell out. I don't think he really intended to try and hold it all up my himself. But he got to town, and the more he drank, the easier it looked. So he just bowed his neck and went after it.

"Now, I don't hold with killin'. I've always been able to make a good enough livin' without it. Buster's got a streak in him, though. I don't know where he got it, but it came out in him today." Dencil's forehead furrowed. "Whatever he's done, he's still my brother, Jim-Bob. I don't aim to see him hang."

Jim-Bob could see pain in Dencil's eyes. "It's a lost cause now, Dencil. I'll do what I can. But even if we hold off the lynch mob, the law's certain to hang him. You're not doin' yourself any good stayin' around here. You're a wanted man, just the same as him, and I ought to be lockin' you up. But I like you, and I want you to move on right now, before somebody comes with the supper and I *have* to lock you up."

Dencil's eyes held a queer light as he gazed at Jim-Bob. "How much money do you make in a month, son?"

"Forty dollars."

"I got five hundred here in my pocket. As much as you'd make in a year. All you got to do is open that cell door, and it's yours."

Jim-Bob shook his head. "Even if I wanted to, you couldn't get away. Do you think I wouldn't already have taken Buster out if I thought it could be done? They'd run us down. There's men watchin' that back door right now to be sure I don't slip him out."

Dencil's eyes narrowed. "I didn't see any men."

"They were there, and you can bet they saw *you*. Oh, they probably didn't see your face, but they know that one man came in. If more than one man tries to go back out, they'll have a hard time gettin' anyplace. Now go on, Dencil, while you still can. Please."

Regret was in Dencil's eyes. "You're a good kid, Jim-Bob. Any other time . . ." He frowned. "But I reckon you've still got some lessons to learn. One of them is—"

He reached down suddenly and came up with a short-barreled six-shooter out of his boot top. He swung it into line so abruptly that Jim-Bob hardly had time to move a hand. "One of them is, don't never trust nobody!"

Jim-Bob swallowed, taken completely by surprise.

Dencil said, "Now fetch me them keys, boy. We're lettin' Buster out."

Looking into Dencil's gun, Jim-Bob felt his skin go cold. "I didn't think you'd do that to me, Dencil."

"I didn't want to. I tried money first. Now this is an emergency. Get me them keys."

Buster Fox was standing, gripping the cell bars excitedly. Sweat had broken out on his forehead, and he was grinning in relief.

The key ring still lay on Mont Naylor's desk. Hesistantly Jim-Bob walked over and picked it up. Looking at Dencil, he felt the evening breeze cool the back of his neck as it searched through the open door.

Suddenly, on impulse more than with intention, he pitched the key ring through the door. It landed somewhere out in the sand, in the darkness. He braced himself, half expecting Dencil to shoot him. He turned and saw desperation in Dencil's surprised eyes. For a second or two, Jim-Bob was no farther from death than the thickness of a cigarette paper as Dencil's finger went tight on the trigger.

Dencil's sudden surge of rage passed. "You go out there and get that key!"

Buster's grin had vanished. Dencil's eyes were unsure. Jim-Bob sensed that he had once again gained the upper hand. He shook his head.

"You can't shoot me, Dencil. One shot would bring them down on this jail like a swarm of hornets. You wouldn't have a chance to get Buster out, or yourself either. Now you better do like I said, get out that back door while you still got time."

Buster saw that Dencil was wavering. He cried out, "Don't go off and leave me, Dencil!"

Dencil allowed the muzzle of the gun to dip a little. The corners of his mouth turned down. Defeat was in his face. "You got a heap of sand, Jim-Bob. It looks like you've won for now. But I'm not leavin' town without Buster. We'll be out there tonight, me and Pony and Hackberry. If that lynch mob gets to crowdin', we'll shoot into it. We'll leave a pile of dead men in that street, boy, like nobody here has ever seen."

His voice was like flint. "And sooner or later, we'll be comin' for Buster. We'll take him peaceful if we can, and otherwise if we have to. You're a good button, Jim-Bob, but I'd kill you to save my brother."

Dencil began backing toward the barred door, stooping down to pick up the gunbelt from the floor. Carefully, his eyes not leaving Jim-Bob, he lifted the bar off. To his brother, he said, "You just hold on, Buster, we'll take care of you." Then, to Jim-Bob, "If you got any friends in that mob, you better stop them before they get to the jailhouse. Otherwise we'll squash them like so many bugs."

He opened the door and vanished into the darkness. Jim-Bob slammed the door and instantly dropped the bar back in place. He turned and leaned heavily against it, his heart hammering away. For a moment he thought his knees would go out from under him. The crushing thought came to him that he was inadequate for the job. This wasn't any make-believe game of sheriffs and outlaws now, no wild daydream of gallantry and adventure. This was a case of real men, angry men, out for vengeance and blood. It was a job that only a man could handle, and Jim-Bob was not sure he was a man yet. Maybe they were right about him. Maybe he *was* just a wet-nosed button packing around a lot more responsibility than he could rightfully handle. Why, of all times, did Mont Naylor have to be out of action on a night like this?

Jim-Bob realized that Buster Fox was watching him, measuring him, and this had a sobering effect. He managed to step away from the wall and stand straight, although the weakness still pulled at his knees. He doubted that Buster could see his face in the gloom, and he was grateful. Bad enough to be so scared that your belly aches. Worse, to know that everyone else knows it.

7

Jim-Bob had no intention of going out into the darkness to hunt for that key ring. There was mightly little chance of finding it in the first place. And he didn't want to take a chance of someone jumping him with no one inside to watch the jail. He knew where Mont kept an extra set of keys in a desk drawer anyway.

Eventually Harvey Mills and Slim Underhill came back bringing supper for Jim-Bob and Buster. They sat down and picked their teeth, waiting. They'd already eaten. Jim-Bob toyed around with his plate a little, not wanting it. He noticed that Buster wasn't eating much, either.

Jim-Bob glanced up at Harvey. "How does it look down the street?"

Harvey frowned, glancing at Slim before he spoke. Slim was shaking his head. "Poor, Jim-Bob, mighty poor. We took a peep in the Tobosa Bar. Tom Singleton's sittin' in the back of it. Not drinkin', not eatin', just sittin' there. And they're gatherin' around him."

"Who?"

"Friends. Maybe some people who don't even know him. Funny how a thing like this draws in even the strangers. And there's some of the Kendrick outfit on account of the cowboy Fox shot."

It seemed to Jim-Bob that the food was unusually dry. It took a lot of coffee to wash it down. "Is Tom talkin' up a hangin'?"

"He's not talkin' at-all. He don't have to; it's in the air. They'll keep gatherin' down there. After a while he'll just get up and start walkin' thisaway. They'll all follow him."

Jim-Bob felt cold, even though it was a warm night. "I don't reckon you-all will want to be here when that happens."

The partners looked at each other. Finally Harvey said, "You're figgerin' on stayin', aren't you, Jim-Bob?"

"Somebody's got to."

"It'll be a poor place for a man alone. We'll stay with you."

There was little Jim-Bob could say, except "Thanks." He had a hard time keeping his hands still. "Reckon a man could talk to Tom?"

Harvey shrugged. "A man could talk. I don't expect Tom would listen."

"Maybe a man like Walter Chapman . . ."

"The way we heard it, Walter's stayin' out of it. He's sittin' up with Dan's body, over at the parsonage."

"There's bound to be somebody who could talk to Tom."

"Mont Naylor might, but he's not in shape to talk to anyone. We'd just as well face it, Jim-Bob; folks who don't like this thing are stayin' home, keepin' out of the way. Those that are left on the street, they'll come with Tom when he's ready."

Jim-Bob said desolately, "It's hell to just sit here and wait. Somebody's at least got to try. I wish I could talk with Walter."

Harvey said, "Then you go try. We'll watch the jail for you."

"You'll never know how much I appreciate what you-all have done."

Harvey dismissed him with a wave of his hand. "Better get along. There's no tellin' when Tom'll decide to move."

The streets were quiet, deadly quiet. Swallowfork was not normally a town that went heavy on night life, but even so there was usually more movement on the streets about this time of evening. Now Jim-Bob saw almost none. Not a horse was tied anywhere along the street between the jail and the Tobosa Bar. Everybody knew what was coming. No one wanted to risk his horse breaking away and running off during the excitement, leaving him afoot.

Jim-Bob stood in the shadows beneath the liveoaks, looking around. Presently he saw a movement behind the jail, the flare of a match and the glow of a cigarette. They still had a man watching.

Jim-Bob saw no more movement. Somewhere out there, he knew, Dencil Fox was watching too. Watching and waiting to cut loose with a deadly fire that would leave good men dying in the sandy street. Now, in a way, Jim-Bob regretted that he hadn't locked up Dencil when he had the chance. Yet he hadn't been able to bring himself to do it, to put Dencil in the same hopeless predicament as Buster. He knew he still couldn't, even if he somehow had the chance again.

Jim-Bob walked to the town's white frame church and turned in at the small parsonage that stood beside it. Something moved on the porch. Jim-Bob hauled up short. Then he heard a dog whimper. It was old Ranger. How the dog knew Dan was inside, Jim-Bob would always wonder. The instinct of animals had always been a mystery to him. Whining, the red dog rubbed up against Jim-Bob's leg. Jim-Bob knelt and patted him gently on the head. A great lump swelled in his throat. "It's just you and me now, old partner," he whispered.

He knocked on the door and took off his hat while he waited. The gray-haired minister came in a moment. Momentary surprise was in his eyes. "Come in, Jim-Bob. I thought you'd be tied up at the jail. I know you'll want to see Dan."

Jim-Bob had been trying to keep from thinking of Dan. "I came mostly to see Walter Chapman. Is he here?"

"In the parlor. Come along."

The parlor was lighted by candles, with a white cross standing between them. A plain pine casket rested near the candles. Walter Chapman had been seated in a rocking chair, his head bowed. At sight of Jim-Bob he stood up, sadness in his eyes.

"I didn't expect you, Jim-Bob. But it's good that you got to come."

Jim-Bob moved hesitantly toward the open box and looked inside. He felt a deep chill. This was Dan Singleton, yet it wasn't him at all. The features were his. But this still, cold body in the flickering candlelight was like some clay figure, strangely unreal. The Dan Singleton Jim-Bob had known was gone. He turned away, not wanting to look again. He wanted always to remember the other Dan Singleton. "I came mostly to see you, Walter. You know what's fixin' to happen."

Walter's voice was subdued, almost a whisper. "I know."

"Walter, somebody's got to talk to Tom. You're the only one I know that might make him listen."

Chapman was quiet a little while. Then he said, "What would you want me to tell him, that I think he's doing the wrong thing, that I want him to go home and forget it?"

"Something like that."

Walter's tired face was grim. "How could I tell him he's wrong when I'm not really sure he is?"

Stunned, Jim-Bob said, "Do you mean you think he's right?"

"Who am I to say whether he's right or wrong? I've tried to decide, but I can't. All I know is that we thought the world of this boy, and now he's dead."

A sense of hopelessness gripped Jim-Bob. He hadn't expected a turn-down from Walter Chapman, not even after what Harvey had said. "Walter, no matter what you say, deep inside you know it's wrong."

Walter lowered his head and looked down at the floor. "I guess I do. What's worse, I think I really want it to happen. That makes me a coward of sorts, doesn't it? I sit here tellin' myself I'll have no part in it, that I'm keepin' my hands clean. That makes me worse even than the men who will really go out and do the job. At least they're open and honest with it. I'm a coward and a hypocrite."

Jim-Bob backed toward the door, disappointment heavy on his shoulders. "I'm sorry, Walter."

"So am I, Jim-Bob. But that's the way it is. If any-body talks to Tom, I guess it'll have to be you."

Out on the dark street again, Jim-Bob stood a few moments, trying to make up his mind. He felt a strong temptation to get a horse and ride out and not come back for days. But that wasn't the way John McClain would have done it, or Mont Naylor.

Maybe Walter had a point. Maybe Jim-Bob *could* talk to Tom. He knew the chances were against him. But anything was worth a try. He moved off down the street, the red dog following at his heels.

He expected a cauldron of angry activity at the Tobosa Bar, but he didn't find it. The crowd was there, all right. But it was a grimly quiet group that stood around the bar, some drinking a little, some not drinking at all. The little conversation carried in muffled tones hardly above a whisper. As Harvey had said, Tom Singleton sat at a table alone in the back of the room. No one was talking with him, but Jim-Bob sensed the bond of anger that drew the men to Tom.

All attention riveted on Jim-Bob as he walked through the door. Forty or fifty pairs of eyes quietly took his measure. Jim-Bob felt that weakness come back to him. He tried to muster new strength, to keep the anxiety from showing. He looked over the faces. A few were strangers, but most were people he knew. Cowboys, ranchmen, townspeople. Good men, for the most part, men he had known for years. As individuals, they wouldn't consider killing a man. But now, herding together, they were being caught up in a strong tide of anger and revulsion that was steadily swelling, that would soon break over and crush anything that stood up against it.

His eyes on Tom Singleton, Jim-Bob walked between the other men. They made way for him as he moved, then turned to watch what he would do. He felt no hostility in them. Yet he knew that when the time came they would swarm over him and trample him underfoot if he stepped out in their way. He stopped in front of Tom's table. Tom's dark eyes lifted briefly to him, eyes dulled by grief. Jim-Bob saw recognition there. Then Tom looked down again, his gaze fastening on the table, his mind drawing back to some other time, some other place.

"Tom, I've come to see you." Jim-Bob was surprised at the strength he managed to find in his voice.

Tom made no sign that he had heard.

"Tom, I know what you're figurin' on. You mustn't do it."

Tom said nothing.

"Tom, you know Dan Singleton was the best friend I ever had. We grew up together, rode the same horses, slept in the same bedroll sometimes. He was almost as much a brother to me as he was to you. But I know what you're fixin' to do is wrong."

Tom still didn't look at him, didn't say a word.

"Dan wouldn't approve of it, Tom. He wasn't the kind that would."

Tom looked up at him then, his eyes cold. "How can anybody know now what Dan would approve? He's dead. And your prisoner killed him."

"You know I'm duty-bound to protect Buster Fox. You come up against me tonight and somebody's liable to die."

He didn't dare tell them about Dencil Fox. This bunch would go out into the darkness after him, and somebody would be killed sure enough.

Tom's eyes narrowed. "Do you think you could kill me, Jim-Bob?"

Jim-Bob stammered for an answer. He had none.

Tom said evenly, "If you stop me, that's what you'll have to do!" He looked down at the table again, withdrawing into the cold shell from which he had so briefly stirred.

Dismayed, Jim-Bob knew he could not budge Tom Singleton. On the contrary, if he stayed here, he probably would stir things up so Tom and these men might come marching even sooner than they otherwise would.

For a moment he considered arresting Tom on the spot and breaking this up that way. But he knew it would be a futile attempt. He would never get Tom out the front door.

"All right, Tom," Jim-Bob said regretfully. "All I can do is warn you." He turned and started out.

"Jim-Bob!" came Tom's stern voice.

Jim-Bob stopped and looked back over his shoulder. "What is it?"

Tom said, "I don't want to hurt you, button. Don't you get in my way."

Jim-Bob walked out.

Standing in front of the bar, Ranger beside him, Jim-Bob listened to the voices that had been lifted with his departure. He wondered now if he had done the wrong thing in coming here. The men were louder than they had been before. Maybe his attempt had only stirred them up and hastened the inevitable.

He noticed the many horses tied around the bar, and below it. He might scatter them and create some confusion, but what would it accomplish? It wouldn't last long. Despairing, he turned back toward the courthouse. There was, then, no way he could stop these men from coming. And there would be no stopping them at the jail. If only Mont were able to help . . .

He found himself moving involuntarily toward Dr. Spain's house, where Mont lay. He told himself he should leave Mont alone. Yet Mont was his last flicker of hope. Maybe Mont could suggest something. Only God knew what.

The doctor was skeptical about letting Jim-Bob see the sheriff at all. But he relented. "Just take it easy with him, Jim-Bob. He's not in any shape for excitement. He needs a lot of quiet and rest."

Quiet and rest. The irony of that brought a twist to Jim-Bob's mouth. There wasn't going to be much quiet and rest anywhere in town tonight. Not even for a man in a sickbed. Mont lay on a big bed with heavy iron bedsteads. His square face was drained almost as pale as the pillow upon which his gray head rested. His eyes were closed when Jim-Bob eased into the room, but he opened them a little, awakening slowly.

The doctor murmured in Jim-Bob's ear. "He doesn't know what's shaping up in town tonight. Don't you tell him. He'd lie there and worry about it, and there's nothing he could do."

"He'll hear it anyway, when the noise starts."

"I'm going to give him something to make him sleep."

That jerked another prop out from under Jim-Bob. He had been counting on advice from Mont. Now he couldn't even ask for it.

Mont's voice was barely audible. "Jim-Bob. Glad you came, son."

"I'm tickled to see you lookin' so good, Mont." A lie if he had ever told one. He twisted his hat completely out of shape.

Mont's eyes closed a moment. It must have been an

ordeal for him to speak. "How's everything? Prisoner all right?"

"Everything's fine, Mont." Jim-Bob reached up and touched the sheriff's cold hand. "Don't you worry about a thing." He swallowed hard, trying to get a lump down, trying to keep the growing fear out of his voice.

Mont rasped, "You take care of it for me, son. I'll be up and around in a couple of days. Anything comes up, you can handle it."

Jim-Bob nodded, his voice low. "Sure, Mont, I'll handle it. Don't you fret over nothin'." He gripped the sheriff's hand. Then, with a helpless look at the doctor, he turned to the door.

In his small parlor, Dr. Spain reached into a cabinet and took out a bottle and a pair of small glasses. He poured the glasses full and handed one to Jim-Bob. "Brandy. You look like you need it."

"Thanks, Doc."

He appreciated the sympathy he saw in the doctor's eyes. Spain was a good man. He had come here many years ago, a gasping consumptive with only weeks to live. This open country with its high climate, its dry air, had turned those weeks into months and the months into years. He could have made a lot more money now in the city somewhere. But it was the city that had so nearly killed him. He preferred to remain in this country where he had found his life. He had all the money he needed to live out here. And he had much more—much that had nothing to do with money.

"Don't worry about Mont, Jim-Bob," Dr. Spain said. "It'll take a lot more than his 'couple of days,' but I promise you he'll make it."

Jim-Bob's lips were tight. "I'm glad. The question now is, will *I* make it?"

"What can you do?"

"I wish I knew. I was hopin' Mont might tell me."

"And now it's all up to you. A big responsibility for a man so young."

"Too big. I'd just like to saddle me a horse and get out of here as fast as I could run. That would be the easy way."

"You won't do it. You know it wouldn't be the easy way at all. You'd find it the hardest thing you ever did. You'd hate the memory of it. You could run away from Swallowfork and the people here, but you'd never forget. It would be a blot on your conscience as long as you lived."

Jim-Bob's gaze dwelt absently on the glass. "I know. I've got to stay. If I just knew what Mont would do. . . ."

"Jim-Bob, I'm afraid it's too big even for Mont Naylor. He'd try, of course, but in the end he wouldn't be able to stop it. He won't blame you if *you're* not able to. He'll only blame you if he knows you didn't do your best."

Jim-Bob finished the brandy. It warmed him, and he felt a little better. But his hands were still shaky, his stomach uneasy.

Dr. Spain said, "I know it's a tough thing to happen to you, losing your first real prisoner. I remember the very first patient I ever had. He was a drunk who leaned over a saloon balcony to call for another beer. The balcony gave way. I did the best I knew how, and I thought I had him patched up fine. But he died on me."

He smiled then, trying to get through Jim-Bob's

somber mood. "Maybe you could set fire to the livery barn or something. Keep them so busy fighting the blaze that they wouldn't have time to worry about your prisoner."

Something hit Jim-Bob. He looked up suddenly and felt the same dart of elation that a falling man feels when his hand grasps something solid, even if only for a second or two. "Doc, maybe you've got it. I might be able to do it."

"Burn the livery barn?"

"No, no, of course not. But something else, something to get them away from the prisoner for a little while."

The idea quickly grew and became a plan. It was a slim ray of hope, and yet it was at least that much. A few moments ago there had been none at all. Jim-Bob pumped the doctor's hand, a nervous smile breaking over his face. "Thanks, Doc, thanks. If it works, I'll get you a whole case of that brandy come Christmas."

He stepped down off the doctor's front porch and hurried toward the livery barn, old Ranger tagging along at his heels.

Old Leather Dryden took care of Mont Naylor's livery barn and wagon yard when Mont was too busy with his peace officer job to do so himself. Like many another old-timer who had cowboyed too long before he quit, Leather had one stiff leg, and his left arm didn't look just right. But he knew his horses.

According to Mont, Leather had seen the elephant and heard the owl hoot in his day. Jim-Bob could only take Mont's word for that. Leather didn't look like it now. He was dried up and played out. He had read some books, and it showed in his talk. Moreover, he had taken to religion, after a fashion. He didn't make an issue of it, but the cowboys who slept in the wagon yard on their visits to town watched their language when Leather was around, and they kept their bottles out of sight.

Right now there wasn't a cowboy anywhere around the barn at all. Leather had it to himself. From the looks of the horses in the corral, though, Leather had been doing a thriving business earlier. The riders were all over at the Tobosa Bar, Jim-Bob figured.

"Quiet around here," he commented.

Leather nodded gravely. "For a little while maybe. Thought you'd be at the jail." There was question in his eyes.

"Took time out to try to talk to Tom Singleton."

"Didn't do any good, did it?" Leather answered his own question with a shake of his head. "Tom's a single-minded man. And when he gets that mind made up, the gates of hell shall not prevail against him."

Jim-Bob eyed the old cowboy speculatively. "You know what's comin' up tonight, Leather. How do you feel about it?"

Leather frowned, the wrinkles around his eyes deepening and stretching far down his cheeks. "Well, if ever a man deserved hangin', I'd say that man does. But I'm not real sure, Jim-Bob, that any of us, even a judge and jury, has the right to take another man's life away. 'Vengeance is Mine, sayeth the Lord.' One thing for sure, it's wrong to take a man out and string him up the way they're fixin' to do tonight." Conviction burned in his gray eyes. "It's a thing they'll all regret later on. I've tried to tell some of them so. I saw a lynchin' one time. I've spent years tryin' to forget it, but I never have. And I never will."

Jim-Bob nodded in satisfaction. "I thought you'd feel that way, Leather, but I had to be sure. There's just a chance we can beat that bunch tonight. Would you be willin' to help?"

"You bet, son. What you want me to do?"

"Dr. Spain gave me the idea. I'm goin' to try to decoy that bunch away so I can slip the prisoner out."

"I'll do anything but set fire to the barn."

Jim-Bob smiled. "That's what Doc suggested, but it's a little drastic. No, I'll need some saddled horses."

Hurriedly he helped Leather catch up and saddle four of Mont's better horses. One pair he picked for sudden speed. The other two were a pair that weren't so fast, perhaps, but could carry a rider for hours at a steady pace and not give out.

"These two," he said, "we'll hide out back yonder, in the dark. If anybody finds them, we're blowed up."

"Nobody'll find them," Leather promised.

"The other two, we'll need up close to the back door of the jail. Give me about ten minutes, Leather, then bring them on. Stay in the dark—don't let anybody see you with them. Ease up under that liveoak *motte* by the courtyard fence. Just wait there and watch the back window. When the time comes, I'll stand by the window and strike a match, like I was goin' to light me a cigarette. Then you bring them horses and come a-runnin'. They'll be taken off of your hands in a hurry."

Leather was shaking his head. "You won't get far, Jim-Bob. That bunch'll run you down."

Jim-Bob said, "That's what the two fast horses are

for. Sure they'll run them down, only it'll take a while. And when they do, they'll find it's not me and the prisoner at-all. It'll be Harvey Mills and Slim Underhill, if I can get them to swallow the idea. By the time that bunch finds out what happened, I'll be off to a nice head start with Buster Fox. In the other direction."

Admiration showed in Leather's squinched-eyes. "You've got about as much chance as a snowball in h—the hot place. But you know somethin', Jim-Bob? You're lookin' more like your old daddy every day!"

8

Jim-Bob headed back toward the jail, the lonely old Ranger dog not letting him get far ahead. He paused a time or two to spot any lookouts that might be posted. He saw one idling at the closed blacksmith shop, watching the front of the jail. He knew there would be another, or maybe a couple, somewhere out back. Jim-Bob knocked softly on the jail's front door.

"Who is it?" came Harvey's voice.

"Me, Jim-Bob."

The door opened. Jim-Bob slipped in. Slim hurriedly shut the door again, dropping a wooden bar down into place. But not before the dog had gotten in too. Jim-Bob frowned at the bar. "Trouble?"

"Nothin' yet," said Harvey. "But there's been a little prowlin' done outside. Me and Slim thought a mite of precaution would be better than a right smart of cure."

Jim-Bob motioned toward Buster Fox's cell. He could barely see it in the dark. "How's he takin' it?"

"I haven't heard him laughin' much."

Jim-Bob walked back to Buster's cell. He could not see Buster's eyes, but he could almost smell the fear that gripped the man. "Buster, I've got an idea that might save you. But before we try it, I want you to tell me what you did with that bank money."

"You go to hell."

"Buster, you're in a mighty tough spot."

"I'd be in a tougher one if I told you where that money is. It's all I've got to bargain with. You say there's a chance. All right, let's try it. You get me out of here and maybe I'll tell you."

"And maybe you won't."

Buster shrugged. "We'll just have to wait and see."

Harvey Mills showed a lively interest. "What's this chance you're talkin' about? Tom Singleton loosenin' up?"

Jim-Bob shook his head. "Not a bit. I was just hopin' we might outfox him." He dropped his chin and looked up at Harvey and Slim. "You said a while ago you'd do anything me or Mont wanted. Does that still go?"

Harvey glanced uncertainly at Slim. "Let's hear the proposition. Mont give you a plan?"

"Mont's in bad shape. He doesn't know what's goin' on. No, this is my idea." He told them about the horses. "When I light the match, Leather will bring them up. I figure if you two bust out of the back door on the run, grab the horses and spur south as hard as you can go, they'll all figure it's me makin' a break toward Dry Creek with the prisoner. They'll take out after you like hounds after a rabbit. When it's clear, I'll slip out with Buster, get the other horses and head north toward Grafton."

Harvey chewed his lip. "There's a flaw in this thing as big as a Chihuahua hat. Them boys are liable to shoot at us, and there's one or two of them that ain't in the habit of missin'."

"I don't think they'll shoot, Harvey. They won't know which one is Buster, and they won't be anxious to kill *me*. The way I figure it, they'll just keep after you till they finally ride you down. But there's a chance I'm wrong. I'd want you to realize that risk before you said yes."

Harvey studied it a little, then looked at Slim. "Slim, you been shot at the last day or two?"

Slim shook his head. He seldom spoke, but he was smiling. "Not that I know of."

Harvey shrugged. "All right, Jim-Bob, we'll give it a try. If they *do* shoot us, the joke's on you." His grin died then. "What worries me is you off out in the open country with *him*," he said, pointing his chin at Buster Fox. "I'd sooner carry a rattlesnake in my hip pocket then have him ridin' along beside me."

Jim-Bob said, "I'll watch out for Buster. You two just watch out for Tom Singleton and his bunch."

He pulled out his watch and held it up close to his face, trying to read it in the darkness. "Moon isn't up yet, but it soon will be. We need to be on our way before it comes." He frowned at the two men. "You sure about this now? I wouldn't want you to think I was tryin' to pressure you into it."

Harvey said testily, "We told you, didn't we?"

Jim-Bob held out his hand. "All right then. Lead them as far as you can, but if it gets too tight, don't take any unnecessary risk. Good luck to you."

Each man shook Jim-Bob's hand. "Send us a letter from Grafton," grinned Slim.

Jim-Bob raised the shade on the rear window and struck a match. He heard the quick strike of hoofs. "He's comin'," he said. Harvey slid the bar off and pushed open the door.

"Run for it," Jim-Bob whispered urgently.

Harvey and Slim jumped out over the back steps and hit the ground running. Watching from inside, Jim-Bob spotted a quick movement in the shadows. A man trotted out into the open, waving his hand in excitement. "Stop there!" he shouted futilely. "You ain't gonna do this!"

The two men kept running. The lookout shouted louder, "They're gettin' away! Help me, you-all! Stop them, somebody!"

The man drew his gun and leveled it. Jim-Bob sucked in a sharp breath. Then, as he had hoped, the lookout evidently changed his mind, afraid he might hit the wrong man. He fired into the air. "You-all come help me! They're gettin' away!"

Leather came in a hurry, leading the two horses. Harvey and Slim grabbed the reins and swung up, keeping themselves bent low. They spurred out before they even had their right feet well into the stirrups. Leather faded back into the shadows. Jim-Bob knew he would return to the livery barn.

The lookout kept shouting and firing into the air, running afoot after the two riders. Though he could not catch them himself anymore, he had created an explosion of excitement down the street. Jim-Bob could tell from the noise that men were boiling out of the Tobosa Bar. He could hear drumming of hoofs as cowboys caught up their horses. Several men ran by the jail afoot, heading south toward the excitement.

Jim-Bob unlocked the cell door. It squealed as he swung it open, and the sound raised the hair at the back of his neck. "Come on, Buster. We better get out of here while all the excitement is down the street.

Some of those left behind are liable to pop in here directly, lookin' for somebody they can raise hell with."

Buster Fox quavered. "What if they catch us out there?"

"Safer out there in the dark than it'll be in here. Grab your hat and let's skin out."

As Buster reached the cell door, Jim-Bob was ready with a set of handcuffs. He locked Buster's wrist to his own, only a short chain between them. He motioned with his .44. "Don't you take any foolish notions when we get out there. Any kind of commotion and they'll be on us."

Buster almost stumbled on old Ranger. The dog stuck close beside Jim-Bob. Jim-Bob whispered, "Go home, Ranger. Go home." But the dog paid him no heed. Gripping the gun tightly in his free right hand, Jim-Bob led Buster out the door into the darkness. He hugged up against the building and worked his way along in the deep shadows as far as he could.

"Those trees yonder," he whispered. "Duck down and let's get to them."

He waited just a moment, taking a long look and seeing no sign of anyone close by. Then he sprinted across the open space, Buster right beside him. They reached the deep shadows again and crouched to catch their breath and listen. Jim-Bob and Buster were almost afraid to breathe. But Ranger squatted unconcernedly beside them, panting for the whole town to hear.

Buster whispered urgently, "Get rid of that dog!"

"I can't." Jim-Bob wished Ranger would leave, but he knew no way to send him off without raising a racket about it.

From down the street, around the livery barn and

the Tobosa Bar, he could still hear frenzied activity. Men were catching their horses and riding out in the chase. From farther south, well out of town, came the fading sound of running horses and shouting men. Occasionally one of these men would fire into the air as a signal to guide those later ones still trying to catch up. The shots were trailing farther away.

"Stop breathin' so hard, Buster." Jim-Bob spoke quietly. "I'm just as scared as you are."

He thought he saw a movement at the jail. He made out the form of a man entering the open back door. He couldn't be sure, but he thought another man was waiting outside.

"We got out of there just in time," he whispered.

The man came back out of the jail and headed south like the rest, afoot and in a hurry. Jim-Bob could tell that another man or two were with him.

He tugged at the handcuff. "Come on, we better ease toward the livery barn and get our own horses."

Buster asked anxiously, "How long do you reckon your friends can keep them led off?"

"No tellin'. Just accordin' to how the luck runs. We better be doin' some runnin' ourselves."

Buster said worriedly, "I wonder where Dencil's at? He promised he'd be around."

"I figure he's followin' that lynch mob, him and Pony and Hackberry. They'll have it in mind to rescue you when the mob catches up to you and me. They'll get as big a surprise as the rest when it turns out it's Harvey and Slim after all."

He couldn't see Buster's face, but he could sense the prisoner's disappointment. "Looks like it worked out pretty good all around," Jim-Bob commented. "Got rid of the mob and Dencil too. Now let's mosey."

They took the long way to the corrals, staying in the shadows most of the time, keeping well away from lamplight that spilled out of many windows along the street. By the time they reached the back side of the wagon yard, the excitement there was over. The last rider had caught his horse and had ridden away, or else had given up and gone back to the bar. A sharp smell of dust lay heavy in the air. Angry talk floated down from around the Tobosa. Frustrated, the cowboys were probably making plans not only for what they'd do to Buster when they caught him, but also for that smart-aleck kid deputy.

"I don't reckon I'm any more popular up there right now than you are, Buster," he said. "Let's go easy now. We tied the horses in this little mesquite thicket out back of the corrals."

He moved as quietly as he could, but it seemed to him that the pair of them were as noisy as a bunch of big steers, feet brushing through the heat-dried grass, boots crushing an occasional twig or dead limb that had fallen from a mesquite.

They had just reached the thicket when Jim-Bob saw a man moving toward him. His heart leaped, and he brought up the gun. Ranger began barking at the man. Jim-Bob thought his legs would give way.

"Jim-Bob," the man whispered. Jim-Bob recognized old Leather Dryden. He lowered the gun, his heart still pounding away. The breath was nearly gone from him.

"Hush up, Ranger," Jim-Bob hissed. "Git!" Then to Leather he said, "My Lord, Leather, I like to've shot you."

"I had to be sure somebody didn't find the horses. Nobody saw you?"

"We wouldn't be here if they had."

Buster was cursing softly. "That lousy dog. He'll be the death of us yet. If I had a gun I'd kill him."

Jim-Bob replied, "I wouldn't swap him for a dozen of you. Ranger, go on home!"

The dog reluctantly moved out a ways and stopped to watch.

Leather said, "I put Mont's saddlegun and scabbard on your saddle. You may need it."

"Thanks, Leather. I didn't think of it."

Jim-Bob untied the horse he had selected for Buster. He unlocked the cuff from his own wrist and snapped it around Buster's other wrist.

"Mount up."

Buster did, and Jim-Bob swung into his saddle. He loosened the hornstring and shook out a loop in his rope. This he dropped over Buster's shoulders and drew it up around the man's belly.

"Just to supplement the handcuffs," he said. "You try anything and you'll get yanked out of that saddle."

He leaned down and shook Leather's tough old hand. "Thanks, Leather. Just one more favor—when Doc Spain approves, would you go tell Mont what we've done? I expect it'll make him rest easier."

"Mont'll be proud of you, son. But you're a long way from Grafton, and you better git ridin'. God go with you."

Jim-Bob pulled his horse around and headed him straight west at the beginning. Out this way was only a scattering of houses and the least chance of being seen. Buster did not lag, for he knew Jim-Bob meant business with that rope. Jim-Bob looked behind him. As he thought, Ranger trotted along at a discreet distance. He stopped to order the dog home again, but he knew it was useless. Ranger had lost Dan. He didn't want to lose Jim-Bob.

The two riders kept their horses in an easy walk as they skirted the houses. Jim-Bob thought they were going to make it without incident. But then the dogs picked them up. Several dogs moved in and began to bark at the horses. Buster said fearfully, "They'll hear them dogs."

Jim-Bob held his breath. He saw a man open a door and peer out into the darkness. He hauled up short and held still, hoping the man would not see him and Buster. The man stood on his front steps and looked in their direction, where the dogs were setting up a racket.

"What's goin' on out there?" the man called. "Who is it?"

He started to move their way. Jim-Bob didn't think he had actually seen them yet. Just then old Ranger declared himself into the game. He tore into one of the dogs with a vengeance. For a moment it was a madhouse of yelping and excited barking.

The man evidently satisfied himself that it was nothing but a strange dog trespassing in the neighborhood. He growled something about thinning out a bunch of dogs one of these days and went back into his house.

Jim-Bob exhaled slowly and wiped cold sweat from his face. "I knew Ranger would amount to something someday if we left him alone."

He tugged on the rope, and the two started riding again. Behind them, Ranger was still entertaining the other dogs, holding them at bay. "We'll probably lose him now. By the time he gets through back there, we'll be gone. He'll turn around and go home."

Jim-Bob tried to listen for sounds of the mob after Slim and Harvey, but the continued barking drowned out any distant shots that might otherwise have carried this far. By now, he figured, the mob was just riding hard, trying to catch up to those two fast horses. They wouldn't be doing much shooting.

Finally Jim-Bob and Buster passed the last shack on the east edge of town. "From here on out, Buster, it's open country. We better start tryin' to make some time."

He reined north then, straight north toward Grafton. He had it in mind to intersect the wagon road somewhere up ahead and follow it. He moved into an easy lope. Buster was a little slow in following. The rope drew up taut. Buster spurred and moved abreast of Jim-Bob.

"How about this rope?" he complained. "Have we got to leave it on?"

"If you were me, would you take it off?"

Buster did not reply to that, and the rope stayed around him. They stayed in an easy lope for a while. Jim-Bob wanted to put as much distance behind them as he could, yet he knew he could not afford to overtax the horses. If he did that, he had just as well give up before he started. There might come a time, later tonight, when a little reserve strength, a little extra speed, would be a matter of life or death.

They rode up on top of a gentle rise. Jim-Bob drew up a moment, taking a last look at the lamp-lighted town which lay at some distance behind them. He stepped out of the saddle so that he might hear better any noise from behind them. He heard nothing. Damnation, he thought, he would give a month's pay just to know what was going on back there.

Not far ahead would be the wagon road to Grafton. Coming in at a tangent as they were they would strike it somewhere on the flat that lay below them. Jim-Bob would be glad to get on the road. No matter how well a man thought he knew the country, he was likely to stray some and put in a few extra miles trying to ride across it in the dark. Especially a place as far away as Grafton. The moon was coming up. It was getting light enough now that Jim-Bob could make out individual mesquite trees, coal-black against a silver ground. He and Buster hadn't gotten out of town any too soon. "Let's get to the road, Buster. We've killed all the time we can afford."

They were within a couple of hundred yards of the road when Jim-Bob heard the horses coming. He jerked on the reins and nodded toward a pair of mesquites nearby. He and Buster pulled up behind them and waited. Not letting his eyes roam far from Buster, he got down to watch. He made out three men, swinging along in an easy lope. Jim-Bob's horse started to nicker. Jim-Bob reached up quickly and grabbed the animal's nose, stopping the sound. He held his own breath until the riders were past them and out of sight in the dim moonlight.

"Cowboys on their way home," he said. "Probably missed the show in town. They don't know how close they just missed one here." He got back into the saddle. "Guess we can't use the road after all," he said regretfully. "We'll have to take out across country."

A little flicker of hope came to Buster Fox. "There was three of them. You know, that just might be old Dencil, and Pony and Hackberry."

The thought gave Jim-Bob a sudden jolt. He hadn't considered that. "It can't be, Buster. They're bound to be out chasing after that mob. We fooled them like we fooled everybody else."

"Dencil's a hard man to fool. He might just be a little too smart for you, boy."

"Why don't you holler and find out?" Jim-Bob challenged Buster.

That put an end to it, as far as Buster was concerned. But it gave Jim-Bob something new to worry about. What if he *hadn't* fooled Dencil?

9

They angled westward awhile. Jim-Bob wanted to put some distance between them and the wagon road. It wasn't bad for a while, because the land was mostly gentle, flat, or rising and falling only a little. Occasionally they moved through patches of brush, and he kept a close watch on Buster Fox.

In time he sensed that Buster had shaken the heavy anxiety that had gripped him. Buster sat straighter in the saddle, surer of himself. He even began to hum.

"I don't know what you've got to feel so happy about," Jim-Bob commented dryly.

"If you'd just got out of a hangin', you'd feel good too."

"You mean I got you out of it."

Buster replied flatly. "You got nothin' to brag about. You was the one got me into it in the first place. Maybe someday I'll find the way to thank you right and proper. And I don't think you'll enjoy it much."

"You're not goin' to get much chance for anything anymore that you can't do in jail, Buster. You've got a fair trial comin' to you, then a good *legal* hangin'. If I was in your boots, I don't know how much hummin' I'd do."

Buster gave him a dry laugh. "You really think

they'll hang me? Boy, the snow'll be three feet deep here the Fourth of July before they ever hang Buster Fox."

"I don't see that you've got any way out of it."

"I got two ways out. One of them is me, and the other is my brother Dencil. I been in mighty few spots in my day that I couldn't get out of by myself. And them few, Dencil took care of. Don't you go buyin' any flowers for me, boy. It'll be a long time before ever I need them."

Buster began to sing a bawdy dancehall tune about a girl in a red dress. Jim-Bob took it as long as he could then flamed. "Shut up, Buster. Doesn't it bother you at-all, knowin' that you've killed two men today, two good young men that never hurt you or nobody else?"

Buster shrugged. "They won't come back to life, me worryin' over them. A dead man is dead, boy, and you'd just as well forget about him."

Jim-Bob's teeth ground together. "I'm not forgettin' them, Buster, especially not the one in the bank. He was the best friend I ever had."

Buster said, "That's tough. But he ought to've known what he was gettin' into when he went to work in a bank. Bank's a dangerous place for a man to be, boy, all that money around. He ought to've worked in a mercantile or somethin', and he wouldn't have gotten his fool self hurt."

Jim-Bob reined up suddenly. The rope snapped taut on Buster's belly. Buster jerked out of the saddle and landed with a hard thud on the ground. It jarred him. For a moment he sat there, numb. Angry himself, Jim-Bob could feel the burn of Buster's glare across the ten feet that separated them.

"What do you think you're doin'?" Buster demanded. "Did you pull me away from that mob just so you could kill me yourself?"

Jim-Bob's voice was brittle. "Don't tempt me, Buster."

Buster swore under his breath. He got up stiffly and rubbed his hip. "Crazy kid, there ought to be a law against anybody like you packin' a star. You could kill somebody."

"Awful easy," Jim-Bob said. "Come on, let's go."

They rode a couple of hours then without speaking. Jim-Bob gradually eased the direction of travel back toward the north star. He kept Buster riding a little in the lead, so that never would Jim-Bob's gaze need to be away from him, never would Buster be able to spur in suddenly and surprise him. He had learned that lesson from Jace Dunnigan. It was a mistake he would never make again.

Riding, Jim-Bob found himself growing curious about Buster, wondering what it was that made him so quick to kill. Finally he said, "Buster, I been tryin' to figure you out. For the life of me, I can't. How does a man get off the track the way you did? What ever made an outlaw of you?"

Strangely, the question seemed to please Buster, seemed to touch the braggart in him. "You really consider me an outlaw, boy?"

"What else?"

"How many real outlaws did you ever see?"

"I was out with the C Bar wagon one time when a man came ridin' up about dark and asked if he could spend the night with us. I was just a button and had a pretty good-sized bedroll, so Tom Singleton put him in with me. Next mornin', when he left, the other boys told me he was Alkali Gotcher from out west of the

Pecos. I didn't sleep good for three or four nights afterwards."

Buster laughed. "Alkali Gotcher! Who ever heard of anybody losin' sleep over a counterfeit like that? His blood would turn to clabber if he ever went up against a real badman."

"He looked tough enough to me."

Buster snickered. "Counterfeit."

Jim-Bob's nose wrinkled. "You didn't look so tough yourself yesterday when we took you. Or tonight when it looked like Tom Singleton was fixin' to get you. I'll bet you'd have cried like a baby if they'd taken you out."

He heard Buster's sharp intake of breath. "Shut up, boy. Maybe I'll show you just how tough I can really get."

"What's the matter, Buster? Do you hate the whole world?"

"This world owes me a lot, boy. I still got a good many debts out, and I aim to collect on them."

"And kill innocent people doin' it?"

"Let them watch out for themselves. There ain't nobody ever done anything for Buster Fox."

"Dencil did."

"That's different. He's my brother. Brothers are supposed to look out for each other."

"Dencil told me how you two were on your own as kids. But so was I. Lots of people were good to me. Didn't anybody ever help you, Buster?"

Buster scowled. "Not without damn well lettin' me know they were doin' me a favor and that I owed them somethin'. There never was anybody cared anything for me except Dencil. Not even our old man and old woman."

Jim-Bob didn't prod him, but Buster seemed to want to talk now. "First it was the old man. He was a faro dealer. I remember how he and the old woman used to drag us around from town to town when we was just little bitty buttons. Sometimes they would move us in the middle of the night. They hated each other, and I think they hated us. First it was the old man, just took off one night and never did come back. Then the old lady. We went three days without anything to eat, waitin' for her to show up again. She never did.

"There wasn't anybody wanted us. Folks would feed us a meal and start us on our way to get shed of us, hopin' somebody else would pick us up so we wouldn't be left on their hands. We was both too little to work, people said. So when we got hungry enough, we'd steal. We got awful thin sometimes, but we never did starve. Finally we got big enough to really work. We'd stay on a ranch awhile, then they'd decide they didn't like me. They always liked Dencil well enough; it was *me* they picked on. Me and Dencil, we found out how easy it was when we left a place just to take a few of their cattle with us. We never did have much trouble selling them to somebody.

"Dencil always could tell who was a likely prospect to buy our cattle. He said he could tell by lookin' in their eyes. Honest people, most of them was supposed to be. But Dencil could always tell. They knew the brands had been changed, but they hadn't done it themselves, and that made a difference. If anybody ever asked, why, they bought them cattle, and they had a bill of sale to show for it."

Buster laughed harshly. "Honest people! I'm tellin' you, boy, most people are just as crooked as those of us they call outlaws, only they keep it covered up with a coat of white paint. Just let them have a chance to make some fast money and you'll see how quick that white paint turns black."

Jim-Bob said, "A man generally finds what he's lookin' for. There's enough bitterness in you to sour all the milk cows in Texas."

Buster looked scornfully at Jim-Bob. "Maybe you think *you're* honest. Maybe it made you feel real holy tonight when you turned down Dencil's offer of money to let me out. But you turned it down because it wasn't enough, that's all. If he'd made it big enough, you'd have grabbed it and run. You'd find out you're a counterfeit just like the rest. The only difference in anybody is the price it'll take to make them sell out."

Jim-Bob just shook his head. He still could not muster any sympathy for Buster. But maybe he understood a little better what made Buster so ready to lash out at anyone who came near him. He kept the horses moving at a good clip, trotting them awhile, then loping them some, trying to make all the time that he could. But eventually it began to tell on the horses. Jim-Bob could feel his brown laboring to keep up the pace.

He thought he knew about where he was, but in the night this way, in country he hadn't ridden over a great deal, it would be easy to miss the mark. In one way he wished for daylight, that he could know for certain. Yet again, with daylight he would lose the protective cover of darkness that had gotten them this far.

He had intended all along to stop at George Thorn's TX ranch and get a pair of fresh horses. The way he had been figuring it, they ought to reach there about sunup. Maybe earlier. Trouble was, they might pass it up in the dark. Then they would have to make the whole trip on these same tired horses.

"We've made good time," he told Buster, "but it's takin' too much out of the horses. From here on we better just stay in a trot and save them all we can. We'll bear a little to the east and try to strike the dry fork of Paint Horse Creek. If we find it and follow it, we can get ourselves some fresh mounts."

Buster's voice sharpened in alarm. "Where we goin'?"

"Friend of mine has got a ranch up ahead of us."

Doubtfully Buster said, "Those were friends of yours in town, too."

"You gettin' scared again? I thought you were the tough one."

Resentment was in Buster's reply. "You'll see how tough I am. Sooner or later, I promise I'll show you."

Eventually they came upon the fork. Jim-Bob motioned with his hand, and they headed north up its west bank. Summer had shut the rainfall off and slowed the flow of the springs. Water was not running down the bed of the creek now, but all the potholes still held water from the last rain.

Jim-Bob could tell by the stars that the morning hours were wearing along. Luck was running with them, he thought. All that way and they hadn't stumbled onto anything that might look like trouble. Not even so much as a sheep camp.

Dawn was setting the brush afire off the eastern line of hills when Jim-Bob saw the TX headquarters stretched out ahead of them. "That's it, Buster," he said. "Keep on the lookout for some horses."

In a moment Buster pointed. "There's a bunch right yonder."

They moved toward the horses. This was a set of George's broncs, but Jim-Bob knew they weren't going to do any better. He threw up his hand and yelled, *"Hy-yaah!"* The animals turned and headed for the house in a long trot.

"You a pretty good bronc rider, Buster?"

"Never did care much for it. Broke horses was always easy to get."

"Broncs is all we're likely to find here. George Thorn breaks horses for a livin'. He says he sees no future in keepin' them around after they're gentle. One ever gets to where he won't pitch, George sells him."

Nearing the corrals and George's simple frame house, Jim-Bob said quietly, "Whoa up a little. We better make sure first that George hasn't got company."

He looked until he was satisfied, not missing the tension in Buster's face. "All right," he said, "looks clear."

The loose broncs headed straight through an open gate into a corral. Jim-Bob followed along, watching the house. Lamplight shone through the kitchen window. These ranch people never let daylight catch them asleep.

Jim-Bob pitched Buster a little slack in the rope. "Get off and shut the gate behind those broncs."

When Buster had remounted, they rode the extra distance to the house.

"George!" Jim-Bob called, "George Thorn!"

Sue-Ellen was the first to appear in the doorway, wiping her hands on a flour-sack apron. She saw who it was, smiled, then caught herself. "Jim-Bob McClain, what do you mean ridin' up here this time of mornin' and hollerin' like that? For all you know, folks might be asleep."

Jim-Bob came close to grinning at her. "Not around this place, they wouldn't."

Sue-Ellen noticed Buster then, and the rope around his waist. Her eyes widened, and she said nothing more.

George Thorn hobbled out onto his little porch, coffee cup in his hand. He stopped there until he recognized Jim-Bob in the growing light of dawn. "Mornin', Jim-Bob," he said pleasantly. "If you'd come an hour earlier, you'd have caught me in bed." He stared curiously at Buster Fox, at the rope and the handcuffs. "What the Sam Hill you got there?"

"Prisoner, George. Takin' him to Grafton to a safe jail. We need to swap for fresh horses. I'll bring yours back later."

The stiffened old bronc rider frowned at Buster Fox. "I'll bet he's the one that killed Dan Singleton and that boy out at the Kendrick outfit. We heard about it last night."

Jim-Bob nodded. "He's the one. They were fixin' to lynch him."

George's wind-burned face twisted. "Can't say I blame them any."

Jim-Bob said sharply, "He's a prisoner, George. Don't you get any idea . . ."

George Thorn shook his gray head. "Don't worry, thinkin' is all I'd do about it. Sure, you can have some horses. Sue-Ellen, you fix them some breakfast while we get their saddles changed."

Jim-Bob protested. "No time for that, George. They're liable to be along directly, lookin' for us."

"Coffee's done fixed, and she'll have eggs and bacon ready by the time we swap saddles." Handing Sue-Ellen his empty cup, George stepped down off the porch and glanced toward a small shack back of the house. "Wish Chum Lawton would get up of a mornin' without me callin' him three times. He's a fair-to-meddlin' bronc rider but the laziest one ever I seen."

Jim-Bob and Buster rode back to the corral. George hobbled along hurriedly, reaching the gate about the same time they did. He unlatched it and held it open for them to ride in.

Jim-Bob thought about letting Buster help change the saddles, but he decided against it. With half a chance, Buster might try anything. A swinging girth with its brass buckle could be a powerful weapon. Jim-Bob unlocked one of the cuffs from Buster's wrist and snapped it shut again on a post. "That'll hold you while we saddle up."

Jim-Bob unsaddled his own horse. George turned loose Buster's. He looked at the horses Jim-Bob had brought in and said, "I'll have to apologize a little for them. They won't be as good as what you were ridin'. They've been gentled a little, but they're still mostly bronc."

"Just pick us what you think are the best two," Jim-Bob said.

George swung his loop in a figure eight and caught out a young sorrel. "I'd say this is the top horse. Next one is that dun yonder. He's liable to bow up a little and might even pitch a jump or two, but he's the best-goin' bronc here."

Jim-Bob mused, "Better let Buster have him. I'd hate for him to break in two with me and let Buster get away while I had my hands full."

Buster glared at him, not relishing the idea of getting on a bronc.

George said, "It'd tickle me to see this dun bust

him right half in two. Only I don't expect he'll be that bad."

By the time they got saddled and led the horses back to the house, Chum Lawton had gotten dressed and was washing his face and hands in the tin wash basin at the edge of the porch. Drying his face, he eyed Jim-Bob and the prisoner speculatively. "Who caught him for you, Jim-Bob?"

Yesterday Jim-Bob would have flared. Now Chum just left him cold. After what he had been through, Chum was no worse than a gnat buzzing around his ear. Jim-Bob said, "I had help. Better men than you'll ever be."

Sue-Ellen stepped to the door, worriedly watching the two. She saw that there was no anger in Jim-Bob's face, and she eased some. "Breakfast's on the table. You-all better come."

Jim-Bob pulled out a chair for Buster and motioned him to sit down. As he had done at the corral, he unfastened one cuff and relocked it to a table leg. "You can eat with one hand."

Buster colored. "You don't trust nobody, do you?"

"If you had the chance, you'd run like a rabbit."

Buster grunted, "And I expect you'd shoot me like one."

Bluntly Jim-Bob said, "I'd try."

Sue-Ellen had scrambled the eggs. Jim-Bob spooned out a big helping for Buster and added some bacon. "You better eat good. We still got a long ways to go."

Bolting his food, Jim-Bob surreptitiously watched Sue-Ellen. Any time he looked down, he could feel her brown eyes studying him. Funny, he never had especially noticed how downright good-looking she was. He realized he had always needed to compare her with

Tina Kendrick, and alongside Tina's cameo beauty, most any girl would look plain.

Only, what good was beauty when there was nothing beneath it?

Sue-Ellen said, "I heard you tell Dad this is the man who did all those things over at Swallowfork yesterday." When Jim-Bob nodded, she asked, "What was it you said about them tryin' to hang him?"

Briefly Jim-Bob told what had happened.

Sue-Ellen said, "Dan Singleton was always your best friend, wasn't he?"

Jim-Bob nodded soberly.

There was admiration in her voice. "You risked a lot to save this man, even though he murdered Dan. I used to worry about when you'd ever grow up, Jim-Bob. I don't think I'll worry anymore."

Jim-Bob looked at her, and he felt his face warm a little.

Chum Lawton had been listening, his ears perked up. "They were really after him, were they, Tom Singleton and the rest?"

"They wanted him pretty bad."

Chum almost smiled. "Those boys are goin' to be real mad at you when you get back to town." Easy to tell that Chum enjoyed the thought.

Regretfully Jim-Bob said, "I imagine so."

"I expect they'd be grateful to anybody who was to put a crimp in your scheme."

Suddenly worried, Jim-Bob said, "Don't you figure on tryin' anything, Chum."

Chum grinned. "I was just supposin'. Clever as you are, there couldn't anybody put much over on you, could they?"

Jim-Bob lost taste for the breakfast. Funny, the way

Chum Lawton could spoil anything for him. That buzzing gnat had turned into a barking dog.

Sue-Ellen was concerned over something. "Dad, do you think all this might have something to do with those men who came by here this morning and got fresh horses?"

Jim-Bob nearly dropped his coffee cup. "What men?"

George shrugged. "I wouldn't hardly think so. It wasn't no posse or mob or anything. Just three men."

Three men! Jim-Bob's stomach went cold. "What did they look like?"

"Tougher than a leather boot. They left maybe thirty or forty minutes before you rode up. They drove horses into the pen and started changin'. Didn't say howdydo or thank-you-ma'am or nothin'. I got up and walked out there to see what was goin' on. I looked at them, and they looked at me, and I just decided to keep my mouth shut. Besides, they was leavin' better horses than they was takin'."

Jim-Bob's heartbeat quickened. "George, did any one of them look like him?" He nodded toward the prisoner.

George's brow furrowed as he studied Buster. "You might say so. Fact of the matter, I'd say he sure did." His gaze lifted to Jim-Bob. "After you, are they?"

Jim-Bob nodded bleakly. The world had risen up and hit him in the face. But how? How could they? "I'd have bet the best pair of boots in Swallowfork that I threw them off the trail just like I did Tom's bunch."

Buster Fox was grinning. "So old Dencil didn't take the bait after all? I told you you'd get no place messin' around with the Foxes, boy."

"Who's Dencil?" Sue-Ellen asked.

"His brother."

She took in a long breath, fear in her eyes. "Then he's liable to be waitin' for you somewhere up ahead?"

Jim-Bob shook his head. "Not *liable*, Sue-Ellen. He *will* be."

She frowned, thinking something out. Then: "Dad, he can't go on alone. We've got to go along and help him."

Jim-Bob protested, "No, Sue-Ellen, it's *my* job."

George said, "She's right, Jim-Bob. You up against three men, plus this one, you won't have a chance."

Jim-Bob said, "I didn't go into this thing blind-folded. I knew what I might come up against before I ever started. I won't let you go, George. As for Sue-Ellen . . ." He shook his head.

Sue-Ellen said, "I can shoot as straight as any man you can put up against me."

Jim-Bob replied, "And you can get shot, just like any man. Forget about it, I tell you."

It occurred to him that nobody had suggested he take Chum Lawton along. Chum himself hadn't made the offer, either. Jim-Bob wouldn't have accepted, even if he had.

"Hurry up there, Buster," Jim-Bob ordered. "We got to go." He shoved his own plate back. He couldn't help noticing how unsteady his hands were. Buster gulped the last of his coffee. "Any old time, boy. We don't want to keep Dencil waitin'."

Jim-Bob unlocked the cuff from the table leg and snapped it back on Buster's wrist. He nodded toward the door. Buster stood up and moved out.

"Thanks for the breakfast, Sue-Ellen," Jim-Bob said warmly. He wanted to leave, yet somehow he couldn't, not without saying something more to her. "I'm grateful for your offer, Sue-Ellen. Even if I can't take it, I'll never forget that you made it."

She smiled. "You'll accept it. We'll follow along behind you, and you can't make us go back."

Jim-Bob swore under his breath. Stubborn woman. How could you argue with one like that? They were halfway to the corral when Jim-Bob heard Chum Lawton yell, "Stop right where you're at, Jim-Bob."

He whirled and saw a six-shooter in Chum's hand.

10

hum, what do you think you're doin'?"

"I was just thinkin' how popular a man would be if he was to take your prisoner back to Tom Singleton and the men that want him so bad. I was just thinkin' maybe it would make a man popular enough to win an election for sheriff, if he was of a mind to run."

"Elect a man because he turned a prisoner over to a lynch mob? Chum, you're out of your head."

"No, Jim-Bob, just *usin'* my head. You raise them hands up. Raise them real high."

Grudgingly Jim-Bob complied. "I'll get you for this, Chum. I'll see you in the pen for it if it's the last thing ever I do."

Chum grinned. "No you won't. My friends won't let you. You won't do a thing to me. I'll be the sheriff of this county first thing you know, and *you'll* be the one bustin' broncs."

Jim-Bob glanced at Buster. The cockiness had vanished from the outlaw again. He was in a tough spot here, and he knew it.

Chum said, "Fox, you go on toward that corral, and don't you make any false moves. I reckon they'd almost as soon have you dead as alive."

Jim-Bob said grittily, "And you wouldn't mind bein' known as the one who shot him."

Chum replied, "Not a bit, Jim-Bob. Not a bit."

Jim-Bob thought he knew what would happen if Chum got away with this. He would shoot Buster before he had gone half a mile with him. It was the old Mexican border custom, *ley fuga*. Shot trying to escape. Nobody would ever contest him about it. Nobody but Jim-Bob.

Jim-Bob abruptly made up his mind. He would see just how far Chum was willing to go. He suddenly stepped in front of Buster Fox. "You can't shoot him now, Chum, not without shootin' me first."

Chum said, "Step aside, Jim-Bob, I don't aim to hurt you."

"You don't *dare* to hurt me." He eased toward Chum, his hand outstretched. "Better give me that gun, Chum."

Chum's grin fell away. His face tightened. He lifted the gun a little. "I'm tellin' you, Jim-Bob, don't you come any closer. All I want is Fox. I don't want to have to shoot *you*."

"You can't have him. And you know what'll happen if you shoot me. Like it or not, I'm an officer of the law. They'll take you out and hang you, Chum. Hang you up there and choke the life out of you. Ever see a man hang, Chum? You wouldn't like it." Truth was, Jim-Bob never had seen a hanging himself, and he didn't ever care to. But anything was fair now if it would keep Chum flustered until Jim-Bob could get within reach of him. "Go on, Chum," Jim-Bob challenged, "pull that trigger and get me out of the way." He tried to keep his face straight, but inside he was wound up tight as a fiddlestring. Chum might just be crazy enough to do it.

But Chum backed up a step, and then another. Jim-Bob saw that he had Chum on the run. Suddenly he took two long strides and caught up to the man. He grabbed the gun.

Chum held on, struggling with him. Chum cursed as they fought, his face reddening in rage and frustration. Both men gripped the gun, each trying to throw the other off balance. Sweat broke out on Jim-Bob's forehead as he strained. Then he got a solid footing and threw his shoulder into Chum's stomach, hard. The six-shooter broke loose from Chum's desperate grip. But as it did, it fired.

Jim-Bob heard a man cry out. He looped a hard right fist to Chum's jaw and sent Chum spinning. Then he whirled around to see what had happened.

George Thorn sat on the ground, rocking back and forth in pain, gripping his leg. His teeth were gritted. With a sharp gasp, Sue-Ellen ran toward him. So did Jim-Bob.

Buster Fox got there first. Taking advantage of the confusion, he grabbed Sue-Ellen. He pulled her slim body up against him, his rough hands on her throat. "I got the girl, Jim-Bob. You can't shoot me without hittin' her. Now you throw me that gun of yours, or I'll go ahead and choke her."

It had all been too much for Jim-Bob. For a moment he stood there numb, wondering which way to jump.

Buster Fox didn't give him time to do much wondering. He tightened his grip on Sue-Ellen's throat. Jim-Bob could see her face coloring. "Throw me that gun now," Buster demanded again, "and stop foolin' around."

Jim-Bob's own .44 was still in its holster. He held Chum Lawton's six-shooter in his hand.

Sue-Ellen rasped, "Don't do it, Jim-Bob!" Buster's hands tightened, and she choked.

Jim-Bob couldn't take that. He said, "Here, Buster, take the gun," and he pitched it to the ground at Buster's feet.

Buster grinned malevolently. "Old Dencil needn't to've troubled himself. I took care of it myself."

Angrily Jim-Bob said, "Chokin' a girl half to death, you did. But you haven't got out of the country yet."

"You're not thinkin' you can stop me, are you, boy?"

Jim-Bob's heart sank at the thought of losing Buster Fox after all he had been through. "I'd almost rather have seen the lynch mob get you than see you go free."

"I told you all along you couldn't hold me, that it was just a matter of time."

"I wouldn't have lost you if it hadn't been for that crazy Chum . . ."

He looked around for Chum and didn't see him. Chum had slipped away. "I'll come after you, Buster. I'll hunt you clear to Mexico if I have to."

"You come after me, boy, and they'll be measurin' you for a pine overcoat."

Buster was eyeing the gun Jim-Bob had pitched at his feet. He let go his hold on Sue-Ellen's neck and started to bend down, reaching for the gun with his manacled hands. Without turning, Sue-Ellen suddenly jabbed backward with her elbows. Buster clutched at his stomach, grunting in surprise. Sue-Ellen kicked the gun away from under foot, then jumped out of Buster's reach.

Jim-Bob had no time to think. Instinctively he leaped forward, drawing his gun as he moved. Buster dived at the one Sue-Ellen had kicked away. Jim-Bob swung the gunbarrel savagely. Buster's hat went rolling in the dust. Buster stiffened, but his fingers still groped for the weapon. His body awash with anger, Jim-Bob lashed out with the gunbarrel again. Buster groaned and sank to the ground on his belly. Holding the gun, Jim-Bob stood over him and gasped for breath. For a moment it was all he could do to keep from shooting Buster where he lay. But the wild tide of anger peaked, and he let the pistol go loose in his hand.

"You all right, Sue-Ellen?"

She had one hand on her throat, but she nodded. "I'm sorry, Jim-Bob. I shouldn't have let him get so close."

"Not your fault. Your dad hit thataway, anybody would have done the same." Bitterly he remembered Tina Kendrick. "At least you fought him. You didn't just stand there and scream."

"Is that what Tina did?"

He nodded. "So far as I know, Buster never even touched her. She just stood there and screamed her head off."

Jim-Bob turned back to George Thorn, keeping an eye on the fallen outlaw. Buster didn't look as if he was going to get up for a while. "How hard are you hit, George?"

"I've had broncs do as bad, but I never did get to where I liked it." The bullet had torn through the high top of his right boot. Jim-Bob helped George to his feet. The old bronc stomper hopped to the edge of the porch with Jim-Bob propping him up. Jim-Bob caught hold of the boot and pulled it off. He found a small but steady flow of blood.

"Went through the flesh," George observed. His face

was paling with growing shock. "Bet it'll be a good many days before I can ride a horse again. And it looks like I just lost a bronc rider." He motioned with his thumbless right hand. Jim-Bob heard a horse and glanced toward the corrals. Chum Lawton was just climbing up on the dun that had been saddled for Buster. Chum looked across at Jim-Bob, his face full of hatred. The bronc made two or three crowhops, then stretched out down the south road in a lope.

Chum had left the gate wide open. Jim-Bob headed for the corral as hard as he could run. He got there just in time to throw up his hat and stop the other broncs from stampeding out into the open. Jim-Bob closed the gate. Sue-Ellen came up after him.

"Chum's gone after Tom Singleton," Jim-Bob guessed. "Bound and determined to earn him a little glory out of this someway. Looks like I better catch Buster another horse and vamoose *por allá*."

"Jim-Bob, you know there are three men up ahead somewhere, just waiting' for you."

"And no tellin' how many of them behind, huntin' me."

"At least those behind aren't going to kill you."

"They're out to kill my prisoner. I don't intend to give them the chance."

"I can't talk you out of going on?"

He shook his head and roped out a black bronc.

Sue-Ellen clenched her hands, her mouth drawing thin. "Then promise me, Jim-Bob, that if those three men stop you, you won't do anything foolish. If they get you in a tight spot, let them have Buster Fox."

Jim-Bob threw a saddle on the bronc and carefully reached under for the girth, wary lest the black kick his head off. It was Chum's saddle, and Jim-Bob hoped it got torn up before the day was out. "They won't get him without a fight. If I let Buster Fox loose, I'm finished as a lawman. They'll run me out of town. I'll be lucky to get a job breakin' broncs."

"We'd rather have a live bronc rider than a dead deputy sheriff."

He finished drawing up the cinch and turned to face the girl. "Sue-Ellen, you've got no idea how long I dreamed and planned to get this badge. I don't aim to lose it. It means more to me than anything I've ever had."

"More even than life?"

He pondered a moment. "I don't know—maybe it does. I reckon I'll find out if it ever comes to where I've got to make a choice."

He saw tears squeeze into her eyes, and he caught her hand. Suddenly, somehow, he got some of the feeling he used to get when he was with Tina Kendrick, a funny tugging inside him.

"Look, Sue-Ellen, I'm not goin' to get myself killed. Fact of the matter, I expect I'll be back tonight, or maybe tomorrow, to see you. Why, I'll even take you to the next dance they throw at Sothern's, if it'll make you feel better about it."

She tried to smile. "Is that a promise, Jim-Bob?"

"It's a promise, and you can hold me to it."

There was something about her then, her pretty brown eyes, her open lips. On impulse he bent down and kissed her. He caught her by surprise, then her hands came up behind his arms and pressed tightly there while she warmly met his kiss. It was the first time Jim-Bob had ever seriously kissed a girl. All the blood seemed to rush to his head. He drew back, not understanding this sudden compelling urge that gripped him. His breath was short. His face was warm.

"I'll be back, Sue-Ellen."

He said nothing about it, but he knew George's wounded leg knocked out any chance that George or Sue-Ellen would try to tag along and help him. Badly as Jim-Bob wanted help, he was glad neither of them could go. He led the two horses back to the house. George still sat on the edge of the porch, gripping his leg. He had the bleeding stopped.

Jim-Bob asked, "George, you sure you'll make it all right?"

George nodded and dismissed him with a quick jerk of his head in the direction of Grafton. "You better get a move on."

Buster was sitting up, rubbing his head. Jim-Bob said harshly, "Get up from there, Buster. You don't know how close I came to killin' you."

Buster stared dumbly at his hand, streaked red from a gun gash on his head. His eyes were glassy at first. The haze slowly faded out of them. A searing anger took its place. "I swear, boy," he struggled for breath, "I'll kill you the first time I get the chance."

Jim-Bob's eyes narrowed. His voice was tight. "No, Buster, because the first time I think you're about to get the chance, I'll kill *you*."

He lifted Buster to his feet and led the black horse around. The horse had a little hump under the saddle, and that seemed to wake Buster up. A little shakily he gripped the reins up on the bronc's neck, getting a handful of mane with them. His right hand was on the horn. He swung up quickly, getting his right foot in the stirrup without losing any time about it. The pony goated a moment, then settled down.

Jim-Bob got on his sorrel. There was no sign of trouble. He looked down gratefully at George Thorn. "Thanks, George, for everything."

Sue-Ellen was trying to fight down the tremor in her voice. "Remember your promise. I'll be lookin' forward to that dance."

Jim-Bob said, "I'll remember. We'll have us a time, you and me." Then he pitched the loop over the prisoner's head again. "All right, Buster. You lead."

It took a little while to get the kinks worked out of the two broncs. For a time it seemed that both of them were set with a hair trigger. They kept looking for the slightest excuse to break into pitching. Both Jim-Bob and Buster held the reins up tight. When either horse acted as if it was trying to get its head down to pitch, they firmly pulled it up again. The steady pace finally wore the foolishness out of the broncs.

All the way to the Thorn outfit, Jim-Bob had paused periodically to look and listen behind him. Now he was no longer so worried about his back trail as he was the one ahead of him. He pulled far away from the wagon road that led to Grafton. He preferred to strike out across country. He was careful not to top out over any rises that might outline them against the sky. He tried to keep to the lower ground, working in and out of the brush as much as he could.

"No use you tryin' all these shenanigans," Buster told him sullenly. "Old Dencil's goin' to find you anyway."

"Shut up, Buster." Jim-Bob's voice was sharp. Too sharp, for he knew he was letting Buster get under his skin too much. Now, for the first time since they had started from Swallowfork, Jim-Bob pulled out Mont's saddlegun and rode with it across his lap.

They rode two hours under the morning sun before they suddenly came upon a band of black-topped Merino sheep, grazing a green flat in the cool breeze. The sheep nearest them bolted back into the band. The excitement rushed through the entire bunch like the ripples on a disturbed hole of water.

"Let's back out a little and go around," Jim-Bob said. He could see the herder on the other side of the band, quickly sending his sheepdog out on the run to intercept those sheep which might flee from the flock on one side. Jim-Bob rode the other way to try to patch up that end. The sheep quieted, and Jim-Bob eased Buster toward the spot where the herder stood.

The sheep smell was strong around this grazing ground, yet it was not an unpleasant odor at all. Jim-Bob thought that if he lost Buster today, he might have to take up a job herding sheep. It might be all that was left open to him.

He recognized an old Mexican he had been seeing in this country occasionally for several years. "*Hola, amigo,*" he said. "*Como le va?*" He had picked up a little cow-camp Spanish in his time, as had most cowboys. It was enough to keep him from starving to death in Mexican country.

"*Buenas dias,*" came the answer in the pleasant but formal manner which these people always showed to Angelos they didn't know well. The old *pastor* took in Jim-Bob's badge and his prisoner without any reaction showing on his gray-bearded face. "*Qué pasa,* sheriff?"

"I'm lookin' . . ." Jim-Bob started off, then remembered he wasn't talking Spanish. Some of these herders understood English, but they seldom admitted it. They often found ignorance, or the reputation therefor, to be their shield in event of trouble. "*Busco para tres hombres.*" He knew he probably wasn't saying the words right, and he held up three fingers for the three men. He was reasonably sure the old Mexican wouldn't have seen the trio. He thought he probably had gotten far enough off the road to miss them.

But the herder smiled and told him yes, he had seen three men, and if Jim-Bob hurried, he probably could catch up with them. It had not been more than *una media hora*, half an hour, since they had passed this way. But before the young sheriff left, would he not care for some coffee? The three friends had paused with the herder. There was plenty, and surely the *patron* would bring more coffee before this was gone. Jim-Bob glanced at Buster Fox and saw triumph in Buster's gloating eyes.

Jim-Bob's stomach seemed to burn. Perhaps the coffee would help ease this sick feeling that welled up in him. "*Si, amigo,*" he spoke weakly. "I'll take some coffee."

The morning hours ground away. The summer heat grew, wrapping itself angrily around the two riders. The want of sleep was beginning to tell on Jim-Bob. He sweated, and his stomach was aboil from tension and sleeplessness. The steady riding, the constant watching, were relentlessly wearing him down. It came to him that he had been on the go since early yesterday morning.

Buster Fox was working on him, too. A mocking laughter was in his eyes. "What you lookin' so sharp yonderway for? You think Dencil's goin' to let you see him? He'll be up there someplace all right, only you'll never know till it's too late."

Edgily Jim-Bob said, "Why don't you quiet down?"

When Buster wasn't talking to him, roweling him with taunts, he was riding along humming tunelessly. That was just as bad.

Buster said, "Liable to come any time now, boy. See that clump of mesquite yonder? Dencil and old Hackberry and Pony might just be bellied down behind it, with their rifles trained on you this very minute. Or they might be waitin' just over that next hill. You don't know."

"I said shut up!"

"Tryin' to help you, boy, don't you know that? You ought to've realized by now that you ain't goin' to git me to Grafton. Why don't you just be sensible now and turn me loose? You can tell them Dencil took me. There won't nobody know the difference."

"*I'd* know, Buster." Jim-Bob's reddened eyes were constantly on the move, searching out every bush, every arroyo or cutbank.

"That girl back yonder," Buster said, "she's not a bad-lookin' one at that. Seemed to me like she thinks a right smart of you. You got her all wrapped up, I'd say. But what if somethin' happens to you, boy? What's she goin' to do then? You want some other man to get her?"

Angrily Jim-Bob jerked on the rope. It went taut around Buster's belly, but Buster hauled up short. He didn't come out of the saddle this time. Face darkening, he gritted, "Go on then and be a fool. See what good glory does you when you're dead. It's goin' to pleasure me to get to pull the trigger on you."

Jim-Bob stopped often to lift his hat and wipe the sweat from his face, then to scan the country ahead of him. It seemed to him that he was sweating far more than Buster did. Always the shimmering heat waves put themselves in the way when he tried to get a good look. Occasionally he turned and glanced over his shoulder, wondering if Tom Singleton was closing the gap between them. All night he had dreaded the thought of Tom riding behind him, tall, gaunt, relentless as death. Somehow now he almost felt that he would welcome the sight of him.

But Jim-Bob saw nothing in either direction, nothing except the aimless scatter of brush. Cattle lay under many of the bushes, for at this time of year they usually grazed early, then shaded up from the heat of the sun. The cattle worried Jim-Bob. He had seen so many of them this morning that he was used to them. They moved, and he felt no alarm. But sooner or later there might be something under one of those bushes that wasn't cattle. It might be men. Would he glance over them and pass them by, or would he know the difference before it was too late?

Weakness grew, and his stomach was troubling him considerably. He took out the gold pocketwatch with John McClain's name engraved on the back. One o'clock now, past dinnertime. He felt that with a little something to eat he might do a bit better. He was glad now that George and Sue-Ellen had forced him to take time and have breakfast. Without that, he would be in real trouble by now.

They gradually moved closer to Grafton. Jim-Bob still hadn't seen anything. He began to feel a faint renewal of hope. There was a chance that they somehow had missed Dencil Fox. This was a big country. The outlaw couldn't watch it all. It was a slim chance, yet Jim-Bob clutched at it for support. Just ahead of them now ran a crooked creek. Beyond that, a couple of miles, lay Grafton.

"That creek sure does look good," Buster commented. "I'm thirsty enough to spit dry dirt."

Jim-Bob moved slowly, his eyes cautiously working the fringe of green brush along the creekbank. He found himself also eager to reach the water, for he too was hot and thirsty, his clothes sweat-soaked. He knew the horses needed a drink. They hadn't had water since they had left the sheep camp. Jim-Bob gripped the rifle a little tighter as he watched the mesquite and catclaw. "Just go easy, Buster. Work down to the creek slow, and don't forget that rope or my rifle."

Something moved, far down the creek. Jim-Bob drew up abruptly, dropping low in the saddle and raising the rifle barrel, his heart tripping. His mouth went wide. He suddenly found himself gasping for breath. Then a calf moved out into the open. Jim-Bob lowered the rifle and straightened in the saddle. Relief washed through him, leaving him even weaker than he had been before. Buster chuckled, and Jim-Bob felt foolish. The two horses walked into the shallow water. Nowhere was the creek more than a couple of feet deep. Jim-Bob drew rein and looked around him. Seeing nothing amiss, he finally said, "We better let them drink." He slacked the reins. His horse dropped his head.

Then the quiet voice reached out to him from the brush. "Just take it easy, Jim-Bob!"

11

Jim-bob jerked erect in the saddle, hands desperately gripping the rifle. He saw Dencil Fox nonchalantly push his horse out of the mesquite on the far side of the creek and walk him up to the bank. Jim-Bob swung the rifle around to point at Dencil. Dencil had no gun in his hand, although there was one on his hip.

"You just as well put the gun down, Jim-Bob," Dencil said in a quiet, matter-of-fact way. "There's no use us havin' a fuss over this thing. You know you'd lose."

Jim-Bob found no voice for a reply. He heard Buster begin to laugh. The outlaw couldn't control himself. His laughter rose to a wild, high pitch. Only then did Jim-Bob realize how deeply worried Buster actually had been. The sudden wash of relief left Buster a-tremble.

Jim-Bob got settled enough to ask, "How did you find us?"

Dencil replied, "We been watchin' you more than an hour. We just kept edgin' along, out of your sight. We trotted ahead so we'd be here waitin' for you at the creek. This looked like the best place to do it. Now let Buster go, Jim-Bob, and we'll be on our way."

Still tight-gripping the rifle, Jim-Bob resolutely

shook his head. He eased his horse up a little more, getting Buster between him and Dencil. "I've been through a lot since last night, Dencil, and come a long ways. I didn't do it just to turn Buster loose."

"You got no choice, Jim-Bob."

"I think I have. I've got a gun in my hand. You haven't. And I've still got hold of Buster."

Dencil smiled thinly. "I don't need a gun. I sort of came out to talk truce, you might say. Hackberry and Pony Sims are both in the brush, lookin' at you over the sights of their rifles. Now be sensible, button. Nobody wants to shoot you."

Furtively Jim-Bob looked around him. He saw nothing, but he knew Dencil was telling the truth. Pony and Hackberry were bound to be there somewhere. A tingle worked up and down his back. But he said stubbornly, "I'm comin' on, Dencil." He raised the muzzle of his rifle a fraction. "You better move aside."

Dencil shrugged regretfully. "I hate to have to play it this way, Jim-Bob. All right, Hackberry. Show him."

Jim-Bob saw the flash of the rifle at the instant a bullet smacked into the water right under his sorrel's nose. The bronc went straight up, then came down fighting. He pitched wildly, churning the water into an angry boil of mud. Jim-Bob's rifle went first, splashing and sinking out of sight. Jim-Bob made a vain effort to grab it and thereby lost his seat. He bounced once or twice behind the saddle. His right stirrup began to flop. Desperately reaching for any kind of hold, Jim-Bob accidentally raked a spur along the bronc's flank. The sorrel lunged harder, bawling as he jumped. This time Jim-Bob knew he was gone. He turned part way over in the air and came down on his back with a big splash.

Though he had lost the rifle, he hadn't lost his hold on the rope. At the sound of the shot, Buster Fox's horse also shied away. Seeing an opportunity for freedom, Buster put spurs to the black. But choking though he was in the muddy water, Jim-Bob saw the move coming. He got halfway to his feet and braced the rope across his hip.

The jolt knocked the feet out from under him, but Jim-Bob was up again almost instantly. Buster sailed out of the saddle. Crouching, Jim-Bob reached him in two long strides. He grabbed desperately at his holster and found to his vast relief that he had not lost the .44. He jerked Buster up against him and jabbed the six-shooter into Buster's ribs.

Buster was clawing at the rope. Jim-Bob caught hold of it and savagely jerked it taut again. "Back up with me, Buster," he breathed. "You're goin' to be my shield."

His eyes were afire from the water and mud. Wringing wet, his hat gone, his hair plastered down flat on his head, Jim-Bob began to drag Buster back to the creekbank from which they had come.

Dencil Fox had pushed his horse out into the edge of the creek. Now he stopped again, staring in surprise at the suddenness with which Jim-Bob had recovered the advantage. "Don't shoot, Hackberry," he called to the man in the brush. Then, to Jim-Bob, "Use your head, boy. We got you dead to rights."

Jim-Bob glanced over his shoulder as he backed away, measuring the distance to the bank behind him. He kept moving, kept Buster up tight against him.

Buster rasped, "You're playin' the fool, boy. They'll kill you."

...im. "Don't look like it chipped the bone any," Den-
... said with evident relief. "It won't cripple you none,
... it's apt to be awful sore for awhile."

... Pony fished in Jim-Bob's pocket and got the key to
... handcuffs.

... Dencil said, "We'll take you and drop you off at the
... dge of Grafton, so somebody can get you to a doc-
... or." He held the wet, cool cloth against the wound,
... rying to stanch the steady flow of blood. The wound
... was numb right now. Jim-Bob was aware only of a
... steady burning, and of the weakness that made his
... head so heavy.

... Jim-Bob's voice was thin, but at least he found it. "I
... thought we'd shake you last night like we did the
... others. How did you know?"

... "Just luck. We were waitin' out there in the dark
... like I told you we would. When we saw two men bust
... out the back door of the jail, we just naturally figured
... like everybody else that it was you and Buster. We
... went runnin' to help you. For just a second or two
... there, we got close enough that we could see those two
... men. Now, you might have fooled anybody else, but I
... knew my brother. I could tell at a glance that neither
... of them was him.

... "So I asked myself a couple of questions, and the
... answers was easy. Those men were decoys. You and
... Buster was still in the jail. We worked up that way to
... get you as you came out, only you had already done
... t. The jail was empty.

... "Your decoys rode south, takin' that mob with
... hem. So I figured you'd probably head north with
... uster. From there it was easy. Grafton was the logi-
... l place to go. We started out. We figured we were
... ead of you all the way. We started scoutin' for you

Jim-Bob clenched his teeth. "I swear, Buster, if they
get me, I'll live long enough to blow your guts out!"

Buster yelled at the other men. "Get him clean and
get him good, or he'll kill me!"

The three men held their fire. Dencil Fox had pulled
back from the creekbank but still stood his horse there
watching, perplexed. It was plain that he hadn't expected Jim-Bob to hold on like this.

Jim-Bob gritted, "All right now, let's run for it."

He and Buster broke into a trot, getting out of the
water and moving up over the bank. At the last instant
Jim-Bob gave Buster a hard shove that threw him off
balance, temporarily helpless. Buster sprawled down
the far side of the bank. Jim-Bob came right behind
him, keeping low, the gun in his hand. He caught Buster's shoulder and took a tight grip on it with one hand
while he touched the muzzle of the gun to the man's
head. "You just hold still, Buster. Act like you're dead,
or I promise you *will* be!"

On his knees, Jim-Bob wiped a wet sleeve over his
mud-streaked face. He wished for his hat. The sun in
his unshaded eyes was forcing him to squint his eyes
almost shut. He was not accustomed to being outdoors without a hat.

A growth of rank weeds at the top of the bank
served as a screen so he could stick his head up far
enough to see out. The broncs had settled down and
stood across the creek. They had just as well be in New
Mexico territory for what good they would be now,
Jim-Bob thought.

Somberly he stared down at Buster. He still had his
prisoner, but what was it worth to him now? He
couldn't take him any place.

Dencil's voice came to him from across the creek. "It's just a matter of time. Don't make us have to come over and get you."

Jim-Bob's eyes still burned, but he had them blinked clear. He could see all right now. He wished for the rifle that had fallen in the creek. With that, he might be able to make a stand. But he still had his dad's old six-shooter. They might get him, but they'd know they'd been to a battle before they finished with it.

"Time's on my side, Dencil," Jim-Bob yelled. "Brother or no brother, you know Buster's earned everything that's comin' to him. If you rush me, he's liable to die too. And Tom Singleton's bunch is comin' up behind us, so you can't be losin' any time. I've still got the upper hand. You better give Buster up and go yonderway before Tom gets here."

For a little while there was no answer, and Jim-Bob began to wonder if Dencil had slipped away, if he was up to something. But finally Dencil said loudly, "Did you ever have a brother, Jim-Bob?"

Jim-Bob replied, "No."

"Then you don't know how it is. We don't want to do it this way, Jim-Bob. But we've got to turn Buster loose."

Leaning against the cool, damp creekbank, Jim-Bob heard the horses. He stiffened, his heart missing a beat. He raised his head up. Two hundred yards up the creek, Pony Sims was splashing his horse over to Jim-Bob's side. Down the creek, Hackberry was doing likewise. Across, the two men turned at the same time. They bent low in their saddles and came spurring at Jim-Bob. A surge of panic momentarily froze Jim-Bob. He wavered, knowing he couldn't stop both men. He might get one, but the other would surely ride him

down. He remembered the promise he h___ to Buster, that before he went down he wou___ cil___. This was the time, he knew. But he couldn___ bu___

He fired the six-shooter at Pony, knowing ever squeezed the trigger that he was going t___ He raised up a little higher for a better shot. ___ was his mistake. A white-hot streak of pain ___ through his right arm as the bullet caught hi___ spun him halfway around. The mesquites an___ wet creekbank began to whirl about him. He ___ one feeble attempt to grip the gun that was slip___ out of his fingers. It was no use. The gun fell. J___ Bob stumbled and went down on his knees. He tri___ to grab the six-shooter again, but he could not mak___ his fingers obey him. The life seemed to have gone out of them. He touched the gun but could not pick it up.

The riders were upon him then, Pony and Hackberry. They swung down from the saddles and brought their horses in close. One of them kicked the six-shooter out of the way. Jim-Bob heaved to his feet and lunged toward them, determined to fight. But th___ strength was not in him. A light-headedness seemed ___ take the legs out from under him, and he sank to ___ ground.

Gentle hands picked him up and set him on the ___ of the creekbank. A grim-faced Dencil Fox laid d___ a smoking rifle and began tearing away Jim-___ bloody sleeve. "I hated to do it, Jim-Bob, I tell___ really did. I'd almost as soon have shot mysel___ run and soak this handkerchief in the creek ___ up there where the water's clean."

Dencil carefully went about washing the ___ arm. Slowly Jim-Bob felt some strength co___ and finally spotted you an hour ago. We didn't think you'd put up the fight that you did."

Dencil smiled then, frank admiration in his bewhiskered face. "I declare, Jim-Bob, you're the gamiest young rooster ever I seen. I hate to admit it, but you're goin' to make this country a real lawman. Tough, you losin' your first prisoner thisaway. But if folks haven't got sense enough to see what you're worth, I reckon it's their loss."

Soul-sick at the loss of Buster Fox, and physically sick from shock of the wound, Jim-Bob sat slackly, chin down. He had nothing to say. Dencil gently started to pull him to his feet. "Hackberry's bringin' the horses. Come on, we'll get you to town."

Buster Fox broke in roughly. "We ain't takin' him noplace, Dencil. I owe him aplenty, and I'm goin' to shoot him right where he is." He had picked up Jim-Bob's .44.

Dencil turned on him angrily. "Put that gun away, Buster. You've got no call to do this."

"No call?" Buster's voice lifted sharply. "You ought to see where he pistol-whipped me. You ought to see where he nearly choked me to death. You ought to hear the things he's said to me."

"Whatever he said, it couldn't have been any worse than the truth. You likely had it all comin' to you, Buster."

"And he's fixin' to get what's comin' to *him*. Get out of the way, Dencil."

Jim-Bob stopped breathing. He sat helpless and watched the dark hatred boil up in Buster Fox's eyes. He looked into the muzzle of the beloved old gun his father had left him, and he felt the cold hand of death grip his throat.

"No, Buster," Dencil shouted again and stepped protectively in front of Jim-Bob.

The gun roared. Dencil jerked and fell heavily against Jim-Bob. Jim-Bob tried to hold him, but he lacked the strength. Dencil folded and slipped out of his grasp.

Buster Fox stood with the smoking gun in his hand, staring stupidly down at his brother. "Dencil," he cried, "Dencil, what did you do?"

Jim-Bob knelt beside the fallen outlaw. Pony and Hackberry rushed to him. Gently they picked Dencil up and laid him down again, straightening his legs, smoothing the wet sand beneath him. Dencil's hand lay on his chest, where the lifeblood was slowly flowing out between his fingers.

Hackberry looked at the wound, then glanced up helplessly at Pony and Jim-Bob. His whiskered throat was suddenly active as he swallowed a couple of times. He slowly shook his head and dropped his chin.

Dencil's eyes were glazing, but he managed to find Buster. He looked up at his younger brother, his lips parting. Voice failed him at first. Then he whispered, "Buster, you just weren't worth it. Weren't worth it at all . . ."

His head bobbed over.

Hackberry stood up and turned his back. Jim-Bob just stayed there on his knees, looking down at the bank robber who had died trying to save him. Relaxed as it was now, Dencil's face looked years younger. Strange how much he resembled Buster. A man who didn't know them well might easily make a mistake.

Jim-Bob lifted his gaze to Buster. He shouldn't have said anything, but anger moved him. "He may have looked like you, Buster, but that's the only way you were ever alike. He was worth a hundred of you."

Buster seemed to have been in a trance. Now Jim-Bob's voice tore him out of. "It was your fault!" he flared. "If it hadn't been for you . . ."

Buster remembered the gun in his hand, and once more he brought it up. Jim-Bob closed his eyes, knowing he was helpless against this. But he heard the metallic *clen-n-ch!* of a rifle lever and the hate-honed voice of Hackberry. "Drop it, Buster, or I'll kill you!"

Buster whirled on Hackberry. "You double-crossin' . . ." Something in the man's eyes stopped him cold.

Hackberry said, "Just keep on talkin', Buster. I think I'd enjoy puttin' a bullet right through your thick skull."

Buster could not stand up to the icy stare. He tried, but he began to tremble. He dropped the gun. Abruptly he turned on his heel and strode toward the black horse, which Hackberry had brought up just before the shooting. He stuck his foot into the stirrup and swung into the saddle. Urgently rowelling the animal the instant he had gained his seat, he broke into a lope.

Hackberry watched him a moment. Then he raised the rifle to his shoulder and squeezed the trigger. The black bronc jerked in mid-stride and dropped dead in its tracks. Jim-Bob expected to see Buster jump up and start to run. Then he realized, Buster was pinned helpless beneath the dead horse. Hackberry lowered the smoking rifle, his face twisted in satisfaction. "We tried to tell Dencil, but what can you say to a man about his own brother? He's all yours, Jim-Bob. See that he gets what he's got comin'."

Hackberry glanced at Pony Sims, then back at Jim-Bob. "All we ask of you is a good head start."

Jim-Bob nodded gratefully. "You'll have it."

The two men looked down at Dencil Fox. Hackberry sadly said, "I reckon we'll all wind up thisaway sooner or later. They always do, in our business. And it's all for nothin'—nothin' at-all. *Adiòs*, Jim-Bob."

"*Adiòs*."

Jim-Bob stood and watched the two men ride away and disappear in the thick green brush. When they were gone, he leaned down and pulled Dencil's hat up over the still face. It was a painful effort for Jim-Bob to move around. Feeling was beginning to return to the wounded arm. He knew it wouldn't be long until he would be sick. He could hear Buster Fox groaning. He walked over and found the man lying helpless, one leg pinned under the black bronc's dead weight.

"Get me out of this, Jim-Bob," Buster pleaded. "It's heavy. It's killin' me, I tell you."

Jim-Bob watched him impassively. He made no move to help. "Maybe that'd be a good way for you to die."

Buster fought desperately, cursing as he did. But try though he might, he could not budge the leg. He struggled until his breath was gone and his face was almost purple. Then he went stiff, listening. He looked up at Jim-Bob, a sudden fear crawling in his eyes. "You hear that, Jim-Bob? Horses. It's that lynch mob of yours, comin' to get me!"

"I don't hear anything." Jim-Bob really couldn't. There was a ringing in his ears.

"They're comin' though, I tell you, comin' to kill me! Jim-Bob, you got to get me out of here!"

Jim-Bob slowly shook his head. "I rode all night and

half the day, tryin' to save you from that bunch. Now all of a sudden I'm sick to death of the whole thing. I don't care what happens to you."

Buster gasped. "You're a lawman. You got a responsibility."

Responsibility! What a word for Buster Fox to use. Jim-Bob almost felt like spitting on him. "You've never known responsibility in your life. You've never felt obliged to anybody. Your own brother risked all he had to save you, and you killed him."

"I didn't mean to. But he's dead, and I'm alive. Jim-Bob, for God's sake, I want to *stay* alive. Get me out of here, please. I'll do anything, anything, I tell you!"

A thought came to Jim-Bob. "Even tell me where you hid the money you took out of the bank?"

"Sure. You get me out of here, and I'll tell you."

"You tell me first. Then maybe I'll get you out."

Buster was almost crying. His voice was breaking, and tears were beginning to course down his dusty cheeks. "Just before you-all caught up with me out there in that draw, I could tell it was all over. Remember that fence where I pulled the staples out of the posts and pushed the wire down so I could cross my horse over it?"

"I remember."

"There was a badger hole under one of them posts. I shoved the money into it and caved it in with my foot. I thought if I did get away, I could come back later and get it. And if I got caught, I might bargain my way clear with that money."

Jim-Bob said severely, "You'd better not be lyin' to me, Buster."

Buster cried, "I swear it's the truth, Jim-Bob. You know where I crossed that fence. You can find the money easy. Now please, get me up from here. They're gettin' closer. I can hear them."

Jim-Bob picked up his handcuffs, his muddy .44 and the wet rope he had kept around Buster's waist. He caught his sorrel horse. He tried several times to get into the saddle, but he was too weak to make it. Giving that up, he led the horse over to Buster. He pitched the outlaw the loop end of the rope.

"Put that over your saddlehorn."

Buster did. Jim-Bob wrapped his end of the rope around his own saddlehorn and led his horse back. He tightened his cinch the best he could, then made his horse pull against the rope. It came taut once, then slipped back. Buster cried out at the weight falling on him again.

By now Jim-Bob could hear the horses coming, although he could not see them. He led the horse up again. This time he kept the animal pulling hard. He saw the dead bronc's body lift a little, then a bit more. He saw Buster strain. Suddenly then Buster was free and on his feet. He hobbled painfully, favoring the leg.

Holding his gun on Buster, Jim-Bob said, "We can't outrun them all the way into town anymore," he said. "I don't think I could even make the ride. But I got another idea. Let's get into that thick brush yonder."

Deep in the green mesquite, he found a tree about the right size. "Flop down there on your belly."

Buster did. Jim-Bob made him stretch his hands out in front of him. He buckled one cuff around Buster's wrist, the other around the thick trunk of the tree. "You lay flat, and don't you even breathe," he warned Buster.

Jim-Bob led his horse back to the creekbank. He sat down exhausted beside Dencil Fox's body.

The riders broke out of the brush. Jim-Bob thought he counted ten men. Tom Singleton was in the lead. A lot fewer men than had started last night. Tom loped his horse up to Jim-Bob and stopped him. He quickly swung out of the saddle and dropped the reins, reaching Jim-Bob in three long strides. His stubbled face was tired, and trouble was in his dark eyes.

"Jim-Bob, you all right?" He looked down at Jim-Bob's arm, and his mouth dropped open. The wound had begun to bleed again. Tom's voice was shaky. "We heard the shootin' from a long way off and came as fast as we could. How bad is it, boy?"

Jim-Bob's heart was beating rapidly. "I'll make out."

The other men swung down and gathered around. They, like Tom, were dusty and tired. Frowning, Tom examined the wound. "It's just a little way into Grafton. We'll take you to a doctor."

Thinking of Buster, Jim-Bob quickly said, "No, Tom, I'll be all right. You-all can go on back. It's all over."

Tom knelt then and looked at the body. He lifted the hat, glanced briefly at the face, then covered it again. "Buster Fox?"

Jim-Bob only nodded. He didn't want to trust his voice in a lie.

"What happened?"

"Some friends of his tried to rescue him."

Tom looked away a moment. Jim-Bob gazed upon the men who had come with him. To his surprise, he saw relief come into their weary faces. It came to him that they were somehow glad the thing had been taken out of their hands.

Tom turned back, guilt in his face and in his voice. "Except for you gettin' hurt, Jim-Bob, I'm kind of glad it ended up this way. It's been a long night and a long day, and I've had plenty of time to think. A lot of the boys turned back. I found myself wishin' they all would, so I could too. Then we pulled up to the Thorn ranch this mornin', and that girl told us about those three men after you.

"She told us some things about ourselves, too. She told us if anything happened to you, it would be our fault. *My* fault. Funny, I always want to think of you and Dan as just kids. But you were one of the few real men in town last night, Jim-Bob. It was *me* that acted like a kid." Tom stared down at his feet and soberly rubbed the back of his neck. "You did real fine, Jim-Bob. Dan would've been proud of you. I don't expect he'd have found much to be proud of in me."

With his good hand Jim-Bob reached up and gripped Tom's arm. "He was always proud of you, Tom. I never blamed you, and Dan wouldn't have, either." Then he frowned. "Tom, do you mean you've gotten over the lynchin' fever? That if you'd caught up with us, you wouldn't have killed Buster Fox?"

Tom shrugged. "If we'd caught you early, we might have. But all mornin' I've just wanted to catch up with you and keep you from trouble with those men who were out to set Buster free."

Jim-Bob chewed his lip. He decided to take a chance. "If I told you this isn't really Buster, that I have Buster stashed away someplace, what would you do?"

Tom stared at him in puzzlement. "We'd help you take him wherever you wanted to go with him. He's your prisoner, and you've gone through a-plenty to prove it."

Jim-Bob studied Tom until he was sure Tom meant it. He could see remorse chewing away at the older man. He told Tom the truth about Buster. Tom grinned thinly at the end of the story and motioned for some of the men to fetch Buster in. Jim-Bob handed one of them the handcuff key.

Chum Lawton was with the men. He hadn't said anything. Now he stared incredulously at Tom. "You mean this is all you're goin' to do? You're just goin' to forgive him and go on? This is a chicken-hearted bunch if I ever saw one!"

Tom Singleton squared himself up to his full height. "Chum, I've listened to all I'm goin' to from you. If you want to fight with Jim-Bob, I'm sure he'll oblige you when he's able. If you want to fight with *me*, just keep on talkin'."

Chum swallowed and shut up. Nobody ever wanted to fight with Tom Singleton.

Jim-Bob said grimly, "Chum, the day this arm is well, I'm goin' to go lookin' for you."

Chum backed away, plainly wondering where he had gone wrong. The whole thing had blown up in his face, and he still wasn't sure how.

Buster Fox was crying like a child and pleading for mercy when they brought him back out of the brush. Jim-Bob looked away in disgust while Tom Singleton told the outlaw, "We're not goin' to hang you. We've decided to let the law handle that in its own due time."

Tom led Jim-Bob's horse up. "Come along, Jim-Bob. You need a doctor and a good long rest. You'll get them in Grafton."

Jim-Bob nodded. He was bone-tired, and the arm was beginning to throb. He wanted to throw himself across a bed and not get up for days.

"Tom," he said, "I know you're tired too and want to rest. But could you find somebody in Grafton that would ride back to Swallowfork and let Mont Naylor know everything turned out all right? And tell True Farrell I know where Buster hid the money. I'll dig it up as soon as I get back to Swallowfork."

"Sure, Jim-Bob."

Jim-Bob looked down. "One more thing, get him to go by way of the TX. Sue-Ellen will be sick to death with worry. I sure want her to know . . ."

Tom's hand was on the young deputy's shoulder, and his voice was warm. "A fresh horse will get a man there before dark. Anything particular you want him to say to her?"

Jim-Bob smiled weakly. "I don't reckon—yes, there is something. Just tell her a sore arm won't hurt my legs any. And she'd better not figure on dancin' with anybody but me!"

PECOS CROSSING

1

In the 1890s a mile was a distance that a man could respect. From Sonora, Texas, up to San Angelo, and from there west to the Pecos River was a long, rough, dangerous trail, especially when a man paused every so often and turned in the saddle to look back with worried eyes for someone who might be following. . . .

A lot of Texas maps didn't even show Sonora, for scarcely more than a decade had passed since it first began as a trading post on the San Antonio–El Paso Road. Much of it was fresh and new, the unpainted lumber not yet blistered and darkened in the sun. But to Johnny Fristo and Speck Quitman, riding in after spending the winter in a cow camp far down on the Devil's River, it wouldn't have mattered if Sonora had been a hundred years old. It was there, and so were they. A long winter had bowed out to spring, and this was going to be payday.

Speck was as eager as a new-weaned pup loosed on a fresh scent. "She's a peach of a town, ain't she, Johnny? Didn't seem this pretty when we left here last fall."

Johnny Fristo made a more sober appraisal of the scattered frame buildings and Mexican adobes huddled in open sunshine between the rough limestone hills along the river's dry fork. "No town looks like much when you're ridin' out of it with your pockets emptied."

For that matter, they weren't bringing much back. All these cowboys owned, they carried on their horses. Tied behind the high cantle of each saddle was a yellow Fish Brand slicker, a wool blanket and a warbag, bulging with their "thirty years' gatherings." The latter was a misnomer because neither had lived thirty years yet. Johnny was twenty-two and admitted it. Speck was the same and claimed twenty-five.

They had had a run of luck last fall, both good and bad. They had worked all summer with a wagon crew gathering cattle from the rocky hills and the liveoak thickets of the broad Edwards Plateau. After fall branding, the boss paid them off. They drifted into Sonora hoping to find something else. They hadn't found work, but the chuckleheaded Speck had found a man who was willing to teach him about poker. The lessons came high. By the time Johnny Fristo found out Speck had lost all their money, the "teacher" had vanished, bound for San Angelo and points north. The cowboys would have spent the winter swamping out saloons and sleeping on a porch if a hawk-faced cow trader named Larramore hadn't shown up. Larramore was looking for somebody to work cheap and take care of a steer herd he planned to winter down on the river. He was paying pasturage to Old Man Hoskins, who had more grass than he was using. Johnny and Speck spent the winter in a picket shack that was really half dugout, pitifully short of coffee and tobacco but a healthy distance from all temptation.

A few days ago a worried-looking Larramore had ridden into camp with a couple of extra men to gather the steers. He lamented that the cattle market had gone as sour as last week's milk, but he had finally managed to find a buyer.

"You fellers stay and patch up for Old Man Hoskins," Larramore said as he drove the cattle away. "I'll meet you in Sonora Friday and pay you off."

Luckily for Johnny and Speck, the good-natured old rancher had come by the camp. "Forget about patchin' up," he had said. "You punchers have coyoted out here all winter. Go git yourselves a taste of civilization. And drink one for *me*."

Now Speck licked dry lips and glanced toward the first saloon. "Larramore'll be real surprised. Reckon he's got the money for them cattle yet?"

Johnny nodded. "I expect so. Shouldn't make him any difference whether he pays us today or pays us Friday. Comes to the same figure anyhow."

They were a contrasting pair, not much alike except in age. Folks usually took a liking to the swivel-jawed Speck. He talked all the time, though sometimes he got so carried away that his talk quit making sense. Speck was short and bandy-legged, with a round face and freckles. His hair was rusty, his eyes a laughing blue. He could ride any bronc they led out to him and could rope anything that would run. Some folks said Speck had probably been sitting on a fence telling a windy when the Lord was passing out brains. At any rate, he hadn't quite gotten his share. If occasionally some rancher flared up and fired Speck for the tomfool stunts he pulled, he was likely to hire him back in a day or two. He was a good cowboy. A man could put up with a little flightiness.

Another reason ranchmen tolerated Speck's shenanigans was because they had to take Speck if they wanted Johnny Fristo. When you hired one, you hired both. When you fired Speck, Johnny went too.

Johnny didn't often have much to say. With Speck around, he didn't get much chance to talk anyway, and he had long since quit trying. Johnny was taller, thinner of build. He didn't share Speck's flashy ways, but he was always around to help pull his partner out of a jackpot. Johnny would be out doing his job with a quiet competence while Speck was still talking about it. He could ride along with his gaze on the horizon, his mind a hundred miles away, nod agreement to everything Speck said and not actually hear a word of it.

They had spent their boyhoods in the Concho River country up around the army post and cow town of San Angelo, sixty-five miles north of Sonora. Johnny's father raised cattle on a small ranch back from the North Concho. Speck had been brought up in San Angelo by an aunt till he was about fourteen. Then he had landed a job as a horse jingler out on Spring Creek. Once or twice a year Speck worked up courage to make a duty call to his aunt. He would get away as quickly as he could.

"She's a sweet old lady," Johnny had heard him say with a certain reverence. "But she's mean as hell."

Today they came into Sonora by way of the Del Rio road. Eastward, halfway up a hill, stood the new Sutton County courthouse. Horses lazed at hitching racks and posts along the sloping, dusty street. Sweating freighters grunted at the weight as they unloaded store goods from a heavy wagon that had hauled them down from the railroad in San Angelo. A pair of smaller wagons, one tied behind the other, groaned under a load of early-shorn wool.

Speck eyed the first saloon but rode on by it. "Heard a feller say once to always pass up the first one. Shows you got willpower."

Johnny grinned. He knew this saloon had been the site of that cardsharp's *school*. "Speck, if it's all of a whatness to you, I'd rather clean up first."

Speck reined in at the square frame front of the second saloon, stepped down and wrapped his reins through a ring in the hitching post. "You wash the outside and I'll wash the inside."

They had a little money—not much. Larramore had advanced them a few dollars last fall. He owed them for a winter's work, so they would have plenty when they found him. Johnny had counted his money several times before leaving the cow camp, and now he counted it again. Main thing he wanted to begin with was a change of clothes. Those he wore had spent a hard winter, washed periodically in the river, beaten with a rock and slept on to press some of the wrinkles out.

After a while, with new-bought clothes bundled under his arm, he walked into a barbershop which advertised a bathtub. The barber was busy shaving a customer. "Have a seat, cowboy."

Johnny picked up a copy of the weekly *San Angelo Standard,* looking hopefully for items about people he knew. He didn't find his father's name in it, but he hadn't expected to. Baker Fristo was just a little rancher, and he didn't get to town much. Johnny read the trespass and cattle brand notices and shook his head in doubt over ads for patent medicines supposed to cure everything from adenoids to hemorrhoids.

Finishing the paper, he began wondering idly about the man reclining in the barber chair. He couldn't tell much except that the customer was very tall, had a new black suit, and wore a pair of high-laced shoes on feet that probably were more used to boots. A new broad-brimmed black hat and a suit coat hung on a rack by the front door.

Rancher, probably. Or a cattle buyer.

The barber was as talkative as Speck Quitman. "Folks say you've bought a ranch up on the Colorado River, Milam." The man named Milam couldn't answer. The barber was scraping whiskers from his jaw. "Yes, sir," the barber went on, "I was up in that Colorado City country once. Sand country, it is, and good for cows. Man don't go stumblin' around over rocks all the time."

The customer had a firm, deep voice. "Any country is good, Jess, when you own a piece of it yourself."

The barber wiped soap off of his blade. "Used to think that way myself, till I lost my little place in the big panic. Found out it's easier to scrape chins than to try and scrape a livin' off a piece of hard-scrabble land. But, then, I reckon you wouldn't buy anything but a good place, Milam. Bet you and Miss Cora are goin' to be real happy."

"We will," the man said. "She'll be mighty pleased with the place, the way I've got it fixed up for her."

"When you takin' her?"

"We're leavin' tomorrow mornin', takin' the Sonora Mail to San Angelo."

The barber finished. As the customer stood up, Johnny saw that the tall man was around forty—maybe a little more. The outdoors had weathered him badly. His hair showed streaks of gray, but his moustache was still coal black. Crowtracks were etched at the corners of keen gray eyes that looked as if they had seen aplenty of hardship. For a moment those eyes lighted on Johnny. They were not unfriendly, but they looked as if they could read whatever was in a man's mind. Johnny nodded, wondering what it was about this stranger that made him feel suddenly uncomfortable.

"Howdy," said the man Milam, and that was all. He put on his hat and coat, paid the barber and left.

The barber turned to Johnny. "Shave? Haircut?"

"Both. And then a long, slow bath." Seating himself, Johnny jerked his chin toward the door. "Who was that?"

"Him? Why, friend, I thought everybody knew Milam Haggard."

"Name sounds kind of familiar."

"He was a Texas Ranger down on the Rio Grande. Married Miss Cora Hays here, and she talked him into takin' off the star. He's been off up the country, buyin' them a place to live."

Johnny stared out the open door. He vaguely remembered now. "This Haggard, he's got a name for bein' a bulldog in a fight, hasn't he?"

The barber shook his head knowingly. "A man couldn't have a better friend than Milam Haggard. Or a worse enemy. There's no end to what he'll do for a man he thinks is in the right. He's been known to ride fifty miles in the rain to fetch medicine to a sick Mexican kid. But break the law and you got trouble. He hates an outlaw. He sticks to a trail, Milam does. I don't suppose he ever let a man get away, once he ever got the scent. I recollect one time he trailed a pair of horse thieves plumb down into Mexico. I seen him come back leadin' their horses. Their gunbelts was looped around the saddlehorns, and the saddles was empty. Milam never did talk about them hunts. But he didn't have to."

With bold snips of the sharp scissors the barber took off Johnny's winter growth of hair. "Miss Cora, she made him turn in his badge and put up his guns. She was afraid someday somebody would be a-bringin' *his* saddle in empty."

Johnny took a slow soak in the barber's tub, lazily enjoying the luxury of castile soap. Out in a cow camp, a man was lucky to have plain old lye soap that took off the hide along with the dirt. Finished, he tucked the bundle of dirty clothes under his arm, mounted his horse and walked him to the saloon. Speck's horse was still hitched out in front, head down, one hind foot turned up in rest. Johnny shook his head. Likely as not Speck would forget that animal and leave him standing out here all day. Johnny untied the horse and led him to a wagonyard with his own. Might as well turn the horses loose in the stableman's corral and give them some feed; they weren't going anywhere today.

Unsaddling, he asked the stableman, "All right if we bed down over here tonight, me and my partner? We won't bother nothin'."

Hotels were for ranchers, drummers and the like. Cowboys generally slept in the wagonyard or down on the riverbank.

"Help yourself. Just don't be doin' no smokin' around that hay. I'd hate to sell you a burned-down barn." Critically, the stableman looked Johnny over. "You couldn't pay for it noway."

Walking back, Johnny told himself it was fortunate Speck didn't have enough money on him to get into a poker game. Put Speck to work in the country and he was usually worth his wages. But turn him loose in town and he was likely to kick over the traces, bedazzled by the flash of cards and the slosh of whisky. It was like he hadn't grown up, and maybe never would.

Johnny had let Speck have three dollars this morning. He figured that wasn't enough to get him drunk or into a poker game. Entering the saloon, he found out how wrong he was. Speck pushed away from a gaming table and threw his hands up in a gesture of defeat. "That cleans me." He spotted Johnny. "Hey, partner, come here and give me enough for a fresh start. I'm just about to clean these fellers' plow."

Johnny covered his impatience with a grin he didn't mean. "Looks to me like it's *your* plow that shines."

"Aw, Johnny . . ." But Speck could see Johnny meant to be firm. He didn't beg. He leaned on Johnny, looking instinctively to his partner to help him keep his nose clean.

One of the gamblers called to the bartender, "Lige, give them cowboys a drink. I'm payin' for it with their own money."

Speck and Johnny leaned work-flattened bellies against the short granite-topped bar. Speck lifted his glass and said, "Here's to Larramore and his speedy arrival."

Johnny almost choked. He knew he had tasted worse whisky, but he couldn't remember just when. Speck had a fondness for the stuff; Johnny could take it or leave it alone. This kind was better left alone.

A man appeared in the saloon's open door. He started to walk in, then stopped abruptly, seeing Johnny and Speck. Quickly he backed out and walked off up the street.

Johnny straightened. "Speck, that was Larramore."

Speck hadn't noticed. "Maybe he didn't see us."

"He saw us. He backed out like somebody had shot at him. I don't like the smell of it."

Speck frowned. "You don't think he would . . ." He broke off, doubt in his eyes. "You know, he just might."

Johnny nodded grimly. "Let's go find out."

Larramore was walking briskly away. Johnny called, but the cow trader appeared not to hear. Johnny and Speck broke into a long trot and caught up with him in front of a general store.

"Mister Larramore," Johnny said, coming up behind him, "just a minute."

Larramore turned and looked surprised. "By George, it's Speck and Johnny. Wasn't expectin' you-all till Friday."

Johnny said, "Old Man Hoskins told us to come on in. So we're here, Mister Larramore, and we sure do need our money."

Larramore's face was blank. He was watching someone walking up the street. "Money? What money?"

Johnny's voice hardened. "We put in six months of work for you, Larramore." He wasn't using the *mister* now. "You promised us twenty dollars a month. Now we want to get paid."

Johnny was hardly aware of footsteps on the plank walk behind him, or of a man with a badge who passed them and started into the general store. But Larramore had seen him, and he raised his voice.

"I've already paid you. I paid both of you at the ranch. What do you mean now, tryin' to browbeat me into payin' you again?"

The man in the doorway stopped and turned, his attention caught.

Speck Quitman's face boiled full of rage. He grabbed both fists full of Larramore's shirt. "You're a liar! All you ever gave us was a few dollars advance last fall. Now, damn you, pay up!"

Watching the sheriff, Larramore stood his ground. "Get your hands off of me, you halfwit! I won't stand for bein' robbed!"

The insult to Speck made Johnny clench his fists. "*You're* the one who's a thief, Larramore."

The sheriff had heard enough. He stepped up and placed a big hand firmly over Speck's fist, his eyes stern. "Turn him loose, cowboy."

Speck turned angrily upon the intruder, but his mouth shut as he saw the badge.

A cow trader has to be quick on his feet or he doesn't survive. Larramore was quick. "Sheriff, it's a good thing you came by. These boys are tryin' to pull a fast shuffle on me."

The sheriff's grim eyes flashed from one man to the other. "All right, everybody simmer down a little. Tell me what the trouble is."

Larramore spoke quickly, heading off Speck and Johnny. "I hired these two last fall to watch over some cattle I was winterin' down on the Devil's River. The other day I picked up the cattle and paid these men. Now they're tryin' to claim they've still got wages comin'. It's not my fault if they've drunk it up or lost it playin' poker."

Johnny said, "He's a liar, sheriff."

The sheriff frowned. He leaned close and sniffed suspiciously. "You-all *have* been drinkin'. I can smell it."

Johnny said, "Just one is all I've had. It was bought for me. We're not lyin' to you, sheriff. *He* is."

The sheriff studied Speck. "Seems to me I remember you boys. You was in town last fall." His eyes lighted. "Sure, you lost your wad down yonder tryin' to beat one of them Angelo gamblers. You was dead broke."

Larramore cut in, "That's right, sheriff. I gave them a job. Do a man a favor and he'll spit on you every time."

Johnny protested, "He *hasn't* paid us."

The sheriff looked at Johnny's new clothes. "If you haven't been paid, where did those duds come from?"

Johnny could tell the sheriff was almost convinced now, and not in their favor. He started to tell about the advance Larramore had given them last fall, but he realized it would sound hollow. How many cowboys could keep anything all winter out of a fall advance?

Johnny had a sudden thought. "Old Man Hoskins knows. Why don't you ask him?"

A shade of doubt appeared in the sheriff's eyes. "Ely Hoskins? Sure, his word is as good as his bond. But it's a long ways out there."

"If you're interested in the truth, you'll go ask him."

Larramore said, "They're just stallin', sheriff. They're caught in a lie. They belong in jail."

Speck Quitman exploded. His fist came up and caught Larramore full in the face. Larramore staggered backward against the clapboard wall of the general store. For a second Johnny thought the trader was going to fall through the front window. Speck roared forward to follow up his punch, but the sheriff reached out and grabbed him by the collar. With a sudden thrust of his mighty arm, the lawman threw Speck off balance and sent him sprawling backward into the dust of the street.

"That done it!" the sheriff thundered. "I was halfway inclined to go along with you boys, but now I'm goin' to let you sweat awhile in the jailhouse."

Larramore swayed, one hand behind him to brace him away from the wall, the other lifted to his face. His nose was bleeding.

Johnny urged, "Sheriff, Speck's hotheaded, and what he did wasn't smart. But it don't change the fact that Larramore's lyin'. Give us a chance. Go talk to Old Man Hoskins."

The sheriff scowled down at Speck Quitman, who was shakily pushing himself up out of the dust. The lawman pondered. Something about Larramore seemed to make him uncertain. "I don't know what I'm wastin' my time for, but I'll do it. I'll send a man out to talk to old Ely. Till then, you boys are goin' to enjoy Sutton County's hospitality. Behind bars!" He glanced at Larramore. "I'm expectin' you to stay in town till I get the straight of this."

Larramore nodded, holding his handkerchief to his face. "Sure, sheriff, anything you say." He avoided looking at the cowboys.

The sheriff took hold of Johnny's and Speck's arms. "Come on." They walked up the street, the sheriff holding them tightly. The few people who were outdoors paused to look. It was evident the two were under arrest.

A tall man and a woman stepped out of a store and almost directly into their path. The man caught the woman's arm and moved her gently aside. Johnny recognized Milam Haggard. The handsome young woman would be the wife the barber had been telling about. Her eyes touched Johnny's, and he thought he saw sympathy there.

But he found no sympathy in Milam Haggard. The

longtime Ranger stared with stern gray eyes. Any friendliness he might have shown in the barbershop was gone now. It wouldn't matter to Haggard what the trouble was about. He could tell the cowboys were in custody. That was enough for him to pass his judgment.

The sheriff took his hand from Johnny's arm long enough to tip his hat. "Howdy, Cora . . . Milam."

The three walked by. Johnny glanced back, for no particular reason. Milam Haggard was still watching him.

2

A bugle sounded. Johnny Fristo awoke to the rattle of trace chains and the clatter of horses' hoofs. The Sonora Mail was leaving for San Angelo.

Johnny opened his eyes and glanced up at the barred window. Sunrise. He arose stiffly from the hard cot and stretched his back to try to work the ache out of it. The air was cool and fresh. Johnny's movement aroused Speck Quitman, who peered dourly at him a moment, then swung his sock feet down to the floor and started probing around sleepy-eyed, trying to find his boots.

A limping man entered the jail's front door, carrying a covered platter. "You boys up?" the pleasant old jailer asked needlessly. "Brought you-all some breakfast."

He unlocked the cell door and dragged in a small table. He did it carelessly, as if not even considering that the two prisoners could easily jump him and get away. He had brought a big mess of scrambled eggs with pieces of fried beef alongside, and some biscuits. "Hope you fellers don't mind eatin' off of the platter. Too far to pack extra dishes."

Leaving the cell door wide open, he went to the stove and picked up the coffee pot. "Now, don't you boys go gettin' the wrong idea; we don't treat all our prisoners this good. But I figure you-all been out in a cow camp all winter and ain't had no eggs. Besides, like I was tellin' the sheriff, it's probably that Larramore who ought to be in here 'stead of you two."

Johnny and Speck went after the eggs like a pair of starved wolves. The talkative jailer sipped the scalding black coffee, his lips immune to the burn. "I used to cowboy, too, till I got stove up. I looked you two over and decided you was all right. Besides, I heard about some cow deals Larramore was mixed up in. He's no deacon in the church."

Johnny asked, "Hear anything yet from Old Man Hoskins?"

"Nope. Thought he might be in the crowd that was down while ago to see Milam and Cora Haggard off on the Sonora Mail. But he wasn't." He smiled, remembering. "My, she sure did look handsome. Folks was afraid she would wait around and be an old maid, but I guess she was just waitin' for the right man. And she got him." He paused. "You know about Milam Haggard?"

Johnny nodded. "Some."

"*Mucho hombre,* that Milam. Sure did hate to see him turn in his badge. But I expect most of the devilment is over anyway. Country's turned respectable. Milam has outlived his time as a lawman. We don't need his kind of lawin' anymore. This is the '90s now, and we're about as modern as we can ever get."

Eventually the sheriff came, his face creasing as he saw the open cell door. "Ad," he spoke sharply to the jailer, "this is a jailhouse, not a *hotel*. One of these days somebody's goin' to walk right out over you."

Standing up, the jailer said defensively, "I wouldn't

do it for just anybody, but these boys are all right. Like I was tellin' you last night . . ."

The sheriff nodded, his rueful gaze passing from Johnny to Speck and back again. "I remember what you told me, and it turns out you were right. Boys, you can go."

Johnny smiled. "So you heard from Old Man Hoskins?"

The sheriff was chagrined. "Didn't have to. I just found out Larramore sneaked off to the edge of town awhile ago and caught the stage hack for San Angelo. If he'd been on the square, he'd have stayed here like I told him."

Johnny swore. "Damn him! He's tryin' to get off and keep from payin' us what we got comin'."

The sheriff shook his head. "He'll pay. If you boys will get saddled up and put them ponies through their paces, you can get to Angelo ahead of the hack. Go see the sheriff there. I'll write you a letter to give him. He'll see that Larramore pays what he owes you or he'll shove him way back in jail and forget where the key is at."

Speck and Johnny waited impatiently while the lawman scribbled a note. The officer said, "I'd go myself, only I just got word of some trouble down in the south end of the county that's liable to lead to a shootin' if I don't stop it."

Speck said with bitterness, "How am I goin' to explain to my Aunt Pru about me spendin' the night in jail? And all for nothin'."

The old jailer grinned. "Well, look at the bright side: you had supper, breakfast, and a bed, and it didn't cost you a cent."

"Some bed," gritted Speck. "I've slept on rocks that was softer."

The jailer grinned again. "We don't advertise for repeat business."

Johnny folded the letter the sheriff had given him and stuck it in his pocket. "One thing sure, *we* don't intend to come back."

The sheriff followed them down to the wagonyard and watched while they saddled their horses. "Stop in at Pete Smith's ranch halfway to Angelo and tell him I said to lend you a pair of fresh horses. And one more thing: don't try to do nothin' on your own. Just go around that hack and get to Angelo ahead of it. Let the Tom Green County sheriff take care of Larramore his own way. That's his job. You-all leave Larramore alone."

Anger edged Johnny's voice. "He owes us more than wages now, sheriff. He owes us for a night in jail."

The sheriff repeated, "Don't you-all do anything, do you hear me?"

Johnny and Speck heard, but they made no reply. They rode out of the wagonyard gate, touched spurs to their horses and moved into an easy lope on the mail and freight road that led north toward San Angelo.

Twisting along at the foot of the hills, the trail made a slow climb toward the top of the divide which separated the sprawling watershed of the Devil's River from that of the three Conchos. From where the cowboys rode, rainwater would drain generally southward, first to countless draws and creeks, then to the Devil's River and finally by a tortuous, canyon-cutting route to the Rio Grande.

Spring had come with color and hope to this high, rocky limestone country known as the Edwards Plateau. Winter rains had preserved the holdover moisture stored last fall, and now fresh grass rose tender and green amid the tall brown leavings of last year's bluestem growth. Cattle already were slicking off, shedding their coarse winter hair. Frisky calves were fat and shiny.

Johnny and Speck came upon a band of sheep, scattered to graze on an open flat where the grass was shorter and more to their liking. Fat young lambs lifted their heads to watch the riders passing. Many of them scampered away bleating. A Mexican herder stood up at the cowboys' approach and nodded a silent greeting, his eyes narrowed in distrust. Too often the *gringo* did not come in peace.

Johnny asked, "How long since the mail hack passed this way?"

The herder just stared at him, as if he did not understand. Speck broke in to repeat the question in a halting, broken Spanish. The herder did not smile at Speck's mistakes. But neither did he give a clear answer. "*¿Quién sabe?* A while. I have no watch, *señor.*"

Speck seemed disposed to try again, this time in anger, but Johnny said, "Let it go, Speck. That's all the answer we'll get. We're makin' some gain, and we'll catch up."

They moved on, putting the horses into an easy lope and holding them in it as long as they dared. Every so often Johnny would pull down to a trot. Usually he would have to call to Speck, who didn't stop until he saw that Johnny was going to, with or without him.

"Speck, we can't make it if we ride these horses down."

They would trot along a mile or so, then Speck would impatiently spur into a lope again. Johnny noticed Speck wasn't doing any talking. That in itself was a bad sign. The rusty-haired cowboy's jaw took a hard, angry set, and his eyes were narrowed.

Speck was talking inside, to himself. Johnny knew the signs. When Speck was like this the inner heat would crackle and build until there had to be an explosion of some kind. There was no other outlet. That was a side of Speck Quitman most people didn't know about, for it didn't often show. Most regarded him as a scatter-brained cowboy with a lot of bark and no bite. But Johnny had seen him bite a few times. He didn't like it.

They came out atop the divide in a wind-rippled sea of short green grass. Speck reined up and stood in his stirrups, peering out through a scattering of liveoak trees which were shedding their old leaves and putting on a new set.

"Johnny, I think I see the hack up yonder, ahead of us."

Johnny squinted. It took him a minute, but finally he saw it too. Speck turned in his saddle and untied his warbag. He dug around in it, then pulled out a six-shooter, wrapped in oilskin. It was old and tarnished, and on one side a knife-whittled piece of mesquite wood had replaced the original black rubber grip. Relic though it was, Speck prized it above anything else he owned. He had bought it from a broke cowpuncher when he was only fifteen, and he had carried it around with him ever since. He had given it the loving care a man might give a horse. He had never used it in anger, though sometimes Johnny Fristo got a cold, ominous feeling that Speck hoped someday he could. Speck began to punch cartridges into it.

Tightly Johnny said, "Speck, you got no use for that thing. The sheriff told us to go to the law in Angelo, not to try handlin' Larramore ourselves."

"It wasn't the sheriff he cheated. It wasn't the sheriff that had to spend the night in the Sonora jail like some drunk sheepherder."

"Speck, you better put that thing back into your warbag before you do somethin' you'll wish you hadn't. What if you was to accidentally shoot him? A dead man don't pay no wages." He thought at first Speck might be listening to him. But Speck shoved the loaded pistol into his waistband.

"I'm not fixin' to shoot him. But I sure do intend to scare him to death."

Speck's spurs tinkled as he touched them to his horse and surged forward. Johnny held back a moment, trying to figure some way to reason with him. Then he hurried to catch up. "Speck, listen to me. The sheriff made sense. This is the kind of thing they got sheriffs *for*."

"A man ought to stomp his own snakes. And Larramore is a snake."

"We can make a little *vuelta* around them and get to Angelo first. Larramore won't have any idea we're around. We can spring the sheriff on him as a surprise."

But Speck was hot as a wolf, and he was riding, not listening. The thought of that pistol made a cold chill run down Johnny's back. Somehow it always had. He would as soon touch a rattlesnake.

Still, he knew the only way he could stop Speck now would be with a club. All Johnny could do was stay close and try to keep things from getting too badly out of hand. They were partners, right or wrong, smart or otherwise. Several times before, Johnny had come close to riding off in disgust and leaving Speck. But always in the end he would shrug and stay with him.

He stayed with him now.

Ahead of them the trail took a bend around a big motte of liveoak trees to avoid a wheel-breaking gully. Speck cut across, Johnny close behind him. They loped around the heavy motte and came back into the trail ahead of the stage hack. Speck slid his horse to a stop. He raised the pistol to signal the driver to halt.

It would have been hard to gauge which showed strongest in the driver's face—anger or alarm. A robbery on the Sonora Mail was unheard of! "What do you two peckerwoods want?" he demanded. "We got nothin' on board here that's worth stealin'."

Speck Quitman replied in a tense voice that didn't sound at all like his. "Don't fret yourself, mister. We didn't stop you to steal anything."

"Then put that cannon away before you scare the lady!"

Johnny pulled his horse up beside Speck's. "For God's sake, Speck, put that damned old smoke-belcher down. We're fixin' to get ourselves in a mess of trouble."

Under the rolled-up side canvas he could see the frightened face of Cora Haggard, her hands tightly clutching Milam Haggard's arm. Haggard stared at the cowboys, his gray eyes challenging and unafraid. But he was helpless, for he wore no gun. In the seat behind the Haggards, the trader Larramore was trying to crouch down out of sight.

The hack driver had a heavy brown moustache and

a loud, harsh voice. "If you didn't come to steal nothin', put that gun back where it belongs. Somebody might get hurt. Besides, you're stoppin' the U.S. mail. That could get you sent to the pen."

Johnny decided it was time for him to do the talking. Speck wasn't getting them anywhere but in trouble. "Mister, we don't mean to hurt anybody, and we're sure not fixin' to tamper with the mail. But you got a passenger who left Sonora owin' us money, and we want it."

"Cowboy," said the driver, "your private feuds ain't any concern of the Sonora Mail. The man is a passenger. You take up your complaints with the law."

Speck Quitman waved the pistol. "We brought our own law. Larramore, you get yourself down from there, and be right spry about it!"

Larramore stood up partway, his head touching the canvas. "They're lyin'. They come to rob me!"

Milam Haggard spoke in a rock-steady voice: "You heard what the driver said, boys. I don't know anything about the merit of your claim on this man, but I do know that the way you're doin' this constitutes robbery in the eyes of the law. I suggest you stand back and let this hack go on."

"Mister Haggard," Johnny said, "there's already *been* a robbery, and it was us that got robbed."

Haggard studied him a moment with eyes so stern that Johnny couldn't hold his gaze against them. "I remember you. The Sonora sheriff had you in tow yesterday. That doesn't make your argument sound very good to me."

Johnny reached for his shirt pocket. "I've got a letter here . . ."

Impatience jabbed its spurs into Speck Quitman. "Forget the letter. We're takin' Larramore off this stage and gettin' our money!"

Angrily Haggard said, "There's a woman in this hack. You put that gun away!"

Haggard's severe voice got through to Speck where Johnny's pleading hadn't. Speck was a little afraid of the man. He lowered the barrel, but he rode around closer to Larramore. "How about it, Larramore? You gettin' down, or do I have to shoot you in the leg or somethin'?"

Face white, Larramore began climbing out. "All right, I'm comin'." Stepping to the ground, he turned to plead with Haggard and the driver. "Are you goin' to let them get away with this?"

The driver said, "Mister, I got no gun. Neither has Milam."

Johnny held his breath. Now he began to feel the thing was going to go over all right. Maybe there wasn't going to be any more trouble. He rode around to the off side of the hack, where Larramore stood. He dismounted a couple of paces from the cow trader. Speck's anger gave way to anticipation, and he stepped down from the saddle.

"All right, Larramore, a hundred dollars apiece."

Larramore replied shakily, "I got the money in my bag." He turned and lifted a canvas grip out of the hack. Speck shoved the pistol into his waistband and eagerly stepped closer to look as Larramore opened the bag. The trader reached inside. "There now, I've got it."

He brought his hand out with a short-barreled Colt revolver.

Johnny didn't hesitate. He jumped at the trader. Larramore squeezed the trigger. The hammer fell on the empty shell he kept in the cylinder for safety, the empty shell he had forgotten in his anxiety. But the next cartridge would be a live one. Johnny grabbed the man's wrist. They struggled.

The woman screamed. Haggard started putting her off the hack on the other side to get her away from the fight. At the same time he was shouting, "You fools, be careful with that pistol! You'll kill somebody!"

The team caught the excitement and danced nervously, ready to run. Badly as he might have wanted to jump, the driver couldn't afford to. He had all he could handle, holding the team.

Larramore brought up his knee and struck Johnny a hard blow to the stomach. Johnny bent a little and let go. Larramore stepped clear and leveled the pistol. As he squeezed the trigger, Speck Quitman caught him from behind and spoiled his aim.

The flash blinded Johnny for an instant. The explosion set his ears to ringing. But he heard a faint cry from the woman on the other side.

The team ran. The driver jammed one foot against the brake and sawed hard at the lines to prevent them from getting completely away. As the hack pulled forward, Johnny saw horror in Larramore's eyes. Larramore pitched the gun away. Johnny spun on his heel.

Cora Haggard was going down. Milam Haggard grabbed her and cried out, "Cora!" Gently he eased her to the grass.

The three men who had been fighting stood stiff and silent now, stunned. They saw the spread of crimson across the woman's white blouse. The color had drained from her face. Her hand reached up and clutched at Haggard's shirt. She gasped, "Milam, I love you." Then the hand dropped away.

Milam Haggard cried again, "Cora!" He pulled her against him as if to try to hold her away from death. But death came despite him, and she lay lifeless in his arms.

Larramore's wits came back to him. He pointed at Johnny and shouted, "That one did it, Haggard! He's the one who fired the gun."

The lie caught Johnny by surprise, and for a moment he could not speak. He stood with mouth open and dry. He tried for words that wouldn't come. A horrified thought ran through his mind:

Haggard will believe him.

Somehow he managed to stammer, "No . . . no . . . I didn't! *He* had the gun! He was shootin' at *me!*"

But he was too late. Larramore had seized the advantage. He had said it first, and Haggard believed him. Johnny could see it in the violent hatred that welled into the tall man's eyes.

The hack driver fought the team under control and circled back. He jumped to the ground and stared wide-eyed at Milam Haggard, who still knelt, holding his wife. The driver breathed in horror, "Milam, for God's sake . . ."

Johnny cried, "Driver, he thinks it was me that killed her. It was Larramore. Tell him. You saw it."

The driver turned slowly, his face ashen. "I saw nothin'. I was too busy tryin' to hold that team. But you boys held us up, and you was robbin' a passenger. That speaks for itself."

Milam Haggard buried his face against his wife's slender neck. He held her, his shoulders trembling, while the other four men stood in helpless silence. At last the driver took a slow step forward. "Milam, we best put her aboard and take her back to Sonora."

Milam Haggard raised his head. Gently he lowered

his wife to the ground. His gaze fell upon the pistol Larramore had tossed away. Johnny saw the intention in his eyes, and he stepped forward quickly. He grabbed up the gun just as Haggard was about to leap for it.

Desperate, Johnny said, "Mister Haggard, Larramore lied to you. I didn't shoot her."

Tears swam in Haggard's eyes, but a cold fury showed through. His slow-measured words were edged with steel. "I'll remember you."

"Please, Mister Haggard, listen to me . . ."

"I'll take my wife home and bury her amongst her people. Then I'll come lookin' for you. You can stay here, or you can run, it makes me no difference. Whether it takes me a week or a year, whether I ride twenty miles or a thousand, I'll find you two. And when I find you, *I'll kill you!*"

"Mister Haggard . . ." Johnny broke off, for Haggard had turned his back. He had shut his ears and his mind.

Gently the driver and Larramore lifted the woman's body. Haggard climbed into the hack and took her into his arms. The driver turned to Johnny and Speck. "Was I you boys, I'd go back to Sonora and throw myself on the mercy of the court. Maybe the court will have some. There'll be no mercy in Milam Haggard!"

He climbed up, took the reins, turned the hack around and started back down the trail toward Sonora.

Johnny and Speck watched until the hack was gone out of sight. Speck finally broke the silence, and he was crying. "It was my fault, Johnny. I ought to've listened to you." Tears rolled down his freckled cheeks. Fear was taking a grip on him. Speck could shift from one emotion to another like he could change shirts. "We got to go some place, Johnny, and we got to go quick.

Let's head for Mexico. It's only a hundred miles to the Rio Grande."

Johnny's voice was tight with shock. "And what do we do when we get there? We got no friends down there, and we got no money. We don't even speak the language enough to get by."

"But it's Mexico. The law couldn't touch us down there."

"It's not the law we got to worry about most, it's Milam Haggard. That river wouldn't even slow him down. He'd just keep a-huntin' us, and we'd just keep a-runnin'. And wherever we went, we'd be *gringos*. We'd stand out like the Twin Mountains."

Speck's eyes were swimming in tears. "But what can we do? If we stay here he'll kill us."

"Texas is a mighty big country. He can't search it all. There are places west of here where you could drop a whole army and never find it. Maybe in time he'll get tired of lookin'."

Speck said weakly, "I bet he don't ever quit. He looks like the kind that'll stay on a trail till the day he dies."

Johnny's jaw set firmly. That was the way Haggard had looked to him, too. But a man couldn't just sit and wait for somebody to come and kill him.

Speck said, "We got to get us a little money, Johnny. We could borrow somethin' from my Aunt Pru in San Angelo."

Johnny nodded soberly. "We better get ridin'."

It occurred to him then that he still held Larramore's pistol. He stared at it in loathing. He drew back his arm and hurled the pistol as hard as he could, into a liveoak motte.

He swung onto his horse and headed north toward San Angelo.

3

They rode in by night, following the stage road that crossed the South Concho at the flood-ruined settlement of Ben Ficklin. Three miles farther on, they rode by the stone buildings of old Fort Concho, abandoned a few years ago by the army when the Indian problems were over. Civilians lived there now. Most of the buildings were dark, for working people had gone to bed.

But across the North Concho, lamps still glowed along Chadbourne and Oakes and Concho Avenue. Horses stood in headsdown, hipshot patience at hitchracks in front of the Nimitz Hotel, the Legal Tender and the other saloons. Johnny and Speck rested their horses at the steep south bank of the quiet-moving river and waited in darkness, watching. Nearby stood the Oakes Street Bridge, but they had purposely shied away from it, just as they had shied away from all travelers on the road today.

Speck said, "I hear a horse comin' across. That wooden plankin' sure does make a noise at night."

Johnny nodded. "We best skip the bridge anyhow. It'd land us smack on Concho Avenue amongst all the saloons."

"There's a shallow crossin' a little ways upriver. We could use that and not run into anybody."

They moved past the deep section known as Dead Man's Hole to the shallow water. They walked the horses across quietly, trying not to splash. But their stealth was thwarted when a couple of stray dogs picked them up.

"Git!" Johnny hissed, wishing he had something to throw at the barking dogs. "Git, I say!"

Anxiously he looked around him in the darkness, afraid someone would come. A man in a picket shack stuck his head out the door and yelled angrily at the dogs to shut up. He didn't appear to see Speck and Johnny.

The huge Tom Green County courthouse, with its high stone walls and its tall cupola, loomed massively in the dim moonlight. It stood back well away from the river, with most of the town lying east and south of it. Some new development was building up in the courthouse area. Johnny had heard someone say San Angelo's population was around five thousand now, but he doubted it. It wouldn't be that big in a hundred years. San Angelo was a ranch town. With the army gone, it was dependent upon cattle and sheep, upon small farms scattered along the three Concho Rivers, and upon the freighting of supplies to ranches and settlements which lay west and south all the way to the Pecos and the Rio Grande.

Johnny had always enjoyed coming here, for San Angelo was the biggest town he had ever seen. Seemed like there was always something to watch, from a backlot badger fight up to horse races and steer rop-ing. Holiday-seeking cowboys rode in from a hundred miles away, for this was a tolerant town that understood a man's letting off steam after months of isolation on a ranch. Long as he didn't hurt anybody and paid for what he broke, no one bothered him much.

They gave him his money's worth and showed him a time.

Since the shooting, Johnny and Speck hadn't done any talking. They had ridden in silence, each nursing his thoughts, sick with remorse and dread. Johnny didn't know how many times he had seen that woman's blood-drained face before his eyes, how many times he had heard her gasp and had seen her die in Milam Haggard's arms.

Now, in the familiar streets of San Angelo, some of the somber mood lifted. But not all of it.

Speck said sorrowfully, "It sure does hurt to come a-sneakin' in this away, like a pair of cur dogs followin' all the back alleys. I always liked to ride in on Concho Avenue screechin' like a wild Indian and lettin' the whole town know I was somebody come."

Johnny knew the ache that throbbed in Speck now, for Speck had grown up here, had played barefoot in these dirt streets when this was little more than a hidehunter camp and a whisky village for Negro soldiers and white officers in the fort across the river.

Speck's voice was melancholy. "I sure hate havin' to leave here. It was hard, livin' with Aunt Pru, but I always did love this town. I fished up and down these rivers. I knew every horse and burro and dog by its name. I bet I could still show you the big old pecan tree where I climbed up out of the water the time of the Ben Ficklin flood." He shook his head. "A queen of a town, she is . . . a cowboy's town."

Johnny said, "Maybe things'll work out someday."

Speck's voice broke. "You saw Haggard's eyes. We can't *never* come back!"

They held up once and pulled back into an alley as a surrey passed with a man and a woman riding in it. Johnny caught the high lift of the woman's laughter and knew she would be one of the "girls" from down on West Concho, by the river. Bitterness touched him as he thought how off-center fate could be, a lady like Cora Haggard lying cold and still in death, while a woman of this kind went right on living, squealing in empty-headed merriment. Why couldn't it have been this one who had died? On reflection, he knew the thought was childish. One person could not take another's place when it came time to die. This woman had no responsibility toward Cora Haggard. That responsibility lay with Larramore and Speck and himself.

Aunt Pru lived alone in a small frame house back from Chadbourne Street. The house was dark as Johnny and Speck rode up to the rear of it. They tied their horses to the picket fence.

Speck said, "Careful now, and don't trip over a faucet. That new waterworks has piped water right to everybody's back step. Next thing you know they'll be wantin' it in the house." He moved up to the small back porch and knocked. Johnny heard no sign of life. Speck knocked again and called softly, "Aunt Pru!"

In a moment a pair of feet scuffed across the wooden floor. A glow went up as a lamp was lighted. Aunt Pru opened the door cautiously and extended the lamp in front of her to light the young men's faces while she held the door ready for a quick closing. She had pulled a cotton housecoat on over her nightgown. Her hair was rolled up. Sleepy-eyed, she squinted. She said with a start, "Speck!"

Anxiously Speck said, "Aunt Pru, would you please get the light out of our faces and let us come in the house? We got to talk to you."

The graying woman stared suspiciously as she lowered the lamp and opened the door wider. "Very well, come on in." When they were inside she said sharply, "Speck, let me smell your breath." He leaned close. She sniffed. Her eyes showed disbelief. "You don't appear to've been drinking. What on earth are you doing out at this time of night? Decent folk are all in bed."

Speck avoided his aunt's eyes. He glanced at Johnny as if seeking support. But Johnny intended to let Speck do the talking, as he usually did. Johnny had always stood in awe of this thin-faced, sharp-tongued woman.

Her gaze snapped from one to the other. "Well, there's something the matter. Speak up!"

Speck was hesitant. "Aunt Pru, there's been a little trouble."

"Trouble?" Her eyes widened. She glanced with sharp disapproval at Johnny, then back to her nephew. "I knew it; I always knew it. I knew someday you'd run too long with the wrong crowd and come dragging trouble to my door. What have you done?"

Speck's voice quavered. "Aunt Pru, we didn't go to do nothin'. It wasn't our fault, really, but we been blamed for it."

"Speck, you're evading me. What have you done?"

Speck was close to crying. "It was an accident. A woman got killed this mornin'. Man who done it, he hollered right quick that it was us, and they believed him. We're on the run, Aunt Pru. We got to run or die."

The tall, thin woman stared in horror, her hands coming up to her cheeks, her mouth open. "A killing! You've gotten mixed up in a killing!"

"It wasn't our fault. We just got the blame for it, is all."

She didn't seem to hear. She turned away from him, crying aloud, raising her face to look up at the ceiling, then dropping her chin.

"Aunt Pru, we hoped maybe you could lend us a little money. We'll send it back to you soon's we can. We wouldn't ask it of you, only we got cheated out of a whole winter's pay. That's what caused the trouble in the first place."

She turned on him with an unexpected savageness. "Money! You bring disgrace to this house, to our name, and then you have the gall to come and beg me for money?"

Speck took a step backward, astonished at her reaction. "We wouldn't ask you, Aunt Pru, but we're desperate. We'll pay you back, I promise."

"Promise! How many times have you made me promises, Speck, and how few times have you lived up to them? Promised you'd go to school? Promised you wouldn't run around with riffraff?" Her furious eyes cut to Johnny. "You promised you'd look for respectable work, but you joined a group of common cowboys and drank whisky and caroused and made a sinner of yourself. You've drunk and gambled and debauched yourself with those painted women down on Concho and left me in shame."

Speck dropped his chin and stood in red-faced silence while she railed at him: "I knew this would happen someday. You were born with the mark of sin on you, and now it's the brand of Cain. When my sister came to me to have her baby, and no ring on her finger, I knew the mark was on you and you would come to a bad end. But I tried, God knows how I tried. I raised you and kept you because you were my sister's baby. I gave you a home and fed you and tried to teach you righteousness. But all the time I knew someday the stain of sin would show. I knew you were born to hang."

Speck's shoulders slumped. Tears rolled down his cheeks. He looked like a dog driven into a corner and whipped, a dog that had no wish to fight back.

"All these years," she drove on relentlessly, "I've known this day would come. I could have thrown her out and been spared this shame. But I was a Christian woman."

Johnny listened with anger swelling in him. He caught Speck's arm. "Come on, Speck, let's get out of here."

Speck edged toward the door. Aunt Pru shrilled, "That's right, run! Get on your horse and run, but you can't escape your sin. It's been on you since the day you were born!"

Johnny pushed through the door, pulling hard on Speck's arm. In the doorway Speck paused. Head still down, he didn't look up into his aunt's face. But he said brokenly, "Aunt Pru, I'm sorry."

The gaunt woman cried, "Go on, get out of here! There's been enough shame on this house already." She raised her face to the ceiling. "Oh, God, what have I done? Why do you torment me so?"

"Aunt Pru . . ."

"I've done my Christian duty. Now I'm through. Go on, and may God have mercy on you!"

Speck trembled like a child lost. Johnny let go his

friend's arm and took an angry step toward the woman. But he caught himself before he loosed the torrent of fury that strained within him. He said only: "My mother was a *real* Christian woman. She'd have cut out her tongue before she would've said the things you did."

He wheeled, caught Speck's arm again and hurried him out the back gate. They swung into their saddles. Johnny said tightly, "Speck, we'll go out and see my dad. Maybe he can help us."

Speck made no effort to talk. They headed north, leaving San Angelo behind them.

For a long time they rode in silence, bone-weary and sensing the weariness of the horses. Johnny watched the reflection of the moon in the river. Speck slumped in the saddle, his head down, the torment so heavy on him that Johnny could feel the weight of it himself. At length Speck asked, "What you thinkin' about, Johnny?"

Johnny hesitated. "I guess I was thinkin' about that woman, that poor Mrs. Haggard."

"I was afraid maybe you was thinkin' about Aunt Pru."

Johnny shook his head. "I'd forgot about her," he lied.

"I wish you hadn't heard all the things she said. She's probably sorry now."

Johnny's face twisted. *She's not sorry for anybody but herself.* It occurred to him she hadn't asked a single question about Mrs. Haggard—not her name, not even how the accident had come to happen. *She's never felt sorry for anybody in her life, nobody but herself.*

"Aunt Pru's really a good woman," Speck insisted. "You just got to know her, is all. I reckon I've given her a lot of grief."

And she's enjoyed it all, Johnny thought. He had known people who seemed to thrive on misery, who seemed to enjoy feeling sorry for themselves and couldn't be happy unless they were unhappy. It never had made sense to Johnny. But he could recognize the symptoms.

Aunt Pru had them all.

Speck worried, "I just wish she hadn't said what she did in front of you, that about my mother and all." He didn't look at Johnny. "I never did want you to know. I hope you don't think none the less of me, now that you know what I am."

"It doesn't make a particle of difference."

Speck brooded. "Seems like I've known about it as long as I can remember. Aunt Pru, she told me a hundred times how she took in my mother and helped her 'hide her sin.' Then I was born, and my mother died. 'God's mercy,' Aunt Pru always said. She just kept me. Sure, she rode me pretty hard, always houndin' me about this and that and the other thing, warnin' me three times a day about hellfire. But she fed me and kept me in clothes. Always said she didn't want folks sayin' she didn't do the Christian thing by her sister's boy.

"You've seen her with her bad side showin', Johnny. But she's all the folks I got. You've had a family. Me, I just got Aunt Pru. Blood kin means a right smart to you when you have so little of it. She's my aunt, and I reckon I love her."

"Never was any question about that."

"And she loves me; I know she does."

Johnny nodded. "Sure she does, Speck." But he had his doubts.

The horses had put in a long trip, all the way from Sonora. Johnny could feel his mount about to cave in beneath him. A man could drive himself to extremes when he had a reason, but he had to consider his horse.

Sometime around midnight they halted on a sloping river bottom, where ageless native pecan trees stood like silent giants, spreading a huge canopy of fresh green leaves which blacked out all the moonlight. For countless generations the Indians had come to the three Conchos each fall to gather nuts for winter food. Now the faces had changed, but the routine had not. Come fall, people from San Angelo and all around would tramp up and down these riverbanks gathering pecans to eat or to sell.

The two staked their horses. Speck voiced concern. "We oughtn't to be stoppin'. No tellin' who's behind us, or how far."

But there was no choice, not unless a man wanted to walk off and leave a dead horse. They spread their single blankets upon the mat of fallen leaves and stretched out. Johnny was so weary he ached all over. He thought he would drop right off to sleep. But he found himself lying awake, looking up into the heavy foliage, which rustled gently in a cool early-morning breeze. The tensions of the past hours did not leave him as he had hoped they would. Lying there, it was almost as if he were still in the saddle, still plodding those endless miles, still looking back over his shoulder, fearful of what he might see back there catching up with him. His mind gave him no rest. Over and over and over again he saw the blanched face of Cora Haggard. He put his hands over his ears, and still he heard her cry.

Somehow Speck slept, but it was a nervous, threshing sleep. Johnny knew the things that went through Speck's restless dreams. Finally Speck cried out, "No, we didn't mean to!" Johnny reached over and shook him gently. Speck sat bolt upright, blinking in confusion.

"It was a nightmare, Speck. A nightmare, is all."

Speck rubbed his hand over his face and squeezed his eyes shut. "Johnny, I kept seein' her. She just stood there lookin' at me, accusin' me with her eyes, with that blood on her ... all that blood!"

"Easy, Speck, easy. Lie down and try to sleep some more."

Speck shook his head in misery. "If I got to go through that every time, I don't think I'll ever want to sleep again."

He got up and rummaged through his warbag. Finding the pistol that had brought on the trouble, he held it a moment, feeling it with the tips of his fingers. Then he drew back and threw it into the river.

He sat on the ground with his knees drawn up and his face buried, and he began quietly crying.

4

ired, a separate ache for every long mile, Johnny
felt a lift as the little Fristo ranch headquarters
came in sight along a slow bend in the brush-
studded draw. Stretched out ahead were the corrals
he had helped build as a boy. There was no telling how
much of his own sweat had gone into the slow, labo-
rious digging of holes, the ditching, the tying together
of cedar stakes, and the tamping of heavy posts to
make the fences bull-stout. He watched the big cypress
fan of the windmill turning slowly in the noonday
breeze, and he wondered how many times he had
helped pull the suckerrods up out of that deep hole.

The first settlers had taken up the river land. Baker
Fristo had arrived a shade late, with little in assets except ambition and a willing back. He had to accept
rangeland away from the living water. But the day of
the windmill had come just in time. He had found that
his land—though there wasn't so much of it—could
produce as much beef as any that lay along the river,
so long as a man had windmills. It didn't matter so
much where the water came from; the main thing was
to have it. He had worked for wages on neighboring
big outfits for cash to buy cattle and drill wells and
put up the wooden towers.

Johnny and Speck rode their flagging horses into the main waterlot gate. Two high-headed cows with trailing calves eased warily around them, breaking into a run when they were in the clear. In front of the barn the riders climbed down from their saddles, stiff and groaning from the ache. Pulling off his saddle, Johnny could tell how badly drawn his horse was. They had put in an awful day yesterday. Without those few hours of rest along the river during the early morning, the horses might not have gotten here. Johnny dropped his saddle front-end down and draped the sweat-soaked blanket across it to dry. He slipped the bridle off the horse's head. The horse turned away and made for the water trough. In a moment Speck's followed suit. Johnny stood wearily with the bridle in his hand, the leather reins trailing on the ground, and watched the thirsty horses drink.

He saw his father walking out from the small frame house, trailed at a respectful distance by a short, dark-skinned Mexican cowboy. Baker Fristo was the picture of Johnny Fristo, plus twenty-five hard years. Grinding work had put a twist in his back, and he walked leaning a little forward. He favored his left leg, an unwanted souvenir from a bronc of years ago. His features were the same as Johnny's but badly abused by time and weather, the hair almost solidly gray now where it showed from beneath his old grease-stained hat. He had a three-day stubble of beard, for his wife lay buried yonder on the hill, and there was no one to tell him to shave.

The ranch was small, and it wasn't much for fancy. But what there was of it, it belonged to him. It had his sweat and blood soaked into it.

He was a plain man, and he showed his emotions.

He grabbed Johnny's right hand and clamped his left hand tightly on Johnny's elbow. He squeezed so hard that it hurt. "Son, it's sure good to see you home."

"Howdy, Dad. I'm tickled to be here."

The father squeezed again, and Johnny winced. Baker Fristo stepped back for a long, critical look at his son. He extended his hand to Speck. "Howdy, Speck. I declare, you fellers look a sight. Bet you been over in Angelo celebratin' spring. Don't you-all know when to stop?"

"Mister Fristo, I'm afraid we ain't got nothin' to celebrate about."

Baker Fristo looked quizzically at his son. His grin gradually faded. "There's somethin' wrong. What is it?"

Johnny shook his head and looked at the ground. "Dad, it's a long story. I don't hardly know where to start. Reckon we could eat first? We're both hungry as a wolf."

"Sure. Me and Lalo were just fixin' us some dinner when we saw you-all ride up. We'll throw some more in the skillet." He studied his son, apprehension clouding his eyes. "You sure you ain't been drinkin'?"

"No, sir, none atall."

Baker Fristo hesitated, worry still pulling at him as he looked at the two horses rolling themselves in the dirt. It was plain that they had been ridden hard. "Well, let's mosey up to the house." He led the way. Johnny and Speck trudged along, trying vainly to keep up with him. Another day, they would have led him.

When he had finally become financially able, Baker Fristo had built the frame house to please his wife. Lord knew, she hadn't had many of the nicer things. Once it had seemed a big and beautiful thing to

Johnny. Now that he was grown he could see it for the wooden box that it was. The color was faded and peeling too. The house hadn't been painted since his mother passed away. Off to one side of it stood the picket shack which Baker Fristo had first put up for his little family so many years ago. It was built of cedar posts, hewn for a fit and lashed tightly together, the butt ends set solidly in a trench. The space between the posts had been chinked with plaster. In a way, it resembled a small log cabin standing on end. The Mexican, Lalo Acosta, lived in it now.

Baker Fristo sliced steak from a quarter of tarp-wrapped beef hanging on the small back porch. Because he and the Mexican could not eat a whole beef before it spoiled, it was Baker's custom to pool beeves with several of his neighbors. Johnny stood around hungrily watching the meat frying in the pan. Impatiently he took it out of the skillet before it was completely done. Ordinarily the sight of blood running would make his stomach turn over. Like most Texans, he wanted his beef well done. But he was desperately hungry now, and so was Speck. They took the beef in big bites and ate it quickly, like a pair of starved pups.

The longer he watched them, the more Baker Fristo's eyes narrowed. "You boys are in Dutch, I can tell that."

Johnny glanced at Lalo Acosta, indicating by his expression that he didn't want to talk in front of anybody but his father. "We need a couple of fresh horses, Dad. A couple of good ones."

Baker Fristo understood. "Lalo, how about you goin' out and fetchin' up the horses?"

When the Mexican was gone, Baker Fristo leaned

back with his bearded-face long and grave and waited for the story. His jaw hardened as he listened. He blinked faster, the full implication reaching him.

"Poor woman," he said quietly. "No part of it was her fault, but she suffered anyway. Wasn't really your fault either, come right down to it. But you'll be the ones who pay." He placed the palms of his rough hands together and seemed to measure his thick fingers. He glanced at Speck.

"I suppose you went by and told your Aunt Pru?"

Speck nodded.

"What did she say?"

Speck was slow to answer. He got up nervously and paced the floor. "She was awful sorry about it." He looked down. "I reckon I'll go help Lalo."

When Speck was gone, Johnny told his father bitterly about Aunt Pru. "Dad, I never did want to hit a woman in all my life. But I wanted to hit *her*."

Gravely, Baker said, "Son, she can't help bein' what she was born, any more than Speck can. What she's done for Speck she hasn't done out of love. If the truth was known, she likely hates him. But she figures he's her ticket to Heaven. She's figured to buy her way in by feedin' him and bringin' him up, even if she *did* treat him like a dog from the day he was born. Some of what's wrong with Speck today, you can blame on her."

Johnny said, "I'm glad I had you and Mother, and not somebody like *her*."

Baker Fristo looked at his hands again, his jaw quivering. "I've heard of Milam Haggard. I expect most folks have. How long do you think he'll give you?"

"They'll be buryin' her today, I guess. Likely he'll come a-ridin' when the service is over."

"How'll he know where to start lookin'?"

"He can ask the cowboys we've worked with. We didn't make any secret about where we came from, or who our folks was. Who'd have ever thought we'd need to?"

Baker Fristo frowned darkly. "So, he'll likely be stoppin' here about tomorrow. Next day at the latest."

"I expect."

Fristo took a handkerchief from his pocket and blew his nose. He tried to look at Johnny, but he couldn't. He turned and stared out the window awhile. "Johnny, I been doin' a lot of thinkin' lately. I been hopin' you'd get the roamin' out of your system and come home to stay. I need you around here."

"You got Lalo."

"Sure, he's good help but he's not like family. You're all I got left now. I been plannin' how one day soon I'd turn this place over to you. I'll be gettin' too old and stove up. This place would give you a good start. *I* started with nothin'. It's been a hard fight, but at least I've managed to build this little bit. You could build a lot more. You're young yet."

Johnny's throat was tight. "I've missed you, Dad. I've wanted to come home. But first I wanted to prove I could make a hand worth my hire to somebody else. Now I reckon it's too late."

"You could stay and try to talk it out with Haggard."

Johnny shook his head. "You don't know how he looked. If he could have, he'd have killed us and cut us up into little bitty pieces. In his place, I suppose I'd have been the same."

"Once a man starts runnin', it's awful hard to find a stoppin' place, son. He has to keep on runnin' and runnin' till finally he can't run anymore. And in the end he has to turn and face it anyhow."

Johnny's hands shook. "Dad, I just can't face him now. Call me a coward and I guess you'd be right. Maybe someday I can do it. But not now."

Baker Fristo was silent awhile. "It's my fault, in a way. I intended to talk to you but I was afraid you wouldn't listen. Now it's too late."

"Talk about what?"

"About Speck Quitman. I know you like him; *I* like him too. But he's a millstone around your neck."

Johnny stared, wanting to reply but not finding the words.

His father said, "Sure, you made a good pair when you were younger. But you've outgrown him. You're a man now and ready to take on a man's responsibility. Somewhere back yonder, Speck quit growin'. He'll never be a man if he lives to be a hundred."

"Dad . . ."

"Let me finish, son. Some folks say he's simple-minded. I don't go that far. But I *do* say he's got no imagination, no foresight. He's got no idea about the consequences of the things he does. He'd walk into a burnin' house just to get a cigarette lit. Now, that cow trader was the one to blame for what took place yesterday. But think back: if it hadn't been for Speck, it wouldn't have happened, would it?"

Johnny shook his head.

His father went on, "You ought to've said *adiós* to him a long time ago, Johnny. Stay with him and he'll get you killed!"

Johnny nodded a regretful agreement. "You're right, Dad. I've known it a long time. More than once I've started to ride off and leave him someplace, but I never could bring myself to do it. What could he ever do by himself? Now it's too late. Whatever happens to us now, we'll have to face it together."

Baker Fristo brought himself to look at his son, and his wrinkle-edged eyes were sad. Johnny had never seen his father cry but once, that when Mrs. Fristo had died. He thought he could see tears in Baker's eyes now. "Then, son, if there's no other way, you better run. You'll need some money. Whatever I've got, I'll give it to you." He paused. "Any idea where you'll go?"

Johnny shook his head. "West someplace, wherever the trail leads us. Texas is awful big."

Lalo brought in the horses. Badly as he wanted to rest, Johnny knew he and Speck needed to travel all they could. These first days would be crucial. If they could get a long-enough lead on Haggard, there was a chance he never could find them in those vast spaces west of here.

Baker Fristo took a rope out of the barn. He made a gentle underhand loop and caught a long-legged bay. "Speck, here's one that ought to fit you." When Speck bridled the bay and slipped Baker's rope off its neck, Baker reached out and snared a brown. "Johnny, you know this horse, old Traveler. I traded him off of Wilse Arbuckle. He's not much for pretty, but he'll take you all the way and bring you back."

"Thanks, Dad."

They saddled up. Lalo came out from the house with a sack of food—canned goods, cold biscuits, coffee, a little of the beef. Baker Fristo watched while Speck tied the sack on behind his saddle. He shook hands with Speck. "Good luck, boy." He turned back to Johnny. "Write me, son. Let me know you're still alive. Maybe someday I'll be able to tell you it's safe to come back."

Johnny's eyes held doubt. "Dad, we better face what's true. I don't expect I'll ever be able to come back."

Baker Fristo looked down again for a long time. "Well, Johnny, a man does what he has to. Me, I'll just have to give up some dreams. As you get older you find out most of your dreams don't really come true anyway. They keep you goin', but they don't often turn out. Still, without them a man never would amount to much."

Johnny's throat was tight and painful. He wanted to hug his father's neck, the way he had done when he was a boy. But he only gripped Baker's rough hand. "Goodbye, Dad." He swung up into the saddle.

Baker Fristo watched them ride out of sight. Finally, his shoulders slumped helplessly, he turned toward his house, oblivious of Lalo Acosta standing there, sympathy and puzzlement mixed in the Mexican's dark eyes.

"Not goodbye, son. Don't let it be goodbye!"

5

They angled northwestward from the ranch, purposely leaving a clear trail. By and by they came to a public road. They turned into it and stayed long enough to establish an appearance that they intended to remain on it.

Speck seemed numb. He followed along woodenly, doing whatever Johnny did, making no comment, contributing nothing that might help them. At length Johnny said, "We've gone far enough north. There's generally enough horse and wagon traffic on this road to blot out our tracks before long. Maybe by the time Haggard gets to here we'll have him fooled. He'll think we've headed for Colorado City and north."

Speck shrugged as if it didn't matter. "There ain't no use. There ain't nothin' goin' to fool Milam Haggard for long."

"We got to try."

Johnny saw a sandy spot beside the road, and he reined out to the left. "Time we was headin' west, Speck."

Speck only nodded and followed like a pup. Johnny dismounted a hundred feet from the road and handed his reins to Speck. He broke a limb from a mesquite and walked back to the road with it. He carefully brushed out their tracks, eliminating any trace of their having left the road. He moved slowly backward toward the horses, rubbing out all the tracks as he went. From the road there would be no visible sign that anyone had ridden away from it.

"That ought to leave us clear," he said.

Speck's eyes were bleak. "It won't fool him. Ain't nothin' goin' to fool him."

Impatience flared in Johnny. "He's only a man. Any man can be fooled."

"Me and you can. Other folks can. But Haggard can't."

A t this point they were nearly thirty miles up the North Concho from San Angelo. They could not follow a route due west from here, for they would not find natural water before they reached the Pecos, not unless it had rained somewhere. And rain in the country west of San Angelo was a thing to be treasured when it came but never to be counted upon. With luck, they might come across a windmill once in a while. Without that luck, they might starve for water before they ever reached the Pecos.

Still, Johnny knew there was a way. If they angled south-westward they would strike the Middle Concho. It meant extra traveling, but it was worth that. The Middle Concho had its beginnings west of San Angelo eighty miles or more, when weather was wet. Chances were right now that its upper reaches would be dry; to be safe, a man had to figure on that. In olden times the wagon trains and trail herds venturing west from Fort Concho had followed along the Middle Concho as far as there was a river. From San Angelo west, the country turned increasingly arid. With every ten miles you could tell a difference. Early travelers had stayed with the living water as long as they could. At best, they knew they faced long, miserable miles of dry travel between the headquarters of the Middle Concho and far-off Horsehead Crossing on the Pecos. It was foolhardy to start a dry trek any earlier than necessary.

Even now, with windmills increasing over the range, travelers tended to stay with the old trails and the river as long as there was any water in it. It was a conditioning bred into them, like an old-timer watching for Indians long after the last of them were gone.

Johnny and Speck watered the horses in the North Concho beneath the shade of tall old pecan trees whose limbs reached well out over the river. Johnny filled their canteens and listened to the high-pitched hum of the locusts. The afternoon was no more than half gone. If they pushed, they should reach the Middle Concho by dark.

"Speck, you look sick. You feelin' bad?"

"I been feelin' bad ever since that woman died. I'm tired, is all." He grimaced. "Tired. And scared."

"You're not alone, Speck. I'm scared too."

They came upon the river at dusk, and it was time, for both of them were spitting cotton. Johnny rode Traveler over the bank and down to the water. He slid stiffly out of the saddle and loosened the cinch so the horse could drink comfortably. He stepped upstream to the end of the reins, holding them because it was too far from home to let a horse get notions about traveling alone. He dropped on his stomach to drink long and gratefully of the cool water. Finally satisfied, he pushed himself up on one knee and wiped his sleeve across his mouth. Above him, Speck was watering too. The horses were both still drinking.

Johnny called, "Speck, why don't you come down here and drink? The water looks a little clearer."

"It don't matter. I figure on drinkin' it all anyway."

Johnny looked up the river. The stream here was probably not deep enough to wet a man to his waist, and a good jumper with a running start could almost clear it in a leap. It was a quiet stream most of the time, in summer dropping so low that in places it disappeared below the gravel. But once in a great while its vast dry watershed would catch a whopping big rain that brought water cascading down from the rocky hills and put the Middle Concho up on its hind legs to roar.

Johnny had noticed a bank of dark clouds forming far off in the north the last couple of hours and had made a mental note that they would do to watch. It wasn't considered realistic to predict rain in this part of the country, but it never hurt a man to be prepared.

He glanced again at Speck. "Ain't you ever goin' to get yourself watered out?"

Speck raised up, the water dripping off of his chin. "I never did know just how good water could taste."

"Leave some. We're liable to need it again."

Speck pushed to his feet. It was a considerable effort for him. Johnny could see dark circles under Speck's eyes.

"Speck, we'd just as well camp here. I'm gettin' hungry."

The Middle Concho lacked the heavy pecan and other timber that the North Concho had. Anyway, if those clouds moved up during the night and brought a spring electrical storm with them, Johnny didn't want to be under a bunch of trees. He'd take his chances with the rain out in the open. He'd seen lightning kill several steers beneath a tree one time. Thing like that came into a man's mind every time he saw a dark cloud.

They took the horses back up the riverbank. Johnny looked around for dry brush that would make good firewood for camp. He saw some mesquite.

"If you'll get that sack off of your saddle, Speck, I'll start a fire."

Speck turned toward his horse. His face fell in dismay. He glanced at Johnny, unbelieving. "Johnny, that grub ain't here."

Johnny stiffened. "What do you mean, it ain't here?"

"I had it tied to my saddle. Now it's gone."

Johnny swore and looked for himself. "That knot you tied must've come loose. Got any idea where you lost it?"

Impatience had edged into his voice, and Speck reacted with a testy defense. "If I'd known when it come off, I'd have stopped and got it."

Johnny wished he hadn't been so snappish, for he knew the strain Speck had been under. Speck had ridden along so benumbed that he could almost have fallen off the horse and not realized it. Johnny took a long look down their backtrail, what little he could see of it in the growing darkness. "Might've been a mile, or it might've been before we even got out of sight of the North Concho. Cinch we can't go back and hunt for it now."

Speck stared at the saddle as if he couldn't believe it. He reached up and touched the saddlestrings. "We got nothin' to eat. What're we goin' to do?"

"We'll do without."

They staked the horses on the fresh green grass and spread their blankets. Johnny took a hitch in his belt, but it didn't stop his stomach from growling. He looked at Speck with a nagging impatience.

They lay and watched the bullbats swooping down and touching the river, then lifting and banking around for another try. By and by Speck complained, "Johnny, I sure am hungry."

"Go down there and get you another long drink of water. That'll fill you up."

"I already slosh every time I move."

Gradually, as full darkness came, Johnny grew aware of a pinpoint of light upriver. He narrowed his eyes, wondering. Speck noticed it too.

"Campfire?"

Johnny nodded. "I expect."

Speck pondered awhile in silence. "Reckon they got anything to eat?"

"Sure, they wouldn't be out here without some chuck. But they'd remember us if Milam Haggard came along and asked."

Speck agreed reluctantly. "Still, I can almost smell supper a-cookin'."

"Forget it," Johnny snapped.

Speck was plainly hurt. He sat a long time in brooding silence. "Johnny, I'm a real trial to you."

"Go to sleep, Speck."

"I'm the one caused you all this trouble. Hadn't been for me we'd have somethin' to eat right now. Hadn't been for me, Mrs. Haggard would still be alive. We wouldn't have to be runnin' thisaway." He paused. "You know what you ought to do, Johnny? You ought to just go off and leave me!" He paused again, a long time. Then, worriedly, he said, "You ain't goin' to do it, are you, Johnny? You ain't goin' to go off and leave me?"

The fear in Speck's voice roused pity in Johnny. "No, Speck, I'm not goin' off and leavin' you."

Johnny turned first one way, then the other on his blanket, trying to find a position where he wouldn't feel the aches and the stiffness. He had to sleep. Hunger teased him, and he tried to force it from his mind. After a long time he drifted into sleep.

With daylight he awoke and looked up into a leaden sky. The smell of rain was fresh in the air. It would be coming down hard before long, he would bet on that.

His stomach growled its hunger. He pushed to his feet and looked around. In the north the sky was a sodden blue. Already raining yonder.

"Speck, we just as well get started."

Speck Quitman stirred and rubbed his eyes. He blinked and looked around sleepily, trying to get his bearings. Speck was always a slow one to wake up. If there had been any nightmares last night, Johnny was not aware of them. He thought Speck probably had been so tired that Mrs. Haggard hadn't entered his mind. That was a good thing, for Speck had come close to breaking down for a while.

Speck looked at the dark sky overhead, then glanced north. "Bad enough just to be hungry. But to be soaked and cold on top of an empty belly is almost too much to stand."

"We got slickers," Johnny said curtly. "At least *those* didn't come loose from the saddles." *There I go*, he thought then, ashamed, *still laying it into him*.

"I know it was my fault," Speck conceded ruefully. "But that don't make it any easier. I'm starvin' to death."

Johnny found himself looking wishfully in the direction where he had spotted the campfire last night. He couldn't find it now in the daylight.

Speck said, "I think we ought to go over yonder and see who them folks are. Maybe it's some ranch's chuckwagon."

"You know the risk."

"And I know I'm so hungry I can't see straight."

Johnny frowned. He had tightened his belt as far as he could pull it, but it hadn't helped much. "All right, let's go."

They saddled up and rode out, following the river. It took a while. There had been no way of telling in the darkness how far away the fire had been, or on which side of the river it lay. It could have been a quarter of a mile or it could have been three times that much. Johnny didn't indulge himself in curiosity. Like Speck, the main thing which bothered him right now was that he was hungry. He looked often at the sky. The rain smell was stronger. It was a bracing smell, one welcomed by a native West Texan under almost any circumstance, for rain came too seldom.

They saw the tent first, then the old Studebaker wagon standing there with a half-wornout wagonsheet tied loosely over the bows to cover whatever goods were in the wagonbed. Two horses were staked out on grass nearby. A campfire had burned itself down low, a coffeepot sitting on shoveled out coals next to it. Johnny saw several pots and one big Dutch oven, but they looked empty. He wondered if the folks had already eaten, and thrown out what was left.

"Hello," he shouted. "Anybody home?"

It wasn't polite, those days, to ride into someone's camp and not announce yourself.

He saw a flash of skirt at the open tent flap. A girl stepped outside and looked worriedly around. Her gaze fell upon the approaching riders. She lifted her skirts a little and came running. She was young, Johnny saw, maybe seventeen-eighteen. And she was crying.

Speck's horse shied at the flare of skirts rushing straight at him. Johnny's Traveler poked ears forward but didn't otherwise flinch. The girl cried out, "Thank God you've come! Please hurry!" She tried to say more, but her voice broke, and Johnny couldn't understand her. Speck was staring at the girl in total surprise. Johnny swung down. The girl caught his arm and began to pull him toward the camp.

"Please, I've got to have help."

Johnny dragged his feet a little, watching the tent with a considerable degree of suspicion. "Miss, I don't know what your trouble is, but we got trouble too."

With an effort she steadied her voice. "My father's in there. He's dying!"

Johnny glanced back at Speck, who still sat on his horse. "Come on, Speck. We better see what we can do."

Speck frowned. "Johnny, I don't like the smell of this."

"Come on."

Johnny wrapped his reins around a wagonwheel and followed the girl to the tent. A streak of lightning darted to the north, and thunder rolled. A drop of water struck his hand. He paused at the tent flap and looked inside. A man lay on a bedroll spread out on the ground. The hollow-cheeked face was wasted and pale. His beard was the only thing about him that wasn't a liver gray. The man coughed. Reddish foam showed on his lips.

The sight struck Johnny like a blow across the face. Tuberculosis!

This man was a consumptive. Likely he had come to the dry West Texas region like hundreds of others from God knew where, hoping this climate would work the miracle, would bring him a cure. As a boy Johnny had come upon many of them like this, camped up and down the rivers, sleeping on the ground, taking their rest, breathing the dry air and praying for health. Some had found it. Others had found only a lonely grave, maybe a thousand miles from home.

Johnny knew the girl had judged right. This man had waited too long.

The girl dropped to her knees and touched a wet handkerchief to her father's lips. Johnny stared, a strange knot drawing up inside him. "Is he conscious?"

The girl nodded. "Off and on. Right now he knows I'm here; that's about all. He's going. I can feel it; he's going." She bit her lip and touched the handkerchief to her father's face again.

Johnny made himself move a little closer, though a cold chill ran through him. He dreaded this slow, wasting disease, and he had always avoided people who had it. "You've known, haven't you, that he didn't have much time left? You can tell it by lookin' at him."

She nodded again, dropping her hands to her knees and staring forlornly into the pale face. "But they told us this dry air might do it. We hoped so much, and we came so far. All the way from Illinois."

"You got no other folks here, nobody to help you?"

"Papa's all I've got left. When he goes . . . there'll be nobody."

The man coughed again. The girl took one of his hands and squeezed it helplessly. She looked up, desperate. "Please, he's in pain. Don't you know anything to do for him?"

Regretfully Johnny shook his head. "I never had any experience with this. I don't reckon there's much anybody can do but wait. And maybe pray a little bit."

He didn't think it would be a long wait.

Raindrops began spattering against the canvas. Speck Quitman stepped up to the flap and looked inside suspiciously. His eyes widened. Wordlessly he motioned for Johnny to come outside.

"Johnny, don't you know what the matter is with that man in there? I can tell from here, he's a lunger. Got the lung fever. You better keep out of that tent."

"The girl needs help. He's dyin'."

"He'll take you with him if you catch the lung fever. Let's get the hell out of here!"

"Speck, she needs help."

"What can you do? Can you stop him from dyin'?"

"No, but somebody ought to be here. She'll be alone."

"She's no concern of ours. She was alone before we come here. We could as easy of rode on by, and she'd be no worse off than she ever was."

Johnny didn't know what it was about the girl that had struck him so. "I can't do it, Speck. She's got too much trouble for a girl like her to handle alone."

"We got trouble too."

The girl called from the tent, "Mister! Oh, Mister!"

Johnny turned and left Speck standing there. The man was coughing again, harder than before. The girl was talking quietly, trying to hold down panic. "It's all right, Papa. We've got some help. It's all right, Papa."

Johnny knelt helplessly, knowing there wasn't a thing he could do but sympathize.

The man's eyes opened a little. He blinked, trying to focus. He looked a moment at the girl, then weakly turned his head to look at Johnny. His voice was only a whisper. "Who are you?"

"Name's Johnny Fristo, sir."

"You help . . . help my daughter. Help her."

"I'll help her."

"Please . . . don't leave her."

Johnny swallowed. He found himself making a promise he knew he couldn't keep. "No, sir, I won't leave her."

The dying man lapsed back into the shadows. There was no sound except his ragged breathing and the quiet sobbing of the girl. That, and the rain drumming down on the tent.

Rain! And Speck was out there in it! Johnny eased to the tent flap and looked outside. He saw that Speck had unsaddled their horses and shoved the saddles into the wagon. Speck squatted beneath the vehicle, his yellow slicker wrapped around him, vainly trying to keep dry. There was enough wind with the rain that the water drove in under the wagon.

"Speck, you come in here before you get yourself soaked."

Speck was resolute. "No! I'd rather take my chances with the rain. If you had any smarts you'd be out here too."

Johnny shivered, for this was a cold rain, the kind that reminds you it hasn't been long since winter. It was the kind that sometimes caught fresh-sheared sheep and chilled them to death. But he could tell Speck wouldn't come into the tent.

"At least get into the wagon before you get soaked any worse."

He turned back to the girl and wished again he could do something besides just stand here and watch. When you came right down to it, there wasn't much anybody could have done now, not even a doctor. Just wait. So he waited. And at last death came quietly into the tent, touched the girl's father and peacefully took him away. It was hard to tell just when sleep lapsed over into death.

Or, Johnny wondered, was there really much difference?

6

The girl cried softly. Johnny put his hands on her shoulders. He thought he probably should say something, but nothing came to mind, so he let it go. All he could give her was sympathy, and he couldn't put even that into words.

The rain stopped. Johnny walked out of the tent and raised his head. For a moment the sun broke through, and it struck the spot along the river where the camp stood. He looked up through the small break, and the sun struck him full in the eyes. A chill passed through him. He had always taken his Bible teachings literally, and he wondered if there was some special meaning in the way the light touched here, where a man had just died.

It came to him that this was the second death he had witnessed in three days, and he shivered again.

Back in the tent, he found the girl was no longer crying. She still knelt, solemnly looking down at her father.

Johnny said, "I expect you'll be wantin' to take him back to Angelo."

The girl was a long time in replying. "We didn't know anybody in San Angelo. We just came there on the train, and we bought this old wagon and team at a stable. We came on out because Papa thought camping on the ground would cure him."

"Seems like you came an awful long way."

"We stopped once closer in, but the man who owned the land didn't want us there. He made us move. We came here, and nobody has bothered us." She paused. "Besides, I don't have money left to bury him with. It took about all we had to get him here."

"You got to do somethin' about him."

"I know. He liked this spot. It seemed to strike his fancy the minute he saw it. I think he would have liked to be buried here."

Johnny rubbed his neck, considering. Seemed to him he'd heard that when somebody died you had to report it to the law, get death papers and such. Just to bury a man out here this way might have been all right ten or fifteen years ago, but now it was probably against the law. It was too simple to be legal anymore.

But, on the other hand, it would be a minor thing compared to the trouble he and Speck were already in.

The girl's eyes pleaded. "Will you help me?"

He couldn't have turned her down if he had seen Milam Haggard and a big posse come riding over the hill.

"We'll help you." He looked outside at the gray sky. "It might set in to rainin' again directly. I expect if we're goin' to dig, we better get at it."

He went out and looked around for a pick and shovel. He found Speck standing by the wagon, his clothes wet. "Speck, I swear you look a sight. You ought to've come inside like I told you."

Speck shook his head. "You about ready to leave here now?"

At another time Johnny might have smiled, for it

struck him a little funny how Speck had lost his concern over being hungry. "Speck, her father died. We're goin' to bury him before we go."

Speck's mouth dropped open. "Johnny, we got to be a-ridin'. Haggard is liable to be most any place."

"We can't just leave this girl here with a dead body on her hands. We got to help her."

Speck looked for a moment as if he had about as soon fight as argue. But he gave in. "All right, sooner we get it done the sooner we get movin'. I'll dig, but I ain't goin' to handle him none, you understand?" He was about to say something else, but he sneezed.

Johnny said, "You oughtn't to be in those wet clothes. Maybe the girl can lend you somethin' of her dad's."

Speck shook his head violently. "No, sir, thank you, I wouldn't touch it." He took the shovel from Johnny's hand.

They let the girl pick the spot, back away from the river where no flood would disturb the grave.

That was the first time Johnny mentioned to her that they were hungry. She nodded solemnly. "I'm sorry. I should've asked you a long time ago."

"You had aplenty to worry about."

"I should've asked you anyway. I'll go fix something."

Speck started the digging. Johnny walked down to the camp with the girl. In the wagonbed he found a small supply of dry wood. She had been farsighted enough to put it under there before the rain started. In a wooden box were some canned goods, coffee, flour and sundry camp supplies. He put some of the dry wood into the firepit, poured a little kerosene over it and set it ablaze. He could see the girl through the open tent flap. She was pulling the blanket up over her father's face. Johnny turned away, respecting her privacy.

"Need any more help right now?" he asked when she came out.

"I'll be all right."

"I best go help my partner."

She said worriedly, "He's wet. I could get some of Papa's dry clothes for him."

"He wouldn't wear them. He takes some funny notions sometimes. But I'll tell him you made the offer, and thanks."

He had been looking around camp for something that would do as a headboard. All he could find was the endgate from the wagon. He took it out.

"Funny," he remarked, "I don't even know what name to put on this."

A tear started down her cheek. "His name was Edward Barnett."

"I never did hear yours, either."

"Mine is Tessie. Tessie Barnett."

With a rope Johnny and Speck lowered Edward Barnett into the grave. They stood and looked at the ground while the girl started reading the Twenty-third Psalm in a weak, strained voice. She finally broke down. Johnny took the Bible from her hands. He finished reading what she had started. Done, he added the one thing he could remember from funerals he had attended: "The Lord giveth, and the Lord taketh away. Blessed be the name of the Lord." He closed the Book and handed it to her.

She glanced up at him, and their eyes held a moment. Something stirred Johnny, something he had never felt before.

"Thank you," she said. She turned and walked back down to camp.

Speck and Johnny filled the grave and put the headboard in place, bracing it with rocks to make sure it didn't fall down. Speck said, "Reckon anybody'll ever notice it up here? It's a ways off of the trail."

"I don't know. Maybe they won't. But it don't seem right to put a man away and not even leave a headboard to mark his passin'. Man ought to have at least that much to show that he once walked this earth. Else he'd just as well never have been here."

Speck shrugged. "Don't look like he's left much to show for him. An old wagon, a tent. Ain't much to make a man's whole life look worthwhile."

Down the slope, the girl was breaking camp. Johnny said, "Maybe it's not the money and the property a man leaves that's really important, Speck. They get scattered, and who's ever goin' to remember him by that? But he left that girl. She'll remember him as long as she lives. She'll have children someday, and she'll tell them about him. They'll remember. Come right down to it, Speck, I don't guess a marker is really so important after all."

They folded the tent and placed it in the wagon. Speck went out and got the team. Johnny looked worriedly at the girl. "Miss, what're you goin' to do now?"

She didn't look at him. "I don't know. I hadn't let myself think about it. I just know I can't stay here where he died."

"You can sell the wagon and team, I suppose, and go back where you came from."

"I've got no family there anymore. There's nothing to go back to."

"Then maybe San Angelo. It's a good-sized town. I expect a girl like you could get decent work there."

She nodded. He could still see a trace of tears in her eyes. She had a lost look about her. She was young yet to be alone like this, to be left a stranger bewildered in a land that was alien to her, a land where she knew not a single soul.

"I have to live somewhere." She squared her shoulders, forcing herself to take courage. "How far is it to San Angelo?"

"A fair piece. Forty miles, I expect." He looked at her with worry. "Think you can make it there by yourself?"

She was plainly dubious. "I guess I could." She bit her lip. "Do you suppose . . . do you suppose I could get you fellows to go with me? I've never been by myself like this." She looked away as if ashamed. "I guess I'm scared."

Johnny saw alarm surge into Speck's face, and he moved to head Speck off. "Miss Barnett, we're goin' west. We can't go to San Angelo."

"I don't have much money left, but I'll give you what I *do* have."

"It ain't the money. I mean, if we could do it atall, we'd do it for nothin'. But you see . . . well, the truth is we *can't* go back. They're lookin' for us there."

She slowly shook her head. "I can't believe that. You've been kind to me, both of you. You couldn't have done anything bad."

Johnny couldn't hold his gaze to hers. "We did a bad thing, but not on purpose. It was an accident." He didn't want to tell her more than that. He was glad she didn't ask.

Speck's calmness even surprised Johnny. Speck

spoke to the girl in a gentle voice. "We'll hitch up your horses, Miss. Too bad we can't do more." It didn't take Johnny long to figure out that Speck was simply glad to be shed of her and get moving again.

They turned the wagon around for her and headed it eastward, toward San Angelo. The girl said tightly, "Thank you again, both of you. I'll never forget this."

Johnny said, "I wish you would. I mean, if anybody asks you . . ."

"I won't say a thing."

They sat and watched her start. They watched her top out over the hill, a tiny-looking thing and all alone.

Speck wondered, "Johnny, reckon she'll ever make it there all by herself?"

"I don't know. I purely don't know."

"It's a long ways."

Johnny kept watching the girl, and that strange feeling came over him again. Suddenly he touched spurs to his horse. "Come on, Speck, we're not goin' to let her do it."

"What can we do? We can't go with her."

"We can take her west with us a ways. There's bound to be a ranch up here someplace where we can leave her with folks who'll see she gets to town all right."

"Johnny, I do believe you're losin' your head over that girl."

"I just never could sleep, wonderin' if she ever got there all right or if somethin' happened to her. Come on, Speck."

Speck grumbled, but he accepted the inevitable and followed.

7

Milam Haggard was tired, but he had cultivated a rigid self-discipline that would not allow him to show it. Riding a black-legged dun, leading a brown horse with a small pack, he kept his back straight, his shoulders high. His flat-brimmed black hat with the round crown was pulled down low over his eyes, so that he held his chin high to be able to see out under the brim. It gave him the appearance of a man with strong pride, and the appearance was not misleading. But it was not pride which dominated him now. He burned with a grim and silent determination.

He had passed the North Concho village of Water Valley a while ago, and ahead of him lay the Baker Fristo place. He had made some inquiry around San Angelo about this Fristo. Most people had told him Fristo was a hard-working small cowman who had pulled himself up by his own bootstraps and never made trouble for anybody. But Haggard knew circumstances could forge drastic changes in a person. The mildest of men would stand up and fight for a son.

He was sure the situation here would be different from the one he had stepped into in San Angelo when he visited Speck Quitman's aunt. She had broken into uncontrollable hysterics and had cried about the shame that had been brought upon her. It had seemed to Haggard that she showed little concern for her nephew but a great deal about the disgrace that had befallen her good family name.

Haggard had held her in contempt, but he had stayed until he found out that the two cowboys were likely to visit Baker Fristo. Fristo probably wouldn't tell him anything on purpose, Haggard knew. But long ago he had learned that people would usually tell more than they realized, more than they intended. A word, a glance, a set of tracks—and he might discover all he really needed to know.

Haggard rode out of the brushy draw and saw before him the big windmill, the rambling set of corrals, the barn, the fading frame house. He reined up for a long, careful look around. He studied closely the places where a man or men could hide—behind the barn, the house, a stack of unused cedar posts, a pile of barbed-wire rolls. Some of these he carefully eliminated one by one, concentrating on their shadows until he was sure nothing stood behind them that didn't belong. Still, plenty of dangerous places were left. He drew the saddlegun up out of its scabbard, laid it across his lap and gently touched spurs to the dun. He moved forward in a slow walk, watching with the tense care of a man who half expects to be shot out of the saddle.

He heard talk. His gaze caught movement out in one of the corrals. Two men were hanging a new wooden gate. Haggard lightly touched the reins and moved the dun in that direction, the pack horse following. He noted that the man facing him was a Mexican. That checked with what Haggard had been careful to find out. Fristo had one man living on the ranch with him, a hired Mexican.

The Mexican spoke quietly. The other man turned to squint at Haggard. The man made a move with his hand, and Haggard's grip tightened on the saddlegun. But he saw then that the man was only wiping sweat from his dusty face.

Now Haggard could see the face, and he knew this was Baker Fristo. He had seen Johnny Fristo once on the street of Sonora and again a few minutes the day of Cora Haggard's death. That face would be burned into his memory to the last day Haggard lived. This was the same face, except for the many extra years to which the deep furrows testified.

"Howdy," Fristo said. He was not unfriendly. "Git down and rest yourself."

Haggard did not do so immediately. He sat still, his gaze sweeping the corrals, the barn.

Fristo understood. "You can quit lookin'. Ain't nobody here but us, just me and Lalo. Nobody else."

Haggard glanced at the Mexican and saw apprehension in the dark eyes. For a little of nothing, the man would turn and run like a deer.

Fristo said, "I ain't lyin' to you, Mister Haggard."

Haggard let his surprise show a little. "You know me?"

"Never met you, but I know who you are. I know why you've come. My boy's not here. Even if he was, he wouldn't shoot you in the back. He ain't that sort."

Haggard stared at Fristo and then looked around for sign of a gun somewhere. Fristo said, "No guns. Me and Lalo, we're just workin' on the corrals a little. We didn't figure on shootin' anybody."

Pointedly Haggard said, "If you know why I've come here, you might be inclined to shoot *me*."

Fristo shook his head. "I'd rather just talk to you, Mister Haggard."

"Talk won't change anything. You ought to know that."

"I always heard you were a reasonable man, Mister Haggard. I think the truth would change things, if you'd just listen to it."

Haggard made no reply. Fristo gave up waiting for one. "Well, no use us standin' out here in the hot sun. It's dinnertime directly, and I'd just as well go fix us somethin' to eat. You'll stay and eat with us, won't you, Mister Haggard?"

Surprised, Haggard said, "You're askin' *me* to eat with you?"

"It's dinnertime. Nobody ever left my place hungry."

"I've come here lookin' for your boy. And you know why."

Fristo nodded slowly. "I know. I aim to try and talk you out of it."

"It won't work."

"I'll try anyway. You got to stop and eat sometime. You'd just as well do it here."

Haggard stepped to the ground frowning, studying this bent man. He couldn't remember that he had ever run into a situation like this. In a different way it bothered him as badly as his encounter with that wailing aunt. He stopped at a trough near the windmill and let the horses water. Then he followed Fristo to the frame house. He glanced for a moment at the old picket shack nearby. The thought struck him that the two young men he sought could be holed up in there. But instinctively he knew Fristo wasn't lying to him. The pair had gone.

On the front porch Fristo nodded toward a washstand on which were a bucket of water, a dipper and a washpan. "I expect you're pretty hot and dusty, Mister Haggard. Probably make you feel better to wash yourself."

As the guest, Haggard washed first, then Fristo. In the house Fristo motioned toward a rocking chair. "Set yourself a spell while I see what I can fix."

Waiting, Haggard looked around. One thing he saw was an old wedding picture. Baker Fristo in that picture was the image of his son today. Plainly enough, a woman had lived here once. Just as plainly, she had been gone a long time. The curtains on the windows were gray now with dust and smoke. A woman had put them there, but a woman would not have allowed them to get in that condition. The dishes on the shelf bore a nice pattern and showed a woman's touch. But some were chipped at the edges, the result of a man's rougher handling. Haggard noted that far fewer cups were left than plates of the original set. Several plain white cups had been added to take the place of some broken by inveterate male coffee drinkers.

It did not escape his notice that when the leftover morning coffee was hot, Baker Fristo passed up the nicer cups and purposely took out one of the plain kind for his own use. He was evidently more comfortable with those.

I guess I would be too, Haggard thought.

He wouldn't have admitted it to anybody, but the thought of settling down and living with Cora had almost frightened him. He had lived alone a long time, Haggard had. He had lived a harsh, womanless life on the trail and in small one-room shacks in a dozen towns. He had been comfortable in austerity. Often he had wondered how he was going to reconcile himself to the change a man had to make when he married, especially when he married a lady of Cora's kind. He would not have asked Cora to compromise her ways. The adjustment would have had to be his. Sometimes he had lain awake at night wondering how and if he could actually make a success of it.

Now he would never know. He and Cora had never had much chance to find a life together.

Baker Fristo broke into Haggard's line of thought. "Afraid my cookin' ain't much for fancy, but it fills in between the ribs. It's on."

Haggard moved to the table. He had never really been hungry. He had never been one to eat much. Since his wife's death, eating had been a necessity that he forced upon himself.

The Mexican came in and sat at the table with them. Haggard noticed this. He had been at many places where it wouldn't have been done. Haggard ate slowly, forcing the food down because he knew he needed it. Fristo ate in silence, but Haggard could feel the man's eyes appraising him. Haggard found himself liking the man. It would have been easier if he hadn't.

Fristo finished eating and leaned back in his chair, his eyes steady on Haggard. "It's a hard and bitter thing for a man to lose his wife. I know, because I've been there."

Haggard was slow to answer. "Then you'll understand how I feel, and why I do what I do."

"Those boys had no thought of hurtin' your wife. If it had even occurred to them that a thing like that could happen, they wouldn't have stopped the hack. But they figured they'd been done wrong, just the way you feel you've been wronged. They made a mistake, like you're fixin' to. They'll regret it as long as they

live. So will you, Mister Haggard, if you go through
with this."

"They killed her. All the talk in the world won't
change that."

"It was an accident. The blame isn't all theirs. It
wasn't even them that fired the gun; it was that feller
named Larramore."

"*They* told you that, Fristo. You can't really know."

"My boy told me, and he's never lied."

"He never killed anybody before, either."

"They're just boys, Haggard."

"They're men. They're both of age, and that makes
them men in the sight of the law."

"And where *is* the law, Haggard? How come it's not
with you, helpin' you hunt them?"

Haggard looked across the room, his jaw ridged in
anger. "The law looked at it the way you do. The sheriff down there, he said it was an accident. He wouldn't
file a murder charge. But she's dead. Nothing anybody
says can bring her back."

"And killin' my son—will *that* bring her back?"

"He killed her, he and that other one. An eye for an
eye is what the Bible says. It's God's vengeance!"

"God also has His mercy."

Helpless anger simmered in Haggard. He couldn't
sit there and argue over this thing as if it were a cow
trade or something. His wife was dead. The grief and
the anger were still sharp and bitter, cutting through
him like a knife. He pushed to his feet. "I'll be ridin'
on. I'm sorry I stopped here."

Baker Fristo stood up too. "Please, Haggard, listen
to me. Think!"

"I've *been* thinkin'. That's all I've done for days. I've
hardly even slept for the thinkin' I've done. And it

always comes back to the same thing: they killed my wife. I'm goin' to get them, Fristo. And the only thing I'll be sorry for is that it's *your* son."

He turned and started for the front door. He heard Baker Fristo move quickly. Instinctively Haggard stopped. Even as he turned back, his hand darted downward, coming up with the pistol from his hip.

Baker Fristo had lifted a rifle from a set of hooks on the wall and was starting to turn with it.

Haggard thumbed back the hammer of the pistol. "Stop it! Stop it right there!" Fristo hesitated a second, then kept on turning, the rifle still in his hands.

Haggard cried, "Stop it, Fristo! You haven't got a chance! For God's sake, man, I don't want to kill you!"

Fristo froze, but he still held the rifle. Eyes desperate, he looked into the bore of Haggard's pistol. The color began leaving his face. The man was scared. But Haggard could tell he was also determined, and that made him dangerous.

Fristo said, "You'll kill me, but I'll kill you too, Haggard."

"Not a chance. It's not worth the try."

"My son's life is worth *any* chance."

"You haven't *got* any chance," Haggard repeated firmly. "I'd put a bullet through your heart, and you couldn't pull that trigger. But I don't want to do it. Believe me, I don't want to do it." He waited for sign Fristo was going to relent. "Put it down now, Fristo. For God's sake, put it down!"

He could see the realization of helplessness slowly come into Fristo's eyes. And with the helplessness, a glistening of tears.

Fristo laid the rifle on the floor and stood up, his

shoulders slumped, his face stamped with defeat. He looked like an old man. "I tried. I tried."

Haggard found his heart was beating rapidly. He had come within an inch of having to kill this man. It was a killing he would have regretted as long as he lived. "You've got a lot of guts, Mister Fristo. If it's any consolation to you, you can always tell yourself you did what you could. But you never had a chance, not from the first."

"It's not important that I *tried*. What matters is that I failed. And now you'll go on out and kill my son."

Haggard swallowed. He saw the Mexican come up beside Fristo, the fear somehow gone from him. He saw the intention written all across the little man's dark face.

"Don't try it, *hombre*. You just leave that gun lay there or I'll have to kill you."

Lalo slowly backed away. Haggard picked up the rifle. He unloaded it, carefully watching the two men. He started to lay the rifle across a chair, then changed his mind. "I'll take this with me out to the barn and leave it there. I'd be real glad if you-all would just stay here till I get out of sight."

He could see desperation clutching at Fristo. "You can't find them, Haggard. It's two thousand miles from here to the Canada border. They could be any place."

"You mean they went north?"

Fristo nodded, and Haggard felt somehow a little sorry for him. It was a transparent effort, born of unreasoning desperation. Had the pair *really* gone north, not even an Indian torture would have made Fristo admit it.

Haggard knew within reason they wouldn't go

south again; that was where they had come from. Nobody here ever ran east, back into the settled country where it would be easy to locate them. Only one way was left: west. Anybody going west from here would almost surely strike for the Middle Concho, Centralia Draw and ultimately Horsehead Crossing on the Pecos. That narrowed it, made it easier for him.

He said, "Mister Fristo, I'm sorry for you." Then he left.

8

I t was night now, and the storm was coming back. Johnny and Speck sat beside the wagon, watching jagged fingers of lightning shatter the black sky to the south. Short flashes illuminated the underside of ugly clouds that likely were carrying hail. Thunder rolled gradually closer, and the ground trembled.

Speck's cold was settling deeper in his chest. Johnny could hear it when Speck coughed. That was more and more often.

"Sure fixin' to rain again directly," Johnny remarked, watching the sodden clouds. "I reckon we best sleep in the wagonbed, under the sheet."

The campfire had burned down low, but in its dim glow Johnny could see the girl seated in front of her tent, staring sadly into the coals.

Speck's voice was coarsening from his cold. "Johnny, that girl is slowin' us down somethin' awful."

"We can't just ride off and leave her."

"There's some as would."

"We're bound to find a ranchhouse someplace tomorrow."

Speck didn't look at Johnny. "Kind of got you goin', ain't she?"

Johnny hadn't realized it showed. "Worried about

her, is all. Things could happen to a girl out here like this."

"Get all wrapped up in a girl and you'll forget your old partner, that's what you'll do." Johnny wondered if he detected a vague resentment. Speck added, "If she was some middle-aged old maid, reckon you'd be as worried about her?"

Johnny didn't reply to that. He was afraid he knew the answer, and it didn't make him particularly proud.

Speck began coughing again. It shut him up, and Johnny was not sorry. He didn't feel like arguing. He pushed to his feet and walked down to the tent. The girl didn't seem to notice him at first. Her gaze was fixed on the glowing coals.

"Anything we can do for you, Miss Barnett?"

Startled, she glanced up. "No, thank you. I'm afraid the only thing that will help me now is time . . . lots of time."

"You'll just hurt yourself, broodin' thisaway."

"Not easy to put a thing like this out of your mind, though, especially as fresh as it is. I'm not sure I want to, not for a while yet." She looked back at the coals. "I'm sorry to be a burden to you."

"You're no burden."

"I'm keeping you here."

"We'll be all right."

"Will you? What about the man you said is after you?"

"Rain this mornin' washed out all the tracks we made up to the time we struck your camp. Rain again tonight will wash out what we've made today. I expect he'll be hard put to follow us."

That wasn't the whole truth, and he knew it. But he saw no gain in telling her Milam Haggard would follow the river, same as they were doing. It was the natural thing. Speck hadn't mentioned it, either, and Johnny hoped it hadn't occurred to him.

The girl stared into the dying campfire. The smell of burning mesquite blended well with the clean smell of oncoming rain. She said, "My father always liked the rain. Said it seemed to wash the world down and give it a fresh start. Said it needed a clean start as often as it could get one."

Johnny nodded gravely. "I wish *I* could get a clean start." He hadn't meant to say anything. But it came to him that if the girl could find concern for someone else's troubles, she might for at least a while forget her own.

Her eyes were sympathetic. "Can't you?"

He shook his head. "It'll take a lot more than rain to wash away what happened." To suit Milam Haggard, it was going to take *blood*.

"Do you have any folks, Johnny?"

"My dad, is all. And I've said goodbye to *him*. Way things are, I doubt I'll ever get to see him again."

"Then you must feel a little like I do." The cool wind came, and she shivered. "It almost makes you panic to realize all of a sudden that you're alone. Deep down, you know the pain will pass someday. But that doesn't help much right now."

Kneeling beside her, Johnny picked up a stick and idly poked at the coals. "I'll tell you somethin' my dad said when my mother died. It helped me. He said to look forward, try and put yourself into the future. He said imagine it's been a long time, that whatever has hurt you is in the past and the healin' already done. He said you know that someday it'll be like that, so try to pretend now that someday has already come."

"Does it work?"

"It helps. It's a way to borrow strength and ease the pain. Eventually you find that someday *has* come. It's over, and you've lived." He paused, solemn. "I've used it a right smart the last couple of days. Lord knows, a man needs anything he can find that'll help, even a little."

She sat awhile in a dark silence. "Your dad must be a good man."

"The best there is."

She brought her gaze up to his face. "And he raised a son just like him."

They were traveling again by shortly after daylight, the wagon wheels cutting deep into the mud of last night's rain. Turning in the saddle, Johnny worriedly studied the bold tracks they were leaving. A blind mule could follow them. Moreover, when the ruts dried they would set, a little like concrete. They would be a long time in eroding away.

Of course, Haggard probably wouldn't know the cowboys were traveling with a wagon. But their own horses were leaving tracks too. By this time Haggard no doubt had studied the tracks until he could pick these two horses out of a remuda by them. For a little while Johnny and Speck tried riding ahead of the wagon, hoping the girl's team would wipe out their tracks. It didn't work very well, and they quit trying. Johnny doubted an expert tracker like the manhunter Haggard would be fooled very long.

Nothing to do, then, but try to find a ranch where they could leave the girl, then pick up speed as they rode on west. Out there it never rained much. The constant wind would worry away at a set of tracks in soft earth until they were gone within hours.

They traveled all morning along the trace started by the Butterfield stages and followed since by thousands of wagons over the long frontier years. With the warmth of the bright morning sun, the moisture from the rain began to evaporate. The steam of it set Johnny to sweating. For Speck it was even worse. His face was flushed. He wouldn't let Johnny touch him, but Johnny knew his partner was beginning to run a fever of sorts. Speck's eyes were red, his temper short. Times like this, Johnny had found it best simply to leave him alone.

They stopped to eat a little and rest the horses. Speck was in misery, both of body and of soul. Sweat soaked his cotton shirt as he sat in the thin shade of a big mesquite. His eyes were riveted to the backtrail. It was easy to read his mind. He ate little.

"Johnny, I'm afraid I caught the lung fever."

"Where'd you get a notion like that? It takes a long time to develop the lung fever. You took yourself a cold out in the rain, that's all."

Speck nibbled at hope, though unconvinced. "You reckon that's it?"

"Sure, you'll be all right. But you need to rest awhile. Soon as we find a ranchhouse."

"We done rested too much now. Old Haggard is liable to come a-ridin' along most any minute now."

Johnny shook his head. "Not yet. He hasn't had time."

"He don't need time. He'll smell us out like a bloodhound. We need to keep on a-movin'."

"Even horses have to have rest. Here, Speck, eat a little more."

Speck waved food away. The melancholy came over

him again. "You're wrong, Johnny. It *is* the lung fever. I caught it off of that girl's daddy as sure as sin."

Johnny didn't feel like going through the whole argument again, so he let it lie. Before long he was itching to go, even as he knew Speck was. Though reason told him Haggard was still well behind, the thought of the man raised something more than physical fear. The ex-Ranger's reputation was awesome. It was easy to believe somehow that Haggard stood eight feet tall, that he did, indeed, have the bloodhound's gift of scent, that with only a look he put the mark of death on a man.

A chill ran through Johnny, and he said, "Let's go, Speck."

About the middle of the afternoon they saw a trace leading off to the northwest, a faint wagon trail that had been used only enough to show it belonged to somebody. Johnny glanced back at the lagging Speck, hunched in the saddle. He pulled out into the faintly marked trail and motioned for Tessie Barnett to bring her wagon along.

Speck drew over to the side of the trail, his head down. He had nothing to say. Johnny edged his horse back beside the wagon. "Tessie . . . Miss Barnett, here's a trail. Chances are it leads to a ranch yonderway someplace. Not a big outfit, from the looks of the trail. But a ranch, anyway." He looked into her eyes, and he couldn't tell for sure whether she was glad or not. He got an odd feeling that she wasn't, really.

"Think it'll be far, Johnny?"

"No way of tellin'. We'll know when we come to it."

She glanced at Speck. "He's pretty sick. He'd be better off in the wagon."

Johnny frowned. "I expect he would." He looked toward Speck. "Why don't you sit up here with Miss Barnett? I'll tie your horse on behind."

Speck didn't argue. Johnny gave him a boost up, and he could tell Speck needed it. He couldn't have made the climb by himself. "Speck, when we find a ranchhouse, you're goin' to have to rest a spell, and no buts about it."

Speck gritted miserably, "Let's just be a-gettin' on."

They rode an hour, following the dim trail over rocky hills and through dry-looking scrub cedar timber. It hadn't rained so much here. Down yonder from the trail ran a small creek that would empty into the Middle Concho somewhere to the south. Finally, as Johnny was beginning to wonder if the trail really led anywhere, they came upon a ranch headquarters. It sat at the foot of a hill, with chinaberry trees rimming what appeared to be a small seep or spring. For a moment Johnny's spirit sagged. He had hoped for more. This was just a little box house—a one-room affair likely, or two rooms at the most. A small rock shed served as saddle house and barn. A couple of weathered brush arbors out by the shed had been intended orginally to shade the livestock. But they hadn't been kept up, and much of the brush topping had fallen to the ground, leaving big openings for the sun to shine through.

Another brush arbor stood in front of the unpainted frame house. Beneath it a lone man sat in an old rocking chair.

The thought came to Johnny that this was no time of day for a man to be lazing around the house. He ought to be out tending to work. At least, that was the way his dad had taught him. But he knew not all people looked at life that way. From the rundown appearance of the place, Johnny would bet this man spent far more time under the shady arbor than at work out in the sun.

The man stopped rocking and sat motionless, watching their approach. Nearing, Johnny saw that this was a man of forty or so, running strongly to paunch. His hair was starting to gray in spots, and he hadn't shaved in a week or two. His clothes would have stood alone if he had taken them off, which he probably hadn't done in days. He gave no sign that he was glad to see company.

"You-all lost or somethin'?" He said it to Johnny, but his gaze quickly shifted to the girl. Lazily he stood up.

Johnny eyed him closely. "You got some drinkin' water?"

The man jerked this thumb toward the house. "Back there in the cistern." He didn't move to fetch any.

Johnny said, "We been lookin' a long time for a ranchhouse. This girl needs help to get back to San Angelo."

The man looked Johnny up and down. "You look to me like a healthy feller. I doubt there's anything she needs that you couldn't of give her." He stepped out from under the arbor and squinted in the sun, looking closer at the girl. "Been a long time since there was any woman at this place. If I'd of knowed you was comin', I'd of shaved and fixed up a little." His gaze fell on Speck. "You look like you'd fell off the wagon and got run over. What's the matter with *you*?"

Johnny answered for Speck. "He's sick. Got wet and took a bad cold. I was hopin' he could rest here a little."

The man frowned, still not friendly. "Sick folks take a lot of carin' for. I don't have much time."

"You won't have to do anything. We'll do it."

"I got mighty little room here, as you can see. I reckon you could roll him out a blanket under the arbor, though. Don't see how that could hurt nothin'."

Johnny felt anger rising. This was a country where most people were openhanded and ready to help, for company was scarce and friendships prized like coin of the realm. In his limited travels Johnny hadn't run into many like this before. This was an attitude alien to the time and the country. "Thanks," he said dryly. "Thanks a lot."

The man looked at Tessie again. "You said somethin' about the girl needin' somebody to help her get back to Angelo."

"I was sort of hopin' there would be somebody here who could take her."

"Ain't nobody here but me."

"Any neighbors?"

"Not for a long ways. I never did care much for neighbors anyhow. Always come a-borrowin' or wantin' help. And then they're always accusin' you of this, that, and the other." He studied the girl, then turned back suspiciously to Johnny. "How come you don't take her to Angelo yourself?" When Johnny didn't answer, realization came into the man's muddy eyes. "You boys are on the dodge, that's what it is. I can tell."

Johnny swallowed. It occurred to him that this man might try to hold them in hope of a reward. He glanced around quickly for sign of a gun. He saw none.

The man looked at Speck. "Maybe he didn't catch cold atall. Maybe he's wounded."

Johnny said, "He's not wounded. I told you the truth."

"Who did you fellers rob? A bank? The Santy Fee railroad?"

"We never robbed anybody."

"Then you *killed* somebody. That's what you done, you killed somebody!"

Guilt rose hotly to Johnny's face. The girl spoke up. "They didn't kill anybody. They were there, but that was all. They weren't the ones who did it."

Johnny said, "Hush, Tessie."

The man stared at her. "How did you fit into this, girl? You look a mite green to be runnin' with the wild bunch."

Johnny protested, "We told you the truth. We found her along the trail. Her daddy was sick. He died and we buried him. Now we're just lookin' for somebody to take her to Angelo. We couldn't go off and leave her there."

The man's gaze moved to first one then the other, calculating. Mostly he looked at the girl. "I don't want to get in Dutch with the law. I can't go harborin' no fugitives. You boys can water your horses and get a drink for yourselves. Then you got to get off of my place. The girl, if she wants to, can stay here. I'll see she gets to Angelo."

Johnny pointed to Speck. "Mister, my partner's sick."

"He'll be dead if the law finds him here. I don't want him on my place."

Angrily Johnny tried to stare him down. But the man simply ignored him and turned back to the girl. "Honey, if you want to get down from that wagon . . ."

Tessie Barnett looked at Johnny. "I don't know . . ."

Johnny stepped closer to her. "I don't like the looks of it here."

"But, Johnny, you've lost a lot of time on my account already. Maybe you'd better be trying to make some of it up."

"Speck bein' like he is, we can't move very fast anyway."

"But you wouldn't have me on your hands."

"I don't like the looks of this feller."

"Neither do I. But if he'll take me to San Angelo, that's the main thing. I'll be all right. Don't worry about me."

"I don't like it. Don't like it atall."

"What choice do you have? You'd better go, Johnny. I think if he could get his hands on a gun, he might try to hold you."

Johnny nodded. "Been thinkin' the same thing myself." He looked down, then brought his gaze back up to her face. "Tessie, I like you. I wish we could have met some other way."

"So do I, Johnny. Maybe someday . . ."

He shook his head. "There won't be any someday. We're not comin' back, me and Speck. We can't."

She leaned over. To his surprise, she kissed him on the cheek. He felt his face warm again. "Then goodbye, Johnny. I won't forget you."

Confused, he pulled away abruptly. He reined up beside the paunchy man. "I never did get your name."

"Gerson. Gerson's my name. What's yours?"

Johnny decided to pass the question. "Gerson, you better be sure you take good care of this girl." He looked back at Speck. "Come on, Speck, we got to be movin'."

Riding away, he paused several times to look back. The first time the girl still sat in the wagon, watching them. The next time she was standing in the shade of the arbor, but she was still watching. The third time, just before they rode out of sight, Johnny saw the man standing beside her.

Johnny turned in the saddle, doubt tugging at him. He and Speck rode half an hour in silence. Speck was slumped forward, fever riding him. Johnny reined up suddenly. "Speck, we oughtn't to've left her there."

Speck made no reply.

"We don't know that Gerson. Did you notice how he looked at her?"

Speck said hoarsely, "Like a coyote lookin' at a cottontail rabbit."

"I'm goin' back for her, Speck."

Speck only shrugged.

Johnny looked about for some shade, though the day was wearing well along toward sundown, and it was no longer particularly hot. He rode to a big mesquite, took his blanket and spread it out beneath the tree. "Lie down there and rest, Speck. I'll be back directly with Tessie and the wagon."

Speck didn't argue. He almost fell out of the saddle. Johnny hurried to help him. When he had Speck set, he swung back onto the brown horse. "Come on, Traveler, let's travel."

Moving in an easy lope much of the way, it took him somewhat less than half an hour to get back. He saw the wagon beside the brush arbor, the team standing droopheaded, not yet unhitched. The man and the girl must be in the house. Johnny wrapped the reins around a post and stepped up to the open door. He heard Gerson's voice.

"Now, girl, you got nothin' to be afraid of."

Gerson hadn't heard Johnny. The man had Tessie backed into a corner, his big left arm braced against the wall to keep her from stepping aside. His right hand was under her chin, and her eyes were wide with fear.

"Get away from her, Gerson!"

The girl cried out in relief. "Johnny!"

Startled, Gerson turned. Instantly the girl darted beyond his reach. She ran across the small room and threw herself against Johnny. "Oh, Johnny, you came back!"

Johnny's fists were clenched. "What have you done to her?"

Gerson shook his head. "Ain't done nothin'."

Tessie Barnett showed her fright. "He told me he was going to the law and tell them about you, unless I would stay here with him. He said he wanted me to be his girl."

Johnny said grimly, "You go on outside, Tessie. Wait for me."

Gently he pushed her aside. But she stayed where she was. "Johnny, he's too big for you. Don't fight him. Let's just go."

"We'll go in a few minutes." Fists tight, he started across the room toward Gerson.

He had been so angry he hadn't thought about Gerson having a gun. But there it was, a rifle propped against a table. Gerson took one quick step and reached it. He brought it up before Johnny could move against him. A wicked smile split Gerson's bearded face. "Just keep on a-comin', cowboy. I'll blow a hole in you as big as your hat!"

Johnny stopped, his mouth dry. He looked down the bore of the rifle at the finger tightening on the trigger. His heart raced. He felt the same helpless fear that had come over him when the cow trader Larramore had brought that pistol up out of his bag.

Behind him, Tessie gave a frightened little cry.

Gerson said, "All I got to do is pull this trigger. You're on the dodge anyway. Likely they'll give me a *re*-ward."

Johnny's heart seemed to be sitting high up in his throat, pounding so hard he would have thought everybody could hear it.

Tessie pleaded, "Don't kill him! I'll do anything!"

Gerson said, "Kind of fancies you, don't she, cowboy? Maybe I ought to take her up on that. Maybe I ought to just let you ride away."

Johnny found his voice. "I wouldn't leave without her."

Gerson nodded. "I know. That's why I got to kill you. Minute I turned my back, you'd be here again, lookin' for a way to kill *me*."

"She'll do you no good, Gerson. Sooner or later she'll get away. She'll tell, and they'll come lookin' for you."

"I'll take care of that in due time."

Johnny saw murder in the man's eyes. He thought of Speck. "My partner's outside," he lied. "Shoot me and he won't let you get out of here alive."

Gerson hesitated. "The sick one? What can *he* do?"

"He can shoot."

Gerson licked his lips, worrying. He had evidently not considered Speck. "You say he's outside?"

Johnny nodded, hoping his eyes would not give away the lie. He had never felt less sure of himself.

Gerson said, "All right, we better go out and talk to him. If he sees I got you-all covered with this rifle, he'll come along easy enough." He motioned toward the girl. "You first. Ease on out that door."

White-faced, Tessie turned toward the opening. Johnny moved carefully along behind her. A dozen ideas raced through his brain, and he dismissed them all. Any sudden action might cause Gerson to kill him by reflex.

Tessie stepped through the door and down to the ground. Johnny paused in the doorway. Tensely, he said, "Tessie, move to one side."

Gerson grunted, "What's goin' on?" But Johnny stood blocking the door. The girl was instantly out of Gerson's sight.

Johnny looked off to his right and spoke loudly as if to Speck. "He's got a gun at my back. If he shoots me, kill him. He can't get out of this house without you gettin' a clear shot at him."

Johnny waited a moment, trying to work up his courage. He sensed Gerson's indecision. Even with a prisoner in his hands, the man had lost his advantage—or thought he had. Johnny got a grip on himself. "If you shoot me now, Gerson, you're as good as dead. This shack of yours will be your coffin. Now, why don't you put that gun down?"

Gerson muttered, "I don't think there's anybody out there."

"Want to stick your head out and look?"

Gerson swallowed. His hand was first tightening, then loosening on the rifle. Johnny's heart was high in his throat. He had never been a poker player because he never could carry off a bluff. He couldn't understand why Gerson didn't see through him. It came to him gradually that Gerson was as frightened as Johnny was.

Again Johnny managed, "The gun, Gerson."

Sweat popped on Gerson's face. His lips quivered. Finally, whipped, he lowered the barrel. "Tell your friend out there I'm puttin' it down."

"Hand it to me," Johnny said, and Gerson did. Johnny took it. "Tessie, come get this."

Tessie came quickly from around the corner. She took the rifle from Johnny's hand as he passed it through the door.

Johnny turned again and looked at Gerson. The fear began draining out of him, and his anger came in a rush. Before Gerson knew what was happening, Johnny was plowing into him, fists swinging.

Normally, with his extra weight, Gerson would have made short work of Johnny Fristo. But Johnny caught him by surprise. The first blow struck Gerson in the stomach. Half the breath gusted out of him, and he staggered. By the time he got his wits together, Johnny had struck him again in the stomach and once across the face.

With a roar of anger Gerson pushed forward. But surprise had cost him too much. From the first blow, Johnny had the advantage. He pressed hard, punching, slashing, driving Gerson back again to the wall. A cold fury welled up and took over for Johnny. He was only dimly aware of the pain when Gerson occasionally managed to strike him.

Gerson fought a losing battle, and he began trying to find a way out. But each time Gerson turned, Johnny was there, striking him again, turning him back. Gerson sank to his knees, his arms raised defensively over his bleeding face.

Reason slowly returned to Johnny. He backed away, breathing hard. He looked down and found his knuckles bruised and bleeding. Each breath he drew hurt him. He paused a moment, looking.

With a sudden lunge he swung one more hard punch into Gerson's face. Gerson fell over and lay on his back.

Gasping, Johnny said, "Now, Gerson . . . don't you ever . . . point a gun at a man again . . . or take advantage of a girl." He backed to the door. "Tessie, the rifle."

Hesitantly she handed it to him. "Johnny, you're not going to kill him . . ."

He shook his head. "I ought to. I would if he made a move. Get to your wagon now, and let's be movin'."

He stayed with the rifle on Gerson till he heard the wagon move. Then he backed out the door and swung into his saddle, the rifle still in his hands. He wondered what Gerson's reaction would be when he came to the door and saw only the two of them riding away.

Johnny went by the corral and chased away a horse he found penned there. That would leave Gerson afoot. With the creek running, there would be no need for horses to come in for water, where Gerson could make an easy catch.

Johnny pulled in behind the wagon and trailed it at some distance. He rode slantways in the saddle, looking back at Gerson's house, the rifle in his hands. For all he knew Gerson might have another rifle somewhere. Johnny didn't want to be caught with his back showing. He rode like that, watching behind him, till he passed over the hill and out of sight of the house. Only then did he relax a little and look ahead of him at the wagon.

It had stopped. Tessie Barnett sat with her hands over her face. As Johnny rode up anxiously, she lowered her hands a little. They were shaking. Her face was milk-white.

"Tessie, what's the matter?"

She motioned for him to sit on the wagon seat beside her. He tied the horse on behind, eased Gerson's rifle down in the wagonbed and climbed up. To his surprise she opened her arms and pulled herself tight against him, burying her face against his chest. Hesitantly he placed his hands on her shoulders and found them trembling.

"Tessie, it's all right now. It's done."

She nodded, but she held him tightly. Her warm body pressed against him, and the effect was like strong whisky. He felt the warm rush of blood to his face.

"Johnny," she said, holding him as if she feared it would kill her to let him go, "I'm sorry to be like this. I don't know what you must think of me."

"I don't think anything bad of you, Tessie, you know that. You've had a couple of hard days."

"I wish I weren't such a baby."

"You're no baby. I don't expect any girl would have done better, and most of them not half as good."

"I won't break down this way again, Johnny. From now on I'll be strong."

"The worst has already happened. Not likely anything as bad will ever happen to you again."

Her arms were still tight around him. She raised her head a little, and he laid his cheek against her forehead. She said, "Somewhere, though, you're going to have to leave me and be on your way, Johnny Fristo. It's going to be hard for me to say goodbye."

He nodded soberly. "How come it had to be like this, Tessie? How come I didn't meet you a few days ago, when I had nothin' to run from, nothin' to be afraid of?"

"I don't know, Johnny. Maybe we just weren't meant to have any luck."

9

For a long moment a rider sat outlined on the bald top of a rock-strewn hill to the west. Johnny Fristo felt a reflex of fear that stopped his breath and stiffened his hands on the leather lines. Then reason told him this couldn't be Haggard, and he eased. The rider wasn't tall. His shoulders were hunched a little, and his manner of riding showed he wasn't a young man.

He came down through big green clumps of *sacahuista* and reined toward the wagon, taking his time. He rode with the slack ease of a man who had done it all his life, and a long life at that. Gray hair showed beneath an old hat most people would have thrown away a long time ago. He had a salt-and-pepper moustache and tight-drawn skin that looked like saddle leather. His hand lifted in friendly greeting as he approached. Frontier times were fading into the past, but even yet it didn't hurt to let folks know you came in peace.

"Howdy." His voice was pleasant. "You-all lost?" His gaze swept them, and Johnny got the feeling that in two seconds he saw about all there was to see. But looking at the sun-squinted blue eyes, Johnny couldn't tell for the life of him what the man was thinking.

"We're lookin' for a ranchhouse."

"Mine's a little ways over the hill. Would it do?"

"I expect. We got a sick feller here."

The elderly rider eased in closer, stopping his sorrel horse beside the wagon and looking down at the feverish Speck. "You sure do. You oughtn't to be haulin' him around."

"It isn't because we want to."

"Well, we'll take him on up to the house. Sarah'll be so glad to see company, she won't care whether they're sick or well—just so they come."

Tessie Barnett took cheer. "Sarah?"

"My wife. She's the best in the country when it comes to takin' care of the ailin'."

Tessie said thankfully, "We've found a place with a woman."

The rancher studied the girl. "You come a ways, I guess. Bet you're young married folks, headin' west to find a home."

Johnny saw the flush in Tessie's cheeks. "No, sir, we're not married. We just come across this girl a couple of days ago, down the river. She was a-needin' help."

The old rider couldn't hide his curiosity, but he didn't pry. He shoved his hand at Johnny. "My name's Dugan Whitaker."

"Fristo. Johnny Fristo. And this here is Tessie. Back yonder is Speck."

Whitaker's face furrowed. "Fristo! That's got a familiar ring to it. I used to cowboy with a feller by that name back yonder on the San Saba River. Lord, it's been twenty-five or thirty years ago. Baker, his first name was . . . Baker Fristo."

"My dad."

A grin broke across the rancher's wrinkled face. "By George, I ought to've guessed when I looked at you. But it was so long ago the Twin Mountains was just a pair of anthills. You're him all over again. Only, I'll bet you can't ride broncs the way he could."

Johnny wasn't in a smiling mood, but he smiled now. After Gerson yesterday, it was a relief to come across the kind of people Johnny was used to. "No, sir, I reckon he can still ride rings around me."

Whitaker chuckled. "I expect you do well enough. Bein' Baker Fristo's son, you've had a good raisin'. Come on, let's go to the house."

He let the wagon have the dim trail, and he rode his horse alongside. He talked all the way in. It appeared to Johnny that Whitaker was as thankful for company as his wife could ever be.

"We got a settlement now, a ways yonder over the hills on the upper reach of the Middle Concho. But Sarah, she don't take well to travelin' anymore, so we don't often go, and we don't see many folks." He watched Johnny a great deal, plainly pleased at seeing him. "Sarah knew your dad. She'll be real interested in seein' the kind of man Baker Fristo's son turned out to be."

Johnny chewed his lip. In a way it was good luck, happening into old friends of the family. In a way it wasn't. He dreaded having to explain to them the trouble he was in, he and Speck. With strangers it didn't make so much difference. Here, it would hurt.

Whitaker was talking to Tessie. "We have a daughter not much older than you. She up and married, though, and moved west. These ranches can get awful lonesome for a woman alone. Sarah'll be real tickled to see you."

Johnny brooded awhile. "Mister Whitaker, we got a favor to ask. For Tessie, that is." He explained how he and Speck had come across the girl and her dying father. The old ranchman nodded in sympathy. Johnny said, "We didn't want to just leave her there. We been lookin' for a ranchhouse, somebody to take her to San Angelo."

"And my place is the first one you found?"

Johnny frowned. "Not exactly. We came across one yesterday. Feller named Gerson."

Whitaker cut a quick glance at the girl. "You didn't leave her there with him . . ."

"Not long."

"Pity this country is gettin' so all-fired civilized. Ten years ago they'd have left the likes of Gerson danglin' off of some liveoak tree. He's been awful careless where he puts his brandin' irons."

Johnny said, "He got kind of careless yesterday."

Whitaker glanced again at the girl and read his own meaning. His mouth went grim. "There's other ways than hangin' a man. One day I'll have a talk with some of the boys."

They came in sight of a big growth of china trees, a pair of windmills and a water-filled surface tank that had been hollowed out of the ground by horse, mule and man sweat. Dugan Whitaker had a small rock house built of material hauled down a wagon-load at a time from the hills. Johnny flinched, thinking about the untold hours of toil Whitaker must have put in building this place. Yet he knew the pride the old man would have in it, too, for the things a man builds with his own hands are dear to him. They are a part of him, like the hands themselves.

"Sarah," Whitaker called, "we got company."

Johnny expected to see a woman walk out onto the porch, but none did. He thought he glimpsed a face inside, back in the shadows. He couldn't be sure. He knew a moment of doubt. If he *had* seen a woman, there was something odd here.

Whitaker swung down and wrapped one of his leather reins around a post to hold his horse. He turned toward the wagon. "Let's you and me get ahold of your friend here and carry him into the house."

They lifted Speck carefully. He had enough strength to help a little. They got their arms around him and his over their shoulders. Johnny expected to see the woman come out and hold the screen door open. She didn't. Tessie ran ahead and opened it.

Whitaker took the lead. "Right on back thisaway. We'll put him in the lean-to."

Inside, Johnny caught a glimpse of a woman seated in a chair. Only a glimpse, but it was enough to anger him a little. What kind of hospitality was this, anyway? The least she could have done was to come over and see what the trouble was. He helped Whitaker put Speck on the bed.

"Sarah," said Whitaker, "we got a sick cowboy on our hands."

The woman's voice came from right behind Johnny, and it startled him. He hadn't heard her walk up. He turned and saw her still seated, but the chair was close now. It was a chair with wheels.

"What ails him, son?" she asked Johnny. Johnny was so surprised he couldn't find his voice. The woman smiled gently. "Don't worry, this chair doesn't bother me much anymore. Not like it seems to be botherin' you."

Johnny took off his hat. "I'm sorry, ma'am. I didn't go to stare at you."

"I'll bet you're not a very good poker player. Your eyes give away what's in your head." Her smile widened, and she wheeled the chair in closer to the bed. She repeated, "What's the trouble with your friend?"

Johnny told her. She touched her hand to Speck's head. "Got fever, all right. How's his breathin' been?"

"Short, kind of. He's been in some pain."

She nodded. "I expect he's knockin' at the door of pneumonia. But he may not have crossed over the line yet. Maybe we can hold him back. First thing, you and Dugan get the clothes off of him." She wheeled the chair around and faced Tessie. "Young lady, you want to help? You can reach up into a top shelf in the kitchen and get me some whisky. I'll show you where it's at." She wheeled the chair out about as fast as Tessie could walk.

After the men had removed Speck's clothing and covered him with a blanket, Sarah Whitaker came wheeling back. Tessie brought a steaming cup.

"Now, young fellow," the ranchwoman spoke gently to Speck, "I want you to raise up and drink this. Take it slow, but drink it all." She took the cup from Tessie's hands and passed it over to Speck, keeping a hold on it so he couldn't spill it. Speck swallowed. His flushed face twisted, and for a moment he was about to spit out what she had given him. "Drink it," she said again. Slowly Speck did. The sweat was already popping out on his face.

Mrs. Whitaker said, "That's more whisky than anything else. It'll help boil the fever out of you. Now, girl, if you'll pull up the covers on him, we want to have him sweat the fever out."

Soon Speck was complaining about the heat, and perspiration was rolling from his face. When he made a weak move to push away the covers, Sarah Whitaker firmly pulled them back into place. "It's just something you'll have to go through. Later you'll feel better for it."

After a while Johnny walked out onto the front porch. Now that he had time to look around, he saw things he had missed at first. He saw a slanting ramp by which the wheelchair could roll with comparative ease off and onto the porch. Inside, he had seen how the plank kitchen cabinet had been lowered so everything would be in reach for Sarah Whitaker.

Dugan Whitaker came out onto the shaded porch after him and paused to roll a cigarette. He offered the tobacco sack to Johnny.

Johnny said, "I don't guess it's easy for Mrs. Whitaker, the way she has to get around."

Dugan shook his gray head and licked the edge of the paper. "But she does all right. It was better when our daughter was still livin' here. She was a world of help. You can't keep a girl around forever, though. When they grow up, they got a right to a life of their own. You got to let the fledglings leave the nest."

Johnny fumbled in his shirt pocket for a match. "I don't mean to ask questions that ain't none of my business, but how did it happen? Mrs. Whitaker, I mean?"

"Runaway horse and a buckboard. Had a young horse, not broke long. He boogered at a jackrabbit and commenced to run. Flipped the buckboard over on Sarah out yonder a ways." He pointed. "There where you see that whiteface bull a-grazin'. She crawled all the way to the house for help. Last step she ever took was when she walked out to that buckboard. It's the last step she'll *ever* take."

"Real bad luck."

"Don't waste time feelin' sorry for her. *She* doesn't. Everybody's got a cross of one kind or another to carry. Sarah took the one that was marked for her and made the best of what she had left. She said if it was the devil's work to cripple her, she wasn't goin' to give him the pleasure of seein' her miserable. I guess a strong spirit is worth more than strong legs." He drew thoughtfully on his cigarette. "We all got somethin' to carry, some trouble that hangs over our heads. Even as young as *you* are, I expect life hasn't been all honey and sweetmilk."

Johnny found the cigarette had lost its taste. He wondered if Whitaker was subtly fishing. Face clouding, he flipped the cigarette out into the clean-swept yard. "Mister Whitaker, before you do anything more for me and Speck, I better tell you about us. You may not want to keep us around."

Whitaker didn't look up. "You fellers are in some kind of trouble, ain't you? I sensed it from the first."

"Then why did you bring us in?"

The ranchman shrugged. "Always did consider myself a pretty good judge of men. I had a good feelin' about you, even before I found out you was Baker Fristo's son. You couldn't have done anything very bad."

Johnny told him about their trouble on the Sonora–San Angelo road, and about Milam Haggard. Listening, Whitaker turned grave.

"Boy, you know Haggard's reputation?"

"I'm afraid I do."

Dugan Whitaker's face was long and sad. He held what was left of the cigarette between his fingers and stared absently at the smoke curling upward from it. He held it so long that the tiny fire went out, and the cigarette turned cold in his fingers. "Goin' to be several days before your partner is in shape to ride. You got that much time?"

"I don't know. Might have, if the rain wiped out our tracks down on the river. Haggard might be several days pickin' up the trail we left after we got away from the Middle Concho."

"He might, and again he might not. They say he's got a sixth sense about him." He glanced up in apology. "I didn't mean to talk like that. You know your trouble well enough without me harpin' on it."

"I know the problem all right. I just don't know the answer."

"Seems to me it was your partner that got you into this scrape. You might be able to save yourself if you'd go off and leave him here."

Johnny shook his head violently. "I wouldn't do that."

Whitaker nodded. "I didn't think you would. No son of Baker Fristo ever *could*."

I f he was often harsh and demanding of others, Milam Haggard expected no less than perfection in himself. Now that he had found the trail again, he was angry, and the anger was vented in his own direction. Another man might have cursed his quarry or blamed bad luck for the five days he had wasted. Haggard had never been prone to this kind of luxury. In his view the blame was his own, and that was where he placed it.

To be sure, rain had been the main factor. It had wiped out the tracks. But Haggard did not blame the rain. He told himself he should have been more watchful. Upon finding the tracks washed away, he had pondered awhile, then gone forward on the assumption that the fugitives would continue straight upriver. But he had gone all the way west to the head of the Middle Concho and beyond that almost to the Pecos without ever finding a trace. Surely, he had thought, he would have to cut their sign somewhere.

He was certain he knew one cause for his mistake. Those months of trying to become a ranchman—of turning his back on the service of the law—had rusted him a little. But the old training and the hard-learned ability were coming back to him now. It would take something more than two cowboys to throw him again.

Backtracking, working north of the river, he had come across the trail firmly set in the dried mud. For a minute or two the wagon tracks had fooled him, for he had no reason to associate the trail of a wagon with the men he was after. But after some study he had become convinced Fristo and Quitman *were* riding along with a wagon now. Only they and God knew what for. Something else bothered him, too. Several days ago, at about the time he lost the tracks, he had ridden upon a new grave and its headmarker, the endgate out of a wagon. He had worried briefly over the possibility that the cowboys had come across someone and killed him. But considering it, he had told himself it didn't make sense for them to kill a man, then bury him and mark the grave. Hide the body, yes, but not mark the place for all to see. He had decided there was no connection.

Now, finding that the two had been traveling with a wagon, he remembered the grave and wondered again. It seemed foolish for two men under pursuit to encumber themselves with a slow-moving wagon. Unless, of course, there was something of value in the wagon that they didn't want to ride off and leave. That could even provide a motive for killing.

There was still another thing hard to fit into the equation: a woman's shoe prints. A woman was traveling with this wagon; he had no doubt of that.

He had trailed a lot of fugitives in his time. None had ever been harder to figure.

Restless now and angry at himself for the wasted days, he resolved that this would be only a setback, not a defeat. Milam Haggard knew he had time. Time, in this sort of case, was usually in the favor of the hunter, provided he faced no deadline at which he must turn back. Haggard had no deadline. He was a free agent, responsible only to himself and to God. He could follow these cowboys from now till next year, from here to Hell's front door.

And he would, if he had to.

Riding along watching the trail, he began—without intending to—wondering about himself. He had never been much given to analyzing his own motives. He had always thought in straight and simple lines. There had never been anything devious about Milam Haggard. He had always set a firm course, and everyone who knew him could predict just where he would stand. He had stood for the right and opposed the wrong, and he had not compromised, ever.

Yet now he wondered. Amid the grief for his wife—and, yes, there *was* grief—he found himself taking some sort of grim satisfaction out of this search, almost an enjoyment. He knew this shouldn't be, and it concerned him. It was as if he had somehow been out of his element awhile and on this trail had returned to it.

He told himself this was *not* his true element. He had always told himself he took no pleasure in the hunting of men. He had never killed a man except when he had to, and he had always hated it.

But now he was on a trail again, and in all honesty he would admit to himself that he felt a satisfaction he knew shouldn't be there.

He shook his head. What *was* this, anyway? The whole notion was foolish. He had been well rid of the Ranger job. It was a job for a coyote, not for a man, riding a-horseback from daylight to dark through more long days than he could count, facing furnace heat in the summer and bitter cold in the winter, all the time trying to watch the ground for tracks while his vigilant gaze searched ahead of him. Though he would never have told anyone, there had always been a chill playing up and down his back whenever he rode into a place where someone might lie in wait for him. Every time he trailed a man, that secret fear rode with him. Haggard was cold and methodical when he stood against a man face-to-face. When he could see his enemy, fear was alien to him.

But always there had been that dread of being shot from ambush without a chance. The longer he had ridden with the badge pinned to his vest, the darker the dread had become. The luckier he was, the more certain he became that someday his luck would run out. No gambler could win forever. That was what Haggard had been—a gambler—betting his life that he was just a shade better than the other man.

He had grown sick of it, and the dread of ambush had become a cancerous thing, gnawing at him day and night. He had been glad when Cora had insisted that he turn in his badge before they were married. It gave him a reason to do what he had wanted to do a long time before.

Yes, sir, he had been well rid of that job. Cora had been the best thing that ever happened to him.

Now she was dead, and he was at it again, following a dim trail that inevitably led to the death of two men. It was a miserable thing, and he knew it. Why, then, this half-ashamed satisfaction?

The saddlegun lay across his lap as he rode down toward Gerson's frame house. Warm dry winds out of the north and west had almost obliterated the tracks now, but enough trace was left for Haggard to follow. He saw a man sitting beneath a brush arbor, shading himself from the morning sun. It was a time of day when most men would be out working. Haggard wondered whether this one was sick, lame, or lazy.

The paunchy man stood up at sight of Haggard. People had always said they could tell Haggard was a lawman almost as far as they could see him. There was something about the way he carried himself.

Riding up, Haggard could see a little of both awe

and fear in the man's red-veined eyes. Awe and fear were often companions, and hatred usually was not far away.

The man spoke first. "Gerson's my name. Law, ain't you?"

"I'm Milam Haggard." Haggard made no move to shake hands. He found that he disliked this man on sight. He didn't know why; he just had an instinct that way.

"Haggard? I've heard of you. I bet you're huntin' them two cowboys that come through here the other day. I didn't help them none, didn't even give them nothin' to eat. I knowed the law was after them, knowed it the minute they come a-ridin' up here."

"How many days ago?"

The man counted on his fingers. "Five, it was. Maybe six. They're bad ones."

Haggard frowned, his sharp eyes catching the healing remnant of a cut on the man's cheekbone. Fist cut, most likely. "They've got a wagon with them, and a woman, haven't they?"

Gerson nodded eagerly. "They do. I knowed there was somethin' the matter the minute they come in sight. . . ."

Impatiently Haggard broke in. "How about the woman?"

"They had some kind of a story about how her pa had died back down the trail, and how they brought her along to protect her. But if you ask me, they killed him. And they got that girl with them against her will. I tried to take her away from them, but they beat me up. Took both of them to do it, but they beat me up."

Haggard frowned. "How come you didn't go to the law?"

Gerson was hesitant in answering. "I figured the law would be a-comin' here soon enough."

Haggard clenched his fist. "Five . . . six days. It's a lot to make up."

"You can do it. That wagon's slow. And one of the cowboys is sick."

Sick. That made a difference. Haggard wondered how the sick one had been much help in beating up Gerson, but he didn't ask. He figured Gerson had exaggerated that part of the story to make himself look good. Chances were, if Haggard looked, he could find Gerson's description on a "wanted" flyer somewhere.

Gerson said, "One other thing, Haggard. When they left here, they took my rifle."

Rifle! Haggard's mouth went hard. No doubt about it, they meant business now. A woman with them, probably against her will. And a rifle.

It all meant one thing: when he found them, he would have to shoot fast and shoot straight!

10

They had spent almost a week at the Whitaker ranch, and now Speck seemed strong enough to try a hard ride.

In the rosy glow that came before the sunrise, Johnny Fristo tightened his cinch and looked across his horse at Speck swinging a saddle up onto the long-legged bay which Baker Fristo had given him. "Speck, you real sure you can make it now?"

Speck reached under the bay's belly for the saddle girth. "To get away from Milam Haggard, I could ride to Timbuktu."

"You still look a little peaked to me."

"Rather be sick than dead."

Johnny looked back toward the house and saw smoke curling up from the chimney. Out on the other side of the barn Dugan Whitaker was milking a Jersey cow. Johnny could hear the rhythmic strike of milk against the tin bucket as Whitaker squeezed with first one hand, then the other. Up on a shelf over Whitaker's head would be a steaming cup of coffee. Whitaker customarily carried a cup with him when he left the house. Wherever he finished the coffee, he would leave the cup. About once a week he would use up all the cups he had, and he would have to search the barns and corrals, making a roundup. Johnny had helped him with one yesterday.

Johnny said, "Time we get over to the house, they ought to have breakfast ready. Then we'll pull out."

"Let's eat and get started. I can almost smell old Haggard's breath on the back of my neck. Why he's not already here I'll never know."

A gate opened. Whitaker let his Jersey cow amble slowly out into the pasture. He shut the gate before her calf could get out with her. Whitaker came then, the bucket three-quarters full of milk and foam. He hadn't brought back his coffee cup, but Johnny didn't remind him of it. He figured a man was entitled to at least one bad habit, and this was the only one he had noticed in Whitaker.

The ranchman said, "Well, boys, this'll be your last woman-cooked meal for a while. Let's go get it." He was smiling, but Johnny thought the smile was strained. Whitaker hated seeing them leave, just as Johnny hated having to.

Except for worrying about Haggard, this had been a pleasant week for Johnny. He had spent his time working around the place, patching corrals, bracing a barn, pulling the windmill suckerrods, and changing leathers. He had felt guilty sometimes about not riding out with Whitaker to work cattle. But he hadn't wanted Speck to remain here alone and helpless if Haggard came. Though, if Haggard *had* come, Johnny had no idea what he could have done. One thing sure, Johnny didn't intend to fight him.

He had enjoyed the Whitakers. Dugan Whitaker had been a man much like Johnny's own father. Sarah Whitaker had amazed him constantly with her cheerful way and her uncanny ability to get around and do what she wanted in that wheelchair. He thought Whitaker must have had trouble keeping up with her when she had the use of her legs.

Most of all, Johnny had enjoyed being with Tessie Barnett. The hardest part of leaving was going to be in saying goodbye to her. He didn't know just when he had fallen in love with her, and it didn't really matter. What counted was that he had done it without wanting to, knowing there was no future for them, hoping for her sake that she didn't feel the same way but somehow wishing for his own sake that she did.

Tessie and Sarah Whitaker had breakfast on the table and waiting for them—eggs, steak, gravy, biscuits, coffee. Sarah Whitaker smiled just as Dugan had, and it was easy to see she had to work at it. "Eat aplenty, now. There's a lot of hungry country to the west of here."

Johnny glanced at Tessie. As his gaze touched her, she turned half around, hiding her face from him.

Dugan Whitaker set his bucket of milk on the cabinet for straining. "I don't want to seem like I'm pushin' you fellers, but it's gettin' daylight outside. I think for your sakes you better eat and get a move on."

Johnny had noted at least one sign of renewed strength in Speck: appetite. All his life Speck had made a good hand at the table or around the chuck wagon. As for Johnny, he felt a wintry sadness about leaving, and he had to push to make himself eat.

Mrs. Whitaker said, "Tessie and me, we've made an agreement, Johnny. She's not goin' to San Angelo."

Johnny looked up sharply.

Tessie said, "They've asked me to stay here with them, Johnny."

"That's right," Sarah put in. "She's got no place particular to go anyway. All she could earn in San Angelo would be a livin'. She'll get that here. She's been a world of help and company to us, like our daughter used to be."

Tessie nodded, and her eyes glistened a little. "That way, Johnny, you'll know where I am."

Johnny had worried about how she would fare in San Angelo. "That's fine, Tessie." He finished eating before Speck did. He said, "Speck, I'll go bring up the horses while you finish."

He walked out to the barn, taking his time, looking around him slowly. He wanted to remember this place. In time to come it might be a refuge for him—in his mind—a place for a restful mental retreat when the world seemed to close in around him. He glanced up at one of Whitaker's coffee cups balanced on a low rafter beneath a shed, and he smiled.

He had taken several minutes before he led the horses out the gate and closed it behind him. He swung up on Traveler, leading Speck's bay. A movement at the house caught his eye. He jerked his head around and saw Tessie running toward him, skirts flaring. "Hurry, Johnny, hurry!"

She pointed, and he saw the horseman outlined atop the hill, the sun rising like a golden ball of fire behind him.

Johnny didn't need binoculars. One glance and he somehow knew with a dreadful certainty. This was Milam Haggard!

The horses, fresh and rested, spooked backward as the girl rushed toward them. "Run, Johnny! You've still got time. Run!"

For a moment Johnny sat there confused and undecided, his hands tight on the reins. What good would it do now to run? Haggard would catch them. Yet, if they stayed and waited, what could they do?

"I'll get Speck," he said, and touched spurs to Traveler's ribs. He moved into a long trot, leading the bay toward the house.

"Speck! Come a-runnin'!"

But Speck didn't come. Johnny reined up at the house and shouted again. Sarah Whitaker pushed the screen door open with her chair and wheeled out onto the porch. "Johnny, he's taken the rifle and gone out the back."

"The rifle?"

For the first time in days Johnny remembered the rifle he had wrestled from Gerson. Except for this, they would have ridden off and forgotten it.

Dropping the bay's reins, he pulled his horse about and spurred around the house. "Speck! Speck, come back here!"

He glanced again toward Haggard. The ex-Ranger was quartering across toward the ranch headquarters, his dun horse in a steady trot. A pack horse followed. Speck was hunkered down behind a cedar. Johnny saw that in a few moments Haggard would ride in front of him. It occurred to Johnny then that Haggard had not seen Speck.

Speck—if he could hold himself in check long enough—could wait where he was and shoot Haggard out of the saddle at almost point-blank range.

For just a moment Johnny knew a sense of relief. That was an out. With Haggard dead they stood a chance.

But he knew this wasn't the way. The death of Haggard's wife had not actually been their fault, but this would put blood on their hands that would never wash away. They might be forgiven for the death of Cora Haggard, but never the murder of this man.

"Speck, hold up! Don't do it!"

Shouting, Johnny spurred into a run. "Speck, for God's sake put it down!"

Haggard saw Johnny moving toward him, and Johnny saw the man's hands come up holding a saddlegun. From behind him he heard Tessie scream. Speck brought up his rifle and leveled it across a branch of the cedar.

Johnny cried again, "No!"

Speck's rifle spat flame. Haggard rocked back, dropped the saddlegun, slumped forward and spilled out of the saddle. Haggard's horse jumped clear, wild-eyed with fright.

Speck straightened and began running toward Haggard, levering another cartridge into the breech. Johnny saw Haggard try vainly to push up onto his hands and knees.

Haggard still lived, and Speck was going to shoot him again.

Johnny spurred savagely. Speck hadn't listened to him before, and he wouldn't listen now. Speck heard the horse running. He stopped to look behind him, his eyes wide and desperate. Seeing Johnny meant to stop him, he turned and began running, trying to reach Haggard and finish him before Johnny could ride him down.

Speck stopped and raised the rifle to his shoulder. As he brought it level with Haggard's bent body, Johnny reached him. Johnny leaned from the saddle and grabbed at Speck as he rode by. He succeeded only in knocking him down. The rifle roared, the bullet plowing harmlessly into the ground. In desperation Speck scrambled on hands and knees, trying to reach the rifle. Johnny quit the saddle and came running. He got to the rifle just as Speck's fingers closed on the stock of it. He kicked, and the rifle went flying.

Speck turned his face upward, and Johnny saw that his partner was frantic with fear and rage. "Let me kill him, Johnny! Let me kill him!"

Johnny grabbed his friend's arms and tried to hold him. "Speck, come out of it!"

"We got to kill him, Johnny!"

Speck began fighting like a tiger, swinging his fists, kicking wildly. For a fleeting moment Johnny had time to wonder where Speck's strength came from. Then he was too busy fighting back.

"Speck, stop it!"

Speck threw himself at Johnny, punching savagely, shouting incoherently. Murder boiled in Speck's wild eyes.

There was no time now for regrets. Johnny put them aside soberly and fought as if he had never seen Speck before, as if this weren't the best friend he had in the world. He tried to avoid Speck's face with his fists. He punched Speck in the belly and the ribs with all the power he had. Speck had to be stopped.

Speck began losing the sudden desperate strength born of his fear. The fever weakness pulled him down. He slumped to his knees, hugging his arms against his sides, tears streaming down his face.

"Kill him, Johnny! You got to kill him!"

"Speck, haven't we done enough to him already?"

"It's him or us!"

"Then it'll have to be us!" Johnny turned away and reached down for the rifle. He opened the bolt, then smashed the weapon against the trunk of a cedar. He swung it again and again until he knew for sure it was broken and bent beyond any possible use. He pitched it away and stood a moment with pounding heart as he tried to get back his breath.

He walked to Haggard, dreading to look at the man. Haggard was on his knees, hunched over in pain. He wore a pistol, but he had made no move to draw it. He seemed paralyzed. Johnny drew the pistol from its holster and pitched it off into the brush.

"Let me see, Mister Haggard. How bad did he hit you?"

If Haggard heard, he gave no sign of it. His face was flour-white, his thin lips drawn tight against his teeth in a grinding agony. His right hand was gripped against his left shoulder, and blood dribbled between his clawed fingers.

"I'm sorry, Mister Haggard. I swear to God, I'm sorry."

Dugan Whitaker came, half running, half hopping. Tessie came, too, though she halted behind Haggard as if afraid to look at him. Johnny raised his eyes. "Mister Whitaker, we got to get him to the house." He glanced back over his shoulder. "Speck, you done it. Now you come help."

They carried Haggard as far as the porch. Whitaker said, "Tessie, you run in and fetch a blanket out here. That slug's still in him, and I got to have daylight to find it."

They laid Haggard out and tore the shirt off of him. They brought whisky to give him for the pain, but he passed into unconsciousness without needing it. Dugan Whitaker tried probing for the bullet, but his old hands would not hold still.

"Johnny, it's up to you. You can save him, or you can stand back and watch him die. But remember: if you save him, you know one day he'll still come lookin' for you."

Johnny grimly studied Haggard's gray face. "Give me the probe."

He got the bullet out. They washed the wound with whisky, then Sarah Whitaker used handfuls of flour to stop the bleeding. When they could, they carried him into the lean-to. They placed him on the same bed where Speck had lain.

"Mrs. Whitaker," Johnny said apologetically, "you got another one to tend. We don't bring you nothin' but trouble."

"The Lord's wish, not yours."

Johnny watched Speck closely, wondering if he might try again. But the spirit was gone from Speck now. He had made his try and failed. He stood with his shoulders drooped, eyes dulled by hopelessness.

Dugan Whitaker said, "Well, at least you got time now. It'll be a long while before he goes after you again."

Haggard stirred. Consciousness slowly returned to him. He blinked, trying to focus his eyes. Johnny stood beside his bed. "It's me, Mister Haggard. Me, Johnny Fristo. I just want you to know I'm sorry for what happened."

Haggard winced with pain, but he forced himself to hold his eyes a moment on Johnny. And Johnny saw the same implacability he had seen that day on the Sonora road.

Haggard's voice was thin, but it had a fierceness to it. "I won't be here long. One day soon I'll be lookin' for you again. And I vow, boy, I'll find you!"

Johnny turned away sadly, his head down. Why try to tell him again it had been Larramore who had killed his wife? Haggard hadn't believed him before. He would believe him even less now. Johnny dug into his pocket for the money Baker Fristo had given him.

"He'll be needin' a doctor, Mister Whitaker. You get him one, and pay him with this."

"You'll need that money yourself."

Johnny shook his head. "If it hadn't been for us, he wouldn't be here. Take it, please." He stopped and picked up a sack of food which Tessie and Mrs. Whitaker had prepared. "Come on, Speck. Let's go."

Outside, he tied the sack onto his own saddle, not trusting Speck to do it this time. He said goodbye first to Sarah, then to Dugan Whitaker. Last he took Tessie's hands. "Tessie, it's been awful good to know you. Take care of yourself."

"Johnny . . ." She would have said more, but the words died. She leaned forward and kissed him on the lips, then pulled her hands free and turned her back, her head bowed.

Johnny rode away, looking over his shoulder. Speck followed him like a whipped dog. Johnny kept looking back, seeing the Whitakers watching him, seeing that Tessie had turned once more and was watching him too.

Suddenly Johnny stopped his horse. "Speck, wait here. I'll be back."

He turned Traveler around and spurred into a long

trot. He stepped to the ground in front of Tessie. He grabbed her into his arms with such a violence that his hat fell off and hit the ground at his feet.

"Tessie, Tessie, I don't want to leave you."

"And I don't want you to leave. But what can we do?"

"I'll send for you, that's what." He held her at arm's length and looked into her glistening eyes. "Someday, somewhere, I'll come onto a place that's so far out of the way Haggard'll never be able to find it. When I do, and when I get settled, I'll write to you, Tessie. I'll send for you."

"Promise, Johnny?"

"I promise. Now that I've known you, Tessie, I couldn't live without you anymore."

"I'll wait, Johnny, and I'll be ready. I'll follow you if you go ten thousand miles."

He held her again, once, then he turned on his heel, swung up into the saddle and rode away.

Inside the house, Milam Haggard's teeth were clenched against a searing pain. But the pain did not keep him from hearing.

11

They quartered west by southwest, skirting the upper reaches of Centralia Draw and pointing in a general way toward ancient Horsehead Crossing. They rode dry all day through greasewood and stunted mesquite and patches of prickly pear. Not even a windmill showed on the skyline. They were west now of any living waters which would feed into the Middle Concho. This was the desolate stretch of lizard and rattlesnake and chaparral-hawk country which had brought misery and desperation to untold numbers of travelers making their way toward the unfriendly river known as the Pecos.

Before night they reached the China Pond. In front of them, and all to the south, stretched a long line of flat blue mountains. Their profile was low, but Johnny knew they were rough, impassable for wagons and difficult for horsemen. All trails led across the desert toward a scalloped opening near the northern edge. This would be Castle Gap, known for centuries as a pointer to Horsehead just beyond.

"This is a good place to stop, Speck. We got water here."

Speck only nodded. He had sulked all day, speaking perhaps half a dozen words since they had left the

Whitaker ranch. This was remarkable for Speck. Instead of riding alongside Johnny, he had hung back half a length. When Johnny would slow to allow Speck to pull up even with him, Speck would draw back and keep the distance about the same. His brooding eyes avoided Johnny.

They made camp at the China Pond. Automatically Speck rode off to try to gather up some firewood. He came back without any, and Johnny used dried cow-chips for fuel to cook a little supper. Later Speck sat back from the tiny fire and ate listlessly, keeping his own counsel. Johnny watched him, wondering what dark thoughts plodded through Speck's troubled mind.

"Speck, you still mad at me because of this mornin'?"

Speck didn't answer.

"I had to do it. We're not killers."

Speck's gaze touched him a moment. Resentfully he said, "You fought me. You used to call yourself my friend, and you fought me."

"I'm still your friend."

A pent-up anger began boiling over. "No, you ain't. You think you're better than I am. I've felt it comin' on ever since we stopped in Angelo. Aunt Pru told you about me, and my mother. Now I'm not good enough for you anymore. I'm trash."

"Speck, that's the silliest notion I ever heard of."

"No, it isn't. There was a time you wouldn't have fought me for nothin' in this world. Now you'd like to take that girl and ride off and leave me. But you can't because you know we're in this together. You're stuck with me and you hate it. You hate *me*."

Johnny's impatience melted away, for his pity was stronger. "You're all mixed up, Speck. I like you the same as I always did. If it's any consolation to you, what your Aunt Pru said didn't make any difference atall. I've known about your mother for years."

Speck stared incredulously. "You mean you always knew, and you never let on?" Johnny nodded. Speck exploded. "That makes it even worse. All these years you been actin' like my friend, and all the time you was probably snickerin' at me behind my back."

He stood up and stomped off to where he had pitched his blanket to the ground. He spread it out and flopped down on his back, lying there and staring angrily up at the darkening sky.

Johnny's jaw took on a hard set. No use arguing. Speck had a haywire way of thinking, sometimes. He'd come around by and by.

At least, Johnny hoped he would.

Next morning they went on to the gap. Johnny noticed horse and cattle bones all along the way. This had always been a cruel trail. Curiosity held him in the gap awhile. Nearby he found the burned remnants of several wagons. He wondered if these were the result of some long-ago Indian attack, a bandit raid or if someone had just gotten careless with fire. If a raid, there was no question about the outcome. If an accidental fire, what had the victims done afterward? Here, so far from civilization, the loss of wagons and supplies in those earlier times could have meant the same eventual outcome: death. There was no way to know for sure now, for the charred wooden skeletons and the dark ashes had been reduced by long years of probing wind and occasional rain. Johnny sat on his horse and looked, and he let his imagination sweep him away. For a while he wished he could have been born fifty years earlier.

But eventually he heard Speck grumbling about how

they ought to be going, and he grudgingly came back to reality, back to his own problems. Trouble, he knew, was something each generation shared.

No one had a monopoly on it.

Johnny pointed across the gently rolling stretch of greasewood which lay below. "Down yonder, Speck, is Horsehead Crossing. Been a lot of history made along here."

Speck was still grumpy but a little more disposed to talk this morning. "Maybe you can see the history, but all I can see is a lizard-lick of a country that ain't worth a Mexican dollar if you got back ninety cents change."

They followed the bone-strewn trail twelve miles and came at last to the river. Here was fabled Horsehead with its sloping banks which led down to swift-moving water. This was the only place for a long journey up or down the river where the banks were such that wagons and livestock could go down into the water with a reasonable chance of coming out again on the opposite side.

A big scattering of animal bones lay along here. At this spot some thirty years before, Charles Goodnight had lost part of a Longhorn cattle herd in alkaline water and treacherous quicksands, and had pronounced the Pecos River the graveyard of a cowman's hopes.

Johnny saw a trail that angled off upriver. "This ought to lead the way up to the salt lake, Speck. That's where Dugan Whitaker told us to go."

Speck shivered, though the morning was warm. "Let's get ridin', then. This place makes my skin crawl."

They followed the wagon trail northwestward, roughly paralleling the snaking river and its line of salt-cedar trees. As they approached the Juan Cordona salt lake, the hard alkali soil began giving way gradually to more of sand. Heat waves shimmered on the horizon as the salt basin came into view.

They met a Mexican burro train moving downriver, the plodding little beasts carrying a heavy burden of white salt in huge twin baskets of rawhide and green willow. The ragged Mexican at the head of the train stared briefly at the cowboys, his eyes all but hidden under the wide, floppy brim of an incredibly old sombrero. He nodded, spoke a two-word greeting and walked on. Johnny watched the short-stepping burros move by him, the salt baskets bobbing from side to side with the rhythm of their walk. The Mexican *mulateros* were grayed with dust, their tattered shirts soaked with sweat and clinging to their bodies. Only one wore shoes, and these had been patched with rawhide. The rest had only simple *huaraches,* a thick sole held to the foot by leather thongs, protecting against thorns, sharp rocks and burning sand.

Johnny said solemnly, "Whenever a man gets to feelin' sorry for himself, he needs to take a look at somebody worse off than he is."

Speck grunted. "I bet they ain't got Milam Haggard lookin' for them."

The "lake" was a vast irregular stretch of shining salt, lying in an ancient basin rimmed by sandhills. The level bottom glistened in the sun, though along the edges a thin skim of dust had settled and turned it brown. There was feed here for livestock—a scattering of sand-type bunchgrasses and weeds. There was the tough green beargrass with its rapier-like stems and the tall yucca stalks. And here and there about the lake lay a dotting of camps, salt haulers of all types.

Johnny and Speck rode into two burro camps

without finding anyone who spoke English. The third camp they found had half a dozen heavy wagons already full of salt and several more wagons in the process of being loaded by Mexican help. A crew sweated in the sun, their shovels slowly pitching dry salt into the wagons. A dark-skinned man saw the cowboys and came walking toward them. His beard was black beneath a crust of dust and salt. Johnny took him for a Mexican until he spoke. "Howdy. You-all lookin' for somebody in particular?"

Johnny nodded. "We're supposed to find a feller name of Massingill."

The salt freighter stared at the pair, his eyes narrowed. "You-all ain't lawmen or somethin'? Ain't got a warrant for somebody?"

Johnny shook his head. "No, sir, we just got a letter for Mister Massingill, is all. Friend of his sent it. Man name of Dugan Whitaker."

The bearded man smiled. His shoulders sagged in relief. "That's different. My name happens to be Massingill. Folks call me Gyp, on account of the Pecos River water I tote in my barrels." He reached up to shake hands. "Afraid at first you might be star-packers. I'm already shorthanded, and I sure didn't want you takin' off none of my help. You say you got a letter?"

Johnny handed him a letter which Dugan Whitaker had spent an hour in writing by lamplight the night before Johnny and Speck had left the ranch. "We're in kind of a jackpot, Mister Massingill. Dugan Whitaker, he thought you might be able to help us."

Massingill squatted in the shade of a wagon. It took him almost as long to read the letter as it had taken Whitaker to write it. His index finger followed the lines as he slowly read, his lips forming the words. At last he looked up. "A jackpot, you say? Looks to me like it's a right smart worse than that. I've seen Milam Haggard. How far behind you is he?"

Johnny explained about the shooting at the Whitaker ranch.

Massingill frowned suspiciously. "You-all must've known old Dugan a long time."

Johnny shook his head. "Never met him before."

"You sure must've convinced him you was all right. Or maybe you held a gun at his head to make him write this letter."

"No, sir, he wrote it of his own accord. He was awful good to us, him and Mrs. Whitaker both. This is the first time we ever been in trouble. They knew it."

Massingill studied them awhile, his eyes keen. They burned like the sun through a magnifying glass. Finally he nodded. "Well, if you convinced old Dugan, I guess that'll do for me. He's not an easy man fooled." He folded the letter and shoved it into his pocket. "And if Haggard has been laid up with a bullet in him, that means you got some time. We don't have to do things in a hurry. I'll make you a swap. You help me, and I'll help you."

Johnny nodded eagerly. "Anything you want."

"Well, the way I see it, Haggard will be a-lookin' for you-all to go on west. That's where any smart man on the dodge would go. So we'll fool him. Soon's I get these wagons full I'm takin' this salt south, down the Pecos River. There's ranches off down in there that a man wouldn't find in a hundred years if he didn't know where to look. It's a big country, some of it so big and dry that a hawk won't leave the nest without it carries a canteen. I'll take you down there with me, and I'll get you a job on some outfit where the whole United States army couldn't find you."

"That's mighty good of you, Mister Massingill."

"Gyp! And don't thank me till you find out how good your hands fit a shovel handle. I'll swap you a ride on my wagons in return for your muscles and your sweat. Sooner we get them wagons loaded with salt, the sooner we start down the river.

"You'll find the shovels over yonder!"

12

Patience was part of a manhunter's stock in trade—difficult to learn, but indispensable. Milam Haggard had learned it long ago. It served him well now in this small settlement on the Centralia, for without it he could not have forced himself to remain here idle—waiting, watching, biding his time. It had been most of three months now since he had lain bleeding at the Whitaker ranch, listening to fading hoofbeats as the two cowboys rode away.

Even without hearing it, he sensed the speculation which his long stay had started among the townspeople and the ranchmen who ranged their cattle on bluestems and tobosa grass up and down the creeks and draws. He had not chosen to tell them why he had remained here, though doubtless they could guess most of it. Only one person in town, besides himself, knew the full reason.

To be sure, the whole country knew who he was and knew of his mission. They knew his wife had died as an innocent bystander in a fight along the Sonora–San Angelo road. They knew Haggard had been shot at the Whitaker ranch and that he had come riding in here as soon as he was able to mount a horse by himself, disclaiming any further help from the cowboys' friends. It was common knowledge that Dugan and Sarah Whitaker would still argue the fugitives' case to anyone who cared to listen.

It was well known also that Haggard was no longer a Ranger, that he had been unable to get official backing in his search for the two cowboys. At least two Ranger friends, to the knowledge of the townspeople, had come here to talk with him. Common belief was that they were trying to talk him out of his quest.

Why then, people asked each other, was he still here? Granted, his left shoulder was still stiff and appeared to give him some pain. But those who from afar had watched this gaunt, unsmiling man at target practice beyond the edge of town could testify that his eye was keen and his aim was ungodly straight. Haggard lived in a small shack on which he paid a token rent. Though civil enough, he made no effort to cultivate new friendships. He received no company except for a couple of ranchmen who had known him down south in the Ranger service. They stopped in occasionally to see how he was getting along, for they felt a genuine concern. He spent his time reading, exercising the shoulder and practicing at targets.

Some careful observers had noted that he always watched the mail hack when it arrived at the small general store that served as a post office. Inevitably he was among the first to be there as the storekeeper sorted the mail. It had become something of a routine, which seldom varied. Haggard would go straight to the corner where the mail was put up in small individual boxes. "Anything today, John?"

The storekeeper would always shake his head. "Maybe next time."

It had become so repetitious that the early flurry of speculation had died down, and many people largely lost interest. Most agreed he was either awaiting a renewal of his Ranger commission to make his search legal, or during his long recovery period he had sent someone ahead to track down the fugitives and now waited for word as to their whereabouts.

Whatever the storekeeper knew, he wasn't talking.

Milam Haggard had never been a drinking man. He did not believe it wise in his trade. Often he had observed how liquor had made quarry fall easy prey to a gun in the hands of a sober man.

But Haggard was a lonelier man than most people suspected, and once in a while he welcomed a visit from old friends. On such occasions, though he did not drink, he sometimes accompanied his friends to the saloon and sat there to enjoy their companionship.

Thus it was that he happened to walk into the place one afternoon and find himself face-to-face with the cattle trader Larramore.

Larramore was playing cards with two prospective cow buyers. The surprise was mutual. Larramore's eyes opened wide and frightened, his face losing color. In Sonora that day after Cora Haggard's death, Larramore had sensed how close he came to being shot when the sheriff told Milam Haggard about the swindle against the two cowboys. Though Haggard blamed the shooting directly on Johnny Fristo and Speck Quitman, he had immediately grasped the fact that Larramore's duplicity had provoked the incident. Haggard's granite fist had sent Larramore reeling. Larramore had lain terrified, not moving, knowing that if Haggard had been wearing a gun he would have killed him without ceremony and without regret.

Seeing Haggard now, Larramore arose shakily, his voice strained. "Haggard, I been tryin' to stay out of your way just like you told me. I had no idea you was here." His glance dropped anxiously to the six-shooter on Haggard's right hip.

Haggard only stared at him, his eyes hard and hating.

Larramore watched Haggard's right hand. "Haggard, I ain't got a gun on me." That was a lie, for he carried a small .38 in his boottop. But he feared if Haggard even suspected its presence, he might force Larramore to reach for it. It would have been no contest.

Haggard's narrowed eyes seemed to crackle with danger. "Larramore, those cowboys still claim you were the one who really fired the shot. I know you said you didn't, but I want to hear you say it again."

Larramore trembled. "It was *them*. They both had guns."

"That's a lie. Only one of them had a gun. And *you* had one."

"It was *them* that killed her. It was them!" The trader dropped his chin, unable to look into Haggard's face.

Haggard cut his gaze to the two men who had been playing cards at the table with Larramore. One he recognized as a rancher south of here. He took the other for a rancher, too. They sat watching in surprise, not quite comprehending. Haggard asked, "You-all have business with this man?"

One of them replied hesitantly, "He told us he knew where there was some cattle we could buy worth the money."

Haggard's voice was raw. "You'd better have nothin' to do with him. He's a thief, a liar and a cheat!"

Larramore jerked his head up. "Haggard, you got no right . . ."

Haggard's eyes cut back to him, and they were deadly. Larramore's words stuck in his throat. Haggard's voice sliced like the razor edge of a skinning knife. "Leave town, Larramore. Leave this part of the country. Next time I see you, I'll probably kill you!"

He turned sharply and started for the door. Larramore stared after him, frozen.

Haggard had just reached the door when the bartender shouted. Instinctively he jumped to one side, whirling as his right hand dropped and came up with the six-shooter.

Larramore crouched awkwardly, having reached down to his boottop for the .38. No gunman, he fired wildly. The bullet smacked into the doorframe and sent wood splinters flying. He never got a chance to fire again. Haggard's pistol roared like thunder inside the small saloon. Larramore stepped back under the driving impact. He began bending forward from the waist, the .38 slipping from his fingers. He screamed. Then the scream died off, and he pitched forward onto his face.

Haggard cautiously moved toward him, kicking the .38 out of the way. He stooped and turned Larramore over into his back, the strain bringing a stabbing pain to the old shoulder wound. "How about it, Larramore? *Was* it you who killed her?"

Larramore made a feeble effort to speak. Then he went limp. He died with his eyes and his mouth open.

Haggard pushed to his feet, the shoulder throbbing

a little. He shook his head and spoke to no one in particular. "It doesn't matter, I guess. They *all* killed her."

I t was a rare occasion when Dugan Whitaker came to town. Since Milam Haggard had ridden away from the Whitaker ranch on his dun, slumped over the saddle horn in pain but too proud to remain any longer under that roof, he had seen Whitaker only once. They had nodded civilly and gone their separate ways. Taking care of his place virtually alone, Whitaker didn't have much time for coming to the settlement.

But this morning, sitting in front of the shack and watching the dark clouds which built threateningly in the north, Haggard saw the Whitakers pass by in their buckboard. Dugan and Sarah Whitaker gave him a polite nod, but nothing more. The Barnett girl only stared, and Haggard thought he saw fear leap into her face. During the time he had been at the ranch, wounded, the girl had kept her distance as if he had been a rattlesnake.

Haggard regretted that. He saw fear everywhere these days, since he had killed Larramore. He wanted respect, not fear. But that was part of the business. He had come to expect it, even if he didn't welcome it.

He hadn't been back to the saloon. He doubted he would ever go. As he heard it, the bartender hadn't even cleaned up the blood. He had purposely left it to soak a dark stain deep into the wood. Now it had become an attraction for the idle curious. This brought a rush of resentment every time it crossed Haggard's mind. He was not an exhibitionist. Killing a man had never pleased him. He had always dreaded it, and he had regretted it when it was done.

He had thought there might be a grim pleasure in killing someone who had had a part in Cora's death. But to his surprise the sight of Larramore dead on that dirty saloon floor had brought only the same old revulsion to sicken him.

Of late he had spent much time thinking about his ranch up on the Colorado River. He had a few cowboys hired, and he felt sure they were taking care of it for him. But he wished he could go up there, find out how things looked, see if summer rains had greened the grass and fattened the cattle. He had grown to hate his vigil here. The thought of following another long trail in a lonely search for fugitives was abhorrent to him.

But again, there was his training, and his pride. He had made a vow over the fresh mound where they had laid Cora to rest. He had never broken a vow in his life. He wouldn't break this one, though sometimes he had to conjure up a vision of Cora's face to give him the strength that he could carry on this way.

Watching the Whitakers' buckboard wheel on down toward the heart of the settlement, Haggard suddenly remembered this was the day for the mail hack. And it was due about now, give or take an hour. He didn't want the Whitakers receiving their mail before he got there.

Squaring his hat, he started up the dusty road afoot. To his satisfaction he found the Whitaker buckboard sitting in front of a different store. Dugan Whitaker and Tessie Barnett were lifting Sarah Whitaker down into her wheelchair. Haggard looked east on the wagon road that led in from San Angelo. He saw dust. He wondered if that would be the mail hack.

Well, this was going to be cutting things pretty fine.

He sat down on an empty bench at the front of the store to wait. His gaze drifted up and down the street, cutting back often to the Whitaker buckboard. He hoped they wouldn't come over this way before the hack got in.

The driver pulled up, the dust drifting on ahead of him. He nodded at Haggard and carried the mail bag inside. Haggard kept his seat awhile, giving the store-keeper time to put up the mail. There wasn't any hurry about it, so long as the Whitakers didn't come. Even so, it seemed it took an awfully long time. Finally the hack driver came out and nodded again, wiping his mouth. The storekeeper always had coffee ready for him. He took time to drink it before he traveled on. Haggard glanced through the window constantly to see if the mail had been sorted. The seat of his pants prickled with impatience. When he saw the store-keeper leave the mail corner, he arose and walked inside.

The storekeeper's eyes met his, and Haggard knew even before the man nodded. "It came, Mister Haggard."

"You're sure?"

The storekeeper nodded again. "It's addressed to Miss Tessie Barnett, care of Dugan Whitaker."

"Let me have it, John."

"Well, now, I can't be doin' that. It's agin the law."

"Damn the law! Give me that letter!"

"I promised I'd tell you when it came. I didn't tell you I'd give it to you. It's still the U.S. mail, Mister Haggard, till the girl puts her hands on it. There can't nobody touch it. Not you and not me."

Anger swelled in Haggard. He was sorely tempted to walk across and take the letter anyway. But judgment stopped him. Unreasoning anger was another luxury he had never allowed himself. "All right. I'll wait."

He walked to the door and started to go outside. But he saw Tessie Barnett on her way, walking rapidly several steps in front of old Dugan Whitaker. Haggard stepped back, looking quickly around him. He saw an open door leading into a storeroom. "Not a word, John." He stepped through the door and out of sight.

Tessie came in, Dugan Whitaker hurrying along in a vain effort to catch up with her. "Tessie," he laughed, "go easy. Have some pity on an old man."

Tessie might as well not have heard him. Eyes sparkling in anticipation, she searched out the storekeeper. "Do you have any mail for me? Tessie Barnett?"

The storekeeper took his time, glancing at the open storeroom door. He knew what was about to happen. "Yes, ma'am, I believe maybe I do." He walked over to the corner and sought out a letter from among a dozen. Regretfully he placed it in her eager hands. "This what you've been waitin' for?"

Excitement leaped into Tessie's face. "Uncle Dugan, it's from *him*; I *know* it is!"

Haggard stepped out of the storeroom, unnoticed by Tessie and Whitaker. The storekeeper turned his back and walked away, wanting no part of this. Tessie ripped the envelope open, her hands trembling. "Uncle Dugan, it *is* from him, it *is*!"

Milam Haggard stepped up beside her and snatched the letter from her hands. "I'll take that!"

She whirled. Seeing him, she raised one hand up over her mouth. Her eyes were big as dollars. "You!"

Dugan Whitaker made a grab for the letter. "Haggard, you got no right!"

Haggard stepped back and turned half around, keeping the letter out of his reach. "I *have* got the right."

He skipped the opening lines, for they spoke of loneliness, and he knew all there was to know about that. His gaze dropped farther down in the letter:

This is a good ranch. A little on the plain side, maybe, but your going to like it here Tessie. Theres a good adobe house the owner says we can live in. Kind of little but big enough for two. I think we can slip down to Langtry and get Judge Bean to marry us without anybody paying us much notice.

You would never find the place by yourself. So will meet you at Horsehead Crossing on the Pecos. Maybe Mr. Whitaker can bring you or get somebody to. Will be there about Sept. the 15. Bring your wagon. Will wait till you come and please hurry.

Horsehead Crossing! Haggard crunched the letter in his hand. September the fifteenth! Why, that was yesterday! This letter must have traveled halfway around the world before it reached here.

So Fristo was already there, waiting! And Quitman with him, if Haggard was any judge.

He knew a quiet moment of triumph, then his face turned grave. A chill passed down his back as he turned to Tessie Barnett and saw the dismay in her eyes. It struck him that she was a pretty girl. Silently he handed her the letter. Sympathy touched him. Pity she had gotten mixed up in this. Pity she had to know the heartbreak that was coming. But she was young, and she would survive. In time she might even learn to understand the necessity of it. Anyway, there was no choice. The die had been cast. Haggard had long since developed an instinct for the inevitable. The thing was coming to an end now, as sure as the sun would rise and set tomorrow.

The girl's eyes pleaded. "Mister Haggard, you can't do it. Please, say you're not going to do it!"

She had as well have talked to the big wood heater that stood cold and unused in the center of the store. Haggard looked at Dugan Whitaker. "I'm sorry it's this way, Mister Whitaker. I think you'd best take her home." He turned his back and walked to the door. Tessie stared after him, the letter crushed in her hand. The dismay had turned to terror.

"No!" she screamed and went running after him.

Haggard hurried his step a little, wanting to get away from her. He went down off the porch and into the dusty street, his eyes set on the barn where his dun horse was kept stabled. Clouds were darkening overhead.

"Mister Haggard, wait!"

He tried to outwalk her. How could a man argue over a thing like this? How could he explain why he had to go on? For God's sake, didn't she already know?

She grabbed his good arm. Head high, he kept walking, his strength pulling her along. "Please, Mister Haggard, listen to me. What good will it do to kill him? Will *she* come back? Will another wrong make things right?" He walked on, trying not to listen. "I love him, Mister Haggard. If you loved *her*, you should understand that."

He swallowed, trying to shut his ears. She stepped

in front of him, still holding his arm. He tried to step around her, but she was faster and blocked him. He wrested his arm free. She grabbed it again. Weary of the contest, he stopped.

"Why, Mister Haggard? Tell me why!"

"You know why. He helped to kill my wife."

"He didn't shoot her. Larramore did."

"All you know is what he told you."

"I know *him*, and I know he told the truth."

"Whoever actually fired the shot, they were all responsible. They all killed her. They'll all pay."

"He had mercy on *you*. Won't you have mercy on him?"

Haggard frowned. "*He* had mercy on *me*?"

"Speck Quitman tried to kill you. Johnny stopped him. He knew you meant to kill him, but he wouldn't let Speck kill you. He even took the bullet out of you." Haggard made no reply. She argued, "And he left every cent he had with the Whitakers to pay a doctor to take care of you."

"I didn't accept it. I paid my own way."

"But he *tried*. That's important, isn't it? He tried."

Grimly Haggard said, "Would his money buy my wife back to life? She's dead. Nothing he has done since will change that."

"Will his dying change it?"

He held silent a moment, wanting to say something but not knowing what. "Miss, I'm sorry for you, but there's nothing I can do. There's a blood debt to settle. I'm goin' to see that it's paid!"

He glanced at her face again, and he saw that her terror was gone. In its place was a stiff anger, and perhaps even hatred. "You know what you are, Haggard?" She had dropped the *mister*. "You're a killer. You're a lawman because that makes it legal for you, but if you couldn't be a lawman you'd be an outlaw. You won't listen to reason because you *have* no reason. You're like an animal; it's your nature to kill. It's a disease with you.

"You pretend you're doing this out of love for your wife, but you're lying to us, and you may even be lying to yourself. You've hunted men so long it's turned you into some kind of a wolf. Maybe it's better for her that she *is* dead. She couldn't have lived with you very long. In your own way, you'd have killed her yourself!"

Anger rushed to his face. He lifted his hand as if to strike her, but he stopped himself.

"Go ahead," she taunted him, "hit me. Shoot me, even. If you've got to kill somebody, maybe *I'll* do."

Abruptly he turned away from her. She shouted, "I swear to you, Haggard, if you kill Johnny I'll see you *dead!* Then who'll kill *me?* Where will it ever end?"

Thunder rolled in the distance. Haggard wished it were louder. He walked on, wishing he couldn't hear her, wishing he couldn't feel the stinging lash of her hatred.

Tessie stood in the middle of the street with her small fists clenched and watched Haggard walk stolidly toward the barn. Dugan Whitaker came up from behind and put his hand on her shoulder. "You can't reason with him, girl. I'm afraid the only way anybody could stop him now would be to kill him."

"Uncle Dugan, maybe *you* . . ."

"Could kill him?" He shook his head. "Tessie, I'd do almost anything for you. But that is one thing I couldn't do."

"I didn't mean that. But we've got to warn Johnny."

"It's a long ride to Horsehead. Our buckboard couldn't get there before Haggard and his horse."

"But a horseback rider might, if he was desperate enough."

"Honey, I'm old. There was a time, but I'm not that tough anymore. Haggard would outlast me and out-run me."

"*I'm* young, and I'm desperate enough."

"*You?*" His face furrowed. "It's a hard trip for a girl."

"I've been here three months. I've learned aplenty, and I've toughened a lot. I've got a good reason to make this ride. A better reason than Haggard has."

Doubt hovered in Dugan Whitaker's narrowed eyes. But there was also understanding. "You won't make it, girl. But you'll regret it all your life if you don't make the try. Come on, I know where I can get you a horse." He frowned. "But what if you *do* make it? Even if you do warn Johnny and he runs, what then? Haggard will keep on comin'. He won't stop."

"Then *we'll* keep running, Johnny and me. I should have gone with him before. I'll stay with him this time."

"That's no life, a-runnin'."

"It's better than dying. We'll live while we can."

13

Mean enough even in normal times, the Pecos River was on an angry rise. Sodden gray clouds loomed heavy to the north and west. A light mist enveloped this desolate greasewood barren which stretched outward in all directions from Horsehead Crossing.

Johnny Frisco stirred a glowing cowchip fire and put on a smoke-blackened can to boil a mixture of ground coffee and brackish Pecos River water. He reached under a tarp for a couple of dry chips out of a pile which he and Speck had gathered yesterday before the rain started. Chips were about the only fuel here fit to use—"prairie coal," some called them. A man could start a fire with dead greasewood, but it burned too quickly to cook with. Other campers at the crossing had long since used up any dead brush which may have stood along the river.

Speck Quitman rolled his blankets and frowned up at the low-hanging clouds. "Johnny, ain't that girl ever goin' to get here? This is the spookiest place I was ever at."

They had been here three days. Johnny was getting tired of it too. "I told you twenty times, Speck, the letter may have got held up. Not much tellin' when that Mexican got to a post office to mail it."

Speck had changed during the three months or so they had worked on that ranch way down south along the Pecos. He didn't eat much, and he didn't sleep. He smoked up all the tobacco he could get his hands on, and those hands were unsteady. Always when the work would lag a moment, Speck's gaze would lift to the horizon, and fear clouded his eyes.

He had run out of talk a long time ago.

Watching steam start rising from the can, Johnny wished they had been able to fetch along a wagon instead of depending on Tessie to bring hers. A-horseback they hadn't been able to carry much camping equipment. For one thing, he wished they had a barrel so they could fill it and let the water settle before they used it. The flooded river was carrying a lot of mud.

It hadn't tasted very good even before. Now it was about all a man's stomach could stand.

Horsehead Crossing wasn't a pleasant place to camp anyway. There was no shelter. From here back to Castle Gap, all Johnny could see was waist-high greasewood and a scattering of tall Spanish Daggers that had a worrisome way of looking like men, especially in the twilight or in a thin mist like this. He had thought at first Speck was going to come unwound here. Twenty times Speck had sworn he saw one of the daggers move, that it was Milam Haggard. Johnny hadn't wanted to bring Speck here in the first place, but Speck wouldn't have stayed on that ranch without Johnny for all the silver coin west of the Conchos.

Johnny felt an ominous presence about this place, a vague but unmistakable sense of death. For three hundred years white men had known this crossing and had used it—Spaniards first, then the Mexicans and finally the Americans. Indians had swum across here for countless centuries before that. No one knew how many men had died within a stone's throw of this spot. Johnny had found a number of graves along the trail, some of them marked, some of them not. The Pecos was deep and usually swift. Many of the men buried here had underestimated the river.

Then, too, there had been the Indians. Until twenty years or so ago, the fearsome Comanches had haunted this forsaken region. Warfare to them had been a game, though a bloody one. The Comanche War Trail to Mexico had led across here. Only God knew how many captive Mexican women and children had been dragged here in hopeless captivity. No telling how many horses and cattle the Comanches had taken here, or how many scalps. A man halfway across the river made a helpless target.

Bleached bones of horses and cattle told a silent story of hardship and death. They set the mood for this lonesome place, and a cheerless mood it was.

Even as men had used this crossing, they had cursed it.

Speck looked into the steaming can and found to his disappointment that the coffee wasn't ready. He looked eastward again, his face drawn and listless. Then he stiffened. "Johnny, I see somebody comin'."

Johnny glanced up a moment and then said crisply, "Speck, there isn't anybody comin'. Will you ever quit seein' things?"

Speck narrowed his eyes, still peering worriedly through the mist. "I'd of swore . . ." His face was grave.

"He's a-comin' though, Johnny. Milam Haggard is comin'. I can feel it in my bones."

"Speck, you've felt Milam Haggard in your bones ever since that mornin' on the Sonora road. There hasn't been a day you haven't looked for him to come."

Speck shivered, and not altogether from the damp air. "There hasn't been an *hour*!" He squatted on his heels and stared eastward, not satisfied that he had been wrong.

Watching him, Johnny felt a touch of pity. Sure, *he* had worried too, but not like Speck. Haggard had become an obsession with him. It seemed the farther they got away from Haggard, the more certain Speck became that they would be found.

Speck poured coffee into a tin cup and sucked his fingers to ease the burn he had taken from the hot can. "Johnny, what if Haggard does come? We ain't even got a gun."

"He lost us, Speck. He's got no idea where we're at. Besides, what would we do with a gun if we had it? We're not goin' to shoot him, not again."

"*I* would. If he was to die, we could live. As long as he lives he's hangin' over our heads like them clouds up there. I'd've killed him that other time if you'd left me alone."

Johnny had argued this out with Speck a hundred times. But nothing was ever final with Speck. Whatever was dwelling on his mind, he always came back to it, picking over the cold bones again and again. "And then what, Speck? He was right; we were wrong. Instead of *him* comin' after us alone, there'd have been a hundred or two of them, and we'd of been dead now instead of sittin' here at Horsehead."

"Might be better dead than to live the way we do,

afraid every time we see a stranger. Seein' him all day and *her* all night."

Sadly Johnny shrugged. "Speck, I wish I knew what to tell you."

Speck kept watching the horizon. At length he pushed to his feet excitedly, dropping his cup and splashing coffee out onto the wet ground. "Johnny, it *is* somebody. Look!"

Johnny squinted. Speck was right. Yonder came a rider.

Speck blurted, "It's *him*; it's got to be. Let's saddle up and skin out of here!"

"Be sensible for once, Speck. It won't be Haggard. How could he know?"

"He just knows, that's all. He ain't human."

"He's human enough to get himself shot." But arguing with Speck was as fruitless as talking to that stack of cowchips under the tarp. Speck grabbed up his saddle, blanket and bridle and hurried out to where his horse was picketed. Johnny watched him throw the rig up onto the horse's back.

"Speck, even if it *was* Haggard, where would you go?"

"I'd head out across that river."

"It's too high. You couldn't swim it."

"With *him* after me I could swim the Mississippi."

Johnny gave up arguing. Time was when he could talk sense to Speck, now and again. Lately he couldn't reach him at all. Johnny turned to watch the oncoming rider. Something about the horseman struck him oddly.

"It's a woman, Speck. She's a-ridin' sidesaddle." The rider came nearer. Johnny exclaimed, "Speck, it's Tessie. It's Tessie!"

Speck had just finished tightening the cinch. With relief he said, "High time she was gettin' here. Only, where's her wagon?"

Johnny trotted out afoot to meet her. Recognizing him, she called his name. Johnny reached up for her and brought her down from the saddle and crushed her in his arms. "Tessie, we'd all but given you up. But why did you come by yourself?"

Her voice was urgent. "We've got no time to talk. Milam Haggard's on his way."

His stomach went cold. "Haggard?"

"He got hold of your letter, Johnny. I've ridden as hard as I could to get ahead of him. I passed him in the gap. And he knows it."

Speck had heard. His face drained. "Johnny, I told you I felt it. He's comin'." His voice cracked. "He's comin', and we're goin' to die!"

Johnny spoke impatiently, "Speck, hush up that kind of talk. We got to think."

"It's too late for that. You do what you want to. Me, I'm high-tailin' it across that river. It's still on the rise. Time he gets here maybe he won't be able to follow me."

"It's already too late, Speck. Water's too high."

"With the river we got a chance. With Haggard we got none atall."

Speck swung into the saddle and touched spurs to the bay horse.

Johnny stared after him, not quite believing. "Speck, have you gone plumb crazy? You come back here!"

Speck kept riding.

"Speck," Johnny called anxiously, "if you've got the sense God gave a jackrabbit you'll come back here!" He ran after Speck afoot. Speck saw that Johnny intended to stop him. He spurred again, putting the horse into a long trot. As Speck looked back, Johnny caught a glimpse of his friend's fearstricken face. "Speck, for God's sake stop!"

For an instant Johnny remembered what his father had once said about Speck: *Sometimes he doesn't make good sense. He'll pull a fool stunt and kill himself someday.*

Speck spurred down the wet bank. The bay balked at going into the swirling brown water. Speck kept jabbing him with his spurs and slapping the horse's rump with his hat. Finally the bay jumped off into the river. For a moment it looked as if they were going to be all right. Speck had swum rivers before. Getting out into the fast current, he slipped out of the saddle to give the horse a better chance. He clung to the horn and the saddlestrings.

Something happened. The horse panicked and began threshing. Somehow Speck lost his hold.

Johnny watched openmouthed from the bank. "Tessie," he shouted, "bring my rope. It's on my saddle."

Tessie jerked the hornstring loose and came running with the rope. Meeting her, Johnny grabbed it and ran down the riverbank, stumbling, rolling, regaining his feet.

"Speck! Over here! I got a rope!"

Speck's arms windmilled wildly. Foamy water swirled around him, carrying him swiftly down the river. He saw Johnny and raised his hand. Johnny swung the loop and sent it sailing. But just as it touched the water, Speck went under. When the cowboy came up again, he had missed the rope.

Desperately Johnny re-coiled it and went running again, racing the current. A second time he threw the rope. This time Speck clutched it, and for a moment Johnny thought he had him. But Speck lost his hold. Once more he disappeared beneath the muddy water.

Johnny went running again. This time he knew Speck wouldn't have strength left to hold the rope. Johnny ran until he was sure he was ahead of him. He dropped down over the slippery riverbank, pulling the loop tightly around his own waist and quickly half-hitching the other end of the rope to a salt-cedar. Catching a glimpse of Speck above him, Johnny plunged into the water.

He had no idea the flood could pull so hard. It seemed a futile fight against the swift current, but somehow he made it out into the river. The muddy, salty water burned his eyes, and it was hard for him to see. But he glimpsed Speck almost upon him. He grabbed an arm. "Speck . . ." Water filled his mouth and choked him. He pulled Speck up against him and began trying to fight the current with one arm. It was a hopeless fight. He felt himself going under. But stubbornly he held on to Speck.

He reached the end of the rope. The current pulled him so hard it felt as if the rope would cut him in two. But he kept fighting, and slowly the drag of the current against the rope drew him back toward the bank. He threshed desperately with his free arm. He choked on the bad water, but finally he felt his feet touch bottom. With all the strength that was left in him, he fought his way to the bank.

Tessie was there, wet from the rain, muddy from climbing down the steep bank. She grabbed Johnny's free arm and helped him pull up. He dragged Speck after him. Breathing hard, his heart pounding from exhaustion, Johnny pulled Speck up over the bank and out onto flat ground. Still choking, he turned Speck over onto his stomach and started trying to squeeze the water out of him.

"Here, Johnny," Tessie said, "you're done in. I'll try."

Speck's horse climbed up onto the bank and stood exhausted, hanging its head.

Tessie pumped awhile, till Johnny got over his coughing and regained his breath. Then he tried it. He was getting no response. His heartbeat quickened, and desperation began taking hold of him. "Speck," he cried, half under his breath, "you got to come out of it. Speck!"

But Speck never stirred. Tessie reached for Speck's wrist and felt for a pulse. When she looked up her face was stricken. "Johnny, there's nothing more we can do."

Johnny had sensed it. Now tears came in a blinding rush, burning his eyes. "I tried. Speck, I tried." His throat went tight. He sat on the wet ground, his knees drawn up, his face buried in his arms. Tessie's hand was light and comforting on his shoulder.

After a long time Tessie's voice came soberly, "Johnny, I see a rider coming. It'll be Haggard."

Johnny slowly raised his head and blinked, clearing his eyes. The mist had almost stopped. He could see the tall rider pausing in camp, studying their tracks. In a moment the rider saw them. He reined the horse gently around and came on in a walk, following the river. Across his lap he held a saddlegun.

Tessie bit her lip. "Johnny, what're we goin' to do?"

Johnny clenched his fist. "Earlier, I'd have run." He glanced at Speck. "Now I don't feel like runnin' anymore. I'm tired of runnin'."

"Johnny, I've got a gun. Dugan Whitaker gave it to me."

"No gun, Tessie. Whatever happens, I don't aim to fight him. We were in the wrong."

"But now *he's* in the wrong. He told us himself: they wouldn't even give him a warrant. The law isn't looking for you. Only Haggard is."

Johnny looked sadly at Speck Quitman lying still and silent in the mud. "I wish I'd known that before."

"But don't you see, Johnny? You've got a right to defend yourself now. He's already killed Larramore. In a way, he killed Speck. Now you've got to kill *him* before he kills you."

Johnny shook his head and pushed to his feet. "No, Tessie. I won't kill him."

"Then run, Johnny! Take Speck's horse and run!"

"How far could I get? I've run too long already, and for nothin'. I'm through runnin'. I'm going to stand and face him. Whatever is goin' to happen, let it happen here. Let this be the end of it."

He turned and waited for Haggard.

Milam Haggard had camped in the gap, figuring on riding down to the Pecos crossing in the early hours of morning. He knew the two he sought were down there, for he had seen a pinpoint of firelight. He could have ridden on down and finished it in the night, but he didn't trust himself. He was tired, and the shoulder was still bothering him some. A man could make a mistake in a situation like that, when he wasn't at his best. Better to wait and rest a few hours. He would be ready in the early morning. They would not.

That was the time to take them, when there was still sleep in their eyes.

This, then, was the hour he had waited for. This was the final reckoning, when all debts would be paid and the slate wiped clean, when the burden of vengeance at last would be lifted from his shoulders. It had become an oppression of late, as painful as the slow-healing wound that had bent him. He was weary of it. He would be glad when this was over and he could go home—home to the ranch. He would be glad when he no longer had to call up a mental image of Cora's face to keep driving him on.

He had been aware of someone riding far behind him yesterday, but he hadn't thought much of it. People still used this old Butterfield Trail. He hadn't even considered the girl until he saw her ride through the gap and past him this morning. Daylight had not yet come, and he would not even have seen her had she not ridden within fifty feet of his camp. She had been unaware of him until about the same time he had seen her. She had moved into a lope. He had considered saddling up and racing her to the crossing, but she had a good start on him. He would wear out his horse and maybe himself as well.

Let her go, then. He had lost the element of surprise, and he regretted that. But they couldn't go far. He had an idea the river would be up, from the looks of the heavy clouds to the north. So he would catch them soon. Sure, it was two to one, but they were only cowboys. They knew horses and cattle and ropes, but *he* was the one who knew guns. He wouldn't give them a chance to ambush him again.

"It's almost over now, Cora," he spoke aloud. "In a little while you can rest easy."

But he thought of the girl riding far ahead, and he remembered the bitter words she had flung at him in the settlement.

Who is going to rest easy? he asked himself. *Will it be Cora, or me?*

A killer, Tessie Barnett had called him.

Maybe it's better for your wife that she is dead, the girl had shouted. *She couldn't have lived with you very long. In your own way, you'd have killed her yourself.*

"It's not true, Cora," Haggard said. "We'd have had a good life. I'd have changed, for *you*."

He had been sure he could do it. Well, almost sure. But Cora had died, and he *hadn't* changed. That much, at least, he granted the girl.

Certainly he had killed, but always for the right. He had never killed a man who didn't deserve to die, and he had never killed a man who didn't have a chance. He had killed, but he had never murdered. Of that, he was proud.

Moving toward the crossing, he reached down and drew the saddlegun from its scabbard beneath his leg. He brought it up in front of him and rode with sharp eyes watching through the thin mist. He had let these men shoot him once. He wouldn't make that mistake again. The air was wet and chill and he hunched his shoulders, wishing he had brought a coat or a jumper. But perhaps all the chill wasn't from the weather. He sensed death about this miserable place. His eyes were drawn to two unmarked mounds at the side of the hoof-worn trail. The toll of Horsehead Crossing.

Today there would be new graves.

He thought of the cowboys as he had seen them that day on the Sonora road. They were young. They hadn't meant to kill Cora. But she had died. Had it not been for them, she would still live.

Young, they were, and fated to grow no older.

Well, he had seen even younger ones die, young men who had more right to life than these, men who had done no wrong.

He saw the camp ahead, the chips aglow in the shallow firepit. He saw a horse picketed, no saddle on its back, and another horse standing with a sidesaddle. He saw tracks where a third horse had gone down to the river. There were boot tracks too.

At first he figured they were huddled down behind the riverbank, waiting to ambush him. His hand tightened on the short rifle.

Downriver he saw a movement. He made out the girl standing there, and beside her a man sitting on the ground. Watching them cautiously, he reined gently around and moved in their direction. He wondered where the second cowboy was, and the hair stiffened at the back of his neck. He considered the probability that they were trying to lure him into a trap. But presently he saw the body lying at the girl's feet. He saw a bay horse standing on the riverbank, head down, water dripping.

He thought he could guess what had happened.

Rifle ready, he rode on slowly and drew rein twenty feet from Johnny Fristo and Tessie Barnett. He looked down a moment at Speck Quitman.

Johnny Fristo said with an acid bitterness, "Yes, he's dead, Mister Haggard. You wanted to kill him, and you did."

"*I* killed him?"

"With fear. The fear of you drove him to it. So carve

another notch on your gun. The credit belongs to you. Enjoy it."

Haggard's mouth tightened. For a moment he felt cheated. Then he knew relief of a kind, for in his mind this had been a just way. "Now there's only you left, Fristo."

Fristo stepped away from the frightened girl. He said flatly, "I'm here."

Haggard frowned. "I don't see your gun."

"I haven't got a gun. Never did have one."

Haggard's eyes narrowed. He hadn't considered this possibility. He nodded toward the body. "Then your friend had one. Get it. I'll give you that much time."

Johnny held still. "He doesn't have one, either."

Haggard eased down from the saddle, keeping the rifle ready, pointed toward Fristo. "He *had* one. He shot me."

"I smashed the rifle. He hasn't had one since."

Haggard stepped away from the horse, frowning. "I've never shot an unarmed man."

"If you shoot me, that's the way it's goin' to have to be."

Haggard's hands flexed nervously on the saddlegun. Somehow he found himself on the defensive here in a way that puzzled him. Few times in his life had he ever wondered what he should do; he always seemed to know. Now he faced indecision, and it was hard to cope with.

Tessie Barnett said, "Mister Haggard, you killed Larramore. You killed Speck Quitman. Aren't two men enough to pay for what happened to your wife, especially when it was an accident in the first place? How much more blood is it going to take?"

Haggard did not look at her. He kept his eyes on

Johnny Fristo as he answered her, for he was not completely convinced that Fristo did not have a gun. "This one is still left. I've never hunted a man in my life that I didn't finally get him."

"Is it your wife you're really thinking of, Mister Haggard?" she demanded. "Or is it yourself?"

He did not reply.

Tessie said bitterly, "Two men dead, and you're fixing to murder another. Wouldn't your wife be proud of you now?"

Haggard tried not to listen. He reached across with his left hand and drew the pistol from the holster on his right hip. "Here, Fristo." He pitched the pistol to Johnny's feet. "Now you've got a gun."

Johnny Fristo never looked at it. "If you want me dead, you'll have to shoot me like I am. I'll not fight you."

Haggard's teeth clamped tightly. He *had* to finish this thing, had to get it behind him forever. But he couldn't just shoot down a man who wouldn't fight back. "I'll trail you. I'll hound you till one day I catch you with a gun!"

"You'll never catch me with one. I intend to never touch one as long as I live." Johnny's voice tightened. "Mister Haggard, I've lived in hell ever since that day your wife died. I've run from you, and I've died a thousand times. Ever since it happened I've been lookin' back over my shoulder, expectin' to see you come ridin' over a hill to kill me. And when I haven't seen *you* I've seen your wife. Now all of a sudden I'm more tired of runnin' than I am scared of dyin'.

"You want to kill me? Then do it right now, right here. If you don't kill me I'm goin' home where I belong. I'm goin' to tell the world what I've done and learn to live in spite of it. I'm through runnin', and I'm through bein' scared. So shoot me if you want to. But if you're ever goin' to do it, do it now!"

He waited a moment for Haggard to move. Then he turned his back and started walking slowly toward Speck Quitman's bay horse.

Haggard brought up the rifle. "Fristo, stop!"

Tessie cried, "No, Mister Haggard. If you shoot him now it'll be murder. I'll tell them all how it was. You won't be the hunter then. They'll be huntin' *you*!"

Haggard didn't want to do it this way, but a desperation was driving him. "Fristo, for God's sake turn and face me! Don't make me shoot you in the back!" He wanted to get it over with. He felt a revulsion against himself even as he aimed the rifle at Johnny Fristo's back. But he had to end it now.

From the corner of his eye he saw Tessie Barnett reach into her jacket. He heard the click of a hammer.

What Haggard did then was pure reflex. He swung the rifle toward the girl. In horror he realized what he was doing, but he was unable to stop the motion he had started. It was lightning swift and automatic. He tried to force himself to raise the muzzle as he squeezed the trigger. The saddlegun roared. The butt of it jarred his shoulder, sending a sharp pain slashing through the old wound.

He heard himself cry out in disbelief even before he lowered the rifle. He froze, horrified at what he had done.

The pistol dropped from the girl's hand. She stared at him in wide-eyed surprise, the color suddenly wiped out of her face. Her left hand lifted toward her shoulder, and she gasped.

Johnny Fristo shouted, "Tessie!" He took two

long strides and grabbed her as she started to sag. "Tessie!"

Haggard came out of his shock. He threw the saddlegun away and stepped toward the girl. "My God! Oh my God!" Blood began to spread through the shoulder of her jacket. "I didn't mean to, girl. I couldn't stop it. I tried to raise the muzzle."

Ashen-faced, Johnny Fristo was easing her to the ground.

Haggard tried to get control of himself. "I didn't mean to. It was an accident."

He realized then how futile that sounded, and where he had heard it before. He put his hand over his face.

In a moment Johnny Fristo said husky-voiced, "It isn't so bad, Mister Haggard. You *did* raise that muzzle. You just kind of grazed her."

Haggard swayed. "I thought I'd killed her." He rubbed his hand over his face again. "How could I have lived with myself?"

Johnny Fristo held the girl tightly in his arms, relief in his eyes. In a little while he said, "Maybe you'd have learned—the way *I've* had to learn."

Reaction nearly got the best of Haggard then. He trembled in realization of what he had almost done. He had almost murdered a man. Had it not been for the girl, he would have shot Johnny Fristo in the back. And then he had almost killed the girl.

Cora, I meant it for you! All that I've done has been for you!

"Fristo," he said finally, "we'd better do something about that wound of hers. She's going to be sick."

Johnny Fristo's voice was tight and grim. "I reckon I can take care of her, Mister Haggard. If you've finished your business here, maybe you'd better just go."

Haggard flinched. Then, "Yes, I guess I'm finished."

He glanced at Speck Quitman lying on the muddy ground, and he looked once more at the girl. "I'm finished." He turned toward his horse. He thought of his pistol lying on the ground where he had tossed it at Fristo's feet. He thought of the smoking saddlegun he had dropped.

But he did not pause to pick them up. He hoped he never had to look at another gun.

Swinging into the saddle, he gave one quick glance to the violent Horsehead Crossing, then reined his horse eastward toward the cleft that was Castle Gap. His shoulders were bent, and his head was down.

He never looked back.